KILL
FOR ME

By Tom Wood

The Hunter
The Enemy
The Game
Better Off Dead
The Darkest Day
The Final Hour

Ebook short story
Bad Luck in Berlin

KILL
FOR ME

TOM WOOD

sphere

SPHERE

First published in Great Britain in 2018 by Sphere

1 3 5 7 9 10 8 6 4 2

A CIP catalogue record for this book
is available from the British Library.

ISBN 978-0-7515-7247-6
C format ISBN 978-0-7515-6570-6

Typeset in Sabon by M Rules
Printed and bound in Great Britain
by Clays Ltd, Elcograf S.p.A.

Papers used by Sphere are from well-managed forests
and other responsible sources.

Sphere
An imprint of
Little, Brown Book Group
Carmelite House
50 Victoria Embankment
London EC4Y 0DZ

An Hachette UK Company
www.hachette.co.uk

www.littlebrown.co.uk

For Ionica

KILL
FOR ME

ONE

The beach was white sand, stretched in a crescent around the bay. Dark waves lapped against the shore as feral dogs foraged along the water's edge, searching for scraps left by backpackers. On the furthest spur of sand two wild horses ran back and forth in some ritual Victor couldn't hope to comprehend.

The seller he was meeting called himself Jairo. He was old and tanned, short and hairy. He had a beard that rose to his cheekbones, pure white and bushy. His shirt was opened to his sternum, revealing a thatch of colourless chest hair. Gold neck chains gleamed from among the curls. His eyebrows were still black, and almost met in the middle. He smelled of rum, else local *aguardiente* – Victor hadn't spent enough time in Guatemala to be able to differentiate between them by scent alone.

The last of the sun was disappearing over the horizon, but the heat of the day remained. Victor's clothes were light-weight and loose, pushed taut against him by the breeze.

It came from the east, from out across the Caribbean Sea, somehow cool and warm at the same time.

Jairo was from across the border in Honduras, and he dressed like a bum. His shirt was dotted with grease stains from a couple of days' worth of messy eating. Threadbare denim shorts hung to his knees. The legs that protruded from the shorts were thin and weak. He wore rubber sandals that revealed the skin of his heels was cracked and split. He had tattoos on his forearms. They were too old and faded, and his skin too tan, for Victor to make out what they portrayed.

He was no international arms trafficker. He was no Vladimir Kasakov. He was no Georg, even. He was just a small-time gun runner. He was just a man in possession of an expensive rifle. How he came across the weapon, Georg hadn't passed on to Victor, and Jairo hadn't offered its history. He hadn't even wanted to show it to Victor without seeing the money.

'I check the weapon is in good condition,' Victor had said. 'Then you get to see the cash.'

Jairo shook his head. 'That's not how this works.'

They spoke in English, because Victor didn't want Jairo to know he spoke Spanish as well as he did. Better, even.

'It works how I say it works.'

Jairo was silent. He glanced at the wild horses.

'Don't forget that you want to sell the gun more than I want to buy it. I can walk away at any point and keep my money. You'll still have a rifle you don't want.'

Jairo thought for a while. He didn't blink a lot, but he rubbed one palm with the other thumb.

He shrugged. 'Okay, you can check it. Make sure it's legit.'

He was nervous while Victor did. He couldn't stop moving.

He couldn't stop fidgeting. If he wasn't shuffling his weight, he was rubbing his palms together. If he wasn't rolling his shoulders, he was scratching the back of his neck. Victor took in all the tell-tale signs and acted as if he didn't see them, as if he didn't understand. He wanted to buy time. He wanted to assess the situation.

The Accuracy International AX50 was a big piece of engineering. It came in a case made from toughened military-grade polymer large enough to hide a person inside – dismembered, but doable. Victor had squeezed bodies into less. Inside the case, thick foam rubber encased the component parts, isolated and identifiable to Victor's gaze. He checked each part in turn, acknowledging that every one was as it should be, as expected. Accessories came in a separate compartment, and were, like the weapon itself, all good. Too good.

He kept his thoughts to himself for the moment, still assessing. Jairo was growing even edgier, because in the dim light he couldn't see Victor's eyes in the shadow of the khaki cap and he couldn't read the expression beneath.

'What do you think?' Jairo asked when he couldn't stand the silence any longer. 'You like it?'

'It's beautiful,' Victor said.

Jairo was picking something from his teeth. 'You gonna buy?'

Victor kept his gaze on the rifle. 'How much do you want for it?'

'A hundred thousand is the price agreed by the middleman. You have the cash? You buy?'

The rifle retailed for a fraction of that, even with all the accessories, but there was a heavy premium on black-market weapons. Jairo was adding a considerable premium to that premium, but for such a weapon it was a seller's market. If Victor wasn't prepared to overpay he was never going to be able to acquire what he needed. Whatever he had said, he wanted the gun more than Jairo wanted to sell it.

He rubbed the gun oil from his fingers. 'Where did you get the weapon?'

Jairo shrugged and adjusted his footing. 'What does it matter? I'm not gonna ask you where you got your money from. You brought it, yes? In your truck?'

Victor nodded.

He had his pickup parked where the sand dunes became prickled with long grass. Jairo's own vehicle – another pickup – was parked on the beach itself, out in the open as agreed. Victor had arrived early, but Jairo had been earlier. He had been drinking. There was a sheen to his skin and a glaze to his eyes.

'Let me see it.'

Victor shut the case and thumbed the catches. He dragged it from the load bed of Jairo's pickup. Even for Victor's strength, it was heavy. The rifle alone weighed almost twenty kilos. He carried it in his left hand. He led Jairo to his truck. Led, because Jairo didn't move fast. He followed at a slow pace. In part because his stride was short like his height; in part because he had poor footwear for traversing sand; in part because of all the nerves.

'A hundred grand is a lot of money,' Victor said as they walked, 'even for a weapon like this. Black-market rates are black-market rates, I get that, but this rifle is brand new. There's still packing grease on the components. Someone tried to wipe it away, but you can't do that. You have to use it. You have to get it dirty first. You have to put it together and fire rounds and strip it apart again and scrub and clean and oil it. Then you get rid of the packing grease. Good try all the same.'

Jairo acted confused. 'What does it matter if it's brand new? You're getting a good deal.'

'That's my point. The price is too good, black-market rates and all, for a brand-new weapon. This has never been used. It's mint in the box. So, where did you get it?'

Jairo shrugged. 'I don't own the gun,' he explained. 'I'm only the seller.'

The light was fading fast and the blue pickup Victor had bought for cash looked almost black. He set the heavy case down in the load bed and dragged forth a sports bag. He shoved it into Jairo's waiting grip and ripped open a packet of beef jerky from a container of supplies.

'Want some?' He offered the packet to Jairo.

Jairo glanced up. 'Looks disgusting.'

Victor shrugged as he chewed. More for him.

Jairo wasn't hungry. He was wasting no time, unzipping the sports bag and peering inside, smiling when he saw the bundles of American dollars.

'You know,' Victor said after swallowing, 'at first I wondered if you were part of a sting operation. A non-proliferation thing. That's always the biggest risk when buying this kind of hardware. I figured there could be binoculars and cameras on me, officials and cops waiting out of sight behind the dunes, ready to rush in when I showed the money. Until then, I'd committed no crime. So, I was weighing up my odds, wondering if they had a clear shot of my features, wondering what repercussions I would face further down the line. Just because I had committed no crime didn't mean there wouldn't be fallout. A man like me can't afford to be on someone's radar.'

Jairo was half listening, because he had noticed something about the bag. He reached inside.

'All those nerves you had,' Victor continued. 'I figured they had you over a barrel, and you'd get them off if you gave up your buyer. Me. But then I found the packing grease. No way an official sting operation would use brand-new weaponry like that. No way they could get hold of it, even to lure out an utterly deplorable person such as myself. They would use what they had, what they had confiscated. So, this has to be something else. I overthought it. The simplest explanation is usually the right one.'

Jairo pushed his hand deep into the bag, drawing out one of the thick bundles of cash. They appeared to be straps of hundred-dollar bills, a hundred bills per strap, secured with a rubber band. Jairo peeled back the first bill to see that the rest were nothing more than rectangular pieces of blank paper.

'No, no, no,' Jairo muttered.

'You didn't think I would bring a hundred grand in cash to make a deal in the middle of nowhere, did you? That's how you get yourself killed.'

'You've made a huge mistake.'

Victor said, 'When I've already made so many, why stop now?'

'You don't know who you're dealing with.'

Victor's tone was wistful. 'If only the reverse were true, Jairo, we could save ourselves an awful lot of inevitable unpleasantness.'

TWO

The sun was little more than a red line on the horizon. The horses had gone with the approaching darkness, but the feral dogs still scoured the beach. They had no fear of the night and were hungry and determined. The waves had lost their remaining luminescence, blackening as the day became night.

'Where's the rest of the money?' Jairo asked, speaking with fast, desperate words. 'In your truck? Nearby? It had better be, for both our sakes.'

Victor shrugged like Jairo had done several times.

'It's not here at all?' Jairo gasped. 'That wasn't the deal. I bring gun. You bring cash. You don't know what you've done.'

'But that's not all you brought, is it?'

Jairo was silent.

'The simplest explanation is usually the right one,' Victor repeated. 'This is a shakedown. This is a robbery.'

'It's not me,' he said.

'Excuse my sarcasm when I say, no kidding? No offence, Jairo, but I wouldn't have bothered with the charade if I thought you were behind it. I would have simply killed you and carried on with my day, a rifle in my truck and a spare hundred K to spend at the blackjack table.'

Jairo stared.

'I jest – half-jest – but the funny thing is that now you know I know you're not showing the same nerves as before. Why's that? Who wants the money?'

It was never unexpected that those Victor dealt with would seek a better deal. It was never a surprise to be betrayed. He kept only a few acquaintances, and of those, he only used them from time to time. He had to deal with new people to do his job and to stay alive. He had to find a constant stream of suppliers. Suppliers who operated in the same underground world as his were untrustworthy by default. Some were even less trustworthy than Victor.

'Marxists,' Jairo explained, shaking his head in some private conflict. 'Crazies. They call themselves the Army of the Poor.'

'The guerrilla group from Honduras? They disbanded decades ago.'

'Doesn't mean that there aren't those out there that wish they hadn't, that would like to start a new war, a new revolution. Like I said: they're crazy.'

That was how they had the rifle then, Victor realised. Part of a larger arms cache; maybe stolen, maybe hijacked, maybe donated; lying unused and waiting somewhere in the jungle, waiting to be put to use; waiting to be activated when they had enough numbers, enough resources to reveal themselves and pursue fruitless goals.

'They're raising funds,' Victor said. 'For the cause.'

Jairo nodded. He thumbed one of the bundles of blank paper, as if he had been wrong, as if dollar bills would magically appear and fix the mess he had found himself trapped within.

'This isn't the first time you've done this,' Victor said. 'Even with your nerves, you did everything else right, so you've had practice. How many times has this set-up worked?'

Jairo hesitated. 'You're the fifth person they'll have robbed.'

'Then you shouldn't have been nervous with me. You should be an old hat by now. My fifth job was a walk in the park. Figuratively and literally. Gorky Park, if you're interested.'

'I don't want to be part of this,' Jairo said. 'I hate them. But I have no choice.'

'There's always a choice,' Victor said, then understood. 'Ah ... you weren't scared the shakedown would go wrong, that I would see it coming. You're scared of what happens when it goes right. You don't have the stomach for it. That's why you were drinking, isn't it?'

Jairo was silent. He couldn't look Victor in the eye.

One of the feral dogs was barking at gulls trying to steal the morsels of food it had found for itself. The gulls swooped down in daring raids as the dog chased them away.

'They're not going to simply rob me, are they, Jairo? They're going to kill me. That's why it's worked four times before: no one left to report the crime.'

'I—'

'Don't bother. I don't want to hear it. I want to hear how they're going to do it. I didn't see any signs that anyone is nearby, so they're keeping their distance.' He glanced around. 'Let me guess: I give you the cash, I take the rifle. I think it's all fine, then I drive into an ambush when I try to leave the beach, when my guard's down. Sound about right?'

Jairo could only nod.

'I like it,' Victor said. 'Whoever thought it up knows their stuff. Can't do much with my hands on the wheel. That's why I don't like driving. You're getting nervous again, Jairo. Calm down, I'm not going to kill you.'

Jairo was confused.

'On one condition,' Victor explained. 'After I've killed your friends, I want your assistance cleaning up the mess. I don't just mean the physical mess, but the fallout. I have a job to complete, and I can do without the added attention. It's proving to be difficult enough as it is.'

'I don't understand.'

'You don't need to understand at this moment. All you need to know is that this is a genuine deal. I don't really have rules, Jairo. There's not much I haven't done. There's even less I won't do. If there's a worse person out there I haven't met them, and I've met plenty, but if someone plays straight with me then I'll probably play straight with them in return. I'd like to call it a do-no-harm kind of philosophy, but in the business I'm in that would be beyond ironic. So let's say that if I agree to a deal then I'll honour it, and while I don't necessarily expect the other party to do the same, there'll be the severest of repercussions if they don't. What I'm trying to tell you is that if someone leaves me alone, I'll leave them alone. You could say I try to keep my word, but I'm also a very bad person. If I weren't presenting you with a genuine offer, if I were trying to trick you, I would say something like "I'm not going to kill you *now*" or "I'll help you get out of *this*" which would allow me to keep my word and still kill you later. Juvenile, perhaps, but who wants to grow up if they don't have to? But that's not what I said. I'm offering you the unprecedented chance to continue your miserable existence. All you have to do is back the winning team. So, are you going to switch sides?'

Jairo was even more confused. 'They have guns.'

'A shocking revelation,' Victor said. 'I can see that you are unconvinced. That's understandable, as you don't know me, so I'll allow you to think about it. You can give me your answer in a few minutes' time.'

'You're as crazy as they are.'

Victor nodded. 'More so, I assure you. But that's enough talking. Let's maintain the charade, shall we?' He secured the case in the load bed and then offered Jairo his hand. 'Pleasure doing business with you.'

Jairo stared at his outstretched hand.

'At least try to play along, Jairo. There's a good chap.'

A tanned hand took Victor's, and they shook. Jairo's grip was limp. He was shaking his head before Victor had finished. 'No, they already know.'

He looked at Jairo. He looked at the open shirt and the loose shorts, the tattoos and the chest hair, the sandals and the hairy legs. Nowhere to hide a conventional recording device.

'You were supposed to give them a signal when you looked in the bag,' Victor said. 'But you didn't. They know I haven't brought the money. They're here.'

Jairo didn't respond, but he didn't need to say anything. A loud rustle came from the dunes, from beyond the long grasses, announcing the approach of several figures with guns.

THREE

They looked as Victor would have expected. They dressed in military fatigues as if they were a legitimate army, but the clothes didn't fit right; they didn't quite match – olive green with woodland green, US Army-issue jackets with Colombian khakis – and attempted to be a uniform, but failed on the details. They had jungle boots and marching boots and hats of various types – caps, berets and smocks. There were six in total, all armed with cheap assault rifles: Galils and FALs, all as old as Victor. They were clean, though, which was the most important detail. Whatever the failed attempt at a uniform, whatever the age of the weapons, these guys had at least some proficiency. Amateurs, but not incompetents.

Their arrival startled the feral dogs, who scattered, leaving whatever they had found to the gulls. Victory through perseverance.

The leader of the six was obvious. She walked – strode – ahead of the others, her face pinched by undisguised anger. The woman looked young, but so did her men. None of them were older than twenty-five. One of the men was still a teenager. They were a group of idealists that had become extremists, which in Victor's experience was more of a short walk than a long journey. He had been paid to kill enough of the latter to know the steps.

She had a confident gait and held a rigid posture. Camouflage paint dirtied her face. Her hair was short and straight. Binoculars hung by a leather strap from her neck. Unlike her men, she carried no rifle, but had a sidearm holstered on her left thigh. She drew the pistol as she neared and aimed it at Victor with her left hand, but the safety stayed on. He was in no immediate danger because killing him meant they wouldn't get the money.

The commander stopped when she was close, but not too close. Victor raised his palms.

'Don't shoot,' he said without inflection.

'Where's your weapon?' she demanded.

Slow and obvious, Victor lifted one flap of his shirt to reveal a Glock tucked into his waistband. He had bought it in the back streets of Guatemala City, where small arms could be purchased cheap and were readily available.

'Lose it,' she said.

Victor did. A good pistol, but no use in a six-on-one gunfight. He threw it towards the dunes, high in the air, so it didn't go far. His gaze was on the woman, so he didn't see the Glock land, but he was listening hard for it to do so. Twelve or thirteen metres, he noted, should he need to sprint for it. He wasn't sure how this was going to go just yet, so he wanted to keep his options open.

'Where is it?' she demanded.

He played ignorant – 'Where's what?' – but not dumb,

13

because his answer only angered her further. He wanted her angry.

'The money,' she spat. 'Where is it?'

'Far away from here. Safe. Secure. Hidden.'

She edged forward. 'Where?'

'I'll take you to it, if you like.'

'Tell me or I'll put a bullet through your skull.'

Victor shrugged. 'Then you won't get the hundred thousand.' He glanced at the bag Jairo was still holding. 'Well, the other ninety-nine thousand, to be exact. I'm guessing a grand isn't a good consolation prize.'

One hundred thousand dollars wasn't a lot of money to Victor, but to some aspiring terrorists living in tents in the jungle, it would go a long way to keep them sustained. Someone had recently told him that revolutions were expensive. When the average citizen in this part of the world earned less than ten thousand dollars per annum, it wasn't hard to see how such a group would kill for the kind of cash Victor had brought to them. Or hadn't brought.

The woman said, 'I don't have to shoot you in the head. I can shoot your dick off if I want to.' She stepped closer. 'You'll be begging to tell me then. You should know that I'm a great shot.'

Victor remained silent. He didn't have to say anything. They both knew it was a bluff. The old weapons and the mismatched clothes answered for him. They were desperate for funds. She wouldn't risk hurting him too much. If he died of shock or blood loss then they would miss out on much-needed cash. This was a new situation for her – the shakedown-cum-ambush had worked every time until now – and she wasn't sure of the best way to handle this particular scenario. Victor had been in similar situations. He knew what to do. She was making it up as she went along.

'Okay,' she said, having worked out her next move. 'You take us to the money.'

'No,' he said.

'No?'

She was shocked. His refusal wasn't part of her next move.

Victor said, 'If you want the cash, you do it my way. I'll take you to it. But only you. Your guys wait here. They can build a fire from driftwood. Sing songs about workers controlling the means of production until we get back.'

She smiled with contempt, stepping closer, and answered with a predictable, 'No.'

Which let him ask, 'You're not scared of me, are you?'

She hesitated, because there was no correct answer. If she agreed, she would lose face in front of her men. If she denied, there was no reason not to go with him.

She smiled at Victor, as if this was a misunderstanding that had spiralled out of control, and lowered the pistol. 'We can fix this, can't we? You want the rifle. We want the money.'

He nodded. 'It was supposed to be that simple. It could've been that simple. Play straight with me and I play straight with you.'

Jairo, standing at the edge of Victor's peripheral vision, tensed.

The woman holstered the gun, fast and easy. 'It still can be. See? We'll all go to fetch the money. I'll go with you. My men follow in another truck. Okay?'

'Sure,' Victor said with a smile of his own, as though she had convinced him it was only a misunderstanding, that her intentions were to make the original deal work.

Pleased to have the situation under control, she turned to face her men, to tell them what to do next. She had a new plan.

The only problem with it was that she now stood too close to Victor, who took a fast step forward – up behind her – closing the distance enough to snatch the gun from her unfastened holster in his left hand while he grabbed her hair with his right.

In an instant, the muzzle was against her cheek.

'Change of plan,' he said.

FOUR

The five guerrillas with rifles went into a panic – muzzles coming up, shouts, threats. Victor ignored them because he had their commander as a human shield. She was a lot smaller than him, but that didn't matter. None of the five were calm enough to risk a headshot, especially in the semi-darkness, especially because Victor didn't keep himself, or his hostage, still.

He had her hair bunched tight in one fist, pulling back to keep her head from being in line with her hips, robbing her of her strength, her stability. He kept the muzzle pushed into her cheek despite the tactical naivety of doing so – the closer the gun, the more opportunities she had of going for it – but it was for show, to make a statement, both to her and her men.

She said, 'Don't do anything stupid.'

'I haven't before,' Victor said. 'I'm not going to start now.'

Her body was a mass of tension, but she didn't struggle. She didn't fight. She knew she was at his mercy.

'We can work this out.'

'That's what I've been trying to do all this time. It never had to reach this stage. I only wanted to buy a rifle.'

She said, 'Take the rifle. It's yours. Take it and go. Keep the money.'

'Your sudden generosity is rather touching.'

'You don't have to kill me.'

He wasn't planning on killing her. At least, not yet. Not when there were five automatic weapons waiting to shred him to pieces the second he executed his hostage. Which was why such hostage situations never worked. It was nothing more than a bluff. If the hostage taker were suicidal they wouldn't have taken a hostage in the first place. The hostage taker needed the hostage alive, because it was the only thing keeping them alive in turn. The problem was that most hostage takers didn't realise this until it was too late, until they had already trapped themselves.

The five guys with the rifles didn't understand this dynamic and neither did their commander. If any of them had, escape would have been impossible for Victor. He'd been on their side of proceedings once before, but he hadn't needed the experience to know how these things played out. It was little more than common sense.

In time, however, the guerrillas might work out that he was as much a hostage as the commander, so it was important not to hang around and give them the chance.

Victor said, 'Tell your guys to drop their weapons.'

'Then you'll let me go?'

'I'm not leaving here until your men have dropped their guns. If they don't, you're leaving with me.'

Once they were disarmed, he would have time. He could place his shots. Her pistol was, like the rifles, an old gun. A

Colt 1911. Solid, reliable, but it only held seven rounds in the magazine. Which gave Victor two spares if he failed to land all headshots on the guys with rifles.

'Drop your weapons,' she called to her men.

They hesitated, which was the natural reaction. He could see them struggling between the need to obey and protect their leader, and the fear of leaving themselves unarmed. She repeated herself, louder and more forceful. It was enough for the five men to start lowering their guns.

Victor readied himself. He would be shooting with his left hand, which was not his preference, but he was almost ambidextrous. Five targets. Seven rounds. Not easy, not without risk, but doable.

Except for the one element he had neglected to account for:

Jairo said, 'Let her go or I'll shoot you dead.'

A quick glance over Victor's shoulder told him it was a genuine threat. Jairo had pulled a weapon of his own. An automatic; Victor could identify the model in the dim light. He knew Jairo had been armed, but hadn't expected him to draw it. He wasn't the sort. Dutch courage, maybe.

Nothing about Jairo suggested to Victor that he was any kind of marksman, but the man was only a few metres away. Victor's back was a wide enough target that at this range even a poor shooter could hit.

A one-eighty spin would put the woman between Victor and Jairo's pistol, but would only expose Victor's back to the five guerrillas. He twisted ninety degrees instead, enough to keep both sets of enemies in his vision with a half-turn of his head. It was hard to move fast on the sand without losing his footing.

'Stay out of this,' Victor said.

'What are you going to do now?' the hostage asked him.

'I mean it,' Jairo insisted. 'Let her go.'

Victor could see the five guerrillas were edging forward. The change in situation had given them a new play to make. They weren't going to shoot Victor if he turned around long enough – too much chance of a through-and-through hitting their commander if they grabbed their guns in time – but they were going to rush Victor instead. He wouldn't be able to drop them all if they did, even if he didn't have to worry about Jairo shooting him in the spine.

'You're going to die,' the hostage hissed at him.

'I'm starting to get that impression.'

He had tried reason. He had tried being reasonable, and it hadn't worked. Now, it was time to bring emotion into proceedings.

Victor released the commander's hair and wrapped his arm around her ribcage. Once he had a tight hold, he took the muzzle from the woman's face, pushed it against the back of her left thigh, and squeezed the trigger.

The dense muscle of the hamstrings and quadriceps, combined with the thick layer of subcutaneous fat, suppressed the gunshot, muting it to a wet popping sound. The .45 calibre round exploded her femur and burst through the front of her leg, spraying blood and flesh in its wake.

Victor was strong enough to keep her upright with just one arm, but she was becoming heavier by the instant. He had severed her femoral artery because he wanted the sight of so much blood pumping out of her leg to focus her men's attention, but it also made her unable to support her own weight. Without his assistance, she would have collapsed straight to the ground.

The guerrillas, and Jairo, didn't know what to do. They were stilled with shock and horror at the sight of the wound and all the blood; overcome with fear and concern for the commander, who passed out within seconds.

Victor called, 'No time left to argue. We do it my way. She'll bleed to death within a minute unless a tourniquet is applied. Throw down your weapons.'

The guerrillas hesitated, but only for a moment. Once the first had dropped his rifle, the other four followed suit. Jairo was the only one left with a gun in his hand.

'Lose it,' Victor said.

Jairo kept it pointed at him.

'She doesn't have time for this.'

The gun didn't move.

One of the guerrillas yelled, '*Do what he says.*'

Jairo didn't listen. His aim held firm as the commander bled. She was pale now. She didn't have much longer, that was obvious. Victor could see that. Jairo could see it too.

I hate them. But I have no choice.

Victor understood. Jairo had switched sides, after all, but he had switched to his own side. He saw an opportunity that he hadn't seen before. A moment ago, he had wanted Victor to release her – not because he cared, but he was playing his part. Jairo wanted to be on the winning team and he didn't want to have to justify why he hadn't acted to ensure victory. But that was then. Now, she was bleeding to death. Now, Jairo saw a different endgame. No guerrillas tormenting him, threatening him, forcing him to lure unsuspecting gun buyers to deaths for which he had no stomach. He saw freedom, and all he had to do was nothing at all.

Jairo wanted her to bleed to death. He wanted free of the

yoke around his neck. He was going to stand there and let her die. Victor didn't care about his motives, only what that meant. When the commander died, or when it was obvious that she could no longer be saved, the five guerrillas would be grabbing their guns and, even with a head start, Victor wouldn't make it far.

Change of plan, he had told the woman. He needed a new one for himself.

When reason was exhausted and emotion failed there was one final card to play.

Violence.

FIVE

Six rounds in the Colt and six targets.

Jairo, with a gun in his hand, was the most immediate threat, so Victor shot him first – a single snapshot because he didn't have time for anything else – letting go of the woman as he turned to face the five unarmed guerrillas. The commander dropped to the beach. Her skin was almost without colour, but her lips were blue. Her fatigues were drenched in blood, as was the sand around her.

The five young men were already primed, and were reacting without hesitation, going for their weapons. Harder targets now they were moving fast and ducking, squatting or kneeling. No way to kill them all before one had a rifle up and firing.

Victor put a double-tap at each of the closest two and dashed for the cover of the pickup, sliding on the loose sand, and going down behind the vehicle.

Bullets were coming his way before he had recovered. They thumped into the truck and blew up chunks of grass and clouds of sand from the dunes, or zipped above his head. A window broke above him. Pebbles of glass rained down over him. He shuffled behind one of the tall, thick tyres. A round burst through the rubber and a rush of escaping air hissed across his face.

Multiple assault rifles roared in a maelstrom of gunfight. This was rage. This was vengeance. They weren't picking their shots but expressing themselves through firepower. There were far too many bullets flying for Victor to track their rounds; the one thing he knew for certain was the barrage couldn't last. One long squeeze of an assault rifle's trigger was all it took to empty the magazine when the mag held thirty and was losing rounds at the rate of several hundred per minute.

The firing ceased. Not all at once, but the guns went silent within a couple of seconds of one another.

Victor could swap out a Galil's mag and be shooting again in under three seconds. Untrained guerrillas dosed up on adrenaline and rage might do the same in five, or even ten. Either way, the few seconds he bought wouldn't matter. He would need at least thirty to make it to anything resembling cover.

He peeked out round the blown tyre, looking beneath the truck's engine block to see that there were three shooters, all reloading. The other two were prostrate on the beach. His double-taps had dropped them both. In the twilight he couldn't tell if they were alive or dead, but they were unmoving.

The three active were reloading, in varying stages of readiness. Victor fired the last round from the Colt beneath the truck, but the angle was too extreme to score a hit.

It bought him some extra time, however, causing the three guerrillas to flinch and react. The teenager dropped his replacement magazine.

Victor, still crouched down, shuffled to where Jairo had fallen, and where the man's pistol lay nearby. The truck blocked line of sight, but not for long. Even untrained enemies knew how to flank when they held a significant numerical advantage.

A moan told him Jairo was still alive. He was conscious, writhing in slow, pained movements. Victor's shot had hit him in the face, but the bullet had somehow missed the brain and spine. There was almost no blood. Just a little brightened his stubble. Jairo was conscious, but he was in shock. He could likely stand, but didn't know how.

Victor scooped up the man's dropped weapon, and almost smiled. It was an FN Five-seveN. Something of an unexpected bonus. Not an easy thing to acquire, even on the black market. Jairo had made a special effort for his personal weapon. He knew his guns, after all.

'Good choice,' Victor said to Jairo, who could only moan in response.

It didn't have the government-only-issue twenty-round magazine, but ten bullets were ten bullets. After checking there was a round in the chamber, Victor turned back. He pictured the three gunmen on the far side of the truck, spreading out. Two circling one way, while the third went the other. They wouldn't be rushing. Even with the numerical advantage, they would be scared. They had lost their commander and were down to half their number. There was a good chance this was their first proper firefight. Shooting paper targets all day long and the occasional ambush couldn't prepare them for what it

25

was like to have someone shooting back. They were learning the hard way that they were out of their depth.

Still, bullets were bullets whoever fired them. The only difference between getting shot by an amateur instead of a professional was the indignation.

Victor shuffled back behind the blown tyre and reached up. His hand found the handle of the passenger door and he eased it open just enough to enable him to slip inside the cab. He kept low, lying across the seats on his shoulder. No rounds were coming at him, so they hadn't seen him. They were too focused on what lay on the other side of the vehicle to think about what could be going on inside it.

He had left the keys in the ignition in case he needed to make a fast exit. The fob was metal – nickel or some alloy – that was shaped like a naked woman. Cheap and tacky, but shiny enough to catch what little light there was to help Victor locate it without exposing himself any more than he had to do. It had belonged to the truck's previous owner.

He heard footsteps crunching on sand. The three gunmen were close. One had circled around the back, while the other two were in front of the truck. Perfect.

Victor twisted the ignition key.

The starter motor spun and the engine revved and the headlights came on as twin intense beams of white that washed over the two guerrillas in front of the truck.

With pupils dilated to capture as much of the twilight as possible, the men were blinded as well as startled; for a moment frozen in place, unable to see and unable to move, and perfectly illuminated.

Victor sat up only as much as he needed and shot them both through the windscreen.

He didn't have the time or angle to aim properly, so put four rounds at each to make sure they went down and stayed down.

The guy at the back of the truck opened fire in response, shooting his rifle on automatic, bullets plugging holes in the rear windscreen and ripping through the roof above. Victor dropped back down, letting the truck protect him until the gunman had wasted his magazine.

Once the firing had ceased, Victor slid out of the truck's cab, expecting to find the guy four seconds into his five-second reload, surprised and vulnerable and easy to kill, but instead he saw a Galil on the sand and a figure sprinting away in the red gloom of the truck's rear lights. He had tasted his first firefight and found it not to his liking.

The guerrilla was fast – the teenager – increasing the distance with every passing second, energised by fear, thinking he had enough of a head start, but he didn't know what gun Victor was armed with; he didn't know it had an effective range of fifty metres. He was even running in a straight line along the crest of the dunes, a sharp silhouette against the darkening sky.

Victor aimed the Five-seveN and squeezed the trigger twice.

It should have been over then, but one of the other guerrillas was still alive.

SIX

He was one of the two guys who had taken a couple of bullets from the Colt at the start of proceedings. He had gone down, he hadn't been moving, but now he was awake, alive and angry. The bullets had hit him at the top of his chest. They hadn't hit his heart because he was alive and they hadn't hit his spine because he could stand. Victor was disappointed with his poor shooting, even for snapshots. The hydrostatic shock of overlapping waves of energy from the double-tap had put him down and knocked him out, at least, so it was a lesson in protocol if nothing else.

The guerrilla had a rifle, pale with caked-on sand, that he raised and pointed at Victor. The Five-seveN hung by Victor's side, barrel cooling and the scent of cordite mixing with the salt air. The guerrilla gestured to it, and Victor dropped the pistol. It was empty, anyway.

The young man with the rifle was bigger than his dead companions. He was better fed, better nourished. He hadn't been in the jungle for as long, or was stealing food from the others. Sweat gleamed on his face. There was no triumph in the young man's expression, and he said nothing. He enjoyed the moment, though, the anticipation. Victor waited.

The guerrilla squeezed the trigger and nothing happened.

'Sand gets everywhere,' Victor said. 'Weapon maintenance 101.'

The misfire did little to change the guerrilla's mindset. He wasn't done yet.

He charged Victor and swung the rifle like a club, gripping the barrel housing to grip in both hands and the stock as the business end. Which made a certain kind of sense, because the stock was the heavier end. It would generate more force on impact – but there was little chance of an impact with a weapon that slow. Holding it the other way around would have reversed the balance, making it hit lighter, but the attacks would be faster. They might have a chance of connecting then.

He reserved his earlier assessment – the rifle-club was never going to hit him – because the guerrilla didn't have a clue how to fight. He put all of his effort into the first blow. When it missed, he couldn't compensate for all the force he had generated that hit nothing. He swung himself off balance. It left him defenceless. He hadn't even attempted to test his opponent's speed.

Victor slipped the clumsy attack, and waited for the next. He was in no rush.

The guerrilla kept swinging and missing. He had zero skill, but he had determination. He had will. Sometimes that was enough. Most enemies would have given up by now, but Victor could see in the man's eyes that the corpses nearby had been friends. Victor understood the strong bonds of brotherhood that were forged by living and fighting alongside comrades. It created an unrivalled loyalty, and an unequalled ferocity. Victor had almost died trying to save his teammates. He had been willing to die.

Within seconds, the guerrilla was exhausted.

Victor hyperextended the closest knee with a kick to the outside of the joint. The leg didn't quite collapse into a sideways V, but it was close enough.

The guerrilla lost the rifle as he hit the beach on his back, with Victor moving to end up on top of him, knees pinning the guy's upper arms in place. A soft landing thanks to the sand, but the guerrilla would have fared better on concrete, because Victor grabbed a handful of sand and threw it into his face on the end of an open-palm strike. It didn't just get into his eyes, nose and mouth, but was driven into them with intent. The coarse particles scratched his eyeballs and caked the sockets; it filled his nostrils and naval cavity; it coated his tongue and blocked his throat.

He went into a fit of sneezing, coughing, and retching.

He couldn't see Victor, let alone have enough control of himself to fight back. He was desperate, however, and one arm came free in the thrashing, working its way out of the loose sand. That arm rose to flail in front of him, searching for a target. More an annoyance than a danger, but Victor batted it aside, and used his advantage of position to throw a couple of downwards elbow strikes. Bones broke. Blood mixed with the sand and mucus covering the guerrilla's face.

Victor stood and flipped him on to his stomach, then used the heel of his shoe on the back of the guerrilla's head to force his face into the sand. It bloomed around him. He writhed beneath Victor's foot.

Victor heard the gulls above and the feral dogs scuffling in the distance. He gazed at the black waves lapping on the beach. A beautiful place, even in the darkness, so isolated it was almost otherworldly in its serenity. Victor liked isolation. For him, peace was a challenge impossible to realise, but the further away from other people, the more chance he had of finding – if not peace – contentment.

He breathed in the sea air and was content.

The guy beneath his heel struggled for a few, fruitless seconds. When the struggling achieved nothing, he screamed for a few, muffled seconds more.

FIVE WEEKS EARLIER

SEVEN

There were some things in life that money couldn't buy, but Luis Lavandier had yet to find one of them. He was a wealthy man, rich by any reasonable standard, but compared to his employer he was but a pauper. She paid him handsomely for his services, and bestowed upon him all manner of lavish gifts and generous bonuses. In return he gave her words of wisdom. It was a scam, he knew, because he was no wiser than she, but he was able to project erudition and he was a patient man who kept his cool – or at least the appearance of cool – at all times.

Such cool and patience were tested on a regular basis.

Today, for example, had been most trying for the Frenchman. He was shaken, though he didn't look it and didn't act it. He kept his stress and anxiety buried down inside him to maintain his unflappable exterior. He stood with his arms folded before him while he observed Dr Flores examining Heloise. Flores was composed but concerned. Heloise was the epitome of composure. Whereas Lavandier's was a front, Heloise was the real deal. He had seen her enraged many times, but he had never seen her scared. Lavandier had never known anyone so fearless. It made him want her all the more.

The clinic was the most exclusive in Guatemala City, maybe in the whole of Central America. It occupied a six-storey building on a quiet street in one of the city's most desirable neighbourhoods. Heloise had been a patient of its owner, and chief practitioner, Dr Flores, since she had been a little girl. Flores had treated her father, Manny Salvatierra, for most of his life, as well as his wife and daughters. Now, he treated only Heloise. Lavandier wasn't sure why he had chosen her over Maria, and he didn't want to know.

Flores was old, but healthy. He didn't act his age. He moved with the vigour of a man half his years. He had more energy than Lavandier, who liked to consider himself fit. Although a kilogram or five off the waist wouldn't hurt, he thought as he drew in his stomach.

'I know what you'll say so I hesitate,' Flores said as he concluded his examination of Heloise.

She sat on the end of a medical cot, still and poised, gaze fixed on the wall ahead. She neither complained nor showed signs of discomfort as Flores made sure she was okay. He had checked her pulse, her breathing, her blood pressure. He had cleaned her wounds – shallow cuts from broken glass. He could do nothing for the contusions, but they were minor.

'Just say it,' she said.

He was already shaking his head in readiness for her response. 'I think a neck brace would be a good idea.'

'Impossible.'

'You see? I knew you would ignore my recommendation. I'm only your doctor, after all. What do I know? I wonder why you even came here when you know so much more than I do.'

Lavandier watched the exchange with silent amusement. Flores was unique, but he didn't know it. Heloise never tolerated such impertinence from anyone else. He could stray into outright rudeness and Heloise would show no reaction. She would feel no wrath. Yet even her worst enemies were unfalteringly polite to her, even in threats. Her temper was equal only to her cruelty.

'Why do you want me to wear one?' she asked.

'You've had some whiplash from the crash. There is a little tenderness at the back of your neck. We could X-ray to be sure, but I believe you may have some bruising around your C4 and C5 spinal vertebrae. It's not showing through the skin, but we shouldn't ignore it. It wouldn't take much of a knock to make it worse.'

'But why do you want me to wear a brace?'

Flores said, 'I think you'll find I just explained why.'

'No, you explained why I require one, not why you want me to wear one.'

Flores was confused. He was an excellent physician, a clever man, but Heloise's world was not his own. Its rules, its perils, were beyond his understanding.

The Frenchman decided to help out. 'You want to keep her safe, yes?'

Flores nodded. 'Of course. But—'

Heloise interrupted: 'If I'm seen in a neck brace, I'm hurt. I'm weak. It sends a message that they came close, that it won't take much to finish the job. How long will the neck brace keep me safe if it inspires further attempts on my life, if it shows my men that it's only a matter of time before I fall? Will they fight so hard for a lost cause?'

Flores didn't know how to respond.

'I appreciate your concern,' Heloise said as she stood from the cot. 'I assume there is medication I can take?'

'Yes, for the pain.' He filled out a prescription form, but Heloise would take no pills, Lavandier knew. She played along so Flores would not worry about her. Lavandier took the form because he was not only advisor, but personal assistant. He had never agreed to this, of course, but he would never mention such activities were beneath him. He would never argue the terms of his contract. The only term that mattered was that Heloise was his employer – his goddess – and she could make him do whatever she desired.

Would she ever let him leave? It was a question he thought much about.

After the morning's attack, security had been doubled. Sicarios lined the hallway and stood outside on the kerb. More gunmen stood either end of the street too. Lavandier opened the door to the waiting limousine, and Heloise climbed inside.

A beautiful day, as many were at this time of year. Lavandier, always a lover of the warmth, relished Guatemala's equatorial sunshine. He sported a fine bronzed hue, year-round, which was an all-over tan thanks to the privacy afforded to him by extreme wealth and high walls.

The vehicle was more akin to a tank than a car. From the outside it had the classic, long shape beloved by the rich the world over. It was always highly polished, always gleaming. The windows were tinted. The licence plate was personalised.

It was at home pulling up outside a premiere or black-tie function, but it was so much more.

Not only had all exterior panelling been replaced with thick armour, the chássis itself had been remodelled to support the huge amount of extra weight. The engine had been replaced with a double-capacity machine, with more cylinders, a supercharger, to drag the hidden bulk. Every window was an inch-thick laminate of alternate layers of glass and polymer. None of these features were unique in the armoured limousine world, but most armoured limousines had not been built for cartel bosses in countries that could almost be classified as war zones. The underside of the limousine was armoured too, and again differed from similar upgrades, because that armour was shaped in a V to help direct and distribute the force of an explosion from a mine or IED.

Had Heloise been travelling in it this morning, they might have been spared a trip to Dr Flores' clinic. But Heloise liked to drive. She liked sports cars. She didn't like Lavandier's words of caution.

He kept his *I told you so* to himself because he liked his tongue inside his mouth where it belonged. Heloise had long nails as hard as claws and his poise was tested to its limits when she used them on her enemies.

Beyond protection alone, the limousine had offensive capabilities. The sunroof, which like its civilian model, was large enough for a person to stand through, also had a machine gun fixed to its underside. When the sunroof was open, the machine gun could be folded out and deployed. Lavandier dreaded the day when Heloise instructed him to make use of the weapon. He had been taught to fire it by one of her armourers, but his aim was awful even while safely practising in a field. Against enemy sicarios out for blood, he would be no help. If their survival ever depended on Lavandier's competence with a weapon, they were all corpses.

Which was one of the many reasons he said, 'This situation has become untenable.'

'If you have a winning strategy, dear Luis, I wonder why you are only now voicing it.'

'I'm no soldier,' he said. 'I'm no general. But you pay me to advise you, to offer an outside perspective, and I think that's what is missing here.'

'Are you telling me that you can no longer provide that service? Because I am both surprised and disappointed that your loyalty is so transient, so temporary. Can we even call it loyalty if it can falter so easily?'

'My loyalty is eternal,' Lavandier was quick to explain. 'As well you know. What I'm talking about is familiarity. In this war we know our enemies like they know us. There are no surprises. This morning's attack was not unexpected. It is just the latest of many, and there will be many more to follow.'

'We will respond in kind,' Heloise said. 'We have to demonstrate our strength. We need to show there is consequence.'

'I know, and I agree, but we will land a blow without – forgive my impudence – conviction. We will kill some sicarios, maybe slaughter some traffickers, but they will be replaced. They are always replaced. Ours and theirs.'

'You're telling me nothing I don't already know, Luis, and you misunderstand me. We don't simply need a response, but a statement.'

'Of course,' he said. 'I do understand that.'

'Not merely externally,' Heloise explained. 'But internally too.'

'In which case, I'm not sure I understand what you mean.'

'My men need to see an immediate show of strength.'

He began to catch up. 'Even if it's pointed in the wrong direction?'

'Any direction I point is the correct one.'

Lavandier bowed his head in apologetic reverence. 'Yes, patron.'

Heloise said, 'Now tell me what you're proposing.'

'The other side is winning because they have the advantage of strength. Their influence is wider. Not because they have an outside perspective.'

She looked away, dismissive. 'Mercenaries only fight as hard as you pay them. They have no allegiance. They will not lay down their lives to protect mine, and they will turn on us the instant a better offer comes their way.'

'I'm not suggesting you hire an army. We have enough sicarios as it is. I'm talking about a professional. Someone we don't know, who no one knows. Someone who won't be seen coming.'

'An outside perspective,' Heloise said.

Lavandier nodded. 'And if self-preservation isn't enough, there is a more practical matter to consider.'

'I'm listening.'

'What did our friend in the mayor's office say?'

Heloise looked away.

'Continued violence, let alone an escalation, makes it harder for him.'

'He's paid more than enough as it is and we have nothing to show for it.'

'And we never will if we stop him doing his job.'

'He gets us a licence, that's all. It's a piece of paper ultimately.'

'A piece of paper with an estimated two-billion-dollar annual gross.'

Lavandier said nothing more because there was no need. He was paid to advise Heloise. He could convince her of nothing. Every decision was hers.

She said, 'I don't know of any professional who would be capable of ending this war.'

'Nor do I,' Lavandier admitted. 'Which is a problem, granted, but also the key to the success of the idea. If we don't know, then nor do our enemies.'

Heloise looked intrigued. She didn't look intrigued often. 'We would require a foreigner then. Someone from far away.'

Lavandier said, 'My thoughts, exactly.'

'Someone already proven in such work.'

He nodded.

Heloise said, 'And we keep this between ourselves. Just you and I will know he exists. If there is any merit to this suggestion of yours then it must remain a secret.'

Lavandier nodded again. 'Then you're on board with the idea?'

'That depends,' Heloise began. 'That depends on who you find.'

EIGHT

Forgers had a certain flair, a certain anima. Victor had never encountered one who was overweight. He had never dealt with one who was quiet or reserved. Most had counterculture leanings. Some were idealists. At least at the start of their careers, before age began to strip away that youthful rebellion and before they understood just how valuable their skills were to those with money to spend. This one met all of Victor's expectations and then added some contradictions of her own. This forger was female and she was young. He didn't know her age and wouldn't ask, but he was good at estimating. It was one of the many things he needed to be good at if he wanted to stay alive. Which he did.

At first glance, he had put her in her early twenties. Twenty-two. Maybe only a few months beyond her birthday. She was slim, but her cheeks were rounded. There were no lines on her face and her skin had an unmistakable plumpness to it that no cosmetic procedure could emulate. He knew about such procedures because he had undergone many in his lifetime.

Not to appear younger, but different. Each cut or injection to alter his face, little by little, so that even he didn't recognise himself any longer.

Only his eyes were still his own, and in them he saw nothing.

The young forger had the counterculture look, although this was not an area of his expertise. He knew little about the changing waves of fashion, but until semi-shaved heads and facial tattoos were as common as not, he was willing to hedge his bets that the forger had made an effort to forgo mainstream styles. Her hair was shaped into an afro quiff, bleached platinum blond in a stark contrast to her dark skin. The music she played from her computer was unrecognisable to his ear. Whatever it was, he hoped it didn't catch on. He found it hard enough to travel on public transport fighting the urge to use earbud cables to choke out the rude and disrespectful.

She didn't refer to herself as a forger. She claimed to be an activist. She interspaced their professional discussions with political commentary and words like 'revolution'. She spoke of 'rising up'. She dreamed of 'bringing the system down'. She wanted to expose 'every last lying politician'. Victor neither agreed nor disagreed. He paid no attention to politicians unless he was hired to kill them.

The forger had no name that she had told him, and he feigned ignorance on the matter, but there wasn't a lot that he didn't know about her other than her exact age once he decided to use her services. Any forger had almost unequalled potential to do him harm. To do their job well enough to get him through airport security meant they had to know information about him he didn't want anyone to have. Therefore, he had to have insurance. If they had his biometric data he needed to know where they lived and who they cared most about in all the world.

Her handle was Poison Snowflake.

'You can call me Poison,' she had told him. 'Or Snowflake.'

'Okay,' Victor said.

'But not Flake.'

'Okay,' Victor said again.

She had a twisting pattern of white-ink snowflake tattoos on her neck that ran from behind her left ear and down her spine, where they disappeared beneath her T-shirt. Victor couldn't help but wonder how far down they went.

Poison had a studio apartment in Amsterdam, which was also her work studio. She had photographic equipment set up in one corner, next to sophisticated printers, laminators, and other technological wizardry needed to create and modify bogus identification of all kinds.

'I started out making fake IDs when we were teenagers,' she explained. 'It was easy and fun.'

Victor pretended to be interested. 'Uh huh.'

She took his photograph and printed off a passport-sized version. She spent a long time examining it, searching for something he didn't know and didn't ask to know. She seemed happy enough, though, and fixed it to a blank but genuine Canadian passport that Victor had supplied. She could offer passports of her own, but none that he wanted. A Canadian passport had particular value as it granted visa-less access to many countries. As such, it had cost him a considerable price, but not as great a price as the black-market fixer who had sold it to him had ended up paying.

'I want double what we agreed,' the man had told Victor.

'That's too bad.'

The fixer might have made a useful contact otherwise, but people were greedy, Victor had learned many times. As he went out of his way to project a non-threatening demeanour, it was not uncommon for those he dealt with to attempt to take advantage of him. He didn't take such things personally – he accepted it as an expected price of dealing with criminals – though his inevitable response tended to be greeted with less acquiescence.

Please don't ...

Poison's work was interrupted by a compulsion to check her phone – phones – at regular intervals. She had several mobile devices that pinged or chimed or flashed or vibrated. All of which seemed to require her immediate attention. Victor didn't understand what it was like to have such need for instant gratification, for endless dopamine hits. He was at his most satisfied with a coffee or a book.

He waited a while. It wasn't his nature to hurry someone's work or complain about the manner in which they went about it. He recognised his own limitations and needed the expertise of others. He would pay Poison well for good work. It mattered little to him if it took her an hour or two. If patience was a virtue it was the only way in which he was virtuous.

She didn't look at him as she said, 'You can take a seat, you know.'

'I'm fine standing.'

He was a little stiff from sparring in a nearby dojo. A private session with the owner, after hours. It was a favour of sorts, a year in the making.

She didn't respond, but he saw the tension in her shoulders. He was fine standing, but she wasn't fine with him standing. He glanced around at the low sofa and faux-leather bean bags before his gaze settled on the stools at the breakfast bar. He perched on one and saw her relax.

Perhaps he wasn't being quite as unthreatening as he had intended. Or perhaps Poison's instincts were better than average. It was rare for people to see through his façade of normalcy, but it was not impossible. For a moment, he thought of a time in Berlin and someone who he had not only failed to convince of his normalcy, but who had seen straight through him.

He turned his thoughts back to the present. Memories were distraction. Distractions could be fatal.

He looked around the studio, searching for a topic to springboard small talk, but Poison was too young, too different, for him to even fake common ground. Instead, his eyes found her and the way she would roll her shoulders every so often.

'The radius and ulna,' he said.

She glanced at him. 'What?'

'You're getting shoulder discomfort because the bones in your forearms – the radius and the ulna – are pronated so you can use your keyboard and mouse. That's an unnatural position. If your arms are hanging free at your sides, your thumb is in line with your elbow pit. When you use your computer, your hands are rotated out of this position, which twists those bones out of their natural position, creating tension. That travels up your arms and ends up in your shoulders, causing the discomfort you're experiencing.'

She stopped her work and examined her wrists and arms, as if noticing how they worked for the first time. When she understood what he had said, she asked, 'Then what's the solution?'

'You need an ergonomic keyboard and a new mouse to go with it. Maybe a new chair.'

'Right. You've had this too?'

Victor nodded. He hadn't, but he knew how the body worked, and the most efficient ways to break bones and dislocate limbs, to tear ligaments and snap tendons. A physical therapist in reverse.

Poison said, 'I'll look into it,' and turned back to her computer.

Even with the phones distracting her every few seconds, she worked fast. He saw no hurry in her actions, just skill. It was impressive watching her work.

The introduction of biometric passports had made Victor's careful existence increasingly difficult. Once, it had been comparatively easy to acquire a genuine identity or a convincing set of fake documents. Black-market forgers were common and easy to find. Times had changed. Obtaining a genuine passport was more problematic. To craft one, a forger now had to have the ability to clone chips and photograph retinas with an infrared camera. The skills required and increased costs meant most suppliers Victor had dealt with had gone out of business. His own expenses had risen too. A thousand dollars had been enough at one time to obtain a complete set of genuine identification papers – passport, birth certificate, driver's licence – but now it was closer to a hundred thousand. It was an unavoidable cost of his profession. He couldn't afford to get stopped at an airport. He couldn't risk being caught pretending to be someone he was not.

Poison had all the equipment necessary and all of the skills to clone the biometric chip of the stolen Canadian passport of a man of Victor's approximate age and physical appearance and produce a forgery. She overcharged him, but Victor overcharged every client that had ever hired him. Besides, he would rather deal with a forger who felt confident enough in her abilities to charge too much than one who didn't operate with the same self-belief.

He found her charming in a way he recognised as patronising. Her youthful idealism and rebelliousness were hard to dislike. He liked the tattoos and the piercings too, the bizarre haircut and striking clothes. She wanted to make statements with her appearance. She wanted to cause a reaction. Victor didn't have the same luxury. He spent a considerable amount of effort to blend in, to remain unnoticed. He didn't understand what it felt like to have a fashionable hairstyle. He didn't know which colours suited him.

He had never looked his best.

She turned on her swivel chair. 'It's going to take a while to clone the chip.'

Victor said, 'No problem.'

She regarded him with pursed lips. 'Say, here's an idea: wanna do something crazy while we wait?'

He was about to ask what she was talking about, but she was already standing to take off her clothes.

He took the cue to do the same.

NINE

'You don't want to screw with me,' Poison said when they first met.

Victor hadn't felt the need to say something similar. It would have been pointless without breaking character. He didn't want her to know he was the most dangerous person she could meet. Instead, he gave subtle clues so she thought he was running, that he needed the passport so he could flee the country, so he could go into hiding. He didn't know how successful he had been, but she didn't enquire. She was a professional.

But after the barrier between professional and personal interaction had been abolished, Poison asked him why he needed a new identity.

'I'm making a fresh start,' was his answer.

It was a term he'd heard a lot. People often talked about making fresh starts. Victor knew this because he spent a lot of time listening to conversations – on trains, on buses, in cafés, in the street – and not much time talking himself. So, he knew he was making one of his own. At least to the extent such a thing was possible for a man of his profession. He wasn't changing careers, because he didn't know how to do anything else; he wasn't changing residence, because he lived nowhere in particular; he wasn't changing his relationship status, because he had never had one. He was changing the nature of his profession, however. He had always been a free-lance operator, working with different brokers, performing contracts for multiple clients, but the last few years had been different. His independent status had been eroded. The once sacred difference between broker and client had blurred. He hadn't understood just how trapped he had been until he had found freedom again.

There was a newfound exhilaration he hadn't felt in a long time.

Poison checked the computer while Victor dressed. She didn't bother to dress herself again except with her T-shirt. It was a half-hearted attempt to protect what little modesty remained. The snowflakes did go all the way down her spine.

'Your fresh start is almost ready.'

He buttoned up his white dress shirt, leaving the top button unfastened. He wore a tie only when it was unavoidable, and in those cases it would be a clip-on if he could get away with it without drawing attention. He left his suit jacket hanging from the back of a chair and laced his shoes. He always felt a little guilty when wearing outdoor shoes inside a home. He couldn't rid himself of the memory of a time when such an action would have significant repercussions. He spent almost as much effort not thinking about the past as he did on remaining unnoticed, but some things were harder to ignore than others.

Poison said, 'Just so you know, I do have a boyfriend. It's kinda serious. This was just a . . . whatever. Is that okay with you?'

He nodded.

The studio apartment was spacious, with bare brick walls, high ceilings and lots of windows along one wall. The building had once been a textiles factory. Poison didn't own a lot of furniture. Her personal sense of style didn't translate to her living and working environment. It was clean and spartan, with nothing present that didn't serve some function. He imagined even the potted plants had a job. Poison kept all her windows closed, despite the heat. To limit eavesdropping, he presumed. Hence the plants to help oxygenate the studio.

People like Poison were often difficult to locate, but Victor knew where to look and how to ask the right questions. He had identified a number of immigration lawyers of questionable conduct, and after a while observing those seeking the services of these lawyers, he identified an individual who some of them ended up meeting. This man offered several services, including providing bogus documentation. After a polite conversation and an exchange of money and threats, he revealed his supplier. The supplier was small time. He faked work permits and arranged marriages of convenience. A few nights shadowing him and Victor knew where those permits were forged, and further surveillance of that backstreet print shop and he noticed a young woman who frequented it more than anyone could need.

Poison was a careful woman operating an illicit trade, but she was fearful of the authorities, not someone like Victor, who slipped a note into a pocket of her jacket while she enjoyed a chai latte or two. She didn't call the number he had supplied with the note, even when he left a second one while she watched a movie at the cinema. He approached her in the convenience store where she bought her groceries.

'I know you've been following me,' she had said.

Victor didn't tell her that was only because he had made sure she did. 'Then you know by now I'm not a cop.'

He had to prove he wasn't wearing a wire when he had first been invited into her studio.

'Lit scars. Where'd you get that one across your abs?'

When Poison had finished, she presented the passport without fanfare. Victor examined it. He was no expert, but he was no layman either. He saw the excellence in the product and nodded his approval. He reached into his pocket for payment. He handed the envelope to her. She didn't count the cash inside. She didn't even open it.

'About this,' Poison said in a certain tone.

'Is there a problem?'

She said, 'No problem, but a proposition.'

'Go on.'

'I usually do this for the cause,' she explained. 'I do this to help the brothers and sisters fight the good fight against the governments, against the corporations.'

He saw where this was going.

'And here you are in your suit, looking like the living embodiment of everything we're fighting against.'

'I'm not your enemy,' Victor said.

'But you're part of the system that is.'

'Then why did you agree to work for me?'

'Principles aren't cheap.'

'I have only as much money on me as we agreed.'

She nodded. 'I figured as much, so how's about the same

time next month you pay me again, and the same the month after and every month after that so the system doesn't find out that you're travelling through it with the wrong passport.'

'You want a sponsor,' Victor said.

'I know you can afford it, and revolutions are expensive.'

He thought for a moment. She was right: he had more than enough money to cover this expense. She thought she was overcharging, but he would have paid a lot more for work this good.

Poison watched him think. 'You know I have hidden cameras in here, yeah?'

'Two covering the door, one in the northeast corner, one in the lightshade and one in the smoke alarm.'

'How do you ... ?' She stiffened a little, but held her ground. 'In case you didn't know, they're all continuously recording and backed up.'

'To your computer.'

'Not just mine.'

Victor nodded. 'Yes, that's right. Your boyfriend's computer receives the same information over the internet. Encrypted, but then stored on his hard drive.'

She didn't respond.

'Marco,' Victor said. 'He likes to call himself Nemphese when he's not running around as mobile tech support. You met online. On a hacker forum.'

He saw her glance at one of her phones. One that had been buzzing the most throughout the last hour.

'He's pretty annoyed, right? After driving all that way out of town to see a new client that never showed. Long way back home to his apartment with the leaky ceiling. Just round the corner, isn't it? Above the Indian restaurant. He's not as security conscious as you. He's too trusting. He didn't have the same rough upbringing as you did.'

Poison was silent for a long time.

Victor rose from the stool. 'We were talking about sponsorship.'

Poison couldn't shake her head fast enough. 'Forget it. I was just kidding around. I wasn't serious.'

Victor said, 'I'm always serious.'

'Okay,' she replied, backing away. 'I made a bad call, but I've got the cash and you have the passport. We're done. The deal's still good.'

'I'm afraid we need to renegotiate the terms.'

He walked towards her. No longer in character. No longer unthreatening.

'Please don't ...'

TEN

Lavandier had not become consul to the matriarch of one of the most powerful cartels in Guatemala by being stupid, but he knew he was weak. Which, to his mind, was a kind of stupidity. He knew of his weakness, but he couldn't resist it. His weakness was nothing unique, nothing original. He had a taste for young women of the professional variety. His means of employment and location meant there was a near limitless supply to keep him entertained. He was a rich man, but he could have retired long ago if his tastes weren't for only the best and most expensive. Even a rich man could become poor that way.

Lavandier was paid to advise and to manage. Heloise Salvatierra was the boss, but true bosses did little actual work. That was the point of becoming boss. All the money, but none of the sweat. Lavandier sweated for his money. He dealt with traffickers and sicarios, cops and accountants. He kept the day-to-day operations running as smoothly as they could. Busts, killings and missing product were all common. Too common, even, but that was how the drug trade worked. Losses had to be factored in. They had to be expected and planned for, and that was the true skill of Lavandier. That was where his value lay. He made sure that any setback was not an actual setback. No shipment was ever too big, no trafficker too important, no sicario too valuable, to fear losing.

Heloise let him do his job his way, which was rare. Bosses may not want to work hard, but they wanted the work to be done their own way. The way they had done it to become boss in the first place. Heloise might be a different case because she had inherited her title, but no one respected her any less for that. She had been Lavandier for her father. She knew how the business worked and had the respect of those beneath her before she stepped into her father's shoes. Everyone respected her because those that hadn't were no longer in the cartel. Instead, they were buried in the jungle. She had been just as ruthless as her father had been. More so, maybe, because she was a woman and wanted to prove herself. She had done that and more. She had been one of those to wield the chainsaws.

Lavandier had no such ruthlessness. He kept his distance from the messy side of the trade. He didn't even like it when he cut himself shaving. Heloise found his squeamishness amusing. She liked to belittle him. She liked to show him photographs he didn't need to see. She forced him to watch videos that made him retch while she laughed the whole time.

Heloise and Lavandier greeted one another with air-kisses.

'You're looking good, Luis,' Heloise told him. 'I like your jacket.'

Lavandier wore slacks and a blazer over a polo shirt. All new, all the best money could buy. He liked to be smart casual. He didn't end up working for a cartel only to wear a suit. He hated suits. He hated what they represented: working hard only to die tired. No thanks. If Lavandier died tired, he would make sure it would be after a marathon session with the city's best escorts.

Heloise continued, with a wicked little grin: 'And your hair is particularly glorious today. You look positively radiant in your youthfulness.'

Lavandier had embraced the silver in his hair a long time ago, but he refused to be grey. His stylist would add some touches of colour every time he went for a trim, just to top up the silver-gold look that gave him both vigour and wisdom. Heloise teased him about his dyed hair with intermittent cruel taunts. Her humour, like the rest of her personality, was merciless.

He smiled through it. 'And you're delectable, as always. Maybe more so.'

'You flatter me.'

'My dear, I love you with all my soul.'

Heloise laughed. 'I think you mean with all your loins.'

Lavandier bowed his head. 'They share the same space.'

They met in the casino, in the Goddess Suite that Heloise called home. It was a horrific space to Lavandier's eye. So gaudy and ostentatious. All gold paint and excess, designed to appeal to those with plenty of money but no taste.

She led him to the living area and they took seats on armchairs so uncomfortable they could only be outrageously expensive.

'Who have you found?' she asked him.

He said, 'I have two candidates for your consideration. Both men. Both foreigners. At least as far as I can tell.'

'Tell me more.'

'The first I located through our friend in Moscow, so I will refer to him as the Russian. He has an extensive résumé and many notable hits. Long-range rifle kills being something of a speciality, but many achieved by other means also. He comes highly recommended.'

She considered this information for a while, which the Frenchman exploited by gazing upon her without judgement. She was a beautiful woman, with black hair and flawless skin. She dressed like a movie star attending a premiere. Always squeezed into something that showed off every curve. She liked to tease him as much as she liked to belittle him. He spent much of his time in her presence adjusting how he sat.

'The second?' she asked after a while.

Lavandier snapped out of his trance. 'This one was offered by a broker known as Phoenix, who you will remember was used on occasions by your father.'

Heloise nodded.

Lavandier added: 'But I know very little about the man she recommends. Hence, I shall call him the Wraith.'

'How intriguing.'

Heloise thought for a moment. Lavandier stared at her lips. They had been turned to a permanent pout and always smeared with a bright colour. She was in her late forties, but looked ten years younger. If Lavandier's weakness was for escorts, then Heloise's was for cosmetic surgeons. Although it wasn't for vanity, he learned, but for competition. Heloise's sister, Maria, younger, prettier, had been their father's obvious favourite. Heloise no longer had the chance to win her father's approval, but she could still fight her sister's beauty. Lavandier was far too wise to ever comment, but it was a battle Heloise could never win. Partaking only ensured eventual humiliation.

If sibling rivalry was her flaw, it was her only one. Heloise didn't drink and she didn't take drugs, following the example presented by the most effective bosses, like her father. With near limitless funds and access to product, excess was common and almost always led to self-destruction. Heloise was too smart to give her enemies an easy advantage over her. Lavandier was glad about that, because if Heloise was usurped, he would be too. He thrived – and survived – as long as she did, so he did everything he could to ensure this. He paid close attention to grumblings and those with too much ambition.

'If Phoenix is suggesting him then there must be a reason,' she said. 'He must be capable. He has to be good.'

'This is my thinking too. The only thing more important to her than discretion is her reputation.'

Lavandier waited for Heloise to consider the information and come to a course of action. His role was to provide advice, but he knew when it was unnecessary, and also when it could be misconstrued as condescension. Lavandier was French, from rural Normandy. He was a foreigner, an outsider, and this both hindered and helped him in his career. His nationality, his Europeanism, gave him an exotic air and afforded him an instant respect he did not deserve. But conversely he had to work harder to gain trust.

He was in no rush. He watched her think. He enjoyed watching her think.

After almost a minute of silence, Heloise said, 'I like the

sound of the Wraith more. But I want to meet him first. I'm not hiring someone I have no measure of.'

Lavandier nodded. The Wraith was his own preferred choice. 'I'll arrange a face-to-face.'

ELEVEN

The second forger Victor dealt with proved to be far more respecting of their agreement. There was far less personal interaction too. The second passport and accompanying documents provided Victor with an Australian legend, which would be used as a backup identity. He would keep it in motion, using automated courier services to send it across international borders in sync with his own movements, arranging for delivery and collecting it only when it was needed.

With a second clean legend, Victor burned his old passport. It was a fake, but an exceptional one, and though he had never before used it while working, he had owned it for a few years and now more than ever it was essential to rid himself of any connections to his previous employers. A fresh start, as he had told Poison.

Everyone who mattered thought he was dead. Or, couldn't be certain he was alive. Only one woman knew for sure, but he didn't envision their paths would ever cross again. His true vulnerability came via his broker, but they had a good arrangement. Phoenix knew there would be a heavy price for betrayal and much to be gained through cooperation.

If he wanted to work, if he wanted money, then there was always vulnerability. He couldn't operate without drawing attention to himself. He couldn't work without putting himself at risk. It was the nature of the profession.

A profession that presented a new opportunity. It was the first job arranged by his new broker, and it came with a proviso. The client wanted to meet him first.

The meeting took some effort to arrange. The client had many stipulations and unnegotiable conditions, and Victor had plenty of his own. Meeting a client in person was a cardinal sin. Or, at least, it had been before he had been forced to change his protocols to keep powerful enemies on side. Now he was freelance again, now he was making his fresh start, he didn't want to start breaking rules from the outset, but to his surprise the client was willing to come to him, to meet at a time and place of his choosing.

He had selected a suite in Madrid's Ritz-Carlton hotel for the face-to-face and a time of six fifty-five p.m. If the client was a minute early, or a minute late, the meeting would not take place.

The client insisted on being accompanied by an advisor, which Victor accepted, but only if the client's security detail waited in the hotel lobby. Both the client and he agreed no weapons would be present at the meeting, but he would not be honouring the agreement. He had a small arsenal of guns in the suite's master bedroom that would be taken out of there only if needed. He would have no weapons on his person, which he felt kept to the spirit of the rule. He meant the client no harm, unless they left him no other choice.

It took fifty seconds for the private elevator to ascend from the lobby to the suite, which meant Victor had plenty of time to witness the client's arrival at the hotel himself, and still return to the suite.

He had chosen the Royal Suite to host the meeting. It had two bedrooms, three bathrooms, two lounges and a French balcony. An expensive outlay – there was little change from five thousand euros for one night – but Victor had many requirements that only this particular suite could meet.

The advisor entered the suite first. He was a slim man in his mid-forties, with tanned skin and long greying blond hair that was slicked back from his forehead and curled at the nape of his neck. He had a confident, professional manner, neither offering his hand in warm greeting nor displaying any trepidation. It took a certain presence of will to show so little when meeting with a contract killer for the first time.

Heloise Salvatierra walked behind him. She looked like a celebrity travelling incognito, with large sunglasses hiding her eyes and a wide-brimmed hat, which she removed as soon as she was through the door, releasing a lot of glossy black hair over her shoulders. The sunglasses were taken off next and Victor saw the curiosity in her eyes. There was no fear – she was used to dealing with dangerous individuals – but the curiosity gave way to unease. Victor was not whom she had expected.

'You're not as I had imagined.'

Victor said, 'I can see that.'

'I mean, you don't look very scary.'

'That's kind of you to say.'

'I've known many killers,' Heloise said. 'So I know when I'm wasting my time. But with you I can't tell.'

He saw this too, but didn't comment. It was not his nature to feel challenged, and not his nature to feel the need to accept a challenge.

Heloise reacted to his lack of reaction with more curiosity, but it wasn't easy to see. Her face didn't move a lot. Her eyebrows remained perfect frozen arches. She was tall and thin, but her proportions were imbalanced by breast and posterior augmentation. Her nose was straight and delicate. Her lips were full and her teeth even. Her cheekbones were prominent and her jaw defined. Each feature was perfect on its own but the overall face was piecemeal. The surgeon had done a fine job, but she could not be shaped into someone she wasn't. And no surgery could soften the strength in her gaze.

Victor said, 'Let's take a seat.'

He gestured to one of the lounge areas and led the client and her advisor to where two blue upholstered armchairs faced a matching sofa across a coffee table. Like the rest of the suite, the room was lavish in decoration and impeccable in taste. Even Heloise, who no doubt was used to the best that life could offer, seemed impressed. Which was one of the several necessities the suite afforded.

The only thing in the room that disturbed the carefully chosen aesthetic was a red North Face rucksack that rested against the wall by the door.

Victor took a seat on the edge of the sofa. They sat opposite him. The light from the French doors behind him was in their eyes, which was how he wanted it. Heloise sat on the chair to his right. Lavandier took the other.

He seemed more relaxed, whereas it took Heloise a moment to sit comfortably in her dress, which didn't offer a lot of room to manoeuvre.

Victor didn't begin the conversation and neither did Heloise. They looked across the table at one another; her trying to read him from appearances alone and him letting her try. She would realise it was a fruitless exercise before too long. He checked his watch.

Lavandier took this as a cue to open proceedings, although it hadn't been. 'Thank you for agreeing to meet us.'

'No problem,' Victor said. 'I appreciate you coming all the way to me.'

Heloise said, 'It's really not that much bother when you have a private plane.'

'I can imagine it affords a certain amount of freedom to travel.'

'Shall we make small talk or talk business?' she asked.

'I have the suite until tomorrow so it's entirely up to you.'

Heloise sat back in the armchair and Lavandier spoke for her. 'We requested this meeting because we don't do things by halves. We know of your broker, but we do not know you.'

'I'm afraid that's unavoidable,' Victor said.

Heloise said, 'How many men have you killed?'

'I don't think that's particularly important.'

She was undeterred. 'A dozen? More?'

Victor shrugged, dismissive. 'One or two.'

She recognised the understatement. 'What's your success rate?'

'Pretty good.'

'Who was your last target?'

'A man.'

Heloise sighed, frustrated.

Lavandier said, 'Would you tell us about one of your more challenging assignments?'

'I'm afraid that's impossible.'

'We came all the way from Guatemala to find out more about you,' Lavandier replied. 'So, maybe, you could help us out in that regard? You agreed to meet us, after all.'

Victor said, 'I'm not prepared to discuss any of my previous contracts, personal history, and I won't tell you my favourite colour.'

Heloise shook her head. 'We're wasting our time here.'

'But rest assured,' Victor continued, 'your knowledge of me is greater than the majority of my previous clients just by nature of this meeting.'

'Well,' Heloise said, 'you should know I don't make a habit of meeting hitmen.'

'Duly noted, but you should know I'm not fond of that term.'

Heloise's nod said *I don't care.*

'You understand our problem,' Lavandier continued.

'How so?'

'Insomuch that we cannot hire someone without first knowing if they can do what is needed.'

Victor said, 'You may take my word for it.'

Heloise regarded him from beneath her frozen eyebrows. 'Duly noted.'

Lavandier smiled and held open his hands. 'It seems we have an impasse.'

'I thought we might have one,' Victor said, then added: 'Do you mind if I take out my phone?'

Heloise said, 'Should I?'

He kept his movements slow and obvious, removing a mobile from his inside jacket pocket. He looked at Heloise for a moment.

'Would you mind moving your head a little to the right?'

'Yes, I would mind. What is this?'

Victor said, 'Your choice,' and spent a moment operating the phone's touchscreen. He then checked his watch and waited.

Lavandier watched him. Heloise watched him.

Victor waited.

A church bell chimed as the time reached seven p.m. It chimed again.

On the third chime, Victor tapped the phone's screen.

TWELVE

The chime hid the sound of a gunshot.

A subsonic round, fired by a suppressed rifle fifty-eight metres away, on the far side of the street. Still loud, even with the reduced muzzle report and the lack of sonic boom, but unnoticed and unheard in the echoing boom of a chiming church bell.

The bullet struck its mark a split-second after leaving the weapon, having passed through the open French doors, above Victor's head, travelling at a downward trajectory that took it within centimetres of Heloise's left ear.

The red North Face rucksack was filled with sand that trickled in a hiss from the bullet hole and on to the floor.

The thunk of impact startled Lavandier, but Heloise was already reacting to the whizz of the round passing by her. Her advisor was slow to understand, but Heloise knew exactly what had happened. She was on her feet and out of the perceived line of fire.

'You tried to kill me.'

She hiked up her dress, and from under the hem, drew a small nickel-plated pistol from an inner-thigh holster. She aimed it at Victor.

'We agreed to no weapons.'

She said, 'We agreed to a lot of things. Like no partners with rifles.'

Victor said, 'I have no partner. I don't play well with others.'

'Who took the shot?'

'I did.'

'Who hired you to kill me?'

'No one,' he answered. 'And you'll remember I asked you to move your head a little to the right.'

She said, 'Explain yourself before I shoot you dead.'

'This is Spain,' Lavandier said, gesturing for calm. 'We can't do that kind of thing here and expect to walk away. There are rules here.'

'Stay out of this, Luis,' Heloise told him without taking her gaze from Victor. 'The grown-ups are talking.'

Lavandier sat cowed.

Heloise said to Victor, 'I told you to explain yourself.'

'You may not have said so in our prior communications, but you came here to get a measure of me. You came here to find out more about me. As you said: you don't know me. I'm a private person, Miss Salvatierra. I'm not prepared to share details about who I am or what I've done. Hence, we were going to have a problem. Therefore, and I hope you'll forgive my impertinence, I prepared a demonstration instead. To expedite the conversation, if you will.'

She glanced at the phone in Victor's hands. 'You took the shot.'

He nodded. 'There's a museum across the street, and it's

70

sadly not tall enough for what I needed, but there are apart-
ments further away. The angle isn't ideal, but thanks to the
large balcony and French doors this suite offers, it let me set
up a rifle in one of the said apartment buildings, aimed this
way. The weapon is hooked up to an automated rig. I zeroed
the rifle manually, of course, but the rig is controlled wirelessly with my phone. Look.'

He turned the phone around and held it up so she could
see the screen, and the zoomed-in image of the suite from
the rifle's perspective. A camera was part of the rig. Heloise
looked at herself.

'It's touch activated,' Victor said. 'I would show you, but
we'd need to wait half an hour for the next church bell. Unless
you want someone to report the sound of a gunshot.'

'Which was why you were so very particular about the
time of the meeting.'

Victor inclined his head. 'I believed it would suit both our
agendas to demonstrate what I can do, instead of explain
what I've done.'

Lavandier, now caught up, said, 'We're leaving,' and stood.
'No one puts my patron at risk like this. You should know
there will be severe repercussions for your arrogance. Come,
Heloise. Let's take our leave of this circus act.'

He made towards the door, but Heloise hadn't moved,
although the small pistol was no longer pointed at
Victor's head.

'Not so fast, Luis,' she said. 'I'm unharmed.'

He stopped, surprised but obeying, and she approached the
red rucksack. 'May I?' she said to Victor.

'Be my guest.'

She knelt down and worked her index finger and thumb

into the bullet hole. It took her a moment to locate the bullet and prise it free.

'It's real,' she said.

'Of course,' Victor replied.

She stood and presented it to Lavandier. 'Imagine if this had been meant for someone else? The war would be over.'

Lavandier whispered, 'I don't trust him,' in Spanish, into her ear, but Victor had no trouble reading his lips.

Heloise's response was also a whisper, and even easier to read. 'I don't care.'

She returned to Victor and holstered the small pistol. 'I'm at war with a rival cartel. It's been going on for some time, and there are no signs it will end soon, if ever. I have legions of sicarios. They are loyal, and they fight tirelessly on my behalf, but they can't get close to my rival, which is why I need a man like you to do what they cannot. I want you to kill the head of the rival cartel, which will bring the war to a conclusion.'

'I figured as much.'

Lavandier stood silent, arms now folded across his chest.

Heloise continued: 'The head of the cartel is well protected and smart, and though I am loath to admit it, commands even more loyalty than I do. There will be an army between you and your target.'

'No one is bulletproof,' Victor said.

'You'll take the job?'

'Do you agree to the terms presented by my broker?'

Heloise nodded. 'Money is no object. Double your fee. Triple it. I don't care. Do this, and you'll be wealthier than you could ever imagine.'

'That's not what I meant,' Victor said. 'I'm very particular about how I work. If I do this, I do it my way, at my own pace. I've had clients interfering in the past and I won't tolerate it here. Also, I don't want any surprises. I don't want to find out the target has police protection and you failed to tell me.'

Lavandier, following his boss's decision whatever his own reservations, said, 'You'll know as much as we do, I assure you.'

'I work alone,' Victor said. 'Which means no one else is involved in any capacity. No sicarios backing me. You might think it'll help, but they'll only cause problems. You're hiring me to do what they can't, remember.'

'Whatever you wish,' Heloise agreed.

'And no one else like me hired to do the same job. You may want to double your odds of getting the job done, but I don't want anyone else getting in my way. These are my conditions and they are non-negotiable.'

Heloise said, 'You have my word.'

'Do you have a time frame in mind?'

Lavandier looked to Heloise, who nodded for him to answer.

He said, 'The sooner this is done the better, but we appreciate these things take time to do properly. We don't want to put you under any pressure. We don't want you to rush. Fast work is rarely good work.'

'Very generous of you, and I agree with the sentiment.'

'Well,' the Frenchman said. 'I think we all understand one another. So, do we agree terms? Do we have a deal?'

'Based on what we've discussed, I'll take the contract. Please pass everything you know about the target to me at your earliest convenience. I'll make my way to Guatemala once I know more, but you won't know when I set off nor when I'm in the country. You won't know when I'll initiate events nor by which method. I will make those decisions myself and act according to my own designs. I may contact you for additional information as and when I deem it necessary, so I will need a direct line.'

Heloise said, 'Luis will give you his personal cell. You may contact him any time, day or night, and he will do anything and everything to assist you.'

Lavandier didn't react, but that only told Victor he had not previously agreed to such an arrangement. It also told Victor that Lavandier would do whatever he was told without complaint or argument.

'The only assistance I'll need will be information.'

Lavandier tilted his chin downwards. 'My bread and butter.'

Heloise said, 'We will have a dossier finalised within the next few days. Rest assured it will contain everything you could possibly know about the target. You see, I'm in a unique position to help in this regard because the person I want you to kill for me is my sister.'

THIRTEEN

Heloise Salvatierra and Luis Lavandier reconnected with their security detail in the hotel lobby, who outnumbered guests two-to-one. The hotel staff didn't know who the men were nor how to handle them, but upon arriving Lavandier had given the flustered manager a month's salary in cash just to look the other way for a few minutes. So, the security detail had loitered in the lobby, pacing about and unnerving the well-to-do guests.

They were not professional bodyguards, but they were experienced gunmen working for the cartel, with skills and loyalty that had been proven time and again. However, they had been chosen because they had passports and because they had been convicted of no crimes. Transatlantic travel was not something any of them were used to, and as Heloise had to cross borders on occasion, it was essential to have at least some of her legions of sicarios with the documents and clean sheets to accompany her.

The men were agitated. Even when they did travel abroad

with Heloise, it was to Honduras, Nicaragua, Panama or Colombia. Never further afield. Never across oceans. They didn't know what she was doing, nor whom she was meeting. This was all new for them, but they did what they were told without argument or complaint. Their agitation was not helped by the fact they were unarmed.

They had flown on a private jet, which provided much freedom to flout laws and regulations, but they couldn't stride around Madrid with their AKs. They had wanted to, of course, but orders were orders. They hadn't expected the meeting to last more than a minute or so, and it was unprecedented for Heloise to ever be out of sight. If something went wrong upstairs, they would know fast, because Lavandier had a radio with him and the head of the security detail had one too, but what then? They were all tough, hardened sicarios, but fists were no replacement for guns.

If anything happened to their boss, worse would happen to them.

Their relief was palpable when Heloise and Lavandier exited an elevator, and that relief was purely for Heloise. None of the sicarios had any love for Lavandier, and their respect was limited, given he was an outsider.

Heloise barely made eye contact with her men as she headed outside with Lavandier at her side, and the sicarios fell into position surrounding her. A limousine was waiting, and Lavandier tipped the valet.

No sicarios joined them in the limousine. They rode ahead and behind in Range Rovers.

The limousine had been rented for the day. It had been difficult to arrange because there was only one rental company in the city that hired out armoured vehicles. Even away from home, away from the war, Heloise would not ride inside any vehicle that could not stop at least a 7.62mm rifle round. Lavandier wasn't sure about the proliferation of assault rifles in Madrid, but given the difficulty in finding an armoured limousine, he didn't imagine drive-bys and ambushes were all that common. He had spent so much time in the civilised war zones and failed states of Central and South America that it was now hard to remember a time when he had travelled without a heavily armed escort. Once, a seatbelt and an airbag had been more than enough protection. Simpler times, never to be repeated.

Lavandier said, 'What do you think of him?'

'I think I want to sleep with him.'

Lavandier felt warm with a rush of jealousy. 'Even in his bed you wouldn't be safe.'

'That's precisely why I want to sleep with him.'

'And what do you think of him beyond his suitability as a sexual partner?'

Heloise settled back into the comfortable seat and closed her eyes. 'When I was a little girl my father called me the queen and Maria the princess. As he lay dying, he called us this again. He said he loved us both equally.'

'I'm sure he did.'

'Maybe,' Heloise sighed. 'He was a man of few words, but every word he said meant something.'

'I don't understand what you're trying to tell me.'

'He said I was the queen and Maria was the princess. You see, a princess can become a queen, yet a queen can never become a princess.'

'I still don't understand.'

'He may have loved us both the same, but he had more

belief in Maria. I had peaked in his eyes, but for her he saw further greatness.'

Lavandier was as shocked as he was horrified. 'You started the war because of something your father said on his deathbed?'

'You think so very highly of me, don't you, Luis? No, the necessity of Maria's demise is pure business. While she lives, there will never be peace and I will never be true patron.'

Lavandier said, 'I'm relieved to hear you say that.'

'But need and want are two separate desires, and I want to kill my sister too. I want to kill her because of what my father said to us.'

'She didn't put those words in his mouth,' Lavandier argued. 'It's not her fault.'

'I know that, of course. I don't want to kill her to take revenge on her. I want to kill her to take revenge on him.'

Lavandier knew when it was best to keep his thoughts to himself.

Heloise said, 'I think our new friend the Wraith can provide that revenge.'

'I'm no longer sure about his suitability. He's too dangerous.'

'You've said that already.'

'I want to make you understand that from the outset. If things go wrong, I want you to remember I warned you about him.'

Heloise smiled at him. 'Were you scared you might lose me in there, dear Luis?' She laid a hand on his mid-thigh.

Lavandier swallowed. 'He could have killed you.'

'But he didn't, did he? Truth be told, I found the whole experience thrilling. An unusual kind of fun, wasn't it?'

Lavandier adjusted his seating position. 'What about what he said at the end?'

She took her hand away, releasing him from the exquisite torture. 'Are you referring to his stipulations that we stay out of it, that no one else is involved?'

'He was explicit on those points,' Lavandier said. 'So, do you still want me to meet with the second assassin when we return? The Russian?'

Heloise nodded as though she had not even considered the alternative. 'The day I let a hitman tell me what to do is the day I'll happily end my own life. Of course I still want you to meet the Russian. Why hire only one killer when we can have two?'

FOURTEEN

The dossier that Lavandier provided was perhaps the most extensive Victor had ever been given. It wasn't a document, or even documents, but a link to a secure website on the deep web. The site contained an autobiography's worth of personal information on Heloise's sister, Maria, as well as dozens of newspaper and online articles on her and her alleged criminal activities. Their father, Manny, had been the boss of the country's largest and most violent cartel, acting as a go-between for the drug-producing cartels of Colombia and the distributors in Mexico. Guatemala's geographical location made it a perfect staging ground to transfer product from the producers to the distributors. When Manny died of a heart attack, at the young age of sixty, his cartel became fractured by rival lieutenants vying for dominance. Amid this infighting his two daughters manoeuvred unnoticed, creating alliances and encouraging the competition to wipe each other out, until they were unopposed. But instead of running the cartel together, or dividing it between them, they turned on one another and had been at war ever since. Victor was not surprised to find that the information supplied by Lavandier blamed Maria for starting the war, but he neither believed this was without bias, nor cared who had caused their conflict. All he cared about was that he had been hired to end it.

If there was an established playbook for cartel wars, Maria and Heloise had followed it. Their sicarios performed tit-for-tat ambushes, assassinations and sabotage on almost a daily basis. Gun battles in the slums were commonplace. Roadside IEDs in the countryside were frequent. Drive-bys downtown occurred more often than not.

With a never-ending supply of poor young men desperate for drug money, casualties were irrelevant. Losses could be replaced within hours, weapons handed down to the newcomers before the blood of the previous owner was even dry. Knowing how poor some Guatemalans were, it wasn't hard to understand how a youth with nothing to lose might be drawn into gambling his life away. It wasn't hard to understand because long ago Victor had been just like them.

The first step in Victor's preparations was a week in Morocco. He rented a small but secure villa, and left the grounds only to procure food and bottled water. He slept in the morning, having spent his nights studying the site set up by Lavandier, and his afternoons in the villa's grounds, swimming and lying on a sun lounger. He was no Latino, and had no intention of pretending to be one, but he also had no desire to stand out any more than necessary.

Travelling to Central America meant flying. The authorities naturally paid attention to people, especially lone men, travelling from certain countries, but as a Caucasian male

Victor tended to avoid scrutiny although given his tan he was fastidious in his shaving habits. He obeyed every airline rule to the letter. He never complained. He never reclined his seat. He never ate loud snacks.

Still, travelling was not without danger. There were no relaxing journeys for Victor. There were no easy routes. And there were no shortcuts. He did everything he could to avoid straight lines. He had a good legend. The documents supplied by Poison were excellent. Perhaps the best he had ever used. Airports were still dangerous, however. Facial recognition software was improving at an exponential rate. He couldn't hope to stay ahead of it even with his regular surgeries and there was only so much even the best surgeons could achieve. There was no point avoiding the technology making a match of his face if to do so drew the wrong kind of attention – which was any attention.

There were other ways, besides changing his face, to reduce the chances of a hit. Avoiding airports was the best precaution. Not always possible, of course, but he did so when he could. It was one of the reasons he had operated in continental Europe so much. The Schengen Agreement meant he could cross dozens of borders without showing documents or being scanned.

From Marrakesh, he took a ferry to Gibraltar, then trains through Spain and France and then to London, before he sat down on a flight to Jamaica. A stop-off in the Caribbean was always good protocol when crossing the Atlantic. Incoming travellers from Europe were almost all tourists. No one he needed to concern himself with paid any attention to such travellers. He blended in with ease, too. Having to engage in a little small talk with an old Jamaican woman was the extent of his difficulties. She didn't have much of an accent.

'Twenty years in Europe will do that to you,' she felt the need to explain. He hadn't mentioned her accent. 'But it'll be back with a vengeance as soon as I get home. You won't be able to understand me.'

She gave him a taste of her rapid-fire Kingston patois.

'You're right,' he agreed. 'I have no idea what you just said.'

She laughed and touched his arm. The Jamaican woman called herself Belle. He didn't believe it to be her real name. She had a necklace that spelled Belle in shiny nickel. The letters were flowing to imitate handwriting. She put her fingers to the necklace as she introduced herself. Maybe it was short for Anabelle. Perhaps it was just a name she liked. There could be a story behind it, but she didn't tell him and he didn't ask.

He respected people's privacy when it came to chosen names.

As much as Victor didn't like to travel in straight lines, he didn't like to do what would be expected. The most common entry point into Guatemala, from the Caribbean or elsewhere, was by plane, flying into Mundo Maya airport outside of the capital, usually via the United States. If anyone was waiting for his arrival, it would be there. Which was why he paid cash to a fisherman to ferry him across the Caribbean Sea to Honduras. From there, he travelled exclusively by bus, first to San Pedro Sula, where he took the daily bus that ran from Honduras' capital all the way to Guatemala City. There was no border check. The facilities were there – huts, barriers, bollards and so on – but they were unmanned. The bus trundled along without so much as slowing down.

Trains were Victor's preferred method of travelling long

distances, but there were no passenger trains in the country. Cars were pretty uncommon too, which meant buses were the main form of transportation.

He swapped buses at the first available opportunity. He was heading to Guatemala City, but he was not prepared to take a single bus all the way there. He waited in a small border town for the next available transport, which was a *camioneta*, or chicken bus.

The driver's helper, the *ayudante*, was a malnourished boy who scaled the bus to fix luggage to the roof with boundless energy and improbable strength. Some bags were bigger than him. The fat man behind the wheel never stopped yelling at him. *Faster, faster.*

The *ayudante* wanted two dollars from Victor, who had already noted the Guatemalans were paying one. Victor paid him the fare without argument or complaint – he knew it wasn't the kid's policy – and tipped him the same amount. 'Don't tell the driver.'

The bus was so overcrowded Victor had to stand with his head pressed against the roof and bodies pressed against him. He couldn't help but overhear the criss-cross of loud conversations in Spanish. He heard other languages too, K'iche' or Mam – Mayan languages – but he didn't understand the words. The ignorance was rare for him. He spoke so many languages he wasn't used to failing to recognise even a single word. He was operating outside of his comfort zone, however. He would have to get used to it.

The acrid scent and taste of exhaust fumes were ever-present. As was the blare of music seeping from poor-quality headphones, chickens clucking, and the screeching voice of a vendor selling homemade snacks. There was no room for him to squeeze along the aisle, so the food and drink had to be passed down from passenger to passenger to get from seller to customer, as did the cash for payment and sometimes the change as well. Victor played his part, staying in character, fitting in as might any other tourist, while keeping a nervous guy with fidgeting fingers in his gaze. The nervous guy was skinny and small and, unlike the snack vendor, he could work his way between passengers and seats. It was no surprise when he ended up standing next to Victor.

Sometimes it was better to be himself.

Victor leaned close and whispered, 'Take my wallet and I'll take your eyes.'

The nervous guy couldn't get away fast enough.

The bus rattled and the exhaust spluttered and rasped. Victor didn't have a chance to enjoy the countryside – he could see almost nothing through the mass of passengers – but he wasn't here to sightsee. He wasn't comfortable with so many intrusions into his personal space but he tolerated them. He pretended to be at ease when he only felt at ease, only relaxed, by himself. He had to be a loner because he was a killer, but he had been a loner long before that.

Every time someone hailed it from the side of the road, the bus stopped and more space was somehow found.

The driver made good use of his horn and took a liberal approach to traffic laws. The going was slow, however, with the dirt roads and intermittent stops to pick up more passengers or drop them off. One stop was for neither. The driver waded into a field and pulled down his shorts.

Victor couldn't reach his destination in the *camioneta*, nor did he want to, so he disembarked with a group of other passengers when the dirt road intersected with a paved road, and he waited at an ad-hoc bus stop for another service. This one was provided by a grey-haired man driving a pickup truck. Two passengers had already taken the prime seats in the cab, so Victor climbed into the load bed with some locals. Mats had been provided to take some of the sting out of the inevitable bumps, but most of the other travellers perched on their bags or jackets.

Victor sat with his knees to his chest and watched the clouds shift and change above him as the locals sang songs about pretty girls and sunny days.

FIFTEEN

The final bus was better on every level. Unlike the rattling chicken bus that had taken him along dirt roads, this was a new vehicle, a double-decker, with clean paint and plenty of leg room. The seat even reclined. It was quiet too, with every passenger in an allocated seat, enjoying a smooth ride and air conditioning. Victor had purchased his ticket in advance – something he didn't like doing – but the benefits were many. On this bus he was indistinguishable from the other tourists. Most were from North America or Europe, picked up from their hotels for a nonstop journey across the country, happy to pay a premium for a faster, more comfortable service. In this instance, they were heading back to Guatemala City and Antigua, having visited the Mayan temples in the east.

Sitting next to him was an American woman named Joanna, who was returning to Guatemala City from a few days at the beach. They had exchanged some words as they had taken their seats. The inevitable 'excuse me' and 'sorry' and 'was that your foot?'. She introduced herself soon after they were settled.

'It's a long journey,' she said. 'I figure we get the awkwardness out of the way right from the start.'

Given he was nearing his ultimate destination and had a name printed on his ticket, he stuck to his legend instead of making up a name on the spot. He had a standard backstory designed to stifle conversation – accountant, divorced – but Ryan Mathus was neither. He was a commodities trader, newly separated after a long-term relationship. It wouldn't have mattered, he soon realised, because Joanna gave up midway through a film she was watching and set her sights on him instead.

She was watching on a tablet while he read his book – *Sapiens* – and when she took off her headset she exhaled and shook her head.

'That was a giant waste of my time.'

He gave a corresponding expression of sympathy.

'If I'd have wanted to watch a cartoon I'd have picked one. It all looks so fake. Why do they bother?'

'I agree,' he said. 'But people like those films.'

She kissed her teeth. Victor turned a page.

He remembered meeting a woman on a flight to Berlin who had been telling herself over and over that she wasn't going to die. She had a phobia. They had talked statistics and passed the time in polite conversation. For a brief moment, he wondered how she was doing, whether she had overcome her fear or if she was performing the same ritualistic chant, unnerving whoever she was sitting beside. She had made Victor curious, intrigued, but not scared. He didn't scare easily. Maybe at all. He was sure he had been – he had to have been – but he couldn't recall the time or the place or what had scared him. In his previous iteration then, before he had become Victor, before he had stepped so far away from a regular existence there was no turning back.

Thinking of the flight to Berlin gave him the compulsion to glance around the bus once more, looking for well-dressed men over forty, but of those he saw, he recognised none. He caught Joanna's gaze in the process.

'Boring book?' she asked.

'I'm easily distracted.'

'Then I'll try harder.'

Joanna smiled and he found himself holding her gaze longer than he should. She wore a colourful dress and a denim jacket she removed halfway through their conversation. The curls of her hair were bunched up on top of her head and secured with a glittering band. Her ears had many pinprick scars but no earrings. The only jewellery she wore was a necklace. Her feet were bare – she had slipped out of her sandals early into the journey – and her nail polish was gleaming ivory.

'What are you reading?' she asked.

'It's about human history, human behaviour. That kind of thing.'

'Interesting?'

He nodded. 'I'm learning a lot.'

'You're studying?'

'Not exactly. But the more I read, the more I understand.'

Her eyebrows rose. 'About human beings?'

'Let's call it a hobby,' he said with a nod. 'I like to understand how they work.'

She smiled because she thought he was joking and continued to ask him questions.

Victor didn't meet new people often. At least, he didn't have conversations with new people often. When he did, it was almost always on public transport. It made sense that it would be the way he interacted most. Confined, bored, with little to do. Most passengers kept to themselves. They played with their phones. They read. They snacked. Victor didn't present himself as someone interested in small talk with a stranger, but he marked himself out by the simple fact he didn't have his gaze on a screen or buds in his ears. Some people took that as licence. He was also smart and respectable. He spent so much effort appearing unthreatening that the side effect was some mistook this as personable. There was little he could do about it. He gave off as many subtle cues to leave him alone as possible. He avoided eye contact. He never spoke unless there was a need. He never smiled. He carried himself in a dominant way because this made him less approachable, but this was a reserved dominance. A quiet strength. He made people neither uncomfortable nor comfortable. But it was an imperfect system. There was no way to maintain an exact balance.

As a boy he had longed to be noticed, to be someone worthy of attention, to step beyond the invisibility that cloaked him. He had spent his entire adult life trying to regain that cloak. He found he had to distance himself from the newly separated backstory. He diverted the conversation whenever it strayed back to his ex-girlfriend. He had to make up details on the fly. Joanna kept asking about it. She offered sympathy. She assured him he would find someone else. There was more than one person for everyone. There were multiple soulmates. They could be anywhere. He might find one when he least expected it.

He made a mental note to reconsider using such back-stories. Better to stay quiet instead of inventing personal history as he went along. By the time Joanna left the subject alone, Victor knew where the parents of his fictional ex liked to walk on a Sunday afternoon.

'Bet you don't travel on a bus very often.'

'It's quite rare,' Victor lied.

'I'm getting used to them,' she said, relaxing back in her seat to emphasise the point. 'More legroom than an airplane, but you miss out on the view.' She paused. 'What are your thoughts on trains?'

'I've always liked them,' Victor said with more enthusiasm than he should ever show to anyone.

She liked that enthusiasm. '*Me too*. Isn't that funny? No one cares about trains these days. They don't get enough love in my opinion. Why do you think that is?'

He was answering before he could stop himself.

She was easy to talk to, even for Victor who had once had to teach himself how to hold a conversation. He had studied and practised. It hadn't come to him naturally. He had to disguise his aversion to other people. He had to bury away his apathy. He had to feign interest. He had to pretend to care. He had sought out interaction because it was a skill, and he needed to practise to maintain his ability therein. He had to train. He had to learn to appear normal so that when his life depended on appearing so, he could with conviction. So he could indeed depend on himself.

Sometimes he was more personable than was prudent. He could never be rude – it only made him memorable – so he tried to be boring – but not too boring. He wasn't always successful. And sometimes, just sometimes, he didn't want to be boring. Sometimes he wanted to talk to another person, to engage with a fellow human, even if it was pretend, even if he was never himself in these situations. His whole life was pretend unless engaging in violence, unless trying to kill or trying to stay alive. Only then were all pretences dropped. Only then could he express himself without a front, without a filter.

Halfway through the journey, Victor put down his book with no intention of picking it back up again.

Joanna had a big bag of mixed nuts that she snacked on while they talked. 'Help yourself.'

They looked good, but he declined. There was no reason to be suspicious of her – and no way for her to poison some nuts but not the ones she ate herself – but it was a habit he couldn't switch off, even to maintain character.

She wasn't a quiet eater, but she wasn't messy. Victor liked to be clean. He didn't like mess, except when a few crumbs found their way to the exposed skin of her chest and they both smiled when she tried and failed to swipe them away without him noticing.

She was the youngest of six sisters, he learned, but not the youngest member of the family.

'I have a little brother,' she told him with a laugh. 'Can you imagine what it was like growing up with *six* sisters?'

'I couldn't possibly.'

'We. Were. Merciless,' she explained, grinning, but with a little guilt to it. 'And his first girlfriend ... Well, let's just say she didn't last long. I'm surprised we didn't turn him gay.'

'I don't think that's how it works.'

She nudged his arm. 'I know, I was joking. Anyway, he's married now. The wife's lovely. I mean, she had to be lovely, didn't she? We wouldn't have stood for it otherwise.'

Her accent was from California or New Mexico, he noted, but it was subtle. He expected she had been out of the United States for a long time. He didn't ask and she didn't tell him, but some things required no explanation. He did his best not to infer too many details about her – in this case it seemed impolite – but he compiled a mental dossier on everyone he met, threat or not. It was habit. Protocol.

As they were nearing the city, she asked, 'Where are you staying?'

'A hotel in the centre of town.' He wasn't the kind of person to be more specific, even with someone he judged to be a civilian. 'What about you?'

'I have a little condo.'

'You live here?' he said, sounding surprised.

'For work. But I've just had a few short days' break from it and I want to stretch that out as long as possible, so don't ask me about the bank, okay?'

He nodded. 'I don't like to talk about my job either.'

He may have had to learn how to converse, but he had never been naive. He knew what they had been doing. How far he was willing to take it, he hadn't been sure of until now. He was working, technically, but he was always working. Staying alive was a full-time job even if there was no one he was planning to kill. He couldn't cut himself off from the world – he had tried before without success – so he had learned to allow himself to live when he could. People said they could be dead tomorrow to encourage themselves to live more in the moment. With Victor death was never that far away.

I spend every day expecting to be killed, he had once told someone whose face he couldn't seem to forget, *because the day I don't will be the day I am.*

He said, 'Are you working in the morning?'

She shook her head. 'I can't go away and then go straight back to the nine-to-five. Why, you looking to hire me as your guide?'

'Sure, I'm interested in your perspective. I figure you can help me understand the city, and the people.'

'But isn't that the irony?' she said. 'We're only ever interested in the people we don't understand.'

SIXTEEN

Lavandier tried not to move. He tried not to make a sound. He wanted to be unseen. He wanted to be somewhere else – anywhere else – but he wouldn't dare leave. No one would stop him, but the repercussions would be severe. So, he stayed. He watched, hoping he was only a little pale, hoping he could swallow back any vomit.

El Perro had hung his shirt up on a protruding section of piping, so it didn't get creased, or stained. A film of sweat covered his skin, making him glimmer in the gloom. He had been hard at work for a long time now. Aside from the sweat, aside from the bloody knuckles, he seemed relaxed. He wasn't out of breath. He hadn't lost focus. He was a patient man. A vicious man.

A lump hammer lay within reach, but El Perro hadn't used it, and nor would he. It was for smashing ice cubes only. He had already gone through one bag, and the second one was half empty. The sicario assisting him tipped away the melted ice from the little bucket next to the hammer, discarding the bloody water down a drain sunk into the floor, covered with a grille. The sicario used the hammer to smash up the remaining ice cubes before he emptied the bag into the bucket. El Perro waited without word until the ice was ready, then sunk his bloody hands into the bucket. When he was finished, the sicario gave him a rag on which to dry his hands.

El Perro rubbed at his knuckles. Even with the regular dousing in crushed ice, they were swollen. He made no complaints. This was his job.

A weak, strained voice said, '*Please . . .* '

Heloise's chief of security was a former member of Guatemala's special forces. He was never referred to by any name other than El Perro. He was a short man, shorter than Lavandier and Heloise, but his size had no bearing on his lethality. His quick reactions and pinpoint aim had ensured the survival of both his employer and the consul several times. Lavandier was terrified of him, and hated him.

El Perro stood before a chair on which slumped a man who would have fallen off had he not been secured to it with cable ties. The man's face was so puffed up his eyes were little more than slits through half moons of inflammation. The skin of his cheeks and jaw was red and purple. His chin was both black with crusted blood and bright red where it ran fresh. His bare chest and lap was stained with it. The floor was dotted with blood.

The man's mouth hung open in a permanent oval because his jaw had been fractured in several places and could no longer close. Had he been able to, there were too many broken teeth and exposed nerves to risk closing. A crueller torturer might have exploited that, but El Perro, though vicious, though merciless, was not cruel. Hence, the need for crushed ice.

The man in the chair diverted the slits that were his eyes when Heloise approached. He was brave enough to look at El Perro, the torturer who beat him. But he couldn't look at the woman who ordered it.

She gestured to El Perro, but the answer was a shake of his head. The man hadn't talked, hadn't admitted the charge against him because he was innocent and everyone knew it. He was a symbol, nothing more. Heloise wanted a response, and this was it. The man was loyal, fiercely so, which was why he had been chosen. This was Heloise's show of strength: torturing a loyal man to show the other loyal men the price of disloyalty. Heloise had carefully selected a high-ranking trafficker to blame for the attack on her, but hadn't acted in haste. She had waited, to give the accusation more weight, to show she wasn't being quick to judge, so she could claim a thorough investigation had been conducted.

Lavandier was sickened by the savagery but more so by the pointlessness of that savagery. The man in the chair had done nothing except work for a devil in a dress and though the devil demanded loyalty, she showed none in return.

Lavandier said, 'Maybe he's had enough.'

Heloise said, 'Maybe the Earth circles the sun.'

The Frenchman knew to keep his lips closed for the rest of proceedings. He felt no sympathy for the man in the chair. He cared only for himself, for his own squeamishness.

The patron of the Salvatierra cartel circled the man in the chair several times. She ran her long nails along his back, drawing red lines on his skin. The man gasped and stiffened when she did, but not in pain – she only scratched him – and Lavandier stiffened too. He didn't have the stomach for what was coming.

As if feeling the tremor of his unease through the air, Heloise motioned for him to come closer. 'You won't be able to see from there, Luis.'

He didn't say that he knew, that his intention was to see as little as possible. Instead, he inched closer. His legs were heavy with weakness. His steps short with cowardice.

To the man in the chair, Heloise said, 'Tell me it was you.'

He screamed, 'IT WASN'T.'

El Perro punched him.

Fragments of teeth clattered on the floor. Droplets of blood joined them.

El Perro had to grab the guy's hair and slap him on the cheeks to return some coherence to him because Heloise was far from finished. El Perro kept hold of the man's hair to keep his head upright. He had no strength left to do so on his own.

Heloise said, 'Tell me it was you.'

This time the man said nothing. To deny meant more punches, more pain. To admit meant worse.

Lavandier watched, his insides a knotted mass of disgust and fear, his jaw clenched, wanting it over.

'Tell me it was you,' Heloise said yet again, 'or I will have El Perro fetch your sons.'

'Please . . . '

'Maybe I'll let one live if you pick which of them dies.'

Tears found their way out from the slits. They glistened brighter than the blood.

Heloise drummed her long, claw-like nails on the metal table. A hellish, awful sound that made Lavandier's skin crawl and his heart thump. He was almost as scared as the man in the chair.

'Maybe I'll have them fight to the death.'

The nails drummed harder. Louder.

'Or,' she said, pausing, 'perhaps I will be merciful and merely castrate them both. You would perform that, naturally.'

The man in the chair wailed. He had taken the best shots El Perro had to offer, suffering for hours, yet Heloise had broken him in seconds. Lavandier was disgusted, but impressed.

'It was me,' the man said, sobbing. 'It was me.'

'What did you do?' Heloise asked him.

'I told them where you were driving. I'm sorry. Please . . . please don't hurt my boys.'

Heloise said, 'You said it wasn't you.'

'Please . . . '

'You lied to me.'

The man said something else, but it was incomprehensible through the sobs. Heloise gestured to El Perro, who fetched a clean, soft cloth to pass to her, but not just yet. He held it in his left hand, and with his right fist closed tight in the man's hair, he wrenched back the head so the man faced the ceiling, mouth hanging open, unable to close. Lavandier tensed. He felt cool beads of sweat dampening his skin.

The man in the chair made no sound now. He could see Heloise with a single eye, and that eye was as wide as the swelling permitted and unblinking as she stepped closer.

Making sure Lavandier could see, Heloise reached her long, slender fingers into the man's mouth, closed her claws into a pincer, and tore out his tongue.

SEVENTEEN

When Victor woke he was lying on his side, which was curious. He had slept on his back for years. Decades, even. A
pillow could render one ear useless, halving the first and best
chance a person had of realising that death approached. He
was half-covered by a duvet too, which was another breach
of protocol. Any bedclothes acted as a restraint, if only temporary, and to Victor, or someone like him, temporary was
more than enough.

He was naked too, yet another no-no – he slept fully
dressed for several reasons – and in that realisation the final
answers came to him.

He heard her at the foot of the bed. The sound had woken
him, despite her efforts to minimise it. She was quiet. She
knew the sweet spot where moving faster but louder was
better than extending noise by moving too slow. She was
practised. This was something she had done before, and
with success, because she wasn't watching him; she wasn't

staring in anticipation – in trepidation – that he might wake and catch her in the act of collecting her clothes on her way out of the door.

He observed her for a moment, appreciating the curves of her nude silhouette and the way her hair moved, but also feeling a little guilty, a little inappropriate at his uninvited voyeurism. He didn't like to be impolite.

He cleared his throat and the silhouette became a statue.

The hair moved as her head turned and the dim light caught her eyes. They were large because she was smiling, albeit in a nervous, caught-in-the-act way.

'Whoops.'

He propped himself up against the headboard.

Joanna said, 'I didn't mean to wake you.'

'I can see that.'

'You're not offended, are you?'

'I'm surprised.'

'Are you upset?'

He nodded. 'I'm crying my eyes out over here.'

She gave him a look of mock sympathy. 'Aww, I'm so sorry. I didn't mean to make you feel bad.'

'I'm very sensitive.'

She picked up the last of her clothes. 'Are we cool?'

'Of course. I didn't mean to fall asleep in the first place.'

Her eyes glimmered for a second. 'Well, I can't say I'm surprised you did.'

He didn't comment. 'Shall I have reception call you a cab?'

'No, I'm fine. Thanks, though.' She paused, and looked around while she considered. 'Say, do you mind if I take a quick shower? Since you're up anyway, I mean.'

'Be my guest.'

She collected the rest of her things and disappeared into the en-suite bathroom saying, 'I'll be quick.'

While she showered, he took the opportunity to check the suite for signs of any tampering, for anything out of place, but he found nothing had been disturbed nor evidence she had used the time when he was asleep to do anything but gather clothes. He was a little surprised. He didn't check her things because she had taken them with her into the bathroom.

He had made coffee by the time she was done. The suite came with an espresso machine. It was one of the reasons he liked to stay in suites.

She had said she would be quick, and she was. Just a rinse, he saw. She didn't wash her hair. When she exited the en-suite she was dressed.

'If I'm clothed I won't be tempted to stay,' she said, as if he needed an explanation. Or maybe she felt the need to justify herself.

Victor remained silent.

She said, 'You did tell me your name, didn't you?'

He said, 'Yes.'

'Would you like to tell me again? Because I may have forgotten it. I have mash-potato brain right now.'

'Sure.'

She waited, expectant. Her hands gestured for an answer. 'Ryan.'

A single groove appeared between her dark brows. 'You don't look like a Ryan to me.'

'I'll try harder.'

She smiled. 'I've never known a Ryan with a scar, nor one so good at . . . that.'

'I'm the exception that breaks the rule.'

'Let me think what suits you.' The smile became a pout and she stroked her chin. 'Ryan doesn't suit you at all, in fact. If you're anything, you're an anti-Ryan. You're more of a ... I don't know. I don't know what name suits you.'

Victor raised an eyebrow. 'Nor do I.'

'Well,' she continued. 'We need to think of a better name for you. I'm just going to point-blank refuse to call you Ryan.'

'What's wrong with the name Ryan? I'm kind of insulted here.'

She scoffed. 'I don't buy that for a second. You're not so easily offended. If ever.' She edged closer. 'What does it take to offend you, I wonder? Is it even possible?'

He liked the tease in her eyes more than he disliked any intrusion into what lay behind his mask of normalcy. 'I'm really not partial to bad language.'

'Do I need to watch my Ps and Qs around you?'

'Most certainly. No blasphemy either.'

She found this amusing, and he expected further teasing, but instead she asked, 'Would you like to know my name too?'

'I already know your name.'

'Pretend you don't. Pretend we're only introducing ourselves now. So, would you like to know my name?'

'That depends,' he replied. 'Does it suit you?'

She approached him. 'You'll have to be the judge of that.' She offered her hand. 'I'm Joanna Alamaeda.'

They shook. 'Pleasure to meet you, Joanna. I'm Anti-Ryan.'

'I assure you the pleasure was all mine, Anti-Ryan.'

'I think I like that name.'

'Yeah? Great news. Are you going to start introducing yourself that way?'

'I think I'll stick to Ryan, if it's all the same.'

'Spoilsport. I'll have to think of something more suitable to remember you by.'

'Remember me by?'

She shrugged. 'I was assuming this was a one-off. I mean, you're not emigrating here, are you? I'm not about to move to Canada.'

'I could be here for a while.'

He said nothing more. She said nothing.

He turned his palms up. *Well?*

She laughed. 'Is that your way of asking to see me again?'

This was not something he did usually, or even ever. He was more used to call girls than real women. First Poison, and now Joanna. A little reckless, sure, but fun. Lots of fun, and Joanna was different. He wasn't ready to say goodbye.

'Is that your way of saying yes?'

She didn't answer. Instead, she used the pen and note-pad that lay next to the room's phone to scribble down her number.

'I'm a busy girl, so you'll almost certainly get my voice-mail,' she said. 'But I'll call you back. Although, if you say "this is Ryan", I won't know who you're talking about.'

'Then who should I say is calling?'

She said, 'Make something up. Something interesting,' then waved with her fingers and left the suite.

EIGHTEEN

Victor hadn't felt this kind of freedom in a long time. Years had gone by since he had last been so without reservation, without constraint. It was both an exhilarating new experience, and one that caused him concern. Just because he could operate with no oversight didn't mean he should act as if there was no consequence. He had no CIA or SIS handlers to answer to, but they still existed, and the organisations they worked for, and other agencies like them, could still make his life difficult, most of all by expediting the inevitable conclusion. All existence was temporary – Victor knew that better than most – and his own resurrection would not last long if he took it for granted.

There was always consequence. Consequence followed him around as a shadow. It was unavoidable. Inescapable. Every action had an equal and opposite reaction. Every action could prove a mistake, either in the immediacy or later, and mistakes were to be avoided. He made them from time to time – it was impossible to be infallible – and each time he had walked a little closer to the edge. Once, he had thought himself to be beyond mistakes, to be above error, but that had been arrogance, he now knew. His greatest mistake then had been believing he would never make one.

So, with Joanna, he had to be certain. That she hadn't killed him while he was asleep and vulnerable was a pretty good sign she wasn't an assassin chasing one of many contracts on his head, and though she had given him no reason at all to doubt her, Victor doubted everyone. Many years of careful existence had proven he was right not to trust, that it was foolhardy to ever lower his guard. He excelled in his profession because he knew exactly how to wait for such opportunities and how to best exploit them.

He knew Joanna worked for a bank, but not which bank and not in what capacity. She hadn't wanted to talk shop any more than he had. Guatemala City, like any major metropolis, would have dozens of banks. Maybe more than one hundred if Alamaeda worked for an investment bank or other financial firm that could be loosely classified as one. Still, it took nothing more than an internet search for her name followed by 'bank' to provide him with her employer, Banco de Guatemala, and even her job title, Client Relations Manager. Her profile on the bank's website mentioned her passion for cementing long-lasting mutually beneficial relationships with a broad range of clients, and fondness for white-water rafting. The accompanying portrait photograph was a head-and-shoulders shot, complete with glasses and a polite smile. She looked the same and also dissimilar at the same time.

Even if she was no killer, he needed to be sure she was who she was supposed to be, so he found a payphone and called the client services number. Speaking Spanish in a Catalan accent, he asked for Joanna Alamaeda. He had spent enough time in Barcelona to pass as a local. He was told by a polite receptionist that Miss Alamaeda was in a meeting and wouldn't be available for another hour. Victor said he would call back, but was glad she was busy. He didn't want to speak to her if he didn't have to, and he didn't want to lie to her any more than necessary. When everything she would ever know about him was a lie, adding others seemed cruel.

Hanging up the phone, content she was indeed a banker, Victor felt a curious sense of disappointment. It would have made things easier to discover it had all been an act, albeit an elaborate one with motives he didn't understand. He would have known exactly what to do if he had discovered anything to be suspicious about. Simple. Easy. Problem solved.

What did he do now?

There was an operational benefit to seeing Joanna that needed to be considered. He would be in Guatemala for an extended duration, and the more complete his life in the city, the more integrated he would appear. He had meetings scheduled with small businesses, producers and distributors, transportation firms and various specialists in the commodities and coffee trade. If he came to anyone's attention, law enforcement or otherwise, he would need more than just a clean passport to avert any suspicion. Similarly, he wasn't prepared to violate such a cast-iron rule without being certain he wasn't exposing himself any more than necessary.

Besides, he wanted to see her again. His well of humanity was empty, but not yet arid. He recognised this as both blessing and curse. If he had the choice, he would erase that thin connection in order to better survive, but he was also glad he was denied that particular choice.

He had no experience of how to proceed. He understood human courtship rituals in the same way he understood how to kill. But in the same way he had never died himself, he had never been in this situation. He had never wanted to see someone again who wanted to see him in return. Protocol had always solved this for him. Had he wanted to see someone again then he had made sure not to see them. There had been a few exceptions, of course, but not like this. Nothing like this.

He was making it up as he went along. Which gave him the same exhilaration he had felt being free for the first time he could remember, but something else too. A sensation that could only be fear. Which made no sense to him. He had stared down the barrel of many guns with his heart rate barely elevated. The unknown then. He knew everything there was to know about his profession, about killing, about violence. There were no surprises for him there. This was a surprise. This was unknown.

Victor decided to meet it head-on. There was a risk, because every day carried risk for him, but no greater risk. Either he would complete his job and leave, else he would be killed in the process. He couldn't know Joanna for long. What would it be? An affair? A romance? A mistake?

He would find out, he supposed. The only absolute was that it couldn't interfere with his work.

NINETEEN

Through a shell company registered in the Channel Islands he had hired a local realtor, who rented an office in downtown Guatemala City on Victor's behalf. It was a small building that he paid over market rates for, but he wanted a short lease and he wanted an entire building. He didn't want neighbours and he didn't want to tie himself to the city any longer than necessary. He never met the realtor in person nor spoke to him on the phone. Communication was done electronically, and keys to the building were left for Victor at his hotel.

The office provided several benefits. It gave him the ability to expand his legend and also provided him with a safe house in which to prepare and plan and store the tools of his trade. He couldn't keep a rifle in his hotel room without upsetting the maid.

It helped that the office was once owned by a foreign coffee exporter. Such a history wouldn't halt any determined investigation, but it might help avoid one in the first place. If the job went as planned, Maria's death would be put down as an inevitable conclusion to the cartel war, perpetrated by Heloise's people. The authorities wouldn't be looking at outside involvement, if they looked at all. Still, it was always better to be over-prepared and over-protected, than under.

The building was nestled in the shadow of an elevated highway, with sleek office towers gleaming in the sunlight to the west, while south lay a rundown neighbourhood of shanties. A chain-link fence surrounded the building and an open expanse of concrete that could be used for parking spaces or deliveries. There were cracks in the concrete and vegetation pushing through.

The realtor had stated the offices had been unoccupied for some time. Inside, it smelled musty and the air was cool. He looked for subtle clues that anyone had been here in the previous hours or days, but the dust was even and undisturbed; the sinks were dry and without water marks. There was an alarm system, for which Victor had the code, and he used a knuckle to enter it and stop the unit's light flashing. He would keep it disabled. If someone broke in, the last thing he wanted was for the alarm to be set off and the police to respond.

There were CCTV cameras placed around the outside of the building to discourage opportunists, but the image quality was terrible. They were for show, not for catching thieves. A closet-sized room on the ground floor housed monitors and recording equipment. Footage was recorded and saved on a hard disk array, and then recorded over after a week. Victor scrolled through the footage from the previous week, seeing nothing but the realtor arrive and remove the sign advertising the building's availability. Victor would have preferred it left in place – the fewer people who knew it was leased the better – but there was no way to have asked for it to remain without arousing suspicion. He could steal a sign or have one made up to give the appearance that the building was unoccupied, but the biggest danger he had was from the realtor. Perhaps the realtor passed the building from time to time. If he saw a sign for another company or for a bogus number he would start to ask questions about who had rented the office.

All the blinds were already down, and Victor checked each window in turn, making sure they were secure and locked, and taking a mental note of those that opened. He found a room without windows to set up his base of operations. There were better rooms, but he didn't want interior light escaping through the windows to alert anyone outside to his presence.

There was no intelligence like that he acquired himself, so he took the time to explore the city. He couldn't operate somewhere without first understanding it. He wasn't going to be around long enough to know it like a native, but he didn't need that level of insight. He needed to ensure he knew his way around the public transport system; he needed to know what time the stores closed and which hotels were best for his purposes; he needed to understand the influence of the cartels.

It was no surprise that crime was a problem in Guatemala City, as it was in almost every city in Central America, as well as the world as a whole to a lesser extent. Victor had been the target of petty criminals before, both in Europe and further afield. He was not a small man, but he projected an unthreatening persona. Sometimes that could be mistaken for weakness. He knew enough about posture, body language and psychology to display himself in a dominant way, which would discourage pickpockets and muggers, but in return would only make him stand out more to the kind of threats he was actually concerned about. He would prefer to encourage a mugger to see him as a potential victim rather than make himself recognisable to another killer. As an outsider, he not only made himself more obvious to other professionals, but to petty criminals too.

The main tourist areas were guarded by armed security. There were exposed firearms everywhere. Not police, but private guards hired by stores and restaurants to protect themselves and their customers. In the more exclusive and wealthy areas, these were well trained and experienced. Elsewhere, they looked out of their depth. For show, to make patrons comfortable, more than anything else. Some were little older than kids. They paid no particular attention to Victor because he was a foreigner and because he looked respectable and wealthy and acted in an unthreatening manner. Police officers he saw looked for longer. He knew corruption was endemic. Many officers worked for cartels, sometimes indirectly, sometimes overtly. Foreigners were the victims of police shakedowns on a regular basis.

For the first time in a long time a suit was not his primary attire. Elsewhere, it helped him blend into the urban population. Here, it was the opposite. People were neat, they were smart, but suits were uncommon. He opted for the most part for tourist attire – walking shoes, khaki trousers and a casual shirt with long sleeves. Victor disliked short-sleeve shirts even before it became impossible for him to wear them. He wore a suit only in specific circumstances, when it was necessary, when it wouldn't draw attention.

Victor had been to many beautiful cities. Guatemala City was not one of them, but when the sun was setting, and the concrete buildings and characterless streets were in a wash of blood-orange light, the city gained a certain composure, a certain poise.

A week turned out to be enough time to get a feel for the city and the people. He found the many markets were ideal places to help him learn as he made a pretence of being a tourist browsing the wares on offer and sampling street cuisine. In particular, Guatemalan-style hot dogs that came with guacamole. He preferred onions, mustard and ketchup – perfection couldn't be beaten, after all – but the local variation wasn't bad. The best one he tasted was bought for him by a generous fixer who helped him source a Glock handgun and other contraband he would need to complete his assignment.

He found that Guatemalans haggled like it was a sport, wanting more to win than to get the best deal. The men were happy to engage in conversation about their homeland that Victor inevitably steered to acquiring knowledge of the cartels, but the Mayan women avoided eye contact and rarely spoke unless to answer a direct question, and then it was with as few words as possible.

Plenty of civilians knew about the war between Heloise and Maria, or the Devil Sisters, as Victor heard more than once. With so much infamy, it was no surprise to Victor that the war was a stalemate. Both Heloise and Maria kept their best people close at all times while their untrained sicarios battled on the streets. That Heloise had been first to look outside the country for assistance suggested she was the smarter sister, or perhaps the more scared, the more desperate, but her motives were only a curiosity to Victor.

He was paid to kill, not to understand.

TWENTY

Finding Maria Salvatierra wasn't the problem. She owned a horse ranch far outside of the city, nestled in a rural valley, out of sight but not hiding. The ranch occupied three thousand acres of pastures. It even had its own lake. At the centre of the land was a beautiful two-storey mansion, two guest houses, stables, garage and several outbuildings. According to the dossier, Maria spent the majority of her time here. Like Heloise, she had advisors and lieutenants to do the heavy lifting. She spent most of her days riding and swimming. She made the decisions, and was in all ways the head of her cartel, but no one liked to work any harder than necessary.

The problems of getting to Maria at the ranch would be many. Though Lavandier had not been able to provide specifics, there would be dozens of heavily armed gunmen guarding Maria's home and surrounding land. There would be further security provided by alarms, lights, motion sensors and dogs, but again no specifics. The dossier told Victor that

Maria had another layer of protection: private security guys who operated throughout the country.

After his week familiarising himself with Guatemala City, he took a bus excursion to the countryside. Public transport was Victor's preferred method of travel for many reasons, and it was increasingly hard to find cars that were worth the risk of stealing. Sophisticated alarms, locks and tracking systems were improving all the time and with them the pool of vehicles that could be safely stolen was diminishing. It was easier to hop on a bus or take a cab. There were many other benefits too. He was able to keep his senses focused on possible threats instead of diverted to driving. Ramming a bus off the road was a lot harder too, as well as pulling off a successful drive-by attack.

The biggest danger Victor faced was the driver, who was toying with a mobile phone as the doors hissed open. He waved Victor on without checking his ticket, and as he passed, Victor caught the scent of alcohol. None of the other passengers seemed concerned by this, and he took a seat next to an old man in a string vest.

The bus rumbled into motion. Like many of the buses he had seen, it was a repurposed American school bus. Repainted and modified, but the shape was unmistakable. The seats were textured vinyl worn down to a glassy sheen. The old man next to him was having fun sliding back and forth. Victor shuffled further along the seat to give the man more room to enjoy.

It was hotter than outside, and humid. The locals were well conditioned to the climate, and seemed content. Victor sweated.

The journey took several hours. It was a slow drive out

of town and into the surrounding countryside. The roads weren't great. Some were little more than tracks. The bus swayed and jolted, rocked and shook. The old man was having a great time.

Victor departed with three other passengers. The bus stop was at a crossroads that had a scattering of buildings around it. The closest was a petrol station that had a sign for Pepsi, but the logo was decades out of date. The other passengers didn't waste time. They headed as a group away down a bisected road while Victor headed into the petrol station. The guy who owned it, or just ran it, was sitting outside in a plastic chair. He sipped from a glass bottle of Coke.

Opening a chest cooler, Victor selected an ice cream and gave cash to the man on the plastic chair.

Victor said, '*Campo de aviación?*'

The man looked at him, and said nothing.

Victor crossed the road to where a square-fronted building named Ruiz's stood. The window displayed sun-faded posters advertising beer and food. Chairs and tables sat outside, but were unoccupied. The *comedor* was half bar, half café, but neither. It had an open cooler by the door full of cans of soda, bottles of water, juice and beer. Some people paid at the counter and took them on their way. Others sat down at the counter, like it was a bar, while Ruiz prepared deli-style sandwiches on the same surface. Meanwhile, a waitress provided table service, ferrying plates of food from a kitchen behind swing doors, but also beverages from behind the counter. Beer bottles, mostly, but different brands from those available in the cooler by the door. Nothing on draft, and no optics for spirits, but he saw a line of tall bottles behind Ruiz that could be domestic concoctions. The furniture looked expensive, and solid and hardy enough to survive a lifetime in a backstreet Dublin pub. The plastic tablecloths seemed almost insulting in comparison.

There was space for around thirty drinkers or diners, but only two tables were occupied. A trio of young men sat together in the corner Victor would have chosen, and four men who were older, but not by much, sat in the centre of the room, beneath a single ceiling fan.

With his preferred seat taken, Victor took a chair where he could watch the door and see through the windows without too much effort. He knew everyone in the establishment was either staring at him or talking about him, but he ignored their curiosity.

The bus journey had been long and he was hungry. There was no menu, however, so he asked for eggs, beans, fried plantains, baked peppers and tortillas, which arrived fast and steaming. The plate wasn't especially large and the food wasn't piled high, but he left a significant portion of it. A good way of losing weight, he had read, but he did it for practical purposes. He never wanted to operate on a full stomach. He preferred to eat smaller, higher-calorie meals on a more frequent basis.

He was something of a novelty to the waitress, who asked him several times if the food was good, if he wanted anything else, if she could fetch him another drink. The final time she worked up the courage to ask him where he was from, so he had kept it vague to blunt any further conversation. The waitress didn't handle the bill. Instead Victor paid at the bar, and made sure to add on a large tip to offset the distrust he generated on account of his foreignness.

Victor said, '*Donde puedo encontrar el aeródromo privado?*'

Ruiz was young, with a fleshy face, and neat, thin hair. His eyes were red and he had bags beneath them. There was tiredness in his movements but an energy in the gaze he cast. He hesitated, so Victor put some more cash on the bar, which was slid away by a prompt palm.

'West,' Ruiz said. 'Five kilometres.'

'Much appreciated, sir.'

Victor turned to leave, but saw that it wasn't going to be that simple.

TWENTY-ONE

Nothing triggered it and there had been no warning signs, so he was a little surprised to see one of the three young men from the table in the corner approach him. He had slicked hair and the expression on his face said plenty, as did the fact his two friends had swivelled around in their chairs to watch proceedings.

A random attack then, delivered by someone with something to prove. To someone, Victor realised, when he saw that the waitress's gaze was glued to the guy with slicked hair.

There was an inevitable path these things always took. Verbal aggression first as the attacker psyched themselves up, which would lead to a shove, then maybe more verbal aggression if Victor didn't comply, or a punch thrown if Victor shoved back. That was how it went the world over with those who linked violence to self-worth.

'You were flirting with my fiancée,' the young guy with slicked hair said.

Victor didn't respond. Instead, he selected a bottle of

sparkling water from the cooler cabinet by the entrance. There were a few brands available. He chose the one with a cone-like shape, the bottle made of green plastic. He paid for it with cash while the young guy grew even more agitated at being ignored.

'Hey, I'm talking to you.'

He didn't understand the contrast between himself and Victor. The former wanted to humiliate the latter. The latter didn't want to kill the former. It didn't take much to drop someone. Even a strike delivered with just the right amount of force to put an enemy to sleep might kill him if he hit his head the wrong way on the floor, or if he choked on the resulting vomit, or if he had a weak heart that couldn't take the trauma. The last thing Victor wanted to do was leave a corpse behind. He couldn't close the distance to Maria Salvatierra with detectives on his heels, looking to find a vicious foreigner who beat a local to death.

It was never a good idea to fight straight after a meal, so he wanted it over fast. Most fights were won with the first punch, which meant they were won before it was thrown. A fight was won when the decision was made to strike first. Action, instead of reaction. The young guy with the slick hair hadn't made the decision to fight. At least, not yet. His intention was to intimidate, maybe to belittle. Certainly, to get a reaction. Drive the outsider away, acting the big man to impress his friends and fiancée too, if that worked for her. Victor had no decision to make. It had already been made. He walked around on a hair trigger. Not temper, but practicality. He couldn't always pre-empt conflict, but he could always be ready for it.

Victor said, 'Let's just skip to the end, shall we?'

As the young guy was processing the remark, Victor

dropped him with a stomp kick to the base of the sternum. Nowhere near his hardest kick – because he didn't want to paralyse the guy's diaphragm to the point it might never recover – but delivered with enough force to catapult him backwards over a table. He hit the floor wheezing and clutching his chest.

Instinct compelled Victor to follow through, to chase after him, circling the tipped-over table to finish him off on the floor. A stomping heel to a vital area usually did the trick, but was often fatal. Vital areas were vital, after all, which was why Victor was apt to target them. A stomp elsewhere was inefficient and risky; any move that took one of Victor's feet out from under him created vulnerability. Hence, kicks were rare too, and best employed in surprise attacks, when those risks were minimal.

He didn't want to kill his attacker, and he didn't want to cripple him either. So, Victor fought the instinct and remained stationary, leaving the young guy wheezing and gasping and his eyes glistening but alive and uninjured. The waitress rushed to aid him.

Before Victor could tell the other two in the corner there was no need for anyone else to get hurt, they were standing up. Not just them, but the older guys from the other table too. It was a domino effect, but in reverse. As soon as the young guy with the slick hair went down, everyone else stood up. Maybe he was well liked. Maybe his father was someone. Maybe his mother could make trouble for those who didn't back up her son. It was immaterial. Victor wouldn't be around long enough to find out why. A quick glance told Victor that Ruiz wasn't going to get involved, at least. He rolled his eyes, used to senseless violence.

Six against one, but only at the start. These were not timid men and they had been drinking, but once they started going down, it would discourage the less confident from joining in.

Fighting multiple opponents was never easy. Human survival instinct had a way of focusing on the most immediate threat to the point of tunnel vision. That tunnel vision had its benefits, but created vulnerability too; danger in peripheral vision went unseen. But that instinct, that tunnel vision, applied only when danger was felt, when under threat. Victor felt neither of those things.

The trick was not to fight more than one person at a time, so he used the room to his advantage, positioning himself so the fallen table and the chairs were obstacles, barriers, to funnel his opponents so he could deal with them one by one.

The main problem he had was balance. Pull his punches too much and it would only encourage others to join in. They would have nothing to fear. Most people could take a knock or two, especially the kind of guys who had drunk multiple beers by one in the afternoon in a hot bar with no air conditioning. But hit them too hard and it would have the same effect. Then it would be revenge they were after instead of bragging rights, and it would be that much harder to put them down in the first place.

He used the water bottle to drop the first of the young guy's friends with a blow to the skull. The makeshift weapon was only small, but was still half a kilogram of accelerating mass, made rigid from the shaking and the resulting increased internal pressure. Victor discarded the bottle as the man fell. It was effective only in a surprise attack and he wanted both hands free.

One of the older guys was the next closest, and most eager.

He even smiled. Some people enjoyed fighting, but only when they were winning. He had tears on his cheeks by the time Victor stopped hitting him.

That shocked the rest into inaction. Only one was brave enough to approach, and he didn't rush.

Victor could tell by the way this one approached that he was a boxer, even before he brought his hands up into a guard; and when he did attack, the crispness of his punches confirmed he didn't just train to keep fit, or even spar, but to fight. He was lean and quick, with good head movement. He didn't come at Victor in a straight line. He moved from side to side, never stepping forward if he could move laterally instead. As expected, he had an excellent jab – fast and powerful – followed by an equally good right cross. The former being the perfect punch to set up the second's knockout potential. They hit nothing but air.

The boxer was a rangy guy: long legs, long neck, long arms. The length of the arms told Victor he wouldn't be throwing many hooks, many uppercuts. He would jab to find the range and send the right cross to do damage. Long arms were a disadvantage up close. Victor knew, because he had them. One of the reasons he preferred the elbow over the punch, aside from the obvious advantage the elbow had in terms of resilience over the fist, was it could be used at kissing distance. He preferred to be as close as possible. The closer he was, the more options he had.

A classic, diligent guard kept him protected from counterattacks, and more punches chased Victor as he kept out of range, waiting for the right moment. He knew it was coming, because every miss made the boxer more eager to land the next one; every miss focused the boxer's mind on making the next punch better, faster, more accurate. He was calling on every iota of ring time, of practice, of strategy, of experience.

His only experience was boxing, however, so when the right moment presented itself – the boxer trying too hard and overextending to land the first hit – Victor had no trouble sweeping his legs out from under him.

The boxer's stance worked against him – his left foot was too far forward – and he hit the floor hard, the surprise only adding to the impact. The way he wailed and clutched his hip told Victor the boxer wouldn't be ready to throw another punch for weeks.

The boxer should have attacked him first. It would have given the others time to surround Victor. The end result would still have been the same, but they couldn't have known that then. The young guy with the slick hair was standing up as the boxer went down, his hair was a mess and he had a knife in his hand.

He ignored the pleas of the waitress to let it go and stepped closer. The knife was a large, showy weapon with a semi-serrated blade and a jagged point, made to look intimidating. Victor could imagine it scaring people who didn't know any better. He would be more concerned if the knife was smaller, if it had no serrations or jagged point, because then it would have been carried by someone intent on killing, not scaring. The serrations were no good for a blade meant for killing. They would catch in clothes. Victor had seen it happen. An experienced knife-fighter would know that; Victor had only ever fought one professional who had used a serrated blade, but a true expert didn't have to worry about such inconveniences. The best cosmetic surgeons in the world couldn't hide the scars Victor had that proved it.

A blade was still a blade, however. A sharp piece of metal could sever an artery in pretty much any shape. The young guy had the classic stance of the amateur knife-fighter – weapon held at his hip and offhand out before him. The latter to initiate a grab to lock a target in range before bringing the knife into play; the former because the amateur's primary concern was to keep hold of his blade. It was a classic contradiction: an offensive weapon held defensively, but it was universal where amateurs were involved.

Victor knew how to defend against such a combatant. He knew lots of ways to feint and trick and trap and take the knife from the wielder, but he didn't need to refer to his skill set. The young guy had made it easy. He was waiting to counter-attack, cautious now he understood the threat he was facing, so he hadn't even considered the several chairs scattered around the room tipped over or knocked aside in the commotion.

Victor grabbed the closest and hurled it.

The young guy with the messy hair was fast enough to avoid taking the chair right in the face, but he wasn't quick enough to avoid it entirely. A leg caught him on the side of the head, hard enough to draw blood and make him cry out, although damage wasn't the primary objective.

He was too distracted to have any chance of avoiding the second chair, which Victor kept hold of instead of throwing.

He held it by the back, four legs out in front, which he drove into the young guy's torso in a frenzy of hard jabs – no need to worry about counter-attacks with such a range advantage – cracking ribs and causing enough trauma to the abdomen to make the young guy vomit all over himself as he slid down the wall.

The chair survived without so much as a creak. Victor set it down back where it belonged.

'That's a quality piece of furniture,' he said to Ruiz, who was still behind the bar.

'I know,' came the reply. 'I make them myself.'

'No kidding?'

Ruiz nodded.

He didn't seem too surprised or too bothered about the mess, the crying waitress, or the three prostrate figures who were still conscious, but didn't want to be. Those remaining on their feet had no desire to join them.

'What was that all about?' Victor asked.

Ruiz explained: 'They come here for casual work. On the farms. One day the truck turns up and they want twenty guys, the next they only want five. Some of these boys walk a long way for work. They have a long walk back. Some don't want to walk back and tell their wives there's no more money. Some would rather sit here all day and spend what little money they have on beer. They get . . . agitated.'

Victor nodded. It wasn't anything unique to this part of Guatemala. He had been to many parts of the world where there wasn't enough work to go around. It made people who would be placid in any other circumstances be aggressive. It made the aggressive dangerous.

He placed some money on the bar, but Ruiz shook his head and pushed it away.

'You've taught these idiots the best lesson they're ever going to get,' he said. 'So, keep your money. You earned it.'

TWENTY-TWO

If a city was a living entity, then Guatemala City breathed air but exhaled smoke and belched noise. Buses passed by chugging and spluttering while tinny music blared from taxis and citizens shouted to be heard over both. Its energy was an extreme juxtaposition of excitement and danger, wealth and poverty. The relentless humidity slowed no one down. Instead, it accelerated them to hustle harder, haggle smarter and smile wider. Joanna Alamaeda had started off hating it – she liked order, not chaos – but now couldn't imagine living and working anywhere else. It was a place devoid of cynicism. Even the lowlifes looked after one another. Even the cops thought they were doing the right thing. Even the pickpockets smiled as they tried to steal her phone.

Alamaeda still wasn't sure if it was all one great big act – one more scam she wasn't in on – but she didn't mind. She was happy to go along with the ride. Sure, she knew to keep her hand on her purse at all times and where never to walk alone, but that was the same as any city. If there was the option to look at somewhere in its best light, she had learned to take it. Play the victim, and somehow everyone looks like an enemy.

'Five says they keep us waiting at least ten minutes,' Wickliffe said from the passenger seat while cleaning her sunglasses.

'Five whole dollars?' she said back with a smirk. 'Are you sure you can afford to lose it?'

Wickliffe shrugged. 'You only live once.'

She nodded. 'Deal.'

They were expected, but the guys at the gate still acted as though Alamaeda and Wickliffe were strangers, unrecognised, in need of verifying. She recognised the men guarding the entrance to the casino parking lot, and she even knew one of their names, yet they couldn't remember her or her associate. They couldn't remember the two American women who visited them from time to time. No, they had to check their identification under a microscopic gaze. Sometimes they phoned the office to check they weren't imposters. The idea was to delay them, frustrate them, and to show power.

'Do you mind if I sit this one out?' Wickliffe asked.

'Hangover?'

Wickliffe smiled at the gentle mockery. They both spent plenty of time in bars washing away the bitter tastes of the day, but Alamaeda had never seen Wickliffe looking worse for wear. She was a robust woman. Slim, but tough. She could handle herself. She never got sick.

'I don't think my patience can handle her royal highness today.'

She shrugged. 'Up to you.'

It took eight and a half minutes of waiting before they were waved through. Alamaeda worked the wheel with one hand while the other was held out in Wickliffe's direction and she wordlessly dropped a five into her palm.

There was a massive empty lot between the casino and the half-finished parking garage. Alamaeda drove across it and tried hard to imagine it full of valet-parked cars. It seemed so empty, so devoid of life that it was incapable of supporting it.

A better-dressed and better-mannered employee greeted her outside the casino entrance. He smiled at her and treated her as if she were a paying customer. He stopped short of kissing her ass, but he did hold open doors.

A private elevator took her up many floors before the brass-plated doors opened and the head of security stood before them waiting for her.

He was the same height as Alamaeda but twice as heavy, at a conservative estimate. His name was Anthony Angelo Castellon, but no one called him that. Alamaeda had never been more frightened of another human being.

She didn't show it, and he did nothing that made him appear threatening. But she knew his history. She knew what he had done and what he could do. That history was the reason he had been hired as a trusted bodyguard and feared enforcer. He gestured for her to raise her arms.

'You know I'm carrying,' she said. 'I'm always carrying. The guys downstairs told you I'm carrying. Shall I start wearing a button that says *I'm carrying*?'

He acted as though she hadn't spoken.

In seconds, he was tapping the gun slung under her arm in the webbing beneath her jacket.

'There's no round in the charmer,' she said, word for word how she always said it, 'and the safety is on. I'm legally allowed to carry it here and if you try to confiscate it you are breaking the law and I can have you arrested.'

'Take it out,' he said, 'show me.'

Like her, he always said the same thing. She removed the gun and presented it for him to check. He was thorough, but gave it her back.

'Keep it in the holster.'

Alamaeda said, 'I always do.'

He ushered her on, and she smirked to show she didn't care about his needless routine, about the stalling tactics at the entrance. They only succeeding in delaying her. Nothing more. It took a lot more than sitting in her car while they played out the charade or the unnecessary searches to frustrate her. One time she had even taken a quick nap. She didn't see a show of their power, but of fear. If they wanted to intimidate her they should just let her walk right in without so much as a glance. That would show her they didn't care about her, her work, her own power, that she wasn't a danger to them. That's how a power game was won. These guys didn't have that level of game. They were thugs, and their imagination was non-existent.

Their employer, however, was a different animal.

Alamaeda found Heloise Salvatierra waiting for her in the huge living area of the suite. The room was bigger than Alamaeda's entire condo, and the suite as a whole was bigger than the two-storey home in the Calabasas suburbs she grew up in. Every piece of furniture, every fixture and ornament looked so expensive Alamaeda was always afraid of breaking something that cost more than her annual salary.

Heloise smiled when she saw her, and shook her hand. She would embrace her, Alamaeda knew, if only she'd let her. She didn't understand that dedication to the pretence. They both knew exactly who the other person was and what they wanted. It was a waste of both their time and energy to pretend otherwise.

'How nice to see you again, Joanna. You're looking well. Did you enjoy your vacation?'

The pleasantries and compliments were hard for Alamaeda to stomach, but she kept things civil. 'I did indeed, Miss Salvatierra. Thank you for taking the time to see me. I appreciate your continued cooperation.'

'It's always a delight to talk with the Drug Enforcement Agency.'

Sometimes, Alamaeda felt like she might throw up. 'I wanted to update you on our progress regarding the attempt on your life earlier this month.'

'Oh, that? I've been trying to put it behind me and forget all about it.'

'Does that mean you still have no idea who tried to kill you?'

She shook her head.

Alamaeda couldn't help but raise her eyebrows in scepticism. 'You have no clue who ordered half a dozen machine-gun-toting hitmen to attack you while you were driving downtown?'

'I'm at a loss,' she said with unflappable poise. 'Perhaps it was a case of mistaken identity.'

Alamaeda caught the laugh, but only just. She cleared her throat. 'You don't think it might have been your sister, Maria?'

Heloise looked shocked. 'Why ever would my dear little sister want to harm me?'

'Why indeed?' Alamaeda replied. 'Why would the two

daughters of Manny Salvatierra be fighting a war for control of the drug cartel he had ruled as sole patron for almost three decades?'

'My father was in the real estate business.'

This time Alamaeda didn't try to hide her amusement. 'Miss Salvatierra, why do you bother with the charade? What do you hope to achieve?'

'I'm not sure I understand what you mean.'

'You're consistent, I'll give you that.'

Heloise accepted the small praise with a small nod. 'Likewise, the DEA is consistent in its perseverance, if nothing else.'

'We all have our crosses to bear.'

Alamaeda approached the wall-length, floor-to-ceiling window. It was an amazing view, even if Guatemala City was not known for its architecture. Still, there was something impressive about the densely packed buildings and the chaos they framed. Or was it contained? For a moment, Alamaeda gazed down upon it and imagined what it must feel like to be Heloise and what she must think when she did the same.

Heloise walked up and stood next to her. 'What do you see?'

'Impossibility.'

'How so?'

'That's for you to answer, don't you think?'

Heloise said, 'I'm afraid I'm not fond of riddles.'

Alamaeda turned to face Heloise and the huge, empty suite behind her, atop the huge empty casino. 'Of course. You look rushed off your feet.'

Heloise said, 'Why do you come here? What do you think I'm going to say?'

'I honestly don't know. But we can't understand evil unless we face it.'

She seemed offended. 'You think I'm evil?'

'Maybe I'm trying to find out. Maybe that's why I keep coming back.'

'I think you misjudge me.'

'My judgement is pretty sound. I'm willing to trust it here.'

'Yet you don't know the answer to your own question.'

'I'm reserving judgement until all the facts are in.'

Heloise smiled. 'Then when they are I'm sure you'll come to realise that I am nothing more than a businesswoman.'

'And how is the casino business?'

'Taking its time to solidify.'

'Yeah, I bet,' Alamaeda said with a nod. 'Getting a gaming licence is pretty tricky when you're the head of a drug cartel.'

'Well, it transpires that government officials are quite susceptible to the hearsay your organisation likes to spread.'

'Is that why you're keeping a low profile? Is that why there have been no revenge attacks against Maria?'

'I'm not sure I understand what you're saying.'

'Roll back a bit and we were scraping sicarios off the pavement every other day. Your guys would kill some of Maria's and she would kill some of yours. Back and forth, tit for tat, over and over. Now, it's strangely quiet. I've been asking myself why. But, as you say, government types don't like bad press. The fewer corpses and bullet holes, the greater the chance that some corrupt pencil-pusher in city hall will bow to your pressure to grant a gaming licence.'

Heloise's face was unreadable.

Alamaeda continued: 'Of course, you can't just let the attack go without a response. You can't show weakness to either Maria or your own people. You lose the respect of your men and you lose your life. So, I've been scratching my head wondering what you're up to. You're keeping a low profile and crossing your beautifully manicured fingers in the hope that a reduction in bloodshed will be enough to get your casino business going, but you simply can't give Maria a free pass in the meantime. So, what are you doing? I just can't figure it out.'

Heloise smiled. 'Perhaps, Agent Alamaeda, what you're missing is an outside perspective.'

Alamaeda had no idea what that meant.

TWENTY-THREE

Five kilometres wasn't far to walk, but Victor wanted to leave the immediate area as fast as possible. Whatever Ruiz's words about a lesson taught, it didn't mean it had been learned. Maybe they would come looking for revenge, maybe with backup. No real threat, but Victor didn't want to leave a trail of injured young men across the countryside signposting his movements. So, he flagged down a pickup truck which stopped, and he climbed into the load bed, dropping cash into the waiting palm of a boy, who then slapped the cab's rear window with his palm three times and the truck set off.

From a practical perspective, he had made an avoidable error. He went out of his way to circumvent trouble. He saw these things coming and made sure they didn't escalate. Here, though, he wasn't yet in tune with the environment. A stranger in a strange land. He had to be more careful.

Thick clouds had rolled in and covered the sun. He expected rain, but the clouds never broke. He disembarked with another passenger from the back of the truck after they had been travelling for a short time to give himself enough of a lead.

The airfield was privately owned and one of hundreds scattered across the countryside. Some were little more than repurposed fields where small prop planes could take off and land, most coming from Honduras and heading north to Mexico or the Bahamas. This one was a little more organised and had a pretence of legitimacy. It advertised itself as a flight school, but it had taken a lot of time on the phone to arrange a lesson. Despite many pilots registered at the airfield and many planes housed in its hangars, none seemed available to take Victor.

In the end he had been able to organise an hour's lesson, but only for an extortionate fee. One that had been quoted to him to put him off, to get rid of him, but he had agreed nonetheless.

The entrance to the airfield was guarded. A teenager with a badly hidden pistol sat on the same kind of plastic chair the man at the petrol station had been sitting on. He wore a grey hoodie over a white T-shirt. His trousers were black jogging bottoms with a red stripe down the sides. His shoes were pumps with a floral pattern. His hair was long and unruly, held in place by large headphones. He had several days' worth of stubble, but it was thin and patchy across his cheeks.

As Victor neared, the teenager eventually noticed him and shot to his feet. He shouted something about private property and that Victor was trespassing.

'I have a lesson booked,' he explained, with his hands raised in an unthreatening manner because the teenager's fingers were inching closer to the handgun tucked into his jeans.

'You know,' Victor said, pointing to a sign that said Aviation School, 'a flying lesson.'

The teenager was struggling. He was a sentry looking out for cops or rivals. He had probably never dealt with anyone else.

Victor reached for his wallet to hasten the impasse, but the teenager lost his cool and pulled his piece, thinking Victor was doing the same.

This wasn't someone who needed to prove something, like the young men in the *comedor*. The teenager was working, and on sentry duty because he wasn't trusted with anything else. Which meant he had never fired his weapon in anger. He was more scared of Victor's wallet than Victor was concerned of the Beretta shaking in his hands.

'Call,' Victor said, and used his free hand to make the universal symbol for a phone. 'Check.'

The teenager had the gun outstretched, elbows locked, gripping the weapon so hard his fingers were reddening. He didn't know what to do.

'It's okay,' Victor said, inching closer, wallet in his left hand, held up and obvious. 'I'm just here for my lesson.'

The guy wasn't planning on shooting him – he was too scared to actually squeeze the trigger – but the danger of a negligent discharge was increasing with every second.

Just a little closer and Victor could launch the wallet in the guy's direction, which would cause enough of a distraction for Victor to cover the remaining distance, and drop the teenager. Even with the distraction, there was a lot of ground to cover, so by the time Victor reached him there would be no opportunity to do it the easy way. He would have to strike hard, and fast, else risk the gun going off, which would either hit Victor or not, but even the latter was bad. It would mean the flying lesson would be untenable, but also because he had already left an unmistakable sign of his presence with the fight in the *comedor*. Another hurt and bloody local would be like adding flashing lights to that sign. Besides, the teenager wasn't like the guys in the *comedor*. He was weak and skinny and might never fully recover from a few disabling strikes. A lifetime unable to twist off a bottle cap was a steep price to pay for a momentary loss of cool.

'Check my wallet,' Victor said, raising it as he neared, and drawing the teenager's gaze higher and away from the rest of Victor. 'It's all in there.'

Two more steps were all he needed.

Victor took one of those steps closer, readying to spring off on the second step, readying to throw the wallet, when a voice yelled, '*Put that gun down, you idiot.*'

The teenager obeyed without hesitation. The muzzle dropped and Victor wouldn't have to hurt him, after all.

The release of tension transformed the teenager's entire body. His face relaxed. His arms loosened. His stance widened. He even smiled.

'I almost killed you,' he blurted out at Victor.

Victor raised an eyebrow. 'I was terrified.'

The other guy was tall, with a rotundness his shirt couldn't contain. He had a bald head and a few days' worth of stubble growth. Forty-three or forty-four, with a deep tan and dry, calloused hands. His clothes were simple, but expensive. A black jacket hung well on his shoulders. The brown shirt was unfastened at the collar. Dark jeans in a loose cut fell over suede loafers. His skin was smooth and pale.

'I'm your pilot,' he said.

He clipped the teenager around the ear as soon as he was in range, and ripped the pistol from his hand. The teenager backed away fast, almost falling over, and rubbed his ear as he looked sullen and embarrassed.

'Adolescents,' the pilot said to Victor, as if he would understand.

Victor wasn't sure he had ever been a teenager, but he nodded anyway. 'What is it with the young guys here? They're wound up pretty tight.'

'Aren't they everywhere?'

Victor shrugged, as if he understood, as if he agreed.

'Estuardo,' the pilot said, offering his calloused palm and a set of short, fat fingers.

Victor shook it.

'We don't get many foreigners asking for lessons,' he said, 'Mister ... Mathus.'

'Call me Ryan,' Victor said.

Estuardo gestured for Victor to walk with him, and they started along the track towards the airfield. After a few metres, Estuardo stopped and turned.

'*Hey,*' he called to attract the teenager's attention.

When he had it, Estuardo threw the confiscated gun, but not towards the kid. Instead he tossed it far into the long grass, and chuckled as the teenager trudged to collect it.

TWENTY-FOUR

'So, you want to learn to fly,' Estuardo said as they neared a hangar.

'It's been a dream of mine for a long time.'

'What's been stopping you?'

Victor shrugged. 'Work's always getting in the way.'

The pilot responded with a nod. 'What do you do for a living?'

'I'm a salesman.'

'Oh,' Estuardo said, losing interest fast. 'What do you sell?'

'Something no one wants.'

The hangar was open. Estuardo led him inside where two light aircraft were parked. The air smelled of oil and cheap tobacco, body odour and greasy food.

Estuardo held open his arms. 'Which one?'

'Which what?'

'Which plane would you like to learn to fly?'

Both aircraft were similar, but they weren't the same. Both were fixed-wing propeller planes, one painted white, the other blue and with a yellow strip. The white aircraft was a Diamond Twin Star, only a few years old. It was clean and bright. The other vehicle was much older, a Cessna 182.

Victor said, 'The blue one.'

'Favourite colour?'

He shook his head. 'It has character.'

'Not scared because it's old?'

Victor shook his head again. 'You don't get old without having lived.'

He placed his backpack in the rear of the plane, behind the two seats. There was enough room for another couple of passengers, but not with anything approaching comfort. There were no rear seats. They had been removed long ago, Victor reasoned, to create more space for cargo. For the same weight as two passengers and seats, a couple of hundred kilos of product could be flown instead.

Estuardo saw him glance at the empty space, and said, 'They need replacing. The seats, I mean.'

'Ah,' Victor said, as if a mystery had been solved.

Estuardo performed a half-hearted check of the aircraft and strapped himself in. He gestured for Victor to do the same. Victor made the motions, but didn't fasten the belt. Instead, he tucked the clasp under his buttock so the belt looked taut. Estuardo didn't notice.

Victor wasn't scared of flying, but he didn't enjoy it. He didn't like that it kept him contained. It made him rely on the pilot's skills and the vehicle's thousands of moving parts to keep him alive. He didn't like surrendering his fate to forces outside of his control. Most aviation deaths were caused by small and light aircraft crashing. Heavier meant safer, somehow. A rogue trader who Victor had once been hired to kill had been a keen pilot until he crashed his prop plane into a meadow. It was ruled an accident because it had been. Victor had been planning to assassinate the man at his mansion when he had been paid in full for causing the plane crash. He had even received a bonus for making it look like an accident.

Estuardo was a competent pilot. He was relaxed in his seat throughout take-off. He took the aircraft in a steep climb, explaining, 'We're going to start with the basics. No take-offs. Just cruising. Think you can manage that?'

'I'll try my best.'

Estuardo glanced at him. 'Have you heard that thing – what's it called? – which says however hard you can push yourself, you can go another twenty per cent?'

Victor shook his head. 'Then I'll try my best plus twenty per cent.'

'That's more like it.'

Estuardo eased the joystick away from him and the nose of the plane dipped a little until they were horizontal. He peered out of the door window. 'Stunning country, isn't it?'

Victor looked out of his own. 'Very.'

Estuardo spoke to him for a while, explaining the roles of the various instruments, what they did and what Victor needed to look out for when he had the controls. Victor listened and nodded and said 'Uh huh' when required. Estuardo never repeated himself. He was going through the motions but he didn't want to be here. He didn't want to waste his time teaching Victor. He was making a reasonable pretence, however, and Victor didn't challenge him on his lack of passion.

'It's so beautiful up here,' Victor said. 'Do you mind if I take some pictures?'

'I thought you were up here to learn how to fly.'

'Just a couple of snaps.'

Estuardo shrugged. 'It's your hour. Use it as you wish.'

Victor used his camera to take some photographs through the side window. 'Wow, these are coming out great.' He turned in the seat and took some through the pilot's side window. 'Can you just lean back a little?'

Estuardo did so. 'Don't take too long.'

'I won't,' Victor said, dropping the camera and lurching at Estuardo, the belt coming loose.

One arm wrapped around the front of Estuardo's neck as the other snaked around the back. Victor's hands found each other, locking off and he squeezed as he slipped between the seats, pinching shut Estuardo's carotid arteries in a choke hold.

Estuardo went slack after four seconds, and Victor kept the hold on for another four to make sure Estuardo would stay unconscious for what he needed to do next. He hit the cruise switch and took out a small leather case from his backpack. From inside the case, he took out a pre-loaded syringe and stabbed the needle into Estuardo's lower back. He was snoring by the time Victor had replaced the syringe and case.

He used the map and GPS to work out exactly where the aircraft was in the skies over Guatemala, and adjusted the flaps until he was on the right trajectory. He was no pilot, but he knew enough. While the plane had autopilot acti-vated, provided he didn't try anything too adventurous with manoeuvres, there was little that could go wrong.

He didn't have to fly far. They had begun close to where he wanted. He had spent a long time and considerable effort ensuring he organised a lesson from that particular private airfield. It was the nearest one to his ultimate destination.

Within ten minutes he was close enough, so he took a large telephoto lens from his backpack and fixed it to the camera.

The lens was the best he had been able to acquire, weighing almost two kilograms, with a focal length of 1200mm, so Victor could peer down at Maria Salvatierra's horse ranch a thousand feet below and see the faces of those who stood guard or patrolled. He had only a few minutes before they were out of range, but he had a great angle to photograph the entire property.

He changed memory cards twice.

When Estuardo woke, his head snapped up and a trail of drool stretched from his chin to where it had been resting on his shirt. He was confused. He was disorientated. He glanced at Victor, at the controls, at the sky ahead.

Short-term memory loss was often a side effect of losing consciousness, and it was always a side effect of barbiturates. Estuardo had no idea what had happened.

Victor – the camera lens now safely back in the rucksack – pointed out of the side window. 'Did you just nod off?'

Estuardo said, 'Uh, no. Of course not,' as he wiped drool from his chin.

TWENTY-FIVE

At another time, in another life, Victor might have been a photographer. Taking a good picture with a camera was a lot like taking a good shot with a rifle. Aim, timing and a steady hand were everything. There were further similarities too. Positioning, patience, even stealth, all helped to find that right frame. Training, practice and talent all fused together to create skill. Any amateur could take a picture as any amateur could squeeze a trigger, but the difference in outcome between that amateur and professional would be worlds apart.

Victor was no professional photographer, but in a rare moment of vanity he allowed himself to believe he could have been. The pictures he had taken of Maria's ranch were excellent, as were those of the surrounding area. It would have taken days to have gathered intelligence of half the quality, and he would have needed to put himself at considerable risk while doing so. He counted twenty-nine gunmen guarding the ranch. There would be more he couldn't see: inside the buildings or vehicles, else otherwise out of shot.

He saw a Land Rover driving on a nearby road. It was not an uncommon vehicle in rural Guatemala, but it was the same green colour as another Land Rover that was parked at the ranch. A mobile patrol then, doing laps of the surrounding roads as an advance warning system to any threats. Maria, or whoever organised her security, was thorough.

If the Land Rover held another four gunmen – and based on the distribution of the other twenty-nine, Victor estimated another 10 per cent might be out of shot – then there could be up to thirty-six men protecting the ranch.

Victor wasn't sure he had ever been tasked to kill someone so well protected. It was going to be every bit as difficult as he had imagined.

He had been right to acquire the aerial surveillance first, because now he knew what he was up against, but he still needed to collect closer intel. He would need to take an extreme level of care. He was no local, and even untrained guards could see that, and that alone marked him out as suspicious. He was used to operating where he could be anonymous, but in Guatemala, in the rural environs, that was impossible. Everywhere was hostile terrain. Everywhere was enemy territory.

He used the photographs to sketch out a plan of the ranch, using the heights of figures and the length of vehicles to measure distances and dimensions, until he had a pretty good representation of where Maria lived. He left to conduct further recon only once every detail had been imprinted into his memory.

He took his time. He took no risks. He kept his distance, utilising his binoculars and camera to build up a more thorough picture of the ranch and its security. The first and most obvious problem to consider was the veritable army of sicarios that guarded Maria Salvatierra. There was a long, one-lane driveway that led from the ranch, with a gatehouse where it met the highway. An ornate, wrought-iron gate blocked the entrance, which would not stop any determined assault from her rivals, but behind it lay three rows of police stingers to ensure that, even if the gate was open, a conventional vehicle would make it no more than fifty feet along the driveway. Six guards occupied the gatehouse, all wearing body armour and carrying assault rifles. Their training and competence was obvious to Victor. They weren't kids from the slums. These were former military.

The ranch was surrounded by a wooden fence, which offered no real security, but it was patrolled by more guards, again with body armour and assault rifles. They had sophisticated radio equipment too – headsets and throat mics – and were in near-constant communication. The land was flat all the way to the ranch and, from examining topographical maps, Victor could see that this was by design. The natural undulation of the land had been flattened and filled. There was a thousand metres of open killing ground between the fence and anything resembling cover, and that ground was dotted with tiny lumps. They were hard to spot at first as they had been painted to match the colour of the grass. Some were only a few inches in height. Some were up to half a metre. They were arranged in a seemingly haphazard pattern, but this was deliberate. At night, with an infrared lens, Victor saw the criss-cross beams of light that covered the land between the fence and where the buildings lay. The single expanse that wasn't protected in this way was the grazing pastures, but these were enclosed with fences that had motion detectors of their own. Not only were there enough guards and defences to repel a full-scale assault, but there was no conceivable way for a lone assassin to sneak up undetected.

He reexamined the photographs, which besides showing the many armed gunmen patrolling, revealed other activity. Several men stood or sat around an outside table, all facing towards where someone else sat in the shade of a parasol. The parasol obscured the person beneath it, but the shadow was unmistakable as belonging to a woman.

The photographs captured the end of the meeting, and most of the men dispersed through the ranch – going indoors or otherwise out of frame.

One did not.

He left the ranch in a yellow sports car. The licence plate was hidden by the angle, but upon zooming in Victor identified the car as a Lamborghini Aventador. An expensive vehicle for a serious player.

Victor wondered if the visit was a one-off or a regular occurrence as he analysed his research. The only way to get close to the ranch would be with an invite. Not impossible – he had gained the trust of well-protected targets before – but improbable, given that Heloise and Maria had been trying to kill one another for some time now. He could foresee working his way into the cartel, doing jobs and earning respect, slowly being introduced to the hierarchy, proving himself again and again over a long period of time, until he found himself invited to the ranch to meet the boss. What he couldn't envision, however, was killing her and slipping away again without being discovered. It would require too much guesswork, too many assumptions, and be too reliant on improvisation. It wasn't a workable course of action.

Besides, the last time he had operated undercover in such a way, everything that could go wrong, had. He wasn't going to make the same mistake again.

The one hole in all the ranch's security was its dedication to security. The flattened land, the lack of trees and vegetation, left uninterrupted lines of sight straight to the house.

Which was why he found himself approaching an abandoned building.

It was a shack of some sort, made of timber, and half-reclaimed by nature. The elements had stripped away any paint or seal and the exposed wood was cracked and warped. Plants climbed all over it. The single door was locked, but it required nothing beyond a shove to open.

The air inside was thick with dust. He coughed a little as he stepped inside. Light filtered through gaps and cracks in the wood. Nebulas of swirling dust glowed and flickered. It was humid and cooler than outside. The wood was more rotten than dry. The floorboards were soft underfoot.

The ceiling was low, and a dust-caked cobweb rippled above his head.

A home, he reasoned, long ago. There were a few items of furniture, an old stove and some rusted pans. A wooden stepladder led up through a hole in the ceiling to a second floor. He had to crouch to avoid hitting his head on the roof, and shuffled his way past the remnants of a mattress to where a single small window, caked in grime, let in a swathe of bright sunshine.

The catch was corroded and required considerable effort to shift, and he almost broke the window frame forcing it open.

He peered through the gap, over the track and the

vegetation, through the foliage, and after a moment his gaze stopped on the pristine white gleam he was looking to find.

He adjusted his position to get a better angle, and raised his binoculars. It took a few seconds to adjust the focus and turn the white blur to a crisp image of the gatehouse. He would need a rangefinder to be accurate, but he expected one would tell him the building was between point-five and point-six of a mile from his current position.

He angled up his head and the binoculars with it, refocusing so he could see beyond the gatehouse and along the driveway, to where, just over a mile in the distance, was the ranch house itself.

Several cartridges could make it, but a .50 calibre round would be the best option. Even so, flight time would be over two seconds. That was a long time to be pushed by wind and pulled by gravity. Temperature, humidity and barometric pressure all had to be factored in when making the ballistic calculations. And he would have to take into consideration how the force generated by the Earth's rotation would affect the bullet's trajectory.

He would need a stationary target, precise measurements of all contributing variables, exact ballistic information for the round he was going to use, plus time spent practising with the weapon in question.

He could shoot only when the conditions were just right, and only when Maria was in front of the house, unmoving. He knew if he missed he wouldn't get a second chance.

One shot, calculated to perfection, and his job would be complete.

First though, he would need a rifle.

TWENTY-SIX

Her name wasn't Georg, but she had once been known that way. She had chosen the name for some flippant reason she couldn't even recall. Was it because of that old film actor she liked? It didn't matter. She dealt in a world where men dominated and women weren't respected, so it had helped to pretend. It had helped for men to think she too was a man. Men were simple like that. If they didn't know any better, they were happy in ignorance. It hadn't lasted, of course, because nothing ever did.

Her business partner – former business partner – had turned on her, and would have killed her too had it not been for the intervention of one of her customers.

That customer had met her in one of her warehouses to collect explosives, and it had been during their negotiations that the traitorous partner had come to murder her. Two of Georg's closest people had been killed in the ensuing gun battle, but at the end of the firefight the partner and his men were all dead by the customer's hand. Georg lay dying on the floor, shotgun pellets buried in her guts, and would have died in agony had the same customer not dialled her an ambulance.

An act of compassion, of mercy, she had thought in the aftermath, but she later realised it had been done only to create a favour that would need to be fulfilled at a future time. She had paid her debt, and had not heard from him again after that call. She hadn't expected to, but when one of her crew came to her bearing a look of confusion and handing her a phone, she somehow knew who would be on the end of the line.

'Yes?' she asked.

He said, 'I want a gun.'

She recognised the voice. A deep sound. A hard-to-place accent. Not German, though he spoke the language like a native. An American, maybe. She recalled his face and the blank, neutral expression. Pale skin. Dark hair. Beard. A grey suit beneath an overcoat, unfastened. A killer.

Georg said, 'You don't want to ask how I've been?'

'I want an Accuracy International AX50. I won't accept anything else. With a couple of scope options. Long range and infrared. And don't skimp on the ammo. If you can't get hold of match grade then I'll only accept the next best thing: PMC Bronze Line 660 grain boat-tail.'

'I'm a lot better, thank you for asking,' she replied. 'I only need to take paracetamol these days. I've even cut back on the tobacco. Well, I'm trying.'

'Are you writing this down?'

She huffed. 'I never write anything down, but I never forget an order. Although I feel compelled to say I'm not really in the weapons trade. I'm not an arms dealer.'

'You delivered last time.'

'I was paying off my debt,' she explained. 'I'm trying to get out of the gun business.'

'Then I appreciate you making a special case just for me.'

'Why do I feel that it wouldn't be in my best interest to say no to you?'

'Because you're a smart businesswoman and I'm a valued customer.'

She forced a laugh.

He said, 'Can you get me a rifle or not?'

'There's not much I can't source.'

'That's the Georg I know.'

'You don't know me, and that's not my real name.'

He said, 'Then feel free to tell me your real name.'

'I think I'll keep that to myself.'

'In that case, Georg it is.'

She sighed. 'I trust this will be a conventional arrangement.'

'You've paid your debt, if that's what you mean. I'll buy the rifle for a reasonable price.'

'Good,' she said. 'Because what you ask for isn't cheap, or easy to procure.'

'If it was easy, I wouldn't need to call you.'

'You flatter me.'

'Take it however you want.'

'Where will I need to send it?'

'Central America.'

She thought for a moment, picturing contacts, imagining phone calls, negotiations, haggling, arguing, agreements, arrangements, risks and profit.

'Okay,' she said. 'I'll make some calls and see what I can source, but I expect it will take some time to get such a weapon to you.'

'That's fine. I didn't think you'd have one lying around. We can talk specifics when you get back to me. I'll send details on how to make contact.'

'As you wish,' she said.

He said nothing more, and the line disconnected.

'Would a goodbye kill you?' she asked the dial tone.

TWENTY-SEVEN

Using Georg was a little problematic. She was an attachment to Victor's recent past, the past he was stepping away from. That couldn't be helped here. He could source firearms on his own, but not of the quality he needed to kill Maria Salvatierra from over a mile away. He knew how to track down small-time arms dealers like he knew how to track down document forgers. Small-time arms dealers had access to handguns and AKs. They didn't have .50 calibre anti-materiel sniper rifles in their inventory. So, he had to go off script and use Georg for want of an alternative.

While he waited for her to get back to him, he considered his other options.

Victor's business was hard targets. He had assassinated warlords and crime kingpins, spies and killers. Clients didn't hire him to kill civilians because it didn't require a man of Victor's skills and prohibitive expense. He hadn't been paid to kill a cartel boss before, but he had been tasked with assassinating similar people. Those targets were almost as well protected, but they had not been expecting attack. Maria Salvatierra expected violence at all times. The war had been raging for years. Her closest bodyguards were experienced and ready.

Therefore, he wanted to have multiple plans in development at the same time. With someone so well guarded and so expectant of attack, a simple ambush wasn't going to work. He couldn't shadow her movements and strike where and when she was vulnerable because she had no conventional movements. There would be no instances of vulnerability.

He would have to create them.

Three approaches would be sufficient, he deemed. A primary, and two secondary options. It was a delicate balance of having as many workable approaches as possible without spreading his preparations too thin. He wanted to be able to put a plan into motion at a moment's notice, when circumstances were just right, but he wanted to know that plan would work.

Aside from the ranch itself, there was only one other potential strike point, which was a superyacht named *Sipak* that Maria used on occasions. It was a three-hundred-foot behemoth, moored on the Pacific coast. A floating hotel, almost. Luxurious and decadent. The price tag was north of ninety million dollars, but the actual price of such yachts was never advertised. If you had to ask, you couldn't afford it. But it was simple for Victor to find hard intel. Online brokers had detailed profiles for their wares, and at least three yachts of the same design were on sale. A few clicks of a mouse in an internet café and Victor knew everything from its range – five thousand nautical miles – to what helicopter the forward deck was certified for – the Augusta Grand New.

The most important details were the number of crew who served on the yacht and the number of guests the sixteen bedrooms could house: forty-five and thirty-one. Seventy-six people on board was a lot to consider, but the crew could be discounted as threats. They were waiters and stewards, sailors and maids. They wouldn't be carrying weapons and they wouldn't risk their lives by getting in his way. Of the thirty-one potential guests, one was his target. The thirty that remained would not all be bodyguards. Maria would have lieutenants and guests that, like the crew, would be non-combatants. There was no way to tell in advance what the split would be, but even in the best case he could expect significant opposition. Though even in the worst-case scenario it would be far fewer guns pointed his way than at the ranch.

The yacht couldn't provide the same level of security, but Victor had no way of knowing when she might make use of it. If he could find out, then he could stow aboard else swim aboard, and kill Maria with nothing more than stealth. He couldn't get close when she was at the ranch, and even if he could, he didn't want to. Too many guards, too many things to go wrong, too little chance of escape.

Victor could remain hidden in the shack for days on end to wait for the right opportunity to make the kill, but with the yacht he had to know in advance when Maria would be on board. He had an idea of how he might find out, but it would require a lot of groundwork.

The third option would be to use explosives. Victor didn't like bombs, but he didn't like firearms either. Both were nothing more than tools to him. Of the two, using a gun would be his preference. Bombs were loud, they were messy and indiscriminate, and required all manner of factors to be just right for them to be incorporated into a successful assassination. For a gun, it took little more than a clear line of sight.

He had used explosives successfully before on several occasions. He had fulfilled one contract by hiding a bomb inside the cistern of a toilet in order to kill a gangster, but none since. He could see an opportunity with his current contract. If he worked on the assumption that the central point of interest for the group gathered outside of the ranch house was Maria Salvatierra, then she was some twenty metres from where vehicles were parked on the driveway. That was close enough for a car bomb to kill her, as well as everyone nearby.

Victor preferred to avoid killing anyone he was not paid to, but his job could be seen as a series of compromises, none of which were related to morality. When working for intelligence agencies his terms of employment were to ensure a lack of collateral damage. They wanted him to kill only those people they decreed. Other life was somehow more sacred.

It was an unnecessary stipulation. He always sought to avoid civilian death and unnecessary suffering, but only because he was a perfectionist. He wanted to do his job well.

It had been rare in recent times for him to have the freedom from oversight, time frames and methodology. Here, he had all three. Heloise wanted Maria dead, however it could be achieved. Victor was sure Heloise would have no problem with him wiping out her sister's most important lieutenants alongside her. There might even be a bonus for him as a result.

In his safe-house office, he printed out the aerial photographs of the ranch. He pieced some together, drawing and marking them with different coloured pens. He measured and calculated, working out explosive velocities and blast radiuses, debris patterns and secondary damage. He studied literature on successful car bombs and those that had failed. He did the sums for different explosives, accounting for the carrier vehicle and the fuel within.

Yes, he concluded. It was possible to transform a yellow Lamborghini Aventador into a bomb and wipe out everyone who happened to be outside the front of the ranch house when that bomb exploded.

For that to work, however, he first had to track down the car.

TWENTY-EIGHT

What Alamaeda found funny about the drug trade was that the single most important commodity outside of the drugs was humble old plastic. Shrink wrap, to be precise. Not for the product, but for the cash. Vacuum-packing could halve the amount of room a bundle of banknotes took up. Halve the volume, double the amount. Cartels owned whole warehouses whose sole purpose was to pack cash into as small a space as possible. And when hundreds of millions of dollars were moved in hard currency, then the percentages really mattered. If you could reduce the volume of cash by 51 per cent instead of 50, then that was worth millions per annum. The fewer individual shipments, the fewer the chances of that cash being intercepted en route. The fewer shipments, the greater the profits. Every per cent mattered. The manufacturers of vacuum-packing machines had pre-orders for newer, better models the instant they were advertised. When thinner plastic wrap was developed, initial production could not keep up with demand.

The corpse found blocking a viaduct was bound in shrink wrap, head to toe, but the cheap kind. Whoever had done this hadn't wanted to waste the good stuff.

'Ugh,' Wickliffe said. 'That's just nasty.'

She kept her distance while Alamaeda sprayed some perfume on to the index finger of her left hand, which she then held under her nose. She still grimaced when she squatted down to take a closer look. 'Huge amount of facial swelling. Almost certainly fractures to the orbital bones, nose and jaw. And he's missing a whole lot of teeth.'

'Tongue?'

'Nuh uh.'

Wickliffe shrugged. 'A rat.'

'You sound disappointed.'

'I was hoping for something a little juicier.'

Alamaeda gestured. 'If he were any juicer, he'd pop.'

'You know what I mean.'

She did. With Heloise's efforts to get a gaming licence, cartel violence had halved, especially in the city, where it was visible. That meant Alamaeda and Wickliffe paid extra attention when Guatemalan police found a dead trafficker. Mr Shrink Wrap was a known entity, one of Heloise's top lieutenants.

Guatemala was home to several DTOs – drug-trafficking organisations – which meant it was called home by many DEA agents, all working together but all tasked with different regions, different cartels. Alamaeda and Wickliffe had the blessing and curse that was assisting in the dismantling of the Salvatierra cartel. Blessing because it was potentially the largest prize, but curse since it had split into two warring factions.

Alamaeda had been in Guatemala long enough to remember

when Manny Salvatierra had been sole patron. The eldest son of a traditional contraband family, in his early days he had smuggled cigarettes and alcohol around the country, avoiding police efforts to stop his operation thanks to the ever-ready loyalty of locals who would tip him off or even hide him, knowing they would be rewarded for their efforts. His had been a slow journey into the narcotics-trafficking business, but he had risen at a steady, relentless rate until the cartel he headed was the most powerful in Guatemala. His two daughters had been his most trusted and valued lieutenants, both eager to learn the business and eager to please their devoted father.

The Salvatierra sisters, like their father before them, never came close to the business unless they wanted to do so. It was the ports on the Pacific coast and on the Caribbean coast where the bulk of the product was moved in and out of the country. The majority of DEA agents in Guatemala were focused there. Their job was to assist in stopping the drugs moving north to Mexico and the US. Alamaeda wasn't here for drugs, but money. Her job was to intercept the money moving back down south.

At a conservative estimate, almost four hundred tons of cocaine passed through Guatemala every year. Just transitioning the product to the Mexican cartels made it a billion-dollar industry. Cartels with closer relations with the South American producers could bypass Guatemala all together, else use it only as a stopping-off point on the long route north, but the other cartels needed Guatemala, needed the Salvatierra cartel, to be their middleman.

For a brief, violent time, the Mexican cartels sought to establish a permanent presence in Guatemala, both in physical and psychological senses, but they were ultimately unsuccessful. This only made the Salvatierra cartel more powerful. The Mexicans had tried, and failed, to bypass them, and so the price of doing business rose as a result. The rules changed too. When once the Salvatierras supplied only to a single Mexican cartel, from then on they could sell to whoever they chose without consequences.

The Salvatierras controlled huge swathes of the country, including two wide corridors that ran from El Salvador and Honduras all the way to Mexico, ensuring their continued dominance of the main trafficking routes. Alamaeda wasn't interested in the smaller fish in Guatemala's pond. Those with closer links or out-and-out proxies for the Mexican cartels were someone else's problem. The remaining Guatemalan cartels were minnows. The Salvatierras were the whale.

Yet there had never been any charges against Manny, or his two daughters. They were untouchable. Everyone knew they were crooks, had always been crooks, would always be crooks, yet they could walk through a storm without getting wet. They were too big and powerful to be faced head-on, and the other cartels were forced to fight among themselves for the smaller slices of pie. That violence kept the authorities busy. The Salvatierras had never needed to fight, had never needed to attract attention. Until the war.

With an even split in territory and manpower, the war was a stalemate, and while the sisters fought each other they allowed the smaller traffickers to steal business, and – more dangerously – they created openings for the Mexican cartels to once again encroach into Guatemala. The sisters needed a resolution, but that was achievable only when one of them was dead. If they managed to kill one another, that would be the best possible outcome. Alamaeda wasn't betting on that happening anytime soon. It was wishful thinking, at least. Her biggest fear was a miraculous reconciliation. Fractured, the Salvatierra cartel showed vulnerability for the first time. It was weak, finally, but only until one sister killed the other.

Alamaeda said, 'This guy took one hell of a beating.'

'Didn't your guy tell you he was a trusted trafficker?'

Alamaeda exhaled. 'What do you want me to say? Not every piece of intelligence is solid gold.'

'That's an understatement and a half. I'm seeing larvae, but with the cold water he could have been down here for a couple of weeks, easy. Given the shrink wrap, it makes it hard to say without a proper examination.'

'He's old news, whatever happened. No point digging deeper. Whoever did this to him has probably forgotten what he did to deserve it. Come on, let's make a move.'

Back in their vehicle, Wickliffe spent a couple of minutes cleaning her sunglasses so Alamaeda seized the opportunity to check her voicemail.

'What?' Wickliffe asked when she had put her cell away again.

Alamaeda played dumb. 'What do you mean, "what"?'

'You're smiling.'

'Is that so rare?'

'It's a different kind of smile and I know exactly what it means.' She frowned in a mock judgemental way. 'Who is he?'

'Early days, so I don't know much about him yet,' Alamaeda answered. 'But looks like I have a date tonight.'

'In the Guat? How'd you find the one dateable man in town?'

Everyone who lived in Guatemala City called it Guat, or the Guat.

'We met on a bus, if you can believe it.'

'Was he the driver or the kid that stashes the luggage on top?'

Alamaeda rolled her eyes. 'Actually, he's a commodities trader or something. He's Canadian.' She made an attempt at an accent. 'Although he doesn't really talk like that.'

'A Canadian?' Wickliffe huffed. 'I don't like him already.'

Alamaeda said, 'Then let your cynical mind be eased because I've already ran a background check on him.'

'Already? That means you like him or there's something not quite right about him.'

'Maybe both.'

Wickliffe's brow furrowed. 'You thought it might be a honeytrap?'

'It did cross my mind.'

'Too good to be true?'

She shrugged in way of an answer.

'And now your fears are abated?'

Alamaeda said, 'Suspicions quietened.'

'So, he's passed the computer's test but not your own?'

'It's hard for me to trust.'

'You say it like it's a bad thing. It means you're no pushover. Be glad of that. I wish I had been a little less eager to trust when I was your age.'

'You're all of five years my senior.'

'At my age, that might as well be ninety.'

Alamaeda said, 'When the mind gives up, the body follows.'

'Hey, I'm the older, wiser one of this little duo. Don't think you can usurp me with some meme-level philosophy. I practically invented that shit.'

'I can believe that,' Alamaeda said as she put the car in gear.

Wickliffe said, 'Did you tell him what you're doing in Guatemala?'

Alamaeda shook her head. 'What good would that do?'

TWENTY-NINE

The night was warm. The rain had stopped, but the air had been left saturated with moisture. Lavandier was a big fan of Guatemala's equatorial warmth, but he would never get used to the humidity. It ruined his hair. The sleek blond-and-silver waves became unruly spirals. He became unkempt, which was unacceptable.

Inside his brasserie, he was safe from the weather. The establishment had exceptional air conditioning. It had been the biggest expense when converting the premises from its original use as a traditional Guatemalan eatery. Along with the brasserie, Lavandier owned an import firm that specialised in French food. The business operated at a small loss, but Lavandier kept it going because he hated beans, could only tolerate rice, and considered tortilla an insult to bread.

He had lived in Guatemala for many years, and had been in the Americas for years before that, but he had maintained his accent and his preference for his national cuisine. At home, he dined on veal and foie gras, Camembert and Puy lentils.

He sipped Bordeaux and champagne. He made a fierce tarte Tatin and sometimes his own vanilla ice cream to go with it. His heart sank whenever Heloise invited him to accompany her to dinner.

He could never turn her down. He always had to act thrilled at the prospect of time in her company. Whatever his attraction to her, he dreaded going for a meal. He had mastered the art of not curling one's lip in disgust. He was well practised in making excuses for not finishing the food. Variations on 'I'm watching what I eat' and 'I'm afraid my stomach is a little delicate' were his go-to justifications. He was sure Heloise invited him to such meals simply to torture him.

He had opened his brasserie in the city's most cosmopolitan and diverse neighbourhood, where there was plenty of new money that needed to be spent, but still there was no profit. Oh well, at least he had a pied-à-terre that could satiate his need for French finery. He had more than enough wealth to cover a loss, and some things were more important than money. He wasn't prepared to be rich only to abandon who he was inside.

The brasserie was staffed entirely by men. Lavandier had once employed only young and attractive women, but his lingering gaze and suggestive comments were not conducive to maintaining discipline, nor keeping staff on the books. Over time he had learned that the best way to control his salacious intent was to have no temptation. Thus, all men. And thinking one step ahead, he made sure none of them were handsome. He didn't want them to have pretty girlfriends visiting that might test his resolve. He wanted no angry waiter to break his delicate nose.

He was enjoying a fine ensemble of truffles and snails when his personal phone rang. Unusual, because he had several phones and very few knew this number. Heloise never called him direct. He always phoned her, and then only after receiving whatever number she was using that day via SMS from a burner phone used by one of her bodyguards.

It was a necessary precaution, of course, but one that left him feeling a little expendable. He was expected to take risks that Heloise would never take herself.

So, Lavandier let it ring for a moment while he finished chewing and took a sip of wine to wash his mouth clear.

He answered with a polite, '*Oui?*'

Lavandier, though a long-time resident of Guatemala and fluent speaker of Spanish, liked to interject his native tongue whenever he could. It was part of both his nature and the character he played – the flamboyant Frenchman, exotic and otherworldly.

'Do you know which of Maria's associates drives a yellow Lamborghini?'

The voice belonged to a man and spoke in English, which was rare to hear in this city. Although Lavandier did not recognise it he knew he had heard it before in a suite in Madrid.

'The Wraith, I presume.'

'Excuse me?'

'We had to call you something,' Lavandier explained. 'I wasn't sure you were even in the country yet.'

'Is the answer to my initial question a yes or no?'

Lavandier sipped some wine. 'Not one for conversation, are you?'

'You're not paying me enough to sit around chatting.'

'*Touché, monsieur. Touché*. Although I think you would agree your purse is staggering in its generosity.'

The Wraith said, 'I'm worth every penny.'

'The answer to your question is no,' Lavandier replied. 'But there isn't much I can't find out, as I believe was previously made clear. Is the answer pertinent to our greater objective?'

'I wouldn't ask otherwise.'

'Then if you will allow me the munificence of time, I will endeavour to ascertain who owns such an ostentatious means of transport.' Lavandier liked to use uncommon words to make himself appear more of an intellectual. 'I should know within a few days, else I'll never know. How might that sound?'

'I'll call you at the end of the week.'

Lavandier said, 'I'm positively thrilled at the prospect of more scintillating discourse.'

The line went dead.

Lavandier sat and thought for a while, sipping his fine wine and listening to the muted sounds of the kitchen staff cleaning up. The dining area was empty except for him, and no music played through the speakers at this late hour. Throughout the day and evening traditional French tunes would add a background ambience to the – few – patrons who frequented the brasserie. Almost all of whom were tourists tickled by the idea of so French an establishment in the heart of Central America.

What to do? he mused. One couldn't come to such an answer without the lubrication only fermented grape juice could provide, so Lavandier refilled his glass to the top and took a heavy gulp.

Of course, he knew who owned the vehicle in question

as he knew many things. He was far better connected than anyone realised. The question wasn't so much how much should he pass on, but how much did he want to pass on?

Lavandier had much to consider.

THIRTY

The roar of an engine caught Victor's attention. It was loud and powerful, and he turned to see a yellow Lamborghini Aventador pull up outside the hotel. He watched as a valet rushed to help a woman out of the passenger seat and a man climbed out of the driver's door. He was dressed in jeans, leather jacket and cowboy boots. The woman was young, in a tight dress and high heels. The driver shoved cash and keys into the valet's hand, but said nothing. The valet circled the car, looking nervous. Not because of handling the car and the fear of damaging it, but because he knew the driver enough to be afraid of him.

The licence plate read *NUMERO UNO*.

'I don't know who drives the yellow Lamborghini,' Lavandier had told Victor over the phone. 'But I know how you can find him.'

There was no Lamborghini dealership in Guatemala City, and no authorised sellers. Any such cars were imported, which made maintaining them difficult. There was only one mechanic who had access to parts, who was paid in cash but had reasonably organised records that Victor made use of when he broke into the auto shop. There was no name listed with entries pertaining to the Aventador, but there was a phone number for a hotel in the city centre.

Victor took a seat in the lobby and asked for coffee, paying the bill straight away so he could leave at any moment. He drank only a little coffee – it was there for show – and checked his watch on occasions – again for show. He had been in many hotels. He had spent more time in hotel rooms than he had houses. He understood the ecosystem of staff and guests and visitors. He knew the mistresses from the wives, the dressed-down billionaires from the convention goers. He could tell from the way they held themselves whether a night porter would let him have a room for cash off the system, whether a concierge could arrange escorts and drugs. He also knew whether a hotel was of a high class or whether it just dressed the part.

This hotel was the latter. There were chandeliers but no crystal; paintings on every wall, but no originals. The uniforms were smart, but cheap. There were no dessert wines on the restaurant menu. Victor had no problem with pretence. His whole existence was built around it. He was a collection of surface details but no depth. Like the hotel, he needed none to survive, to profit. Depth was a luxury neither the hotel nor he could afford, nor wanted.

He spent twenty minutes nursing his coffee and pretending to people-watch – instead of watching for a person – and blended into the comings and goings of the lobby, unnoticed and unaffected as part of the ecosystem. If anywhere were his home, it was here.

For hotel coffee, it was pretty good. He didn't understand why, but no one who worked in a hotel knew how to make an excellent coffee. It was one of those strange immutable laws of the universe beyond comprehension, beyond logic. The best hotel coffee he had drunk was in Germany, which made even less sense. A man in a suit sat nearby playing with his phone. On a wrist, he wore a plastic band with print that read 'Golf is my vice'.

Chequered tiles created a hard floor, so cowboy boots striding through the lobby were loud and distinctive from some distance. He heard no high heels accompanying them.

The man who owned the Lamborghini strode past Victor, who sipped his coffee and watched him approach the concierge. They exchanged words, too far away for Victor to hear, but he could read the concierge's lips well enough:

I'm sorry to hear that, sir ... I'll take care of it ...

The man in the leather jacket left the hotel, shaking his head to himself and checking his phone. The concierge picked up a telephone receiver and hit a button out of Victor's sight. After a moment, he spoke to the person on the other end of the line.

We have a problem in the Fortune Suite. Give her a few minutes and see to it that she leaves without any fuss.

The suite was easy enough to find. The hotel had plenty of signs. It was on the eighth floor, accessible via stairs and two banks of elevators. Victor took the stairs, because he always did. The stairwell was quiet. He didn't remember the last time he had passed someone on a hotel staircase. People were lazier than they had ever been. The eighth floor was quiet – the suites took up at least twice the space of a normal room. It was the wrong time of the day too – after checkout but before check-in. Maybe the suite had been booked before today. Maybe the man in the leather jacket had special consideration. Maybe he didn't need to book. Maybe they always kept a suite or two available for him or other cartel guys they didn't want to anger.

There were no house cleaning carts, no doors open and no maids working hard who wouldn't mind using their master key card in return for help with the rent, which was a shame. Therefore, he settled for an old-fashioned approach.

He knocked on the door to the suite.

There was no answer, so he knocked again, harder, thumping the door with the downside of his fist to create a noise loud enough that it could not be ignored. A few seconds later, he heard footsteps on the other side. Slow. Tentative.

'Who is it?' a woman asked through the door.

'Hotel management.'

The door opened.

'What do you want?' a young woman asked.

She was small and lithe and no older than twenty. Her eyes were red and she had smudged mascara on her cheeks. She looked awkward and self-conscious in a revealing dress and lots of jewellery. Victor knew enough about disguises to know when someone was trying too hard.

'Is everything okay?' Victor asked.

'Why do you care?'

He smiled. 'May I come inside?'

He was already entering as he said it, which could be construed as aggressive or rude, but it was a calculated move. She already saw him as an authority figure – hotel management – so she deferred to him here before she could decide for herself whether she wanted him to come in or not.

She shrugged. 'Sure.'

When the door was closed behind him, he said, 'There were reports of a disturbance.'

'Yes, I'm sure there were.'

She had her arms wrapped before her, one hand on her ribs, the other on her triceps. It was as close to a hug as someone could give themselves.

There was a bucket of ice and a bottle of champagne on a sideboard, but only one glass nearby. The other was in pieces on the opposite side of the room. Wallpaper had darkened in a patch high above the broken glass, and in streaks that snaked downward.

'Do you need me to call the police for you?'

She shook her head. 'No, he didn't hit me, and they wouldn't do anything if he had.'

'I'm sure that's not true.'

'You're not from here,' she said. 'You don't know how it works for people like him.'

'And how does it work?'

'People like him think they can have anything they want. They don't like it when someone says no to them. They think that buying you a bracelet means they own you.' She rubbed her wrist. 'He took it back.'

'Is he your boyfriend?'

She shook her head. 'No. No way. I'm just the latest to fall for Miguel's bullshit.'

Miguel.

'I suggest you don't see him again.'

'He won't waste his time with me,' she replied. 'He'll move on to the next one and forget I even existed, let alone who I am.'

'Can I call you a cab?'

She shook her head. 'No, I'll walk. I want to walk.' She paused, looking at Victor with a searching gaze. 'Why are you being nice to me?'

'It's my job,' he said.

'Then look out for the next girl he brings back here, will you? She might not know what she's getting into.'

Victor nodded. 'May I ask you a question?'

She shrugged.

'How did you meet him?'

She shook her head, but not at him, at the memory. She looked at her hands. 'I was so stupid. He'd just won at cards and was celebrating. He was all smiles and compliments. I didn't know any better. I mean, I did, but I pretended I didn't. Now look at me.'

Victor did, with a sympathetic gaze he didn't have to fake. 'He likes to gamble?'

'That's all he likes to do. We just came from a game. I hate it. All the pressure. All the tension. I don't know how anyone thinks it's fun.'

'At a casino?'

'No, in a bar. A private game. But he didn't do so well. He wanted me to make him feel better. That's all I am – was – to him.' Her brow furrowed and she looked up again. 'Why are you asking me these questions?'

'I'm trying to understand the situation,' Victor said. 'I'm trying to understand what makes a man like him tick.'

'Don't bother,' she said. 'You can't understand a pig.'

She smiled at that, and he joined her. Before he could ask anything further, there was a knock on the door. She tensed.

'It's okay,' Victor said. 'I'll take care of it.'

She relaxed and he went to the door, checked the spyhole. It was a hotel porter. A young guy with a bowl cut and jutting ears.

'Yes?' Victor asked as he opened the door.

The porter was surprised, but composed himself fast. 'I . . . I'm here to see that Señor Diaz's guest gets a cab.'

Diaz. Miguel Diaz.

'I'll see her out,' Victor said, and reached for his wallet. 'And you'll say that you did.' He took out some cash. 'Okay?'

The porter hesitated, then smiled and took the money.

The young woman had stood by the time Victor had returned. She said, 'Thank you for being so nice to me. I'm going to use the bathroom before I go. I must look a state.'

'Take all the time you need,' he said. 'And do you happen to know the name of the bar where he played cards?'

'Why?'

'I play cards too,' he explained. 'I want to make sure I don't go there.'

'I don't remember the name, I'm sorry.'

'That's okay. Take all the time you need. I'll wait and see you out.'

'Thank you,' she said, then paused, looking back at the smashed champagne flute and the stain on the wallpaper. 'I'm sorry about the mess.'

'Don't be, Mr Diaz will be charged for the damages.'

'Oh. Okay.' She looked relieved, then gave him a mischievous grin and knocked over the vase by the door. It smashed to pieces on the carpet.

'*Whoops.*'

THIRTY-ONE

The young porter with the bowl cut was delighted with the extra cash he had been given to look the other way. He did that a lot. The hotel was a hub of infidelity, drug use, prostitution and worse, all under an exclusive veneer. In the porter's experience, the more a hotel projected an image of class and respectability, the dirtier it was, both in guests and goings-on. So, he was well used to receiving money to pretend he hadn't seen something, to ignore white powder caked to the moustache of a police commissioner; to act as if he hadn't seen the mayor's wife between her bodyguards; to look the other way when a cartel guy beat up his date.

It all weighed on his soul, and if his family were not so desperate for the money, he could not live with himself. His salary was not enough to feed and clothe his young children, nor pay for their future books and schooling. He never broke the law, however. He was no thief. In the absence of greater sins, he could find peace with himself.

Peace in a town run by cartels was hard to come by, but

the young porter found what he could. The cartels were the true power in the whole country, and the entire continent beyond. They ruled through power and fear and unimaginable wealth. Those they could not buy, they killed. They showed no mercy and felt no pity. The porter could pretend, he could ignore, he could look the other way in any number of different circumstances, but not when that meant betraying the cartels.

The porter had no love for them. Like any decent human being, he hated the violence they wrought, but he had no intention of being on the end of that violence. He had read the newspaper articles. He had seen the viral videos. He had dreamed of chainsaws and burning tyres. Such atrocities were designed to send a message, and the porter listened.

He had no idea who Miguel Diaz was beyond knowing his name, but the porter knew Diaz was part of the cartel. He was someone. The porter didn't know how much of a someone, but no ones didn't drive Lambos, and they didn't get special treatment in the hotel. So, the porter made his way to the lobby to have a quiet word with the concierge. He told him that there was a foreigner in the Fortune Suite and the concierge thanked him and told him to forget what he had seen and to go about his day.

The porter did just that, his soul a little heavier, and the concierge picked up the telephone.

THIRTY-TWO

The young woman spent some time in the bathroom before she was ready to leave. She had the door closed, and Victor respected her privacy, but he heard the tap running and not much else, so he imagined her reapplying her make-up and straightening out her appearance. He stood near the door while he waited, listening out for any footsteps in the hallway outside.

When she exited the en-suite, she seemed surprised to see he was still present. 'I thought you'd have gone.'

'I said I'd see you out.'

She shrugged. 'Saying and doing aren't the same.'

'I don't say things I don't mean.'

'You're not really from hotel management, are you?'

For an instant, he thought about lying, but there was nothing to gain. 'How did you know?'

'I've been in these kinds of places before,' she said, embarrassed and regretful. 'You're too nice.'

'Trust me, I'm anything but.'

'I do trust you.'

She said nothing else, and took her jacket from where it lay on the floor near the bed. She put it on, and nodded when he asked her if she was ready to go. He took the stairs because he always took the stairs, and she didn't question him.

'It's best if we don't walk out together,' he told her when they reached the ground floor.

This time she wanted an explanation. 'Why?'

'Trust me,' he said. 'Go ahead of me and get a taxi. There are some waiting out front. And don't see Diaz again.'

She held his gaze, and he saw a resolve there he hadn't seen before. 'Don't worry, I've learnt my lesson. Thank you.'

He saw her lean in, and could have avoided the intrusion into his personal space if he so wished, but he didn't stop her. She kissed him on the cheek.

'Goodbye.'

He stood at the foot of the stairwell, keeping out of sight as much as he could, but watching her go. She crossed the lobby with a confident stride – nothing to hide, nothing to be ashamed of – and his line of sight was clear enough to see her step outside. She disappeared from view for a few seconds, but then he saw her climb into the back of a waiting taxi and a moment later she was gone.

He dawdled for a minute, checking his appearance in a mirrored wall to kill some time and to provide an excuse for his presence to anyone who might pass by. Not bad, he thought.

Victor knew something was wrong as soon as he stepped into the lobby proper. He felt the disturbance in the eco-system before he understood why it had been disturbed. His gaze swept back and forth, taking in the hotel staff and guests, where they were positioned and what they were doing. He analysed physiques and appearances, clothing and postures.

Three guys didn't fit in.

They reminded him of a time in Paris. They weren't dressed like the other patrons and they didn't act like them either. There was no style to their suits, but they wore expensive watches. They were waiting, but they weren't talking. They were observant, but cautious.

He saw them note his presence, although there was no immediate reaction that told him they were waiting for him. That came a moment later, because they looked to where the concierge was positioned behind his desk. The concierge saw them do so – he was expecting such a look – and he glanced in Victor's direction.

The concierge's expression said nothing, but he nodded.

A slight, discreet gesture; pointed, but nothing more than necessary – a diner informing a sommelier that the wine had not been corked.

The porter, Victor realised. The bribe to look the other way had not been enough, or could never be enough. The specifics were immaterial right now. All that mattered was that the porter had told the concierge about Victor's presence in the suite, who had then passed the information on to Diaz.

The three men had arrived fast. Even with the young woman taking a few minutes to ready herself, the response time was more than efficient. So, they had been sent here based on their proximity, not competence. Local guys who handled local problems. The three men would be associates of Diaz – cartel guys or corrupt cops or whoever else was on the payroll. There must be similar teams all over the city. It was too much of a stretch to imagine these were the extent of it, and just so happened to be close to the hotel.

Diaz wanted information. He wanted to know who Victor was. He wanted to know why a stranger had been in his suite. Victor could see it going one of two ways. Either the three would follow him, intending to learn where he lived and where he worked, and from there identify him and his intentions with a certain degree of discretion. Then, they would pass that back to Diaz and he would decide the next course of action. The upsides to this were many. They could find out what they needed without exposing themselves, and if there was nothing to learn they lost nothing.

Else, they would wait for the soonest – not necessarily the best – opportunity to corner Victor for an interrogation.

Stepping outside the hotel he saw that it was going to be the latter, because another man in similar attire was waiting outside, standing by a parked minivan with sliding back doors. The minivan was no taxi and the man standing next to it was no taxi driver. The door next to the kerb was already open.

Victor slowed his pace to give himself an extra second or two to work out the best course of action. He knew without looking that the three guys from the lobby would be coming out behind him, closing the distance fast, ready to bundle him into the back of the minivan before he knew what was happening. Only he did know what was happening.

He could run, and he was confident enough in his own speed and stamina to know none of the four had any hope of catching him. They had the minivan though, which he could not outrun, and even if he ran through places it could not follow – buildings, alleys, parks – anyone on foot could, while the vehicle manoeuvred to head him off.

Should he escape, word would reach Diaz, and he would know someone had an interest in him. He would be on guard. He might pass out word to the rest of the cartel. Victor's description might reach every sicario and informer. The difficulty of his job would exponentially increase, as would the risks to his life.

He could fight. He couldn't take them all by surprise because they were expecting to go into action; they were expecting him to resist. He could act ignorant until he was in range and put a stomp kick in the guts of the guy waiting by the minivan. With nowhere to go but into the bodywork, the force of the kick would put him out of the fight. There would be massive blunt force trauma to his abdominal cavity. Internal organs could fail. He might be dead before paramedics understood what was wrong. The three behind would be trickier. They would be reacting by the time Victor turned to deal with them, but not fast enough to prevent him taking down another. Maybe a strike with the edge of his palm to the closest neck, or if that neck happened to be dense, to the clavicle instead. A shattered bone or shocked carotid would put that guy on the ground alongside the first.

Two left, maybe drawing guns by that point, but fumbling in surprise, muzzles nowhere near high enough for a shot. Depending on the gun, depending on how they held it, Victor could knock it from the man's grip or take it for himself. Three seconds gone by then and three guys down.

One left, with a gun in his hand and raised by that point.

If that guy was good, if he was fast, then Victor would be the one dropping next. If not, then there would be four dead or injured cartel associates lying on the ground outside of a hotel in broad daylight.

Running was not a good course of action, but neither was fighting.

So, Victor let himself be kidnapped.

THIRTY-THREE

He played along to the role they expected. He resisted. He acted scared. He made them work to get him into the back of the minivan, but he didn't fight back. He had to battle the instinct to go for pressure points, to break bones and gouge eyes. It was harder than he thought. He had to fight himself more than he fought them. Calling for help would have added to the performance, but he didn't call for help just in case he got it. A would-be hero might get themselves killed, or a rescue attempt might actually work, and neither scenario would benefit Victor's goals of getting close to Diaz and remaining unnoticed.

One man drove, one guy took the passenger seat, and the other two sat either side of him in the back, gripping his arms as he struggled to the extent a scared civilian might. He told himself he feared for his life, but he was weak; he didn't know what to do.

They bought it. The guys in the back weren't exerting themselves any more than they needed. They weren't even holding him with any real force. This was just another day at the office for them. Fun, perhaps.

The one in the passenger seat showed a gun and told him to calm down, so Victor kept in character. He stopped struggling.

'What do you want?' he asked, making his voice break.

The guy in the passenger seat put his firearm into a holster behind his jacket and turned back around to face forward. He spoke to Victor without looking at him.

'We just need to ask you a few questions. Then we'll let you go. Answer us honestly and you have nothing to worry about.'

'What questions?'

There was no answer.

Victor used the time to examine the four men. The driver was the youngest and the frequent swallowing suggested the dry mouth of the inexperienced. That was why he was the driver. The easiest job. Drive the car, let the others deal with the real work. He had the same kind of cheap suit as the others, but the driver's arms couldn't fill the sleeves. The shoulder pads jutted. The two in the back could almost be photocopies of each other. They had the same blank expressions, and similar builds; the useful bulk of the manual labourer, whether that labour was shovelling sand or breaking bones. The one on Victor's left sucked on a plastic cigarette. The one to his right stank so bad Victor wondered how the other three tolerated it. The guy in the passenger seat was in charge. He got to ride up front, which was always a giveaway, further confirmed by his age – at least half a decade older than the others – and protruding gut. It was the weight of leadership. He let the others do the heavy lifting.

The suits said legitimacy in a city where such dress was

uncommon. These guys wouldn't be sent to the slums. They were exclusively city-based, dealing with hoteliers, government officials and cops. Tattooed sicarios with shaved heads and machine guns couldn't operate in the same circles.

'*Tell me what's going on,*' the frightened man Victor was playing pleaded.

He looked at both men in the back for an answer, gaze pleading, imploring. One shrugged. The other smiled. Both were relaxing more with every passing second. He was just a scared guy, a civilian.

No trouble at all.

Victor drove his thumb into the smiler's thigh, pushing down on the quadriceps with enormous pressure focused on the anterior cutaneous branch of the femoral nerve.

The man screamed. He threw himself up from the seat in his instinctual reaction to escape the pain, butting the roof with his head. Both his hands grabbed Victor's wrist to pull him away, to end the agony, but Victor was strong – far stronger than the smiler could have imagined – and his arm was locked and immovable.

The scream was so loud, so shrill and piercing, that the others were shocked into a moment of inaction.

Victor kept his left thumb in place and slammed his free elbow into the face of the second guy in the back. He had a dense skull and was no stranger to pain or injury, so it took another two hits before his head hung forward, blood and teeth flowing from an open mouth.

The smiler was so relieved, so elated, when the merciless thumb was removed, that he couldn't stop Victor taking the handgun from his shoulder rig nor could he prevent that gun striking him on the temple.

By the time the guy in the passenger seat had his own weapon back in his hand and pointing at Victor, Victor was pointing one at him too.

'Stalemate,' Victor said.

The leader was still trying to process what had happened, what he was seeing. The men either side of Victor were bloody and unconscious. Even if they woke up soon, they wouldn't be any help. The one who had taken the pistol-whip to the temple wouldn't be able to focus, let alone fight. It could be hours before he could stand unaided. The one who Victor had elbowed would be in so much pain after waking he would beg to be knocked unconscious again.

The guy said, 'Drop it.'

'No,' Victor said.

'I mean it.'

'I do too.'

The driver was saying nothing. His gaze was in a frantic back-and-forth between the road and the rear-view. The guy in the passenger seat was giving him no direction, so the driver kept driving. The roads here were almost empty. If the driver knew anything about tactical driving he would start swerving and throw Victor around in the back seat, but he didn't. The ride was as smooth as any he had experienced.

'Last chance,' the leader told Victor.

'No,' Victor said in return, 'it's yours.'

The guy in the passenger seat didn't want to shoot him, at least not yet. He wanted answers and he was scared, whatever his previous machismo. Few people could handle a gun in their face. It took a long time to get used to such a thing. Victor had lost count of the times he had stared down a muzzle.

His own lack of fear was adding to the other guy's, and he couldn't handle it. He wasn't thinking clearly. If he was, he would understand that Victor didn't need him alive. The driver was the important one. Victor needed him to keep the car from crashing. The guy in the passenger seat was window dressing. He was alive only for now, until the streets cleared a little more, until the best opportunity presented itself.

'Okay,' the leader said. 'You win. I'll put the gun down. No one has to die here.'

Victor said nothing. He just watched as the guy in the passenger seat did as he said he would. The pistol went back into a shoulder holster, nice and slow, and his hands came up.

The driver said, 'What are you doing? *Are you crazy?*'

'I'm handling it. See,' he said to Victor. 'We can keep this calm.'

Victor said, 'I'm always calm.'

'We made a mistake,' the guy said.

'The biggest of your life. Who are you?'

'Consultants,' he explained. 'Private security.'

'For the cartel?'

The leader hesitated, but nodded.

Victor said, 'Explain.'

'Okay, okay. Listen, we're not drug runners. We protect the business. Not just from the police, but their rivals. Maria's sister, for one, but there are always young punks looking to muscle their way into the business. Then there are the Mexican cartels, who can go from being best business partners one day to worst enemies the next. We guard the bosses when they come into town, take their kids to school. Dig up dirt on politicians. Stuff like that.'

Maria employed a two-ring approach to her safety. She

had an army of fearless gunmen surrounding her at all times, and a network of private security teams working further out, scouting and bribing, looking for threats and taking care of them before the need for overt force. These were part of the second ring, the guys that Lavandier's website had mentioned. Victor hadn't expected them to be this efficient, this well organised.

'And you kidnap people from outside hotels,' Victor said. 'You have a wide repertoire. I'm impressed.'

'We handle the sensitive work, yes.' The guy in the passenger seat paused, then added, 'We provide security. We act as insulation between our employers and those who would do them harm.'

Victor understood. They were an independent crew operating in the city under the guise of legitimacy. A detective agency on paper, registered private eyes, but putting their skills to use for the cartel. These were the guys who sat down with reporters and in polite but no uncertain terms told them to back off. These were the guys who followed politicians to learn their dirty secrets. These were the guys who paid off the cops. Pressed suits and smooth cheeks, but beyond the surface they would be as ruthless as any sicario.

'Who's your boss? Miguel Diaz?'

The leader shook his head. 'We don't answer to Señor Diaz, but we responded to his request. A stranger is a potential threat not merely to him, but the whole organisation. You understand, we were just doing what we were told to do.'

'How many of you are there?'

He looked around the car. 'We're it. But we're one firm. They have many like us. Different neighbourhoods, different teams. You understand?'

'What would you have done if you found out I was no one to worry about?'

'Call Señor Diaz and tell him exactly that.'

'He wouldn't want to check me out personally?'

'Only if you were a threat, but not necessarily. He would tell us to take care of it.'

'Then call him,' Victor said. 'Tell him it was a false alarm. I'm the girl's cousin. I took her home. Tell him nothing else.'

The guy swallowed and took out a phone from his jacket with the same kind of slow and obvious movements he used to put his gun away. He unlocked the screen.

'Hold it so I can see it too,' Victor said. 'And put it on speaker.'

The leader thumbed the screen a few times, doing just that. Victor saw him access call history and dial the last number received. It rang for a short moment.

The call connected and a man said, 'Yes?'

The guy in the passenger seat said, 'False alarm. No foreigner, but a light skin. A cousin. He took her home with him.'

'Follow the cousin for a few days. Make sure he doesn't go to the police. If he does, deal with him and the girl. If he doesn't, forget them both.'

'Yes, Señor Diaz.'

The call disconnected.

'See?' he said to Victor. 'We can be friends. It's all good. All cool.'

'When would you next speak to Diaz?'

He shrugged. 'In a few days, maybe a week, after we had checked out the cousin as he requested.'

'Good,' Victor said. 'Do you know where Diaz plays poker?'

'No, but I can find out. Listen, whatever it is you're doing, we can help you. We don't just work for the cartel. We have private clients too. You could be one.' He smiled. 'No charge, of course. First job for free. Okay?'

Despite the gun pointed at his face, he looked genuine, as though he had decided Victor was the better master to serve. Which wasn't a bad conclusion to come to, although it would have been much better to have reached it before now.

Victor was planning to shoot him in the heart. A headshot might eject brains and blood all over the windscreen. It might put a hole through the glass. A nine mil in the chest wasn't likely to come out of the other side, but a destroyed heart had the same effect as a destroyed brain, albeit a little slower.

He said, 'I'm thinking about it,' because he wanted to keep the leader calm while he waited for a car to overtake. Victor didn't want to shoot someone with a vehicle full of witnesses in parallel, heart shot or not.

'Well?' the guy said.

Victor didn't answer. Instead, he stiffened, all muscles tensing as his nervous system was overloaded with electricity. His face reddened and the blood vessels in his neck and temples stood out in relief through the skin. The pain was horrific. His eyes watered. Muscle spasms made his whole body shake.

He heard the fizzing clicks of the stun gun jammed against his side, but could do nothing about it. His mind was trapped in a form it could not control.

Time ceased to have meaning. The pain and paralysis seemed endless.

'That's enough,' the leader said.

The fizzing clicks ceased as the stun gun was pulled away.

The paralysis remained. So did the pain. Victor struggled to suck in air.

He glimpsed through watery eyes the blurry shape of the guy to his right, the one who had taken the elbow strikes. He was only semi-conscious, but he hadn't needed a whole lot of wherewithal to fumble out a stun gun and press it against Victor while his attention was on the guy in the passenger seat, who now leaned through the gap between seats.

'Nice try,' he said, and punched Victor in the face.

Whatever semblance of senses he had were further diminished by the blow, but he stayed conscious. He felt no pain because agony already consumed him. His vision blurred. Colours washed into one another. Sounds quietened, replaced by a piercing tinnitus whine.

Then a second punch landed and there were no sounds or colours, only silence and black.

THIRTY-FOUR

Gabriel Hernandez was understandably nervous. No one enjoyed talking to cops. No one sane, anyway. He was in all kinds of trouble and if Alamaeda could peek inside his mind she was pretty sure she would see a chaotic mess of jumbled thoughts, assailed from all sides by the single, most powerful emotion of them all: fear. Some people could hide it, but Hernandez was not one of those people. The fear oozed out of him in every conceivable way. He fidgeted. He sweated. He stumbled over his words, of which there were many. Mostly lies, but some excuses thrown in too for good measure. But only when he knew he had no other choice. He talked a lot about choice, about having none.

'Sure,' Alamaeda replied. 'You had no choice but to take all that drug money. They forced it into your hands.'

'Yes,' he said, nodding. 'That's exactly how it happened.'

Though she was loath to admit it, there could be some truth in that. When the cartels came a-knocking, you did what they wanted or you suffered the consequences. However it had started for Hernandez, it had ended up with him being one of Maria Salvatierra's most valued assets. As the manager of a large bank, he was perfectly placed to aid their money-laundering efforts, which was why they had knocked on his door in the first place, but no one had put a gun to his head and forced him to make such a good job of it. He had spent two decades establishing a high-return investment portfolio that generated Manny Salvatierra, and now his youngest daughter, so much money it made Alamaeda's eyes water. And worst of all, it was untouchable.

She sighed. 'You've done amazing work, Mr Hernandez. I can't help but be impressed.'

He sat straighter. 'Thank you.'

'It wasn't a compliment.'

'Oh.'

Hernandez dressed in smart pinstripe suits and shiny loafers. He had long, glossy hair pulled back into a tight ponytail. A neat beard surrounded his mouth and ran in a thin line along his jaw. He toyed with the gold crucifix that hung around his neck when he wasn't talking.

Alamaeda said, 'Even if we took down every trafficker, every killer on Maria's payroll, even if we dismantled her entire network, brick by brick, she would still be able to retire rich and live out the rest of her days in luxury.' She leaned forward. 'And worst of all, we couldn't do a damn thing about it. Thanks to you.'

'But I can tell you how it started, how I did it. I'll testify.'

'It's a little late for that, I'm afraid.'

He didn't know what to say for the first time. Which was how she wanted it. He wiped some sweat from his face with a handkerchief already sodden with it.

'Maybe,' she began, 'and I really mean maybe, I could have used what you know to bring down Manny, but he's dead. There's a statute of limitations when it comes to indicting corpses.'

'But the portfolio, the money . . . it's all Maria's now.'

She nodded. 'Yes, every single quetzal. Every *clean* quetzal.'

Hernandez slumped. He was risking his life talking to the DEA, and he was starting to realise he would be getting nothing in return.

'We don't simply hand people a new life in the US just because they grow a conscience. We need something in return.'

Hernandez hadn't grown a conscience, despite his claims. He had fallen in love with an employee at his bank, an American in Guatemala on a temporary visa. She was young and pretty and he had just gone through a messy divorce. He wanted to start again, wanted to run away with her back to the States. The only problem, and it was a significant one, was there was no way the cartel would let him leave. To try was a death sentence. Hernandez needed protection.

'You're going to get me killed,' he said.

'Don't be so dramatic. No one is going to know we've had this conversation. You're just going to have to put your plans on hold for a little while.'

'Until when?'

'Until you give me something I can actually use.'

'Like what?'

She shrugged with her hands. 'Give me a name. Give me someone who handles dirty money. Give me someone I can use.'

The handkerchief came out again. This time, he kept it in a tight fist after he'd wiped his forehead. He was silent for a while and Alamaeda let him have that silence. He needed it to take control of his turbulent mind, of his fear. She couldn't convince him that he had no other option. Rather, she could, but if he realised it on his own he would be more cooperative, more useful. More desperate.

'Okay,' he said, eventually. 'I'll give you a name. I'll give you someone who knows more than I do.'

'I'm waiting.'

'Will that be enough to give me a new life in America?'

'Whoa there, Nelly. You're getting way ahead of yourself. This is just the first step on a long road, but it's one you have to take. Give me a name and let's see where it leads. Because it's not up to me. Even if it's a good name and leads to something more, it doesn't mean it will be enough.'

'Then I'm saying nothing. I want guarantees before I put myself in danger.'

'You're already in danger, Mr Hernandez. The cartel could find out at any time that you came to see me.'

The reel of expletives was long and colourful. Alamaeda let him shout. She let him scream. She took it on the chin because she didn't care.

When he had tired himself out, she said, 'Are you done? Because this is going to take a lot longer than it needs to if you keep losing your cool. I'm not going to tell anyone about you, and certainly not your paymasters. I'm talking about the cartel finding out themselves. Maria has a whole network of private investigators, remember? You think they're not keeping tabs on people like you?'

Hernandez was silent.

'Have you discussed the move to the US with your new girlfriend?'

'Of course we've talked about it.'

Alamaeda nodded. 'On the phone? In public?'

Hernandez was silent again.

'At work?'

He looked away.

'And I'm guessing she's talked to friends about it too. Colleagues. A chatty barista, maybe. Whoever. Have you looked at flights? Browsed houses online? I bet you have. Just for fun, right? In that post-coital romantic glow you've fantasised about where you might live, what you might do. Just talk at first, but then one of you grabbed a laptop or a tablet and you—'

'Yes,' he hissed. 'We've talked about it. We've imagined. So what?'

'Then, Mr Hernandez, don't sit there and pretend the cartel can't find out what you're planning. That's what's putting you in danger. Not this conversation. Not me. Your denial is going to get you killed.'

It took three and a half seconds for him to finally break.

He took a breath and said, 'Miguel Diaz.'

'Who's that?'

'Maria's chief money launderer. He's in charge of all the cash that comes south.'

Alamaeda sat back, but kept her expression even. 'You've done the right thing, Mr Hernandez.'

'I hope so.'

'Go back to your life, pretend nothing's happened. I'll check out Diaz and we'll go from there.'

Hernandez said nothing more. He couldn't. However

afraid he had been before, it was nothing compared to the new terror he would have to deal with now that the betrayal was complete.

He was going to need to buy himself a new handkerchief.

THIRTY-FIVE

The first thing Victor felt when he woke up was pain. Not from his jaw – which ached and throbbed – but from his side, his ribs. An intense rawness pulsated out from where the two electrodes of the stun gun had struck him. He couldn't see the site of the wounds, but he knew there would be two red indentations with broken skin where the prongs had impacted, maybe scabbed over, but also singed and black from the electrical current.

The second punch to the jaw had hit right on the point of his chin, thrown by a heavy fist on the end of plenty of power. Despite a lifetime of violence, it was rare for Victor to take such a shot. He could open and close his mouth without inhibition so he knew there were no fractures to his jawbone. There was a little blood in his mouth, however, but the bleeding seemed to have stopped.

After the pain, his other senses returned: hearing first, and then sight. A slow process, made slower by the darkness he lay within and a severe lack of mobility. His first thought was injury, that they had continued to hit him after he lost consciousness, but every muscle flexed as it should. Restrained then, he realised, ankles tied together and his wrists similarly tied behind his back.

His bonds were duct tape. He could tell from the rustling sound the tape made when he tried to move his hands or feet. There was lots of it, wrapped tight around and around to keep him immobile.

He blinked and swallowed, wetting a dry throat with the blood from his mouth. His night vision had kicked in, so when his awareness had fully returned he saw that he was in a small room, maybe ten by ten. Cement floor. Unfinished concrete walls. A pale strip of dim light backlit a single door. No windows. A cell, but not designed to be, because he saw no marks on the walls and smelled no urine or faeces. Either he was in a building under construction, or this was somewhere that needed no niceties. An industrial space. A warehouse or factory, perhaps. The former was more likely, because Victor heard little. There were no rumbles or whines of machinery.

It was impossible to know how long he'd been out for, and he couldn't recall how long the shock had lasted. The longer the shock, the greater the effect. Just a few seconds would be enough to drop someone to the ground and leave them disorientated and in immense pain from uncontrollable muscle spasms. A prolonged shock could impair breathing and lead to further injury and death.

They were in no rush to question him, else he would have awoken from icy water thrown over his head or the like. No rush meant no pressure, so Diaz wasn't involved himself. The private security guys had tossed Victor into a makeshift cell and left him there, because they weren't sure yet what to do with him.

There's a guy at the hotel ... Find out who he is ...

If the crew was any good, they would be checking his credentials, finding out who he was and how long he had been in the country. They would find nothing if they found anything at all. His legend was secure to all but an intelligence agency's thorough and persistent investigation. After the incident in the car, they might feel a pressing need to learn more about him, but once they found out he was Ryan Mathus, Canadian commodities trader, they would be embarrassed at most. If they had even the slightest inclination that his credentials were phoney they would have him already secured to a chair, ready to go to work on him.

Poison's excellent work had no doubt saved him. He'd write her a thank you note, if she were still alive to read it.

There was a sour taste in his mouth, he noticed. Not the blood, something similar to garlic, only unpleasant. Somehow dirty. He knew why. Sodium thiopental was a barbiturate used in anaesthesia, euthanasia, lethal injection, caesarean section and medically induced coma. In low doses it made a person more cooperative under questioning, more prone to being truthful by interfering with the higher cortical functioning of the brain. The half-life of such drugs was short, a few hours, but the side effects could last long after that. He felt a little nauseous, which could be from the drug or from the shock or the punch or all three.

They had drugged him to prepare him for questioning, which meant they weren't going to kill him yet. They wouldn't go to the trouble of drugging him and restraining him unless they planned to keep him alive for a while. They would ask him who he was, why he was in Diaz's suite, what he was doing in Guatemala …

Lying was effortless for Victor. He lived a lie every day. He pretended to be someone he was not, someone normal, unthreatening, more than he had ever shown his true self. He had been lying since he could talk, since he knew that truth could be dangerous and used to hurt him. He played so many parts he sometimes forgot where the act ended and he began. But he had never had to lie under the influence of barbiturates. He had no idea how well the drug would work against his own will.

He had no more time to consider how effective the drug would be because he heard movement on the other side of the door. They must have heard him too, maybe groaning or coughing as his consciousness returned.

The guy from the passenger seat, the leader, came to check on him. The door catch clicked and the door opened outwards. In the doorway, the leader stood with his thumbs tucked into his belt loops, as if he needed the extra support to keep his gut stable.

'I expect you're terrified right about now.'

Victor remained silent.

'You should be,' the leader continued. 'I would be. And we're the nice guys. We're the nice guys, but you should still be scared of us because we work for guys who are terrifying.'

The guy with the gut introduced himself: 'My name is Eadrich.'

A Mayan name, Victor knew.

'Who might you be?' Eadrich asked.

Victor had spent decades trying to forget who he was, decades reinventing himself, decades doing everything possible to sever connections to his past. Now, his real name, his true identity, popped into his mind. The name raced to his lips, but he kept them closed, somehow.

Eadrich held up Victor's wallet, with business credit cards in his legend's name.

'Ryan Mathus,' Eadrich read.

'What do you want with me?' Victor asked.

'Why were you at the hotel, Mr Mathus? Why were you talking to Señor Diaz's girlfriend?'

Victor wanted to tell the truth. The truth was simple. He fought to say nothing. He fought to keep his face expressionless.

Eadrich was silent for a long moment. His gaze remained on Victor's eyes as he stepped closer to his captive. It was neither a show of strength nor mark of frustration. He was someone who didn't like to keep still, even if his protruding stomach suggested otherwise.

'You had some good moves in the car,' Eadrich said when he was ready. 'You're fast. You knew what you were doing.' He paused, then asked, 'How does a commodities trader from Canada know how to fight? Really fight, I mean.'

Victor didn't answer.

'And why does that same commodities trader end up in Miguel Diaz's suite?'

Victor was silent.

'That's an answer I'd really like to be able to provide Señor Diaz with.'

Victor just stared.

'I've provided Señor Diaz with false information once today. He won't be happy about that when he finds out, so before he finds out I need to have the truth ready for him. The sooner I have that answer, the happier I'll be. And you want me happy. You want me really happy. As long as I'm smiling, you're not screaming.'

Victor wanted to comply. His mind was consumed by the need to speak the truth and every ounce of will had to be utilised against the relentless compulsion to be honest. Just remaining silent was an exhaustion he had never known before.

He said, 'I heard a commotion from the suite. I heard crying. I wanted to make sure she was okay.'

He swallowed, mouth and throat dry from the effort of such a simple lie.

'You're a guest at the hotel?'

He nodded. It was easier than trying to say 'yes'.

'Huh,' Eadrich exhaled. 'Because you're not on the register. How do you explain that? You wouldn't be lying to me, would you?'

Victor didn't answer.

'Are you hungry?'

'Yes.' It was a relief to speak the truth.

'Thirsty?'

'Yes.' Victor felt a glorious release of tension, of stress.

'Tough,' the guy said, 'because there's nothing to eat and drink.'

Victor didn't react. He understood power games. The show of dominance was unnecessary – he understood his predicament too – but the guy with the gut had a routine and it would have been pointless to tell him it was pointless.

Eadrich continued the performance by taking a stun gun from a pocket of his trousers. Victor didn't know if it was the same device that shocked him, or if they all carried them.

He hadn't seen the one used against him in the car. This one was the size of an old mobile phone. A compact, expensive device. These guys took their equipment seriously. Victor didn't recognise the exact model – stun guns were not his area of expertise – but it would have a voltage range of around three to four million. Victor knew how stun guns worked in the same way he knew how all weapons worked, but he had never used one in a professional capacity. He knew enough ways to incapacitate a person without needing one, and if he needed a weapon it would be to kill the person, not stun them, but he understood the appeal. That he was lying on a cement floor, bound at the wrists and ankles, was proof they worked, after all.

'I love these things,' Eadrich said. 'I feel like a wizard.'

He depressed the activation button and a crackling lightning bolt of blue electrical current leapt between the two metal prongs.

'You have to be careful, though,' Eadrich continued. 'Some people can't take the shock. If they're old, if they're weak, they can die. I've seen it happen.'

Not just the old or weak, Victor knew. Otherwise healthy individuals could go into cardiac arrest if they were susceptible to arrhythmia, and even those without heart conditions could succumb if they were subjected to prolonged shocks. The body could only take so much abuse.

'They're a useful tool for encouraging cooperation too,' the guy continued. 'Hurts like a bitch, doesn't it? Someone doesn't want to talk, well, a few blasts to the balls and ... You can imagine, I'm sure.'

Victor could, although he would never elect to torture someone via their genitalia. When there were so many other ways to inflict a perfectly adequate degree of agony, it seemed uncouth.

Eadrich said, 'Have you ever taken a man's life?'

Victor kept his lips closed. Silence was easier than lying, and no small lie could cover such an extent of truth.

Eadrich nodded. 'That's what I thought. You cannot imagine the strength of will it requires. You cannot imagine the weight it bears on your soul.' Eadrich stepped closer. 'I've done it, I've done it plenty, and I'm prepared to do so again. But, I'll tell you, I'll be honest with you, I don't want to. There are three types of men, I've learned. Firstly, most commonly, there are those who only want to get home to their wives. Then there are those men who are cruel. Who like causing pain. They enjoy suffering and death. Then there is the third type who can do unspeakable things without hesitation because that man feels nothing. Such men are machines. Such men give me nightmares because I am the first kind. But know this: men like me who just want to get home to their wives will do whatever they need to do to get there. So, I'm warning you, don't force my hand.'

'I don't intend to,' Victor said, again feeling the relief of speaking honestly.

Eadrich put the stun gun away. 'Good, because you need to be aware that this isn't the first time we've been in this situation. I've lost count, in fact. We're good at asking questions and even better at getting answers from the most defiant of men. Do you want to know something about those men?' He squatted down before Victor and motioned with his hand as he spoke. 'They all start with faces like yours right now, defiant faces, and those very same faces are covered in tears and snot by the end of it. Every. Single. Time.'

Victor just stared.

Eadrich stood again, his shadow over Victor. 'We're going to be a little while, Ryan Mathus.' He tapped the wallet. 'Once we've checked out a few things, we'll continue this conversation.' He stepped back through the door, but held it open because he wasn't finished yet. 'I'm going to leave you to think about your situation. I'm going to give you the chance to think of an elaborate story to explain away what you were doing. You're going to have all the time you need to come up with the perfect lie, but it won't work. We do this for a living, and we're very good at it. We'll find out everything there is to know about you, and we will extract every last truth from your lips, however hard you try to hold them in. So, do yourself a favour, and make this as easy as it can be. I told you before that we're the nice guys, and it's true. But that's only while you cooperate. Lie to me and things will get very ugly very fast. Use this time to understand you have no choice. Use this time to help yourself.'

He stepped out of the room, closed the door and applied the catch.

'Consider this the last act of mercy you shall receive.'

THIRTY-SIX

Victor didn't relish capture, but he had been in worse positions. He was still alive, which always gave him the chance to turn a situation around, and uninjured. His side hurt and his jaw ached, but he could handle pain. Pain was just a message but he couldn't afford to drag this out any longer than necessary. Even if he wasn't injured now, how long would that stay the case? Despite the hunger and dry throat caused by the drug he was hydrated and fed, but in a few hours his blood sugar would be low, and dehydration would start affecting his thought process and motor functions. He couldn't afford to be even a split-second slower than he was already. When his chance to escape came, whether through process or opportunity, he had to be ready. He had to be able to take it.

The duct tape held his ankles together so tight he was beginning to feel a tingle in his feet from the impeded circulation. There was no such feeling in his hands because the men had made a critical error in how they had restrained him.

Victor had been interested in escapology long before he

had required such skills in his professional life. When he was a boy, the first book he had stolen had been about Houdini. That young boy had been fascinated. Enchanted, even. He had believed Houdini's death had been staged in the ultimate act of escapology: escaping life's final curtain call. Victor still wasn't sure Houdini had died of peritonitis. He wanted to believe Houdini had disappeared to a solitary retirement, unbothered and untethered by the life he left behind.

Or did Victor need to believe that?

He pushed the question from his mind. His captors had made a mistake, but he still had a lot to do. They had used duct tape because it was readily available and there was nothing suspicious about owning it. The tape itself wasn't their mistake. Handcuffs wouldn't have made any difference. Victor knew how to make improvised lock picks or shims and had escaped from them more than once. Cable ties were no better than duct tape, and held Victor only for as long as he wished to be held. Plasticuffs were perhaps the only restraints that couldn't be forced open, wriggled out of or picked. Still, he had escaped those as well.

If they had bound his hands in front of him, the tape could be burst open if the arms were first raised above his head and then brought down fast against his abdomen, elbows flaring out past his flanks, to direct force straight at the tape. The same principle applied to cable ties too, but with tape it could be avoided by applying it further up the arms as well.

Their mistake had been to tie his wrists behind his back. On the surface, it made sense to do so as not only were the hands restrained but the arms too. When the arms were stretched behind the back, the wrists could not be brought together anywhere near as tightly as they could in front. The

212

shoulder joints saw to that. Moreover, his wrists were crossed, making what came next even easier. An amateur error, which seemed to contradict their competence in other areas, but they might have bound him like this as a special consideration given what happened in the car. Knowing he was dangerous could have meant they had mistakenly sought greater security by keeping his hands behind him, not in front where they might be utilised.

If his wrists had been tied in front of him, he would be free within seconds. Behind would take longer, but required no skill, no strength, just patience. Anyone could do it, but most people didn't realise they could. Trying to beat the tape with aggression or panicked energy was never going to work. The tensile strength was just too high, but the tape was malleable.

Victor wriggled, twisted and pulled, but in a slow, relaxed manner. Small, controlled movements were essential. The friction rubbed at the glue, the tiny stretches loosened the tape's hold. He used no speed. He implemented no strength. He trusted to inevitability.

They had used lots of tape, wrapped tight, so it took a little longer than it might have done, but after about two minutes Victor had loosened the bonds enough to slip out one hand, and the loop of tape was on the floor a second later. He pulled the tape from his ankles next.

They had taken his shoes. What they thought he might do with them, he didn't know – although a shoelace made for an effective garrotte – but he would have slipped them off anyway. On a hard floor, his shoeless feet were as good as silent.

He stood and shook the stiffness from his joints. He must have been out for a while, contorted and lying on a hard floor.

He cupped his hand at the door to listen, hearing nothing. There was no handle on the inside of the door, and peering into the crack between the door and the frame, he could see the catch on the other side as a thin silhouette.

His pockets had been emptied, so he retrieved one of the loops of duct tape from the floor and tore off a strip that he folded lengthwise, flattening the folded edge down by running it between the fingernails of his thumb and index finger. The fold gave the tape enough rigidity to slide through the gap and lift up the catch.

The door swung open a little way under its own weight. A store cupboard then, built with a door not meant to accidentally swing shut and trap someone inside. A thoughtful design, now used to secure a prisoner instead of supplies. The room Victor stepped into was lit with a dull orange gloom. Light found its way into the room through a line of semi-transparent bricks high on one wall. That light was orange, but not from sodium bulbs. Natural light from a setting sun. He had been out for an hour perhaps. Not long, but long enough.

The room was a kitchen, but not a domestic one. All the cabinets and work surfaces were bare stainless steel. The floor was lined with white tiles, which were colder underfoot than the cement had been. Cement was a pretty good surface to be forced to lie on. It was porous enough to trap and hold body heat. Fluorescent strip lights ran in lines across the ceiling. Although the kitchen seemed almost bare, he saw where the chopping boards were stacked and checked the drawers nearby, finding many knives. He ignored the larger blades and anything serrated and took a filleting knife. He wanted something that he could slip between ribs. He wanted something that he could fight with, should it come to it.

The kitchen smelled of chemicals, mostly chlorine. It had been cleaned recently, else always smelled this way. Victor realised he had smelt it in the storage cupboard too, although he hadn't registered it at the time. There was only one way out of the kitchen. A set of double swing doors led to ... he wasn't sure, but there could be people on the other side. Close to the doors, Victor heard a television. A quiet sound, so the set was far away. There was no reason to keep the volume down otherwise. It was still daytime, and he doubted they would have been concerned about waking him from his forced slumber.

Victor pictured an out-of-town building; a nondescript unit in an industrial park, with no through-traffic, no pedestrians, plenty of space in between businesses, fences and lots of ambient noise. No one noticing who came and went and who came and never left.

This was the canteen kitchen then. So, a sizeable unit. Maybe a warehouse, maybe a distribution centre, now owned by a cartel. If the cartel used it for more than just a base for this private crew, if they used it to pack or ship product, then he had a serious problem. As well as the four guys in suits, there could be dozens of workers further into the plant; AK-armed sicarios standing guard to make sure no one stole product and no rivals turned up. TV aside, it was quiet. Even if he were too far away to hear those workers, he would hear vehicles at least. Traffickers had to traffic.

That the sound from the television was quiet told him the room was large, or that there were adjoining corridors or hallways without doors. The kitchen was substantial but no bigger than what he would expect to find in a typical restaurant, so he didn't anticipate finding a huge room on the other side of the doors. It was more likely the television was on loud in another room and the noise he heard was bouncing along hallways to reach him. That was good. That helped. A TV wouldn't be turned up loud if no one was watching it. They were spread out, but he didn't yet know how. If all four were on the other side of the door, then it wouldn't matter that one was a little further away. It would still be four guns versus none.

A knife was good, but not ideal against guys with guns. In some ways, at very close range, a knife could be better. A gun was dangerous only at one end. Any part of a blade could do damage, and the twenty-one-foot rule – the minimum distance needed to draw, aim and fire a handgun when faced with an opponent armed with a knife – meant that if he surprised one of them, the knife would be enough. He couldn't guarantee he would encounter them one at a time, however, and even if he did, even if he had the strength to overcome them, with every kill the chances of the remaining guys becoming alerted rose at an exponential rate.

He needed something else to even the odds.

THIRTY-SEVEN

Eadrich would be back, sooner or later. If he returned alone, Victor would have the best chance. Armed with a knife and aided by surprise, Victor might handle him without alerting the others. By the time Eadrich realised Victor wasn't where he was supposed to be, it would be too late. Victor knew how to kill with a minimum of noise. Over in seconds, attacking from behind before Eadrich knew what was happening. Then, with Eadrich dead and the others unaware, he could take his time and kill the remaining three in the most efficient manner. The only problem, the main and serious problem, was that Victor wasn't as strong, wasn't as fast, as he needed to be. Worse, though, was a fog in his mind. He couldn't trust his technique. A mistimed assault would be ineffectual. He needed something else. He had to compensate for his weaknesses.

There was a lingering numbness in his hands, which had to be from the shock or the drugs. The duct tape hadn't been tight enough, and only his feet had felt the tell-tale tingle.

He found his fingers were slow to close. Making a fist took considerable effort, and it hurt. Perhaps the devices had been modified, aftermarket improvements to increase the voltage delivered. These men weren't police; they didn't care if the people they shocked suffered neurological damage.

He looked around the kitchen a second time. Swing doors were no good for hiding behind. The storeroom was too small and enclosed to be useful. He thought about his enemies. They weren't looking to kill him, at least yet. They wanted answers first. That was their priority. That was his solution.

Once the questioning started in earnest, it was over. He had to make sure things never reached that stage. With no way of knowing whether Eadrich would return alone, or with the others, Victor had to be ready for both contingencies – killing Eadrich without alerting the rest, or killing them all. In either case, surprise was essential. He couldn't pick the terrain, so he had to make the terrain work to his advantage.

In the cupboards he found no food, but plenty of cleaning products. He found gallon bottles of bleach and alcohol, industrial solvents. He found large waterproof refuse sacks and lots of duct tape. He found sawdust and sand in great sacks. There were boxes filled with little pine-scented air-fresheners for cars. There were butcher's aprons, galoshes and surgeon's masks. He found hacksaws with blades made of high-tensile steel. He found wood-chopping axes. In one corner sat a pressure hose, neatly looped around an aluminium housing attached to a compressor. Another hose linked to the water supply at the wall. Plastic containers nearby were marked with hazard symbols. They weren't labelled, so perhaps they were homemade concoctions. Bleach alone was not enough to remove traces of blood and DNA invisible to the naked eye. They had everything they could need in one place. Contained. Private.

This wasn't just a kitchen but a torture chamber. The private security crew wore suits so they looked clean, but part of their job description was getting messy. They weren't just mobile security but mobile cleaners.

No chair bolted to the floor or chain hanging from the ceiling, he noted. Such things would be impossible to explain away if the unit was ever raided. He had to respect how thorough this crew were in their professionalism.

They would sit him on one of the stools, which were all aluminium. Sturdy, light and easy to clean. The stools stood in a line next to a long, rectangular island. Like the rest of the work surfaces, it was all stainless steel. Victor tore off a strip of duct tape from one of the rolls, and secured the filleting knife, by the blade, to the underside of the work surface's overhang. It was impossible to see unless sitting down or squatting. The knife was there as a last resort. There was no guarantee of a silent kill, and the inevitable mess would disrupt any chance of continued stealth.

So far he had no sign that there were any more than the four he had already encountered. Of those four, the two who had been in the back seat had both taken hits, but they were still alive. Unless they had gone to the hospital, they remained a problem. Pain and injury would diminish the threat they posed, but they were also going to be more of a problem than they might have been, because now they would want payback. Also, there was no chance of them labouring under the misconception that he was no threat. They knew he was trouble and so would be on their guard.

He had underestimated them, but they had underestimated

him in return by leaving him alone tied up only with duct tape. One all, but with plenty of time left on the clock.

He looked at the pressure washer and the grating on the floor, then he examined the floor tiles and wall tiles in that corner of the kitchen. Some were newer than others, evident where the grouting between them was a lighter shade. He pictured cracked and shattered tiles, broken by bullets used to execute prisoners no longer able to tell their captors anything useful. In one cupboard he found spare tiles, grout and tools. They had thought of everything.

He spent a moment close to the swing doors, listening. Aside from the distant television, he heard nothing. That didn't mean there was no one on the other side, but it did imply there was a good chance no one was going to enter the kitchen in the immediate future. Which gave Victor time to unscrew the tops from two bottles of cleaning products: bleach and isopropyl alcohol.

He removed his socks, then poured a little bleach on to one of them. A tablespoon's worth was all he needed, which he spread out near the hem. He poured plenty of alcohol on to the hem of the other.

Now, he was ready.

THIRTY-EIGHT

Waiting had never been a problem for Victor. Waiting was easy. He had had lots of practice. Long before he had waited for targets, he had waited to be fed. Waited for the shouting to stop. Waited for the chance to run. He had found those quiet moments calming in time. He could let his consciousness slide to the wayside, leaving his mind empty of thoughts, of distraction, of memory. A silent mind was a calm mind. A calm mind was aware. Awareness was always the first and best defence. A threat that could be seen or heard could be avoided instead of fought. A valuable skill now – a lifesaver more than once – but a saver of sanity in the past.

He waited an hour for Eadrich to return, and he didn't come alone. This time the two guys from the back seat came too. One had bandages wrapped like a bandana around his head, holding gauze in place at his temple where Victor had pistol-whipped him. The second's jaw was similarly wrapped. The whole right side of his face was swollen, indicating a broken jawbone. The bandages weren't quite neat enough and the jaw wraps were wrong for professional medical attention, so this was makeshift first aid. Eadrich hadn't allowed them to get checked out by a doctor while there was work to be done.

Neither tried to hide their anger from Victor, nor their anticipation for vengeance.

Only Eadrich seemed dispassionate, having nothing personal against Victor, who also saw there was no fear either, and no change in his expression or manner to indicate he felt any differently to how he had been during their previous conversation.

'Time to talk,' Eadrich said.

The guy with the broken jaw squatted down next to Victor and used a folding knife to cut through the duct tape around Victor's ankles, which he had reapplied. If the guy could smell the bleach, he didn't react. If he found anything amiss with the duct tape, he didn't show it.

Once Victor's feet were free, Eadrich helped him stand. He didn't release Victor's hands. Whatever his level of confidence, he wasn't *that* confident.

'What is this place?' Victor asked as he was led into the kitchen.

'A place for quiet contemplation,' Eadrich answered.

He positioned a stool and sat down. One of the two bandaged guys pulled out a stool for Victor and shoved him on to it with such force he almost toppled it and himself to the floor.

'Easy,' Eadrich said.

The guy shrugged in apology and made sure Victor was secure on the stool, while the other bandaged guy stood by glowering the whole time. Victor played along, acting as though it was all he could do to maintain his balance with his hands bound.

Eadrich said, 'Why don't you two leave us alone?'

It was an order phrased as a question, so the two guys left the kitchen. Neither hurried, and both glared at Victor as they went. They didn't want to miss out.

'My men that you hurt want to hurt you,' Eadrich explained. 'They want to skip the polite discourse and go straight to work on you. They're not what I would call talented, but they are enthusiastic. They don't think about consequences. They forget why they're beating in the first place. I tell them to beat someone and they won't stop until that person is an unrecognisable pile of mush on the floor. So, I have to use them sparingly. I wouldn't be able to leave them unsupervised, especially with you. That's why it'll be just me asking the questions. At least while you're giving me answers.'

Victor waited.

Eadrich said, 'Would you like a smoke?'

Victor didn't fight the sodium thiopental. 'Very much so.'

Eadrich seemed pleased. He positioned himself so he could make use of the island work surface to roll a cigarette. 'Good. There are few pleasures as pure as unfiltered tobacco.'

Victor watched him roll. Despite fat fingers and an obvious lack of dexterity, Eadrich knew what he was doing. Enough repetition, enough practice, and anyone could get better at any task.

'I know that look,' Eadrich said. 'You're an ex-smoker. You want one, but you know you shouldn't. How long has it been?'

Victor didn't have to think, but he spent a moment as if in silent calculation.

'That long?'

'Too long.'

'Then is the answer to my original question still yes?'

Victor nodded.

Eadrich smiled. As pleased to have corrupted as he was to have a smoking companion. 'The others don't smoke. Young guys today are too concerned with their health to know what's good for them.'

He set the roll-up down on the stainless steel surface and began a second. He was inches from the knife. Far too close for Victor to have any chance of grabbing it unnoticed. While Eadrich rolled, Victor worked the duct tape loose that bound his wrists behind his back.

Eadrich was a little slower with the second roll-up, a little more careful. The result was a smoother rolled cigarette, more even and aesthetic, which he presented to Victor, standing it upright on the worktop to show off the precision.

Victor nodded, as though he were impressed.

Eadrich looked pleased with himself, as though he didn't get many compliments. 'You can have it when I'm happy you're telling me the truth.'

'Okay,' Victor said.

Eadrich lit his cigarette and inhaled, holding in the smoke for a moment before blowing it into Victor's face. 'You know, I was an officer in the army, once upon a time. I used to hunt guys like me, but that was then. In any war, you need to think ahead. You need to think about the endgame. Which side is going to win? Who is going to be left standing when it's over? I looked into my future and then decided to join the winning side.'

'I can understand that.'

'You surprise me. Most people don't understand it. They only see the betrayal. The disloyalty.'

'The first loyalty should always be to oneself.'

'To survive.'

'Exactly.'

Eadrich nodded. 'I like you, which makes this difficult.' He opened his jacket to make sure Victor could see the holstered pistol.

'Then don't do it.'

'I switched sides, remember?'

Eadrich looked at him with a certain amount of regret in his eyes, a certain amount of sadness. Victor didn't know a lot about either, but he recognised them just as he recognised the finality too. Whatever Eadrich's reluctance, he would do what he had to do to get home to his wife.

'Your information checks out,' he said. 'Not a blemish. Not a single thing to make me suspicious. Which makes me suspicious about who you really are.'

Victor was honest. 'I'm a guy in the wrong place at the wrong time.'

He shook his head. 'Not just a guy in the wrong place. A guy in the worst place.'

Victor was silent.

'You're not as scared as you were in the car. I mean, you're not as scared as you pretended to be.'

'Would you prefer me to pretend now?'

'I wouldn't believe it,' he said. 'Just as I don't believe ... this.' He gestured. 'Whatever this is. This act of yours.'

'Act?'

He held out both hands, palms down, fingers spread. With his chin he gestured to the right hand. 'This is anyone else in your predicament.' The right hand shook and trembled. Then he gestured to the left hand. 'This is you.' The left hand didn't move.

'Maybe I'm resigned to my fate.'

'You believe in fate?'

Victor shook his head. 'We make our own fate.'

Eadrich gave him a careful look. 'And what fate will you make for yourself?'

'The fate you allow me.'

'Then consider me the master of your destiny.'

He exhaled smoke through his nostrils and rested his cigarette on the corner of the work surface before taking the second and holding it filter-first at Victor, who took it in his lips. Eadrich lit it and Victor inhaled. It tasted like happiness.

He coughed several times.

Eadrich smiled and took the cigarette away. 'Really has been a long time, hasn't it?'

'My throat . . . is very dry.'

'Of course. That's not unexpected. I expect you'd like a glass of water?'

Victor nodded, forcing out another cough. 'Thank you.'

Eadrich set Victor's cigarette down next to his own and stood up from his stool. At the kitchen sink, he turned on a tap, retrieved a plastic beaker from one of the cupboards.

As he did so, Victor slipped out of his bonds and removed his socks.

While Eadrich filled up the beaker with water, Victor crept up behind him, holding his breath while squeezing and rubbing the hems of the two socks together so the bleach mixed with the isopropyl alcohol.

'Once you've had this,' Eadrich said with his back to Victor, 'we will begin in earnest.'

Before he could turn around, Victor slapped the socks over Eadrich's mouth and nose.

The sodium hypochlorite contained in the bleach mixed with the alcohol to produce a range of dangerous compounds including hydrochloric acid and chloroform. Eadrich couldn't help but breathe in the vapour. The first effect was coughing and retching, but the sound was muffled, before the toxic chemicals entered his bloodstream, causing nausea and dizziness. Within a couple of seconds Eadrich's knees buckled. His arms flailed, wild, desperate, but without strength, without accuracy. The chloroform was in his brain, attacking his nervous system, interrupting synapses.

Victor eased him to the floor. Eadrich was still conscious, but he was disorientated. He couldn't move. He couldn't speak. His face had a sickly pallor and his eyes were red and streaming tears.

Further exposure to the chloroform would have knocked him out, but Victor needed only to disable Eadrich so he could kill him without making a sound. Victor retrieved the filleting knife from under the counter top.

'Remember when you told me there are three types of men?' he said to Eadrich, disorientated and immobile, but conscious, aware. 'I'm the third kind.'

In his weakened state, Eadrich was unable to resist or fight back as Victor placed a palm over his mouth and drove the point of the knife into his chest. His watery eyes widened and he emitted a muffled gasp that became a wheezing exhale as the blade reached his heart. He would be dead in seconds, but Victor had to release him and the knife.

He had to release both because the swing doors began to open.

THIRTY-NINE

Victor was already close to the doors, so he used that to his advantage, dashing towards them as they began opening, and going to one side, so they concealed him as they reached the apex of their swing. One of the two guys with bandages stepped into the room. The one with the gauze at his temple.

He hesitated for a second because Eadrich and Victor were not sitting on stools as he expected to find them. An instant later, he saw Eadrich dying on the floor.

From behind, Victor snapped the socks soaked with chloroform over the guy's mouth and nose. Most people wouldn't be able to resist a panicked inhale, but this guy, forewarned by Eadrich on the floor, managed it. He didn't inhale. He didn't exhale. He held his breath. A temporary solution only, but still a solution. It gave him time to fight back.

He threw elbows backwards, hard and well placed. Victor's ribs were on fire from the first impact, building with every subsequent blow until his whole torso was a raging inferno.

He didn't let go. He fought through the pain. Pain was a message, and temporary. Death was eternal.

In seconds the guy was slowing. He had spent his oxygen reserves on the elbow strikes. He made it to half a minute before he sucked in air. He coughed. He retched. He weakened.

Victor kept the socks in place, tight over the mouth and nose, while the guy sank to his knees. Another few seconds and he would lose consciousness.

The fizzing crackle of electricity gave Victor an instant's warning, but he couldn't react before the sudden shock of the stun gun did its job. He spasmed. His teeth smacked together. Awful and inescapable pain wracked his body. His hands snapped closed into fists, releasing the guy from the chemical fumes, but the rag stayed clenched in Victor's fist.

He didn't know if he fell away first or the guy did, but they both went down to the floor tiles – Victor, foetal and trembling, the guy on his hands and knees, dazed from the fumes, ribbons of mucus hanging from his nostrils and gaping mouth, neither man able to move.

In the car, the pain of millions of volts had been ended by punches knocking Victor unconscious. Now, he didn't have that release. The aftermath of the stun gun left him paralysed and deathly cold, trapped in infinite shivers, the source of his immobility, his agony, inside him, out of reach. He could do nothing but shake and tremble, his eyes watering and his limbs beyond control.

He was aware though. He could see. He could hear. He watched the man on his hands and knees, coughing and retching; spitting and wheezing, fighting his own battle against the poison in his bloodstream, and winning.

The passing of time was hard for Victor to track, but at the point he could get his fingers to extend with enormous effort, the guy was able to wipe the snot and spit from his face. When Victor could rotate his head and begin to straighten his back, the guy was pushing himself back on to his haunches and trying to stand.

Eadrich's gun.

Victor craned his neck to see where it lay, still holstered beneath Eadrich's jacket. Not far. Within arm's reach almost, but Victor's arms didn't work. He tried to roll closer, but no part of his body responded to the command. Instead, he dragged himself. He pushed his fingertips against the tiles and pulled. He inched closer.

The guy used a work surface for support and got to his feet. He had to use a hand braced on the worktop to stay upright, but he was upright. His bearings were coming back fast. His liver was working hard to take the poison out of his blood, and not enough had reached his brain to have an extended effect. Another minute, and he would be left with a headache and nothing else.

Victor reached the gun, exhausted from the short crawl, wanting nothing more than to lie still and rest, maybe sleep. He was so tired. He worked the holster open.

His fingertips touched the cool metal. He pressed and pulled it into his fist. Shaking fingers closed around the grip. His index finger wouldn't bend to fit through the trigger guard. He had to use his left hand to manipulate the finger.

He took a breath to summon strength and rolled on to his back. It pained him to do so, but now he saw the guy again. Victor dragged the gun into line. He couldn't aim. He just had to point. Centre mass. Any hit, one hit, would be enough.

He squeezed the trigger.

Nothing happened.

There was a bullet in the chamber. The safety was off. He realised he didn't have the strength to squeeze the trigger back far enough. Six pounds of pressure was beyond his weakened index finger.

He saw the guy turn around. There was some clarity in his eyes. Another few seconds and he would get clear of Victor's limited field of view. Then it would be over.

Victor wrapped the fingers of his left hand around the end of his right index finger protruding through the trigger guard and wrenched it back.

The gun fired.

The bullet missed. It plugged a neat hole into the metal cabinet to the right of the guy's shoulder. He flinched, but a slow flinch. He couldn't move away fast enough.

Victor shot again.

This time the bullet hit, but low. A gut shot. Messy, because it severed the inferior vena cava. The man's white shirt reddened fast. Victor didn't shoot again. He saw the wound was fatal. He could wait for the bleeding to do its job and he needed the remaining bullets. The guy wasn't going anywhere.

He tried to staunch the bleeding with one hand, and when that didn't work, both. Without a hand to support him on the work surface, he fell.

Blood extended across the tiles towards Victor, who swivelled on the floor, half-rolling to face the kitchen doors, bringing the gun up in unsteady hands, ready for when—

—the second bandaged guy came charging through in response to the gunshots, his own weapon drawn and ready.

Victor shot, again and again, unable to aim so trusting to volume instead, bullets missing but others hitting until the man collapsed back through the swing doors and lay still between them.

It was an effort to keep his arms raised and the gun pointed at the doors, but Victor did so, fighting the weakness and disorientation and the desire to stop and succumb to rest, to sleep. There was still one left. The young guy who had driven the car.

Seconds passed. The driver didn't show, and no sound indicated he was somewhere the other side of the doors. Victor could see only glimpses of a corridor beyond.

He hauled himself to his feet, using a stool to help. It wasn't easy, but he felt his mobility beginning to return.

In the quiet, Victor understood the driver's absence, because he heard a vehicle outside. The low rumble of an exhaust. Tyres coming to a stop on gravel. A car arriving in no hurry. The young driver returning from running errands. If he knew what was happening inside – if the others had managed to get a message to him – then he would have arrived fast, engine roaring and tyres roaring on gravel, else he would have tried stealth and Victor wouldn't have heard a car at all. The young guy knew nothing about what to expect.

Victor was standing unaided by the time the driver appeared. He was hesitant entering the kitchen, having found no one else in the rest of the building, but he was expecting his colleagues to be working on Victor, not dead on the floor.

He did a double take when he saw Victor, when he saw the gun, when he saw all the blood. He had a cardboard carrying tray with four cups of coffee held so far out before him it seemed as though he thought it a legitimate risk that he might spill all four all over himself.

Had, because he dropped the tray and coffee went everywhere.

'I know what you're thinking,' Victor said. 'Bad timing.'

The driver couldn't say anything.

'You're thinking that maybe if you had been five minutes slower you might have missed me altogether. You might have missed … this. But don't beat yourself up. I would have waited all night if I had to. I'm afraid you were dead the moment you turned up at that hotel. It's just taken this long for you to realise it.'

The young guy paled.

Victor said, 'You never know how brave you are until you're scared.'

The driver didn't respond. His hair was jaw length and hung over his face. He was too scared to push it back out of the way. His cheeks were smooth but the strip of skin between his nose and upper lip had a hint of stubble. There was a façade of innocence to him, but if true innocence existed, Victor had never encountered it, or perhaps he refused to see it. He used to tell himself he was the culmination of thousands – hundreds of thousands – of years of human history in an effort to justify who he was, to rationalise his life choices. These days, he needed no such excuse. He didn't need to understand how he became himself. It was a fools' errand even to attempt such self-analysis, but more than that, it was unnecessary. Victor simply didn't care.

'There was a time when I might have let you go,' he said, unsure whether it was the drug inside him compelling honesty or something more. 'You're no threat to me now, and I imagine the first thing you would do after I release you would be to get out of the city, the country, and never come back.'

The driver was silent but his eyes agreed.

'That was then,' Victor continued. 'I've learnt from my mistakes. I'm not going to let you go. I'm not letting anyone go. But I'll do you a deal. If you tell me how to find Diaz, I'll make sure your mother can have an open casket at your funeral. Do you think she would appreciate that?'

The driver nodded as much as his fear let him.

'So,' Victor began, 'is there anything you want to tell me?'

The driver found his voice. He spoke in staccato sentences. 'I know where Diaz plays poker. A private game. A bar by the lake. He's there every Friday night.'

Victor said, 'Your mother would thank you if she could,' and squeezed the trigger.

FORTY

There was beauty in death.

Life had a certain inescapable ugliness. It was messy. Uneven. Death, however, was pure. It was unsullied. He knew this. He felt it. Perhaps only he understood the disparity. Maybe only he could see it. To others, the beauty was in the inverse. Life was beautiful and death was foul. But life created bias. The living thought themselves beautiful because they were delusional. They were ugly. Only he could make them beautiful. It was his gift to them.

He received no thanks for this gift. He received no appreciation. There was no applause. No adoration. Ungrateful faces were everywhere. Inescapable ugliness wherever he looked. The impure. The dirty. The disgusting. If they only knew of their own repulsiveness, if they could only see what he saw, they would end their torment; they would spare one another that ingratitude.

He was no mere murderer. He was a guide. He was a

renovator. He took away the ugliness of life and replaced it with something of higher aesthetic.

Lavandier referred to him as the Russian, but his given name was Sergei Constantin. Though that name had long since been forgotten. Maybe it was out there still, perhaps as a rumour, a whisper of pain and terror and that which should not be named. He was no Russian, but from the Czech Republic, although he had not set foot in his homeland for as long as he could remember. He had never been to Russia, but he had affiliates in that country. Men who found him work and whom he worked for on occasion. This was how Lavandier had found him.

The Frenchman told him, 'You need to be aware that another professional has also been hired for this task. He's here already.'

Constantin said, 'I see.'

Lavandier seemed unsure of his tone. 'Is this revelation a problem for you?'

'It is only a problem if he receives payment while I do not.'

'You need not be concerned about that. Your fee is your fee, as agreed. You will be paid it when Maria is dead, whether it is you who pulls the trigger or not.'

Constantin nodded his head. His skull was large and sat above narrow shoulders, supported by a neck that seemed too thin for the job. He was tall – too tall – and thin – far too thin – but he needed no great strength to squeeze a trigger or slip a blade between ribs. It required but the will to do so.

He asked, 'Did you ask this other killer whether he had a problem with me?'

'I did not.'

Constantin said, 'Why not?'

The Frenchman was composed. 'He is unaware that another professional was to be hired. He must remain unaware.'

Constantin's brow furrowed. His skin was thin and pale. He had deep wrinkles and eyes that always looked tired. The light pooled on his scalp.

'I see,' he said. 'I'm the backup killer.'

'I don't think there is any benefit in considering the situation as such. Your client is eager for success. We see hiring you both as a way to double our chances. We would have brought you in sooner, had you been available.'

'You doubt the other man's capabilities?'

'Not at all,' Lavandier said. 'But we are prudent.'

'A competition then.'

'Again, I don't believe that's the right way to look at this. You will be paid in full, whether it is you who executes or him.'

Constantin nodded. 'I see. It is indeed a him.'

Lavandier sat with a trace of awkwardness, but he said nothing.

'Is he to be paid more than me?'

Lavandier said, 'The answer is yes. We agreed his fee as we agreed yours. His fee was higher. There is no insult there.'

'I agree,' Constantin said. 'But if it is I who fulfils the contract then I wish to be paid his fee instead.'

'That is acceptable to me.'

'You are a reasonable man.'

'We are reasonable men.'

Constantin shook his large head, slow and deliberate. 'If you believe that of me then you have been misled, because I am anything but, I assure you.'

'I would like to reiterate the need for discretion. The

other party is not to know you are working towards the same goal.'

Constantin said, 'We are tasked with the same objective. It is not unforeseeable that our paths might converge at some point.'

'They must not.'

Constantin said, 'I understand.'

He considered this man before him, this Frenchman. He was well dressed and well spoken. He had manners. He had wit. Such things were irrelevant to Constantin, who judged all men by their will alone. Lavandier had no will. All he had was the appearance of resolve. His composure was an illusion. Constantin saw straight through it. Of all his skills, the ability to see that which was hidden he considered his most valuable. To be successful in the business of taking someone's life, it was first necessary to understand how they lived.

'Why is my competitor afforded privileged status?' Constantin asked, quiet and reasonable. 'You approached him first. You were happy to pay him more.'

'He comes highly recommended.'

'And I do not?'

Lavandier struggled to find a diplomatic answer. 'It's not personal.'

'I am not offended. I am but curious.'

'We would not hire you if we thought you were incapable of the task. It is just that the person who recommended him carries much weight. On balance, we must trust those sources we know best.'

Constantin made a slow nod. 'I understand.'

'And you do not mind?'

'You pay my fee, you make the rules.'

Lavandier smiled. 'I'm glad you see it that way.' He gestured. 'If we are done, then I have things that require my attention.'

Constantin didn't move. 'We are almost done.'

He would never admit it, and indeed had no one in his life to admit it to, but Constantin enjoyed his work a little too much. Some professionals took pride in a job well done, but Constantin had fun. He liked killing. Always had, even as a child. His neighbourhood had a disproportionate number of missing cat and dog signs fixed to lampposts. It would have been devoid of barks and meows entirely had he not been caught in the act and thrashed to such an extent he spent a week in bed. It had been an important lesson to the young killer: don't get caught. He had heeded this simple, yet invaluable, philosophy ever since. Besides, he had a cat of his own now, and preferred its company to any human. He hadn't realised it as a child, but he had more in common with domestic felines than his fellow man. Cats, well fed by their owners, had no need to hunt, they had no need to torment their victims, but they did so regardless. They did so because they wanted to. They did so because they liked it. So he liked them in return.

If being thrashed by his mother was a defining lesson, so was the lesson his father taught him: if you like doing something, make sure someone pays you to do it. Once Constantin knew he enjoyed taking lives, it was a natural progression to make it a career. He was self-taught in the arts of murder, and had been a quick student. He would be self-reliant in all things if not for the need for others to handle his business affairs, although they were never just business. If no one paid him to kill, Constantin would do it anyway. He chose the contracts that he believed would give him the most satisfaction, which were not always the ones that were the best paid.

Constantin thought about the other assassin. The one, whatever Lavandier had said, who was the primary on this particular contract. Constantin was not driven by ego, but he recognised the implicit insult. His rival must be of special competence to have his conditions met, and by nature of the arrangement Lavandier had more faith in that assassin than he had in Constantin. But should he kill the target first, he would receive the reward. A competition, whatever Lavandier had assured. A race, for which there could only be one winner.

Of course, Constantin thought, if one participant should trip and fall, then the other runner would be assured of glory.

The Frenchman was growing impatient in the silence. Constantin liked to keep people waiting. He liked to exert his will over the ugly.

He said, 'I'll need a description of the other assassin.'

Lavandier regarded him, curious, suspicious. 'Why would you need that?'

'To make sure that were our paths to cross,' Constantin said, 'they may separate again.'

He held the Frenchman's gaze for a long moment, facing down his will and breaking it asunder with his own.

Lavandier nodded in concession. 'Of course.'

FORTY-ONE

Messy. Unrefined. But they were dead and he was not.

Cleaning up the scene was simple. They had everything Victor could need. He wrapped each corpse in plastic, making sure each cocoon was watertight, and loaded them into their own minivan in the cover of their unit. He wasn't yet sure the best thing to do with the van and corpses inside, but they were better found anywhere but here and a long time from now. The independent status and autonomy that Eadrich had boasted of meant Victor could enjoy a significant window before anyone started asking questions.

Outside, the sun was low, but still bright, and it had been much darker inside the unit. The whine in his ears and the fog in his mind were slow to diminish and cleaning up and moving the bodies had been tiring. His limbs remained a little slow, a little ungainly. He didn't trust his balance. His steps were short and almost shuffling – a drunk leaving a bar.

He saw an almost empty stretch of asphalt that would serve any legitimate enterprise as parking spaces for employees and maybe deliveries and dispatches. Now, just one other vehicle besides the minivan. A second, smaller car was parked further away. Shiny paint. Clean window glass. No doubt Eadrich's ride. Victor pictured the minivan driving around to pick up the others at the beginning of the day and performing the same route in reverse when it was time to go home.

No one was around. No one could see Victor. The unit had a chain-link fence, but the next closest unit was out of line of sight, and there was no through traffic on the approach road. Which was why they had chosen it, of course. Quiet. Remote as it could be so close to a major metropolis. How many people had been brought here, never to leave? Victor didn't know. Couldn't know. He was no humanitarian, although he enjoyed the irony of claiming to be from time to time. He didn't care about those people, but he cared that he hadn't become one of them.

There were no CCTV cameras to concern himself with, beyond a few that formed a perimeter around the building. For show, mostly. They were too high and too old to capture Victor's, or anyone else's, face from inside a vehicle. Any cameras that had once been inside had been removed. The crew hadn't wanted recordings of what took place within. He removed the hard disks that captured footage from the outside cameras, because he could never be too careful, and better for there to be no record of the four guys returning here and never leaving again. He didn't imagine detectives would ever come looking for them, but maybe the cartel would. Best if they simply vanished. They had already called Diaz from inside the minivan to tell him there was nothing to worry about. By the time anyone realised that Victor *was* someone to worry about, he planned to be beyond their reach. Half the world away, ideally, with a new legend, sipping a bourbon from a seat where he could see the door and waiting for the next job to arrive. Which was the only forethought he allowed himself. Thinking about the future, like thinking about the past, was a luxury reserved for those who were safe in the present. Victor didn't know when he had last felt safe – had he ever? – and if he had, he was pretty sure he never would again.

The industrial estate contained many large operations but the unit used by the private security guys was small in comparison. They didn't need a lot of space, and a lot of space used by only a few people attracted attention. Like Victor, they had to avoid scrutiny in order to do their job. He took the corpses away with no concern about being noticed.

He drove far out of the city, far into the countryside, through ramshackle collections of dwellings that passed as villages, along narrow roads that were little more than dirt tracks. When he had seen no cars and no people for hours, he buried the bodies in woodland, in a single grave deep enough in the ground that no animals would smell them rotting.

He arrived back in Guatemala City at dawn, and left the minivan unlocked with its windows down in one of the many poor neighbourhoods. It would be stolen within the hour, he was sure, but even so, a crew of four missing cartel security guys was far from ideal. They might never be found, it might never be determined why they disappeared, but questions would be asked.

For a few days, Victor took a step back from his preparations while the barbiturate worked its way out of his system. Even when he no longer had a headache, when he no longer felt slow or weak, he had to work on the assumption that he wasn't at his best. Therefore, he concentrated on cementing the credibility of his legend. He met with more suppliers. He sent emails. He made phone calls. He did nothing that could be construed as suspicious while he checked the news and watched his back.

He didn't need one, but it was a good excuse to meet Joanna for dinner.

She picked the restaurant and he arrived early. The chairs were low, with a sweeping curve of a back, designed for aesthetics, not ergonomics. They were not comfortable. They could have been heavenly, but Victor would still be displeased. He didn't like being low. It restricted his ability to keep watch on his surroundings. It limited his periph-eral vision. He couldn't see threats coming and he couldn't respond to them. He sat straight-backed, with his head in line with his hips, which was the correct way to sit to be able to stand again at speed. It was rare for Victor to sit back in a chair. It was rare for him to relax. The unrelaxed posture made him look awkward. Awkward made him memorable. He didn't like that either, but he preferred it to needless vulnerability.

'You're even earlier than me,' Joanna said when they greeted one another.

He didn't comment on his preference to arrive at places early, or why.

She sat down. 'Good choice of table too.'

They were both hungry, so ordered food when the waiter arrived asking what they would like to drink. Victor told Joanna to order for him, in part to further reduce the already minimal chance someone would tamper with his food – if he didn't know what he was ordering, neither could they – but also because she had been here longer and knew what was likely to be good. They made small talk for a while.

After their drinks arrived, she said, 'Do you mind if I ask how old you are?'

'Guess.'

She didn't hesitate. 'Thirty-five.'

Neither did he. 'Close enough.'

'You're not going to tell me?'

'I'm an intensely private person.'

'I can never tell when you're being serious or making a joke.'

'That's the idea.'

She raised her hands. 'Again ... don't know.'

'Does it bother you?'

'Now? Not in the slightest. Most guys, I know everything about them before they even open their mouths. And when they do, I can see right through their BS. You're different. But ... if I can't figure you out after a while, then you'd see my stern face. I can look *really* stern if I want to. Think one of your old teachers giving you a disapproving stare.'

'I was taught by nuns, so that would be quite something.'

They ate octopus to start.

He was curious where this experiment in normalcy would lead. He needed to experience normalcy to understand it, and without understanding it he could not pretend to be normal with any conviction. The mask he wore had been well fashioned, created with care, endlessly refined until it had become near invisible, until he could wear it and no one could tell the difference. That mask had limitations, however. It could never be perfect. The world wasn't static. Its population was fluid, dynamic, forever changing. He was the eternal student, observing, changing and adapting to fit in, to remain unnoticed. He could never master that which he did not practise. The best he could achieve was an academic comprehension of his subject matter. He could become an expert observer, but he could not become that he was not.

'I have an idea,' Joanna said. 'Let's play the Boring Question Game.'

Victor said, 'What's that?'

'You know, the typical Q&A you do when you meet someone new. The questions you ask when you can't have a natural conversation and you're still struggling to find a rapport.'

'Such as?'

Alamaeda said, 'Okay, I'll start with the absolute worst one: what kind of music do you like?'

'It's easier to say what kind of music I don't like.'

She upturned her palms. 'Well?'

'Anything that uses a guitar, drums, or electronics.'

'So, any music after about nineteen hundred, right?'

'Thomas Tallis used choirs of eunuchs. Some teenagers singing about their angst can't compete with that.'

She said, 'Did he perform all the castrations himself?'

'I don't think so.'

'But, and I'm just speculating here naturally, I'm pretty sure he would have to check they were all genuine, wouldn't he?'

'In case they were fake eunuchs?'

'Some men have a naturally high voice.'

'True.'

'Or they could be a woman in disguise.'

'Now you're reaching.'

'Okay,' Joanna said. 'Time for an important question: you don't mind dating an older woman?'

'Are we dating?'

'This is a date, isn't it? And that's not answering my question.'

'I didn't know you were an older woman until seven seconds ago.'

She looked at him out of the corner of her eye. 'Does it change anything?'

'I'm sprinting to the door as we speak.'

She smiled at him, both in amusement and relief, the former hiding the latter somewhat, but Victor still saw it. He realised he felt good to be the source of that relief, that simple words could have such an effect. She changed the sub-ject, asking him about his work, about commodities. With no barbiturate in his system, lying was again effortless, but whereas once he had relished the effective application of his skillset, here it felt increasingly like betrayal. He answered each of her questions with questions of his own.

In his own evasiveness, he failed to notice her own.

'You sound dispassionate,' Joanna said. 'About commodities.'

'I'm in it for the money,' he admitted. 'What's your excuse?'

'Oh, I'm a mercenary too. A cold-blooded capitalist out to screw over the little guy.'

'A man I used to know told me that what we do for a living is not a reflection of us, but society.'

'How come you *used to* know him?'

'My job got in the way.'

She smiled. 'You can be quite witty when you want to be.'

'I don't often want to be. My charm is a lethal weapon. Best keep it holstered.'

'Now you just sound like a jerk.'

He nodded. 'Like I said: it's best to keep my charm holstered.'

'How are you liking Guatemala?'

'It's a little humid for me.'

'You're too Canadian for this climate, but you'll get used to it.'

When their main course arrived, Victor looked down at his plate with a measure of disbelief. 'You ordered burgers and fries.'

She mistook his tone. 'You did say for me to order for you. I figured you might be sick of guacamole by now. Sorry if I got it wrong.'

'No,' Victor said with a shake of his head. 'This is exactly my kind of food.'

Joanna reached across the table to prod his stomach. 'I don't believe you.'

'I burn a lot of calories in my line of work.'

'Sure. The commodities business is the modern equivalent of working down a mine. Do you get Trader's Lung too?' She pretended to cough.

He smiled to take the mockery on the chin, and said, 'Your job must be pretty taxing mentally.'

'Not really. Mostly it's staring at databases and filling out forms.'

Victor said, 'That sounds exactly like my work.'

She smiled. 'Look at us, we're the most uninteresting people in this place.'

He remembered the last time he had eaten dinner with someone similar, with someone whose company he wanted to be in. The last time he had been on a date, even if he had paid for it. He could picture the restaurant clearly, as if referencing a photograph; clearer still was the smell, the aroma of Indian cuisine and the scent of her perfume, sweet but delicate. She had looked across the table at him, moisture in her eyes, disbelief. Fear. She had never seen him again. She was alive, he knew, because he had broken protocol and found her, putting himself in danger to do so, but he'd had to know if she were alive or dead, if he had killed her through his actions, through association. She hadn't known she had been found. She hadn't seen him watching her, but few ever saw him when he wanted to remain unseen. A little flower shop in the middle of nowhere. A new name. A new life. Smiling at every customer but with unmistakable sadness in her eyes. *Who are you?* was the last thing she had said to him. *Someone you'll wish you had never met*, had been his reply.

Joanna saw his mind was elsewhere, but he brought it back to the present before she could ask him what he was thinking about. He didn't want to lie any more than he had to, so he asked her questions on subjects he knew she liked to talk about. She told him all about white-water rafting.

After the waiter had cleared their empty plates, she said, 'You know, this thing has a finite shelf life, don't you?'

He nodded. 'I know. You have a job here. A life.'

'I say it as a friendly warning.'

'Noted, and ignored. I don't think I'm going to be in town too much longer.'

'At least this way we won't end up taking each other for granted. We'll have just enough time to get to know the other, but not enough to get bored.'

'We're only interested in the people we don't understand.'

She winked at him and pointed a finger like a gun, clicking her cheek. Then she said, 'Say, since we're on the clock, you wanna skip dessert and eat low-fat frozen yoghurt at my place?'

'Like you wouldn't believe.'

FORTY-TWO

It was a narrow street. Quiet. He took a meandering route from Joanna's place, through narrow residential streets paved with cobbles. The buildings were dark on either side of the street. Windows were closed and curtains drawn. A few exterior lights pushed away the night, but only in places. There was no traffic.

Victor preferred to walk facing oncoming traffic. He never let cars come up behind him if it could be avoided. It was one of the first things he had learned. A simple precaution, but the best ones usually were. This was a one-way street, however. Vehicles had to come at him head on, but none did at this hour.

He walked along the centre of the road. He had a light step, but against hard cobbles, and with the buildings in close proximity, those footsteps were loud and echoing. He could hear little else because this part of the city was residential and it was the middle of the night. It made it simple to pick out a second set of footsteps.

Lighter than his, so he pictured trainers or walking shoes. Twenty or twenty-five metres behind him. The echo was different, however – uneven – which meant the walker was on the pavement, close to one line of buildings with the nearby cars muffling the sound.

A citizen out for a late-night stroll, he discovered, but with four men already killed by his own hand, Victor had to operate with a higher level of caution until he knew for sure no one was looking for him.

With half a dozen cartels operating in Guatemala, plus others still from abroad, violence was endemic. Every day there were killings and kidnappings reported on the news broadcasts and in newspapers, but he found only a single mention of the disappearance of four men who worked for a private security firm. It was only a brief mention tucked away beneath an article about a soap opera star's adultery. The article mentioned the men were known associates of one half of the warring Salvatierra cartel, and their disappearance had already been attributed to their rival traffickers.

How hard the police were investigating, he didn't know, but as a rule the authorities focused their resources on finding justice for civilians. The lack of an official desire to find the perpetrator wouldn't necessarily extend to the cartel itself, but like the police, they might put it down to Heloise Salvatierra.

Victor was careful regardless; even if there was no immediate fallout from the dead private security guys, it might trip him up further down the line. But if Diaz thought there was a connection with the events at the hotel, he didn't act like it. He was playing poker that night at his private game in a bar that overlooked Lago de Amatitlán. It was enough to convince Victor that if Diaz knew about the missing crew, he didn't care. Diaz believed he was unassailable. He thought the cartel's power was his shield.

For days, there were no clouds. The pavements were so hot underfoot it felt as though the soles of his shoes would melt. He expected to leave size twelve prints of rubber with every step. Victor was no fan of the heat. The hotter the weather, the fewer or lighter the garments. It was hard to hide a gun under linen. It was hard to have a knife up a sleeve when there were no sleeves. It was hard not to look out of place wearing a suit jacket at the height of summer. It was hard to be ignored when drenched in sweat.

Perhaps that was why most of his work was carried out in the colder months. He had never set out to avoid work in the summer, but he had preferred areas to operate within, so why not seasons? He couldn't escape the climate in Guatemala, and he stood out enough without adding to that with inappropriate dress. There were limits, of course. No T-shirts. No shorts. Good quality shoes at all times. He had rules that could never be broken. He would rather stand out than be unable to deal with the consequences of being noticed.

Despite the discomfort, there were dozens of opportunities to steal the yellow Aventador, but that wasn't part of the plan. Victor would need significant time alone with the vehicle in order to turn it into a car bomb without Diaz's knowledge. That was for later, after he had learned more about Diaz's habits.

That would have to wait, however, because Georg got back with a choice: he could have an AX50 rifle shipped to him from South Africa, which would take three weeks to arrive, or he could collect one at the border with Honduras anytime he wished. Each option had its own positives and its drawbacks. It was safer and easier for the rifle from South Africa to be shipped to him. All he would need to do was collect a crate from the port. The risks would be negligible. Worst-case scenario would be having to bribe a member of the port authority not to check the cargo, and even that was highly unlikely. A cargo ship brought in thousands of shipping containers. If a port wanted to be profitable, it was impossible to check every container, let alone every item of cargo within them. At best, a tiny per cent of containers were inspected. The downside was the wait. Three weeks was a long time. He might miss dozens of excellent opportunities to kill Maria, and while he waited he risked the chance of his target learning she was hunted. He risked the chance of his documentation being exposed. Even without those particular risks, he didn't like to stay in one place so long. Though most of his enemies believed him dead, he considered it prudent to stay on the move. A stationary target was an easy target.

On the flip side, he could collect the rifle from the border with Honduras whenever he wanted. No downtime. No waiting.

The risks, though, were many. While Georg had sourced the weapon, she couldn't vouch for the dealer selling it. At best, she could make a third-hand recommendation, but she could offer no guarantees. She made that clear. She wanted Victor to be under no illusions. She wanted him to have no grievances with her if the outcome was less than satisfactory. He understood this. He appreciated her frankness. Hence, he could not be sure the weapon would be as promised. It might be old. It might have been poorly maintained. The ammunition could be substandard. Maybe it had been used in a crime, the ballistics in a case file somewhere, with dogged cops trying to trace the weapon. Or it might be there was no rifle, just an opportunist looking to rip him off and score a considerable amount of cash. Or, worse, bait as part of a non-proliferation sting operation.

Even if the dealer was legit and the rifle up to Victor's standards, there would still be problems. He would need to transport it himself, else take the additional risk of involving another party to take the main risks for him. Victor always preferred to work alone. He could trust only himself. At some point, everyone he had ever relied upon had let him down, either wilfully else through plain incompetence.

Georg needed an answer fast. The dealer from Honduras wasn't going to hang around and if the rifle in South Africa wasn't on the next cargo ship out of Cape Town, it would be nine weeks, not three, before it arrived.

Victor liked rushing about as much as he liked taking risks, so he called Georg and said, 'I'll take both.'

She hadn't expected this, and was silent.

'Is that a problem?' he asked.

'Of course not, but it'll double the price. Can you afford both? These are expensive weapons.'

'Money is no object.'

'Then I wish I had quoted you a higher price.'

'Too late now. Just make sure your Honduran contacts are aware that I expect them to keep to the very letter of the agreement.'

'Don't worry about that,' she said. 'I've made sure they know exactly the kind of man they're dealing with.'

FORTY-THREE

The smurf was a long, stringy kid with a crew cut that wasn't even. The back was all messed up. So uneven that at first Alamaeda thought it to be deliberate. But no. Just a home cut. Maybe self-inflicted. She hoped it was self-inflicted. Either that or whoever had cut it for him was a sadist. The smurf wore baggy clothes, so oversized he could have been advertising a miracle diet. All he needed to do was smile and hold out his waistband and he could be on billboards everywhere.

Smurfs were always easy to spot because they were nervous. Their task was easy and the risks were non-existent, but they still sweated. Their fingers couldn't stop moving. Their heads never stayed still. They were nervous because they were new. They got the job in the first place because they were new. No one with even the remotest amount of experience or competence would have been given so lowly a task. If they didn't screw up after a dozen or so runs, maybe they would get to do something a little riskier, a little more profitable. Some of the most dangerous sicarios she had taken down had started their careers as smurfs. Some of the most fearless murderers had begun as scared smurfs wiping sweat off their brows as they entered the bank for the first time.

She just watched. There was nothing to be gained by getting him busted. Even if he talked, which was unlikely, he wouldn't know anything. He would willingly sit silent through the interrogation and land himself jail time he could have avoided in order to make doubly sure the cartel knew he hadn't given anything up. If they couldn't get to you in prison – and they usually could – they would get your family. Everyone had a mother or sister or grandfather. Everyone had someone to lose.

So, Alamaeda watched. The smurf would have a nice roll of cash on him. Seven or eight thousand. Below the limit. Below the radar. He would get a hundred bucks for taking all the, albeit minimal, risks. There was probably a sob story to justify this, and Alamaeda had sympathy with those driven to such a life by circumstances outside of their control, but she had no sympathy for what they would become. No circumstances could justify murder. There was never an excuse. She had grown up poor and she hadn't done so much as steal a stick of gum. Did they still make gum in sticks?

The smurf worked for a guy who got orders from a guy who answered directly to one Miguel Diaz, who was the latest verified addition to Alamaeda's rogues' gallery. Diaz was young for a top player, but he was experienced. He had been a courier for the cartel since age twelve, and now had almost two decades of experience that had begun ferrying handwritten orders on his pushbike, advancing rung by rung up the ladder to organising and handling the transportation of huge sums of cash south – namely from Mexican cartels who bought produce from Maria's half of the Salvatierra cartel – back to his masters. An estimated 80 per cent of drug profits never left the United States, and of the 20 per cent that crossed international borders most of it did so digitally through a number of sophisticated money-laundering schemes. The remaining few per cent came back in hard currency, which posed a huge logistical problem for the cartel. Few people knew when and how these shipments would enter the country, such was the threat posed not only by the authorities and rival cartels, but also greedy sicarios who might forget where their loyalties lay.

Cash was a cartel's life blood, which made Alamaeda think of herself as a vampire. It was her job to bleed them dry.

As both accountant and money launderer, Diaz knew where the money was buried. Sometimes literally. Most cartels had a pyramidal hierarchical structure, and the money laundering part had its own such pyramid inside the greater structure. At the bottom were those who deposited cash into legitimate banks in small enough amounts not to attract attention. Higher up, and fewer in number, were those who found ingenious, and sometimes far from genius, ways to hide the physical cash. Sometimes it was sewn into mattresses or stuffed into the pipes of machinery; other times it was buried in sacks of coffee beans. And often it was simply packed into the load bed of a truck and driven along the roads with little more than a tarpaulin to hide it from those who might interrupt its passage.

A mid-ranking trafficker had been picked up on possession

charges and had given up Diaz's name to avoid prison time, confirming the information Gabriel Hernandez had supplied Alamaeda with as part of his negotiations for protection. Low-level cartel players were not prone to roll over – the fear of reprisals on them or their families was too great – but this particular trafficker had a diabetic son and couldn't leave his wife and the kid to fend for themselves. The trafficker knew the name Diaz and so Alamaeda could add another photograph to the spider web of red string that linked the cartel members together on the whiteboard she and Wickliffe had pieced together in their sectioned-off part of police headquarters.

The local cops didn't like their presence, and Alamaeda didn't blame them. She got in the way of their bribes. She cost them money just by being nearby. They weren't all corrupt, but she worked on that assumption. The first one she encountered had tried to make her pay an on-the-spot fine for a non-existent traffic violation. The detectives working on the same floor were polite and decent but didn't go out of their way to make her feel any more unwelcome than she already felt. She didn't tell them that she didn't have to be here, she didn't have to help. She could be working a nice Stateside post instead. She chose to be here. She wanted to do something tangible, to stop the poison before it did the damage, not pick up the pieces after the damage had been done. She'd tried that as a kid and it hadn't worked. She knew, at a Freudian level, she was still trying to save her mom.

Wickliffe was less of an idealist, Alamaeda knew. Wickliffe wanted the action. She liked the danger. She had spent near enough two decades as a prosecutor before deciding it would be more satisfying to hunt the bad guys down instead of putting them away. Most agents went their whole careers without drawing their piece with the intention of using it, let alone firing it. Down here in cartel country Alamaeda had lost count of the number of times she had drawn, and every time she had been expecting to use it. She hadn't shot anyone, but she knew it was only a matter of time. Across the border in Honduras was where things got really crazy, but Guatemala was pretty close. Wickliffe lived for the adrenaline and she got her money's worth in Guat chasing the Devil Sisters.

The Salvatierras had always played the long game. Whereas Mexican cartels used violence to exert power, the Salvatierras developed mutually beneficial relationships. They kept everyone happy and everyone rich, whether they were suppliers, traffickers or locals. Loyalty obtained through fear only went so far and was easily usurped by the fear of greater violence, because the brutality of the cartels was ever evolving. While loyalty obtained through generosity was no less susceptible to being usurped, in Guat there was no one wealthier. An alliance was a safer bond than those applied from master to servant. Such alliances were numerous and intricate, stretching back and forth geographically and politically across the country. The more individuals and factions involved, the more everyone had to lose if the Salvatierra cartel fell. It was in everyone's interest to protect it. With such a history of largesse, Heloise and Maria were not as rich as they might have been, but they were stable, and their only fear was of the other.

The drug trade was a cash business, and however efficient the process of washing the cash, there was a backlog years' long. A billion dollars in hundreds would take up shipping containers' worth of space. It had to be stored, safe and hidden, but it had to be accessible too. A cartel had to be liquid in all senses. Sicarios were paid in cash. Bribes were paid in cash. Both had to be paid on time, every time, or the whole machine would begin to break down. That was Alamaeda's primary goal: interrupt the cash flow and watch with a smile as the whole sandcastle began to wash away in the unstoppable tide of discontent.

A fine strategy, but the problems were many. She found a million here, a million there. In small bills, a million in cash looked like a huge score, but such losses were insignificant to a multi-billion-dollar business. She had to pose for photos with smiling cops, pretending to be delighted, pretending it mattered. Her biggest bust was north of three million and the photograph of it made the front pages. It was a big deal. National news. Her phone didn't stop ringing. It was the early days of her time in the Guat and she was as pleased as anyone about her success. She even felt proud. Then, the next day, she received a buff envelope containing a memory stick. On the memory stick was a video file. The video showed masked cartel guys pouring gasoline on a huge pile of cash and setting fire to it. Three million up in smoke just to make a point. She didn't show the video to anyone else. After that, Alamaeda wasn't so enamoured with posing for photos. She went out and bought herself a comfortable chair. She was here for the long haul.

Later, she realised they wouldn't have sent the video if she hadn't made an impact on them. They had sent it as a show of strength. If they had really been that strong they wouldn't have felt the need to prove it. Three million might not make a dent, but one day it would be twenty, and then a hundred.

That's why they sent the video. They were afraid she was going to get there.

Swung enough times, even the smallest axe could fell the largest tree.

FORTY-FOUR

For a moment, Victor just looked at the sea. His gaze tracked the incoming swells all the way to the beach. The water was black now, even if the stars had yet to appear. The crests of the waves were still white, however, and the sound of them lapping on the sand was still divine. He longed to lie on a beach in another place in another time, just listening to that sound, nothing to do but that all day long; not looking out for beachgoers in clothes; not thinking about sniping lines; not considering how far it was to cover; not keeping a weapon within reach at all times. What did lazy even feel like?

He spent too long in the distraction, he knew. Introspection was a bad idea at the best of times, and worse while corpses cooled nearby. He consoled himself with the thought that if a beautiful beach in the twilight couldn't conjure up some semblance of humanity from him, nothing could.

The sea breeze made him aware of the perspiration on his face. The guerrilla beneath his heel was still, at last. From first shot to final kill, the whole thing had been over in less than two minutes, but there was no better workout than a fight to the death. Not exactly the definition of High-Intensity Interval Training, but better.

He used the coarse fabric of his trousers to brush the wet sand from his palm. Blood stained his fingers pink.

He was miles from anywhere. Victor had last seen any sign of civilisation an hour's drive along the coast. It was why they had agreed on the location – for him to make a trade without prying eyes, and for Jairo and his Marxist pals to rob and kill him without witnesses. Different goals that happened to align.

He had some jerky left, he realised. The packet had remained in a pocket throughout the gunfight. He took that as a sign he was meant to finish it. He wasn't hungry – combat was never good for the appetite – but he chewed a few more strips. He didn't like to waste food.

It was a cool night, almost cloudless, and the heat of the day seemed a long time gone, but dragging, lifting and carrying corpses was hard work. Even for Victor, a dead body was not easy to manipulate with so many joints and slack muscles. The weight was unevenly distributed. The person was uncompliant from beyond the grave in some last act of vengeance. Victor had plenty of experience to offset a corpse's innate reluctance to comply, but it still took a physical toll. None of those that had been the aspiring Army of the Poor had been big, thankfully. Well-fed enemies were even less compliant.

The feral dogs had returned now the gunfire had stopped. Victor couldn't see them, but he heard them. They stayed just out of sight, in the darkness, watching him. On occasions while he worked he glimpsed saucers of moonlight staring out from the night around him, each time a little larger than the last as the dogs grew closer, braver. They could smell the blood on the sand.

The breeze from across the Caribbean Sea rustled the long dune grasses, and toyed with Victor's hair when he lifted off his cap to swipe away sweat. He collected the bodies and tossed them into the load bed of Jairo's truck, one by one. Their weapons followed, and then the AX50. He was disappointed to have to destroy it, but when the remains of the guerrillas were found – and they would be, sooner or later – maybe the investigators would discover they had been in the business of bogus arms sales, and that they had arranged to sell a rifle to a foreigner. Victor didn't want anyone asking about the rifle or buyer, nor paying attention when a cartel boss was assassinated using such a gun. He would have to wait for the shipment from South Africa, and hope no similar scam was being organised.

He siphoned off diesel from the fuel tank and spread some over the bodies and soaked a rag torn from the fatigues worn by one of the corpses. He shoved it inside the fuel inlet. Diesel didn't catch light with ease, but a burning piece of cloth should do the trick. He didn't have time to do much more. However isolated this place, the sound of gunshots travelled far, and however common such sounds might be in Guatemala, they could bring him trouble if he was not expedient in his departure.

A dog lapped at the pool of blood on the sand where the guerrilla commander had died. It ran off as Victor neared, whiskers glistening.

He went for Jairo last, surprised to find the seller still alive despite the wound to his face. Unlike the guerrilla who had survived two to the chest, Jairo was in no state to try anything.

A bullet in the face did that. The wound reminded Victor of one he had seen before in London. Jairo looked worse than that man had, though. He was pale and his breathing was shallow. The wound was neat and the bullet had missed his brain and spine, but caused significant damage elsewhere. Jairo was swallowing a lot and coughing, so Victor expected a major blood vessel had been nicked somewhere inside of his skull. The blood was draining down Jairo's throat.

When he failed to swallow fast enough, it entered his lungs, and he had to cough it back up. His teeth were stained and his lips were coated. The stubble around them was dark with it.

'Who made the deal?' Victor asked.

Jairo heard, and seemed to understand, but he didn't answer. His breathing was raspy and strained.

Victor continued: 'A German woman arranged it from my end, but who was at yours? You didn't have contact with her directly, so who acted as the go-between?'

He stepped away as Jairo vomited up a stomach's worth of blood and acid over himself. The smell was awful.

'I won't pretend that I can save you any more than I'd pretend that I would,' Victor said, 'but if you tell me what I want to know, I'll put you out of your misery. You won't have to drown in your own blood.'

Jairo's lips moved, but no sound was coming out. He managed to smile. Some last act of bravery or defiance.

'Your choice.'

Victor scattered the rest of the jerky on the beach for the feral dogs, then lifted Jairo off the ground and carried him to the back of the pickup.

FORTY-FIVE

It was a disgusting thing. There was no other word for it. Lavandier hated everything about the casino, from the repulsive façade to the trashy interior. A monstrosity by any definition, but Heloise's baby. The drugs trade was eternal, Lavandier knew, because existence was too cruel and joyless for people to get through it without the aid of intoxication, but traffickers had poor career prospects. Even the richest and most powerful cartel bosses ended up in prison or in the ground. No one retired. No one ever lived the good life. At best, they hid themselves away in luxury prisons of their own design, going insane in a hell of their own making.

Heloise knew this too, and she feared decriminalisation. She believed it was inevitable. It was already happening with marijuana. How long before cocaine received the same treatment? The Central American cartels existed on the fragility of the needs of the South American producers. For all Heloise's wealth, for all her cruelty and her influence, she was a courier.

If – when – the time came, she was never going to be able to compete with FedEx.

So, legitimate business was the future she wanted. But, of course, a legitimate business that was ripe for exploitation by criminality.

Hence, the monstrosity. She had poured a huge amount of her own wealth into building the casino in – funnily enough – a monumental gamble that might very well not pay off. Guatemala City was no Las Vegas or Macau, but that's what Heloise dreamed it could become. The start of that dream coming to fruition was the casino itself with almost one hundred thousand square feet of gaming space, along with a thousand-bedroom hotel. Two years of planning and another two of construction and it was built, it was ready to open, but Heloise was not allowed to open it.

She, or rather the shell company, had been given planning permission and the figurehead Heloise had chosen to run the casino had won a gaming licence ... but then lost his life to Maria's sicarios. Her sister, naturally, wasn't going to let Heloise's ambitions go unchallenged.

Then, the problems started. Government officials got scared. Questions were asked. Bribes began losing their effectiveness. Heloise's replacement was refused a licence. There was too much attention, too much negative press for the mayoral office to allow the casino to open when everyone knew who was behind it.

It'll take time, their man on the inside had said, *but you need to keep a low profile.*

It was easy to acquiesce to this request – Heloise had the autonomy to make sure the entire cartel rein in the operations and put a halt to violence – but weakness in the face of an aggressor only caused more aggression. Maria was emboldened by Heloise's passivity, which had led to the attack a few weeks ago that convinced her to hire the Wraith and the Russian.

The casino had been sitting empty and unused for months. At current estimates, it might be several years before a licence was granted. They were haemorrhaging money, exacerbated by the deliberate slowdown in trafficking. Lavandier worried. Sometimes he couldn't sleep. He didn't enjoy the feeling of weakness. Like everyone else who had risen to the upper echelons of a cartel, he did so out of a craving for wealth and power. Now, he wondered if that wealth would last, and any power seemed but temporary.

Such a situation could not endure.

Five short years ago there had been nothing but dead, empty space. Passengers in airliners circling overhead would have seen featureless scrubland beyond the airport's borders. Then, the construction – hundreds of men and thousands of tons of materials, monstrous cranes and endless noise. The noise had been the worst part. Heloise visited the construction site on a regular basis, so Lavandier did so too. He hated it. Builders looked at him with more disdain than sicarios. They sneered at his ear defenders and his pristine white coat – worn to protect his finery from dust and oil – and made jokes they thought he couldn't hear.

Each and every day for forty-seven months the site had been a buzz of activity. Now, with the casino built, it was dead space again. It was quieter than it had ever been. The resort had been constructed to insulate the guests from the nearby airport. Heloise wanted the casino to feel like a palace, but every day it felt a little more like a cage.

Fortunate then he didn't have to walk through much of it as there was a private entrance designed for Heloise's personal use and that of her entourage, and a private elevator to take her straight up to her suite. Heloise wanted a helicopter pad on the roof, but that had to come at a later point now construction had paused. After the licence had been granted, after the parking garage was finished, after the casino was generating profit. To Lavandier, the ride felt as if he were going not up, but down, deep into the earth. He was feeling a little lightheaded when he stepped out.

El Perro – the faithful guard dog – was waiting when the doors opened. He didn't need to, because there were cameras in the elevator car, just as there were cameras everywhere. El Perro didn't trust technology. He trusted only his own eyes.

'Would you like to frisk me too?' Lavandier baited.

El Perro shook his head – which seemed an impossibility when he had no discernible neck. 'You'd enjoy it too much.'

Lavandier smiled at him. *'Pas autant que j'apprécierais une nuit avec ta fille. Elle a presque dix-sept ans, oui?'*

El Perro didn't speak a word of French, so could only stare in response.

Lavandier added: *'Je serai sûr de lui envoyer une carte d'anniversaire.'*

Lavandier knew little of El Perro's history, but he knew he had seen combat many times, and had even fought in proxy wars for the CIA. The Kaibiles had a fearsome reputation, and a ruthless history dating back to the seventies. He had been part of peacekeeping forces for the UN in the Congo. He had been as ferocious, resourceful and fearless as any of his comrades, and had put those qualities to profitable use under Heloise's leadership. He was at the forefront of any

271

assault on her enemies, and took great delight in executing any sicarios who showed fear. Lavandier hated him because he was terrified of him. Heloise was the patron, of course, and the ultimate judge of Lavandier's fate; so as long as he did well there was nothing to fear from her head of security.

El Perro hated Lavandier as much as Lavandier hated him, because the Frenchman had Heloise's ear. He was the one who spent most time in her company, who sat across from her at dinner, who rode in the back of the limousine. El Perro wanted that. He wanted Heloise's undivided attention, and saw Lavandier as a rival to that. He never tried to hide that aversion, and seemed to revel in it whenever chance allowed.

Heloise waited with her back to Lavandier. She stood before a huge floor-to-ceiling window that ran almost the length of the suite, providing a panoramic view of Guatemala City. In the dying light, the city could almost be considered pretty against the backdrop of distant mountains. But only if Lavandier was in a generous mood, which was rare.

The window was treated, of course, so it was one way. Heloise valued her privacy. The view was partially interrupted by the unfinished parking garage built to accommodate the many guests they hoped to receive, but without the guarantee of a gaming licence, creditors could not be convinced to part with any more money. So, it was a shell of a building, surrounded by cranes and materials. Heloise hated to look at it, to have a constant reminder of her failures, of her lack of omnipotence. She hadn't named her home the Goddess Suite for nothing.

It was both her abode and her base of operations. She had inherited much property from her father, and while Maria had always loved the countryside, Heloise preferred the city.

Lavandier still wasn't sure if she had moved into the casino in an attempt to justify its existence.

The Frenchman considered gambling a questionable pursuit of one's time and money. Drugs he could understand. There was a tangible product – or was it a service? – that market values determined the price of, and consumers determined the value of. Gambling was a different animal. Money was spent in the hope of generating more money. An investment then, but one with poor returns. Lavandier didn't gamble and didn't use drugs. He spent his money on a different kind of product – or was it also a service? – and he was a happy consumer. He saw many people leave other casinos in a rage, or bereft, and rare was it to see anyone leaving with a smile.

Of course, this casino would be more than a casino. It would also be a front through which to wash large amounts of cash. The funny thing was that by his estimates the casino would be more profitable than the drug trade. Many legitimate businesses were. Running a casino was a good business model with guaranteed returns – the odds never lied – and no dealers were tortured to death, no cards were confiscated in police raids, no chips hijacked on their way to the table.

Once this casino was up and running, Heloise planned to buy up others throughout Central and South America, to slowly move her illicit monies into legitimacy. More profits for less risk, but that wasn't all it was about. He understood the real draw of running a cartel. It wasn't about wealth. It wasn't even about power. It was about nobility. For every drug-lord billionaire there were twenty who started tech firms, owned oil companies, or mastered the stock exchange. For every cartel boss who had a private army there were generals in charge of real soldiers. The drug lord, however, ascended both and became an aristocrat. They ruled fief-doms. They created their own laws. They were adored by their subjects. They harkened back to an earlier time.

In a continent without royalty, Heloise had become a queen. She may have inherited her father's empire, but she would have taken it eventually. He had died young and unexpectedly, but better that than by his daughter's hand.

Once, Lavandier had believed he understood his employer, but he wondered now if that had ever been the case. Maybe it had all been an illusion. This whole time he had been duped – not by any conscious deception on Heloise's part; that would be forgivable. No, he had deceived himself. He had seen only what he had wanted to see. He had underestimated his mistress.

She smiled at him, as she always did. 'Take a seat, Luis. Tell me how things are progressing. Make me happy.'

Lavandier smiled back, and although he was advisor to a queen, he was beginning to understand that in reality he was little more than a court jester.

FORTY-SIX

Victor was used to setbacks. No job was without difficulty, and even simple jobs could spiral out of control. He had accepted there were some aspects of his work he had no power over. The shakedown with the AX50 was just one in a long list of treacherous acts of which he had been on the receiving end. He never took such incidents personally. It was problematic to have no rifle, but the foresight to order both that Georg could arrange would pay dividends now. He had to wait, which was far from ideal, but he could make use of the time it would take for the gun to cross the Atlantic.

He still had two different methodologies in process. Though his primary plan of fulfilling the contract was to shoot Maria at long range, he was not wedded to the idea. If either of the two secondary methods proved to be better options, or could be implemented sooner, he wouldn't wait for the AX50 from South Africa. It was always good policy to have options in Victor's business, as was the willingness to improvise should an unexpected opportunity present itself.

While he was working towards such an opportunity, he had to deal with what had happened on the border with Honduras. Unlike his run-in with the private security guys, this had the potential to upset the careful balance of Victor's wider world. He preferred not to kill anyone he was not paid to kill, because doing so always had consequences. Such consequences might come into effect immediately, or later down the line. He liked to head them off when he could.

He waited until he was back in Guatemala City before making the call. He found a payphone next to a sign advertising jumbo burgers, which seemed as close to a personal invitation as Victor had ever had. He paused at the kerb to let a tuk-tuk roll by, powered by a stick-thin man sheening with perspiration. Two heavy tourists used their phones to take photographs from the back.

A young couple were outside the fast-food outlet, smoking cigarettes. The girl was upset. She wanted comforting, but repelled any attempts from the boy to offer comfort, and he didn't know how to handle it. Victor sympathised. He wouldn't know what to do either.

He used his knuckle to dial and waited until a voice answered and said, 'Who's calling?'

'The man she told you to never keep waiting.'

There was no response but Victor didn't have to wait long before the phone was passed to her. Her crew caught on fast.

So did Georg. She knew he wouldn't call unless something was wrong.

She said, 'What happened?'

'It was a set-up.'

Georg was silent for a brief moment, then responded

with a heavy sigh. 'I'm so sorry. I ... You must believe me when I say—'

'Don't waste your breath,' Victor interrupted. 'You don't need to convince me of anything. I know you didn't have a hand in it. You wouldn't take the risk, whatever the benefit. The seller just wanted the money without having to give up the rifle. They had no idea who they were dealing with.'

'Silly them. I did pass on to my contact that you were a serious player who wouldn't stand for any nonsense.'

'Your words fell on deaf ears it seems, else the message was lost in translation. Anyway, the why doesn't matter to me. I'm telling you this as a courtesy. Whoever your Central American intermediary is, is bogus.'

'Just because the seller wasn't playing by the rules, it doesn't mean that my contact is similarly duplicitous.'

'That's where you're wrong,' Victor said. 'The seller had done this kind of thing before. Four times, he told me. I was supposed to be the fifth victim. That's too many for your contact not to know the seller can't be trusted. If you've made arrangements through him prior to this one, then you may have lost those customers. There may even be fallout heading your way if those customers had friends and don't know you like I do.'

There was silence on the line as Georg thought about this. The young couple started shouting at one another.

'What's that noise?' Georg asked.

'True love in action.'

She sighed again. 'I'll make some calls and check, because you're not the first person who needed munitions in that part of the world. If you're right and my contact has indeed been setting up my customers, I'll need to take action. In fact, if he is proved traitorous, then you can have the job.'

'You can't afford me,' Victor said.

Even if she could, there was too much of a connection between himself and the target to accept any such contract.

'As you wish,' she replied, neither displeased nor offended. 'I'll find somebody else, should I need to. And thank you for letting me know about this situation. Although, you're not exactly one to share, are you? I have to say I'm intrigued as to why you're taking the time to keep me informed at all. You've never struck me as a humanitarian. Even when you saved my life it came with a price tag.'

'Then you really shouldn't be surprised that I'm doing you another favour now.'

'Ah,' she breathed. 'I'm in your debt once more.'

'I'm glad you see it like that, because I want to cash in straight away. I want the name of your contact. I want a number. I want to know where he lives. I want to know everything.'

Georg said, 'I don't understand. You said you didn't want the job.'

'It's not a job,' Victor explained. 'It's precaution. If he doesn't know already, he's going to find out very soon that the seller is dead, that his associates are all dead too. Maybe your contact starts to wonder who killed them. Maybe he starts to ask who the buyer is, where he is, what he's doing.'

'I follow you. But I'm afraid I can't pass on that information. If he knew nothing of the true nature of the deal, I can't let you kill him. I'm in the relationship business and it's not a good way to stay in business to give up my contacts without a fair trial.'

'He'll get to make his case. If he knew nothing, then I have no need to kill him. If he knew, then it will only strengthen your future bargaining power. Don't mess with Georg, they'll say.'

'They already say that.'

'Do I need to remind you that people connected to him tried to kill me because of a weapon you arranged for me to buy? Or do you not care about the business of our relationship?'

'I care very much,' she said after a pause. 'And yes, you're right. I understand why you need to do this. You can have his name. It's Vinny Arturo. He'll be easy enough to find. He works out of Panama City. He's a lawyer.'

'They're always lawyers.'

'I've never met him in person, but he works for a large firm that does business all over Central and South America. I've helped his clients in Europe. He's done the same for me over there. It's been a good relationship. I hope you're wrong about him. I really do.'

Victor said, 'Don't expect another call from me for a while, but expect it all the same.'

He hung up the payphone and stepped into the night.

FORTY-SEVEN

A trip to Panama City could wait for a few days. He didn't want to lose the previously gained traction with Diaz. A few days on the street, a few questions, and Victor knew a little more about Diaz and his tastes. His yellow Lamborghini had a certain amount of fame. Kids on the street would rush to the kerb when they heard the roar of the exhaust. They would wave as it rushed past. They loved it when Diaz revved the engine. The day he painted smoking doughnuts on the asphalt was legendary. Everyone knew he was cartel. Diaz made no effort to hide it. He revelled in his fame. People talked about him as though he were something of a Robin Hood, always trying to help the needy and downtrodden, although Victor spoke to no one who had ever been recipient of his generosity, nor anyone who knew anyone who had.

The sky was pale blue, burned to almost white as it circled the sun. He walked casually along cobbled walkways that were narrow and winding. Power cables bowed from building to building. Old women leaned out of windows to watch those who walked below and shouted to one another across the street or on the floors above or below when something or someone caught their eye.

Even in the shade it was almost thirty degrees. The light breeze blowing in from the lake fought to cool the sweat on Victor's skin, but only when he walked on the main streets and through the squares and courtyards. The breeze didn't reach down the twisting passageways between tall residential buildings that were barely wide enough for two to walk abreast. Children stopped playing football to beg him for sweets and money. He gave them some gum.

Knowing Diaz played poker every Friday gave Victor plenty of time to familiarise himself with the bar and the locale without the risk of running into the man himself. He wanted to get to know Diaz, but from arm's length. Victor already had a measure of Diaz's personality, but he needed a lot more actionable intelligence if he was going to transform the yellow Lamborghini into a mobile bomb. Given that Diaz played poker once a week in the same private game, those other players could have useful insights that would help further that transformation. Victor had drinks in the bar several times, getting to know the bartenders and sharing anecdotes with the regulars. The freedom to work without time pressure let him integrate himself in a slow, natural way. By the time he started steering conversations towards Diaz, he wanted to do so without arousing suspicion.

It didn't take long to learn that a private poker game was hosted every night of the week.

Even when he had learned enough about Diaz to get time alone with his car, Victor was still going to need to make a bomb. He had once used Georg to acquire explosives, but he wasn't prepared to do so now, not when he was still waiting for the rifle to arrive that Georg had sourced. There was no point distancing himself from his recent past if he kept creating new links to it. Outside of his usual theatre of operations, it would be a challenge, but then nothing about this particular contract had been simple and he didn't expect that to change.

Private poker games were, of course, private, but that didn't mean Victor wouldn't be able to get a seat at the table, especially once he had found out who played. Most were regular players who turned up throughout the week, sometimes every night, depending on money and circumstance. The stakes were high so only individuals known to be wealthy received an invite, and the turnover was low. Most people who had a seat at the table kept hold of it, but on occasion an outsider would join when the numbers were down. Such an opening was impossible to predict, but it was more than possible to ensure one of the regulars didn't show. Victor had taken steps to ensure there would be a seat free at tonight's game.

He had plenty of experience playing cards, and although he preferred blackjack – it was easier to count cards and beat the odds – he enjoyed the skill and gamesmanship of playing against other people instead of a dealer. The dealer had no stake in the game. He or she didn't care if they lost, and even if there was some satisfaction taking money from a casino built to take other people's money, there was nothing like outplaying someone who wanted to win.

Such times were rare, however. Victor didn't socialise beyond the intermittent need for female company. The handful of poker games he had played in adult life had been almost exclusively because of work. Therefore, he always had a role to play. He couldn't win too many hands nor take too much money. People noticed winners. They resented them. Losers were ignored.

But losers with money to burn were not.

Victor made sure he lost. Bar patrons played cards and dominoes and dice games. Victor joined in with a group of guys in their thirties and forties, with a uniform of clipper-short hair and unshaved faces. Their clothing consisted of jeans, T-shirts and sports jackets. Fingertips were stained with nicotine and nails were dirty with oil and grime. One had tattoos on his forearms, visible where his jacket sleeves were pushed up to the elbows. Another had grey hair. The third had fists the size of mallets. All wore heavy boots with steel toecaps. They stank of cigarette smoke – hand-rolled and strong.

He bought them drinks. He made sure they ended the games with more cash in their pockets than when they had begun. By the end of the night people were buying him drinks with his own money.

The country's alcohol laws required bars to close no later than 1 a.m., but that didn't stop the old guy pouring drinks. He gestured to Victor.

'Beer,' he answered and the old guy fetched him a bottle from a chest refrigerator.

The old guy owned the bar, Victor deduced. He was tall and slim, with tanned skin and a buzz of stubble across his head. His clothes were bright and cheap, as were his shoes. He wore sunglasses, even indoors at night. They had gold-coloured frames and sat low on his nose so he could peer over the top. His eyes were small and dark and never stopped moving.

He set the bottle of beer on the bar for Victor, who thanked him and twisted off the cap. Victor took a small sip. It was as delicious as it was cold, but he had ordered beer only because it was easier to control the concentration of alcohol in his bloodstream that way.

He acted ignorant when the high rollers began entering the bar and the old guy ushered them into the back. The last player to show was short and fat and waddled more than walked. He exchanged words with the old guy who ran the bar. Neither man was happy, and two words Victor read on the old guy's lips were of particular relevance.

No show.

The fat guy sighed. *Have you called him?*

He's not answering.

Get a replacement then. I'm feeling lucky.

I think I have just the guy.

Victor made sure he was looking the other way when the two gazes fell upon him.

FORTY-EIGHT

Things went bad pretty fast.

They were playing Texas Hold 'Em. It wasn't Victor's favoured version of poker. He preferred Five-Card Stud. It was older, more classic, a more intimate game of skill and perception, but the former had become more popular in recent years. Texas Hold 'Em had more spectator appeal. Casinos liked it for that reason, as did broadcasters. It had become mainstream as a result.

The back room that hosted the private game had two tables: one for poker, and another for playing pool. He imagined the latter was for use at other times, or perhaps when things around the poker table became a little too heated and players needed to cool off. Even those used to high stakes games were not immune to rushes of frustration and anger.

Unlike the bar, the room was cool. The walls were bare brick and there had been no sweating bodies radiating heat all evening. There were no windows, but it was located close to the bar's kitchen and rear exit and Victor could hear the noise of nearby traffic and the merriment of passers-by.

Victor settled into his chair. He wouldn't have chosen to sit with his back to the door, but all other seats were taken first and asking for the other players to swap would have been counterproductive to his efforts not to draw attention. He was here to gather intelligence only, but the greater threat of the cartel was ever present. He had killed four of their guys, after all.

Everyone drank, so Victor sipped from another bottle of beer he saw opened while he played. He had a high tolerance and there was no immediate danger, but he couldn't afford to lose even a little awareness because of alcohol. There were plenty of corpses out there who might have seen Victor coming if not for the influence of vodka or whisky. For a fleeting moment, he remembered playing his piano while he drank a bottle of Finnish vodka. The last time he had been drunk. He might never be drunk again.

Despite the stakes, the game was played with good humour and a fun atmosphere. No one liked to lose a hand, but there were no reactions more severe than a curse or the throwing of hands into the air. Victor acted as if he was having fun too, even when he lost, which he did often. He folded when he had a bad hand and also when it was too strong. He had to win some to stay in the game, but he could read his opponents' body language well enough to make sure he didn't win too big.

The table was round but the old guy who ran the bar sat at its metaphorical head. The other players treated him with respect, even reverence, and from the friendly, but no-nonsense, way he ran the game, it was easy to see why. Victor liked him too. Not just because his professional sights focused on him as a valuable source of information. If anyone knew Diaz well, it was this guy.

A couple of weeks or so and Victor would have enough to begin the next stage of preparations. What they would be, he didn't yet know, but he needed time alone with the yellow Lamborghini. Enough time to fit a bomb that wouldn't be found, one that could sit within the car's fuselage until Diaz next went to see Maria.

Even a high-stakes poker game wouldn't go on long enough for Victor to have the time he needed. He could fit a bomb in minutes, but not one hidden so well it couldn't be found. He would need all night for that. He would need to be alone, in private, taking the car apart, rebuilding it again. He would need tools. He needed to know where Diaz parked his vehicle overnight, so when Victor had acquired the explosives he could put them to use.

There were so many variables, so many things that could go wrong with such a plan that Victor had to have a complete dossier's worth of information on Diaz before he even attempted that next stage.

Given the run-in with private security Victor had to be extra careful not to arouse suspicion. He had to take his time, to build up a picture of Diaz's personality, habits, movements and routines without ever coming close to Diaz himself until he absolutely had to do so.

The short, fat man roared in triumph as he called the last card and won the hand. The loser wasn't so happy, but Victor joined in congratulating the winner along with the others.

The old guy leaned across the table to ask him, 'Are you having a good time?'

Victor nodded because he *was* having a good time. He was integrating himself well, at a slow, measured pace. Everything was going to plan.

At least, until he heard the familiar rumble of a loud exhaust.

FORTY-NINE

Diaz wasn't tall, but he was stocky. He was strong. He had a wide back and thick wrists. His hair was short and slicked back. He wore jeans and cowboy boots. He hadn't shaved in a while and rubbed at his stubble. He owned a lot of jewellery. He had several rings and several bracelets, all gold. As were many of his teeth, which caught the light when he opened his mouth.

He entered the back room with the arrogant gait of a man who believed he was always welcome, who always had a seat at the table. The atmosphere in the room changed in an instant. There were words and signs of greeting – everyone knew him – but no one was pleased by his unexpected arrival.

Least of all Victor.

He hid it, of course. He acted as if he didn't have a clue who Diaz was, as if he didn't notice the change in atmosphere at the table.

Diaz gestured towards him, 'Who's this?'

'We were a man short,' the old guy explained.

Diaz shrugged. 'Now you're not.'

'It's not Friday.'

Diaz shrugged again. 'I felt like a change.' He then stared at Victor. 'Leave.'

Victor was happy enough to do so. He was glad Diaz didn't want him at the table because Victor didn't want to be there now either. His plan was to learn about Diaz, but to keep clear of him. Playing poker with him was the last thing he wanted to do.

The problem was that no one else wanted Victor to go. They were making too much money.

The old guy spoke for them. 'The game's in progress, Miguel. You're welcome to join us, of course, but our new friend stays.'

Diaz didn't respond. He continued to stare. His eyes were bloodshot and he was sweating. It wasn't a stretch to imagine Diaz enjoyed using his own merchandise.

Victor said, 'I'm happy to make room. I don't want to cause trouble.'

The old guy raised a hand. 'No, you're going nowhere. This is my bar. My rules.' He looked to Diaz. 'What's it going to be? Shall I fetch you another chair?'

Diaz had come to play poker, to blow off steam or win money or both. He wasn't going to turn around and drive away again, so he said, 'Get a chair.'

The old guy left the room to do just that, and while he did so Diaz sat down in the chair the old guy had vacated so that he was directly opposite Victor, and Victor's thoughts turned away from compiling a dossier and preparing a car bomb and towards preventing a bad situation from getting even worse.

The old guy rolled his eyes when he returned with a new

chair only to find Diaz had taken his own. He didn't comment, however. It was his bar, his game, his rules, but he had to keep his patrons happy. Or in the case of a clearly agitated Diaz, calm.

He wasn't calm, though. Whether it was the drugs in his system, his recent woman trouble, a missing crew of private security men, or perhaps not getting his way regarding Victor's presence, Diaz became increasingly volatile as the game failed to go his way.

He didn't like Victor. He hadn't liked him from the start, and liked him less now Diaz wasn't doing so well. He was quiet and sullen and had an unmistakable air of menace about him. This was a man who was quick to anger and didn't like to lose. A dangerous combination.

When he was forced to fold, he left his seat to shoot pool at the nearby table, returning when it was time for another hand to begin. Leaving the table during play was against poker etiquette, but the other players, used to Diaz's temper, allowed him to let off steam to keep things friendly.

Victor, so used to recognising the signs of escalating danger, knew potting a few balls would not be enough to calm Diaz down. The cartel man needed a win before it turned ugly. Given the cards were not on Diaz's side, he was going to create his much-needed win another way. Victor saw it coming, but not soon enough to do anything about it.

'He's cheating,' Diaz said when Victor won a hand.

He had three of a kind – Jacks – which had been called by a man with two Aces.

The quick-fire banter halted. All gazes fell on Diaz, who stared at Victor with unblinking eyes.

'He's cheating,' Diaz said again.

Victor hadn't been. He had played with a single Jack, only for another to be revealed on the flop, and then the third with the final card. He had lost three or four hands in a row before.

The old guy who owned the bar said, 'What do you mean, cheating?'

'He had a card up his sleeve. One of those Jacks, obviously.'

The old guy shook his head. 'Don't be stupid. We'd have seen it.'

Diaz was still staring at Victor. 'Not if he's good.'

Victor remained silent.

The owner looked at him. 'Do you mind rolling up your sleeves?'

His expression and tone was apologetic. He didn't want to humour Diaz, but he knew he had to.

'Sure,' Victor said, and did as asked.

'Look,' the guy said, gesturing. 'No cards.'

'Check the deck,' Diaz said. 'There'll be five Jacks.'

Victor's gaze said: *I know what you've done.*

Diaz's gaze said: *Good.*

The owner gave Victor the same apologetic look once more and started collecting up the cards. He slid them across the table from where people had folded or already made half-hearted attempts to slide them over.

Victor's gaze stayed on Diaz. Diaz's gaze stayed on Victor.

The old guy pushed all the cards together into one deck and began sorting through them, laying first one Jack on to the table, then the second. Then the third and the fourth.

Then a fifth Jack followed.

Diaz wasn't watching, but he smiled when he heard the gasps and tuts.

Victor nodded at him. It was a good scam, a good trick.

Good vengeance. Diaz didn't like to lose, so he cheated. He kept a spare Jack on him to palm into hand. Not an Ace or even a King. People paid attention to those cards. Most players would play a hand with just a single of either, but a Jack? Not for experienced players. Not guys like these. Victor knew Diaz had slipped it on to the table moments after Victor had showed his triple, when everyone's attention was diverted. Diaz had superb sleight-of-hand skills because even Victor hadn't seen it, and there wasn't a lot he didn't notice.

'This is not good,' the old guy said, peering over the gold rims of his glasses.

Victor said, 'I know.'

'It's about as far from good as it gets.'

Victor took his gaze from Diaz because the men at the table were as tense as they were angry. They were silent, but they didn't need to speak to communicate. They were sprinters at the gate, but they were waiting for guidance, for authorisation. Diaz was the cartel guy, the dangerous one, but it was the old guy who commanded their respect. They were waiting for his decision.

He said to Victor, 'Put your palms on the table.'

Victor had to perform no evaluation of the situation because he had done so already. He did so almost without thinking. Within moments of entering any room he had memorised the layout; he knew where every improvised weapon lay, where every obstacle was located; he knew who to take out first, who was strongest, who was carrying a weapon. He had that data in his mind, continually updated as circumstances changed. He accessed that information now, putting together a plan of action.

He placed his palms on the table.

The old guy motioned for one of the players to stand up, who was quick to obey. 'Hold him down.'

Two strong hands gripped Victor's wrists. He noted that the guy holding him needed no detailed instruction. *Hold him down* could be interpreted a lot of ways, but clarification wasn't necessary because they had done this before.

The old guy's mouth opened, but before he could speak, Diaz said, 'I'll do it.'

Diaz stood and circled the table. He took his time, because he was enjoying himself. He wanted to savour every triumphant moment.

'We have this rule,' the old guy said, 'to deal with cheaters, and to discourage would-be cheaters.'

Diaz said, 'We break their hands.'

Victor looked up at him. 'I worked that part out for myself.'

The old guy took one of the pool cues to hand to Diaz, but he shook his head and pushed the cue away. Instead, he took out his gun.

It was a six-shooter, a revolver. A snub-nosed .45. A heavy piece of metal, good for breaking the small bones of a hand. The weapon was polished and had an ivory grip. Victor had never been a fan of revolvers. Reliability was excellent – they almost never misfired – but reloading burned time and they couldn't be suppressed. The way Diaz held the gun said he had a fondness for it. It was a prized possession.

The old guy said, 'It's not personal, but it's the way we do things. We're not good people here, but we have rules. This table is our church. This game is our worship. It has to be respected.'

Victor said, 'I understand.'

The guy holding Victor was standing to his right. Diaz was

to Victor's left. The table was in front of him. Boxed in, there was nowhere to go. He kept his arms loose to give the impression of passivity to the guy holding him down, but the grip on Victor's wrists remained strong. The pressure pinning his hands down didn't relent. The guy wasn't going to be fooled into lessening the hold.

Diaz said, 'It's not personal,' because it was personal.

He adjusted his hold on the gun so he had it braced in his palm. The barrel was too short to hold it like a hammer. Diaz placed his left palm on the table next to Victor's hands to both brace and help his aim. The guy holding Victor's wrists down strengthened his grip and pushed down harder to compensate for the inevitable reaction.

Diaz wouldn't go for the fingers. The back of Victor's hand made the natural target. Five metacarpals for five fingers, covered with skin. A little muscle, some blood vessels. The gun was big enough and heavy enough to hit four of the five metacarpals at once. The first metacarpal that led to the thumb would be spared in all likelihood but the bones that were struck would be crushed. If Diaz aimed more for the knuckles, the phalanges could be broken too. If he aimed more towards the wrist the carpals might also break.

In either case, surgery would be needed to put all the pieces back together, and months of recovery, maybe irreparable nerve damage and permanent loss of strength and dexterity. Not fatal, because the major blood vessels wouldn't be severed by blunt force trauma, although there would be significant internal bleeding. A person so damaged could play poker again eventually, but such injuries would be catastrophic for Victor. Even if he survived so long a period of vulnerability while his hands healed, he would never be the same again.

He would lose his fitness during that time. He would lose his strength. His skills would erode without practice. And then, after the bones had all healed, it might not be over. He might struggle to hold a gun steady or squeeze a trigger. He could fail to maintain a choke hold.

It would be a death sentence.

Diaz raised his right hand, and the gun within it, high above his head.

At that moment, every pair of eyes was focused on Victor's hands.

Except Victor's own.

FIFTY

Victor's gaze was locked on Diaz's right hand and the gun gripped by it, as it rose up from waist level, past Diaz's chest and shoulder until it paused high above the man's head.

The moment Diaz tensed – an instant before the hand began coming back down to strike Victor's hand – Victor kicked out with both feet, hitting the table's central support and propelling it away.

The table couldn't move far – there were people sitting in the way – but it didn't need to move far to slide out from beneath Victor's palms.

Without the table to resist the downward force, the guy gripping Victor's wrists fell forward, over Victor's legs and into the path of the gun in Diaz's hand.

The heavy revolver struck the man on the back of his head before Diaz could pull the blow, before he could react, before anyone could react. The guy fell into the table, scattering cards and chips. He wasn't knocked out, but he was concussed. He wouldn't be able to cause Victor any trouble.

The other players were slow because it was a lot to process. One second they had been eager spectators, the next their brains were rushing to catch up with what was happening. They had to understand before they knew how to respond.

Diaz understood. He was the cartel man. He had witnessed violence before. He had been in life-and-death situations. He was the only one not stunned into inaction, but he had struck the wrong target and he had lost balance when the table he was bracing against went out from under him.

Victor was out of the chair and going for the gun before Diaz was ready to fight back.

He was strong though, and not easy to disarm. An elbow to the face reduced his resistance and focused his mind on warding off further blows, not keeping hold of the gun. Victor knocked it from his hand and it skidded across the floorboards.

Diaz was strong and he was tough, but though he could fight, he had no idea how to defend against someone like Victor. He covered up, trying to block the incoming strikes, but when knees joined the assault – swift, savage attacks to his abdomen and groin – he collapsed, bloody, winded. Dazed.

Victor spun around to face the others, now rising from their seats, brains caught up and ready to respond; one bent over to scoop up Diaz's dropped revolver.

Two steps took Victor close enough to put a stomp kick into the rising face of the man with Diaz's gun. The nose crushed beneath Victor's heel and the pistol hit the floorboards for the second time. The man doubled over, but Victor resisted capitalising with an upwards knee strike. The knee was one of his preferred weapons, but with the man's position, there was too much chance of hitting him in the mouth. Victor didn't want that. He had learned that lesson a long time ago. It had been no fun prising incisors out of his kneecap.

A player launched himself at Victor from across the poker table. No real threat beyond the size of the incoming human-shaped missile and easy enough to dodge. The man managed to land on his feet, however, so Victor swept his legs out from under him.

Diaz was back on his feet now, holding a knife, so Victor took a pool cue from the nearby table and snapped it across one knee. At full-length it made a great melee weapon: light enough to be fast and nimble, but with one heavy end to create plenty of force. A guaranteed kill-shot to the temple. A decent blow anywhere on the skull could end the fight. But it required two hands to make the most of it. It was a little too long, a little too top-heavy, to wield with one hand with speed and agility, and that's what he most needed against a knife.

The cue had enough reach to outdistance a blade many times over, but good as it was when connecting to the head, anything less than a full-force strike to the rest of the body might not stop an incoming attack. Diaz could take a cue strike to the chest and stay standing.

Unlike the young guy with the slicked hair from the *comedor*, Diaz knew what he was doing. He held his weapon – a polished fighting dagger – well.

So, Victor wanted a weapon in each hand. The heavier end of the cue in his right for striking with, and the lighter end in his offhand for parrying the knife.

Like a pro, Diaz was taking his time. For all his own weapon's advantages, he didn't underestimate Victor's chances. He saw two weapons against one and compensated by switching the knife between hands, from right to left and back again. The message was obvious – Victor wouldn't know which hand the knife would attack from.

That was Diaz's first mistake. He had advertised his intent. He wanted to put Victor off guard. He wanted to intimidate. He failed.

Victor attacked him, going high with one cue and low with the other. Diaz was far too slow, and took both: one to the face, one to the abdomen. He went down harder this time.

A downward strike broke bones in the back of his right hand and he lost the knife.

Victor dropped the cues and scooped the revolver from where it lay and aimed it at Diaz, who had pulled himself up to his knees. He stopped, but this was no paralysis of fear. Diaz wasn't scared, but neither was he stupid. It was only over because Victor had the gun, which Diaz considered a temporary problem.

Victor saw him glance to the others – a silent message to make them understand that too.

'No one has to die here,' Victor said.

There were five of them at point-blank range and six bullets in the revolver, but Victor didn't want a massacre. He didn't want cops investigating the scene. He didn't want the cartel to question who'd killed their man. He didn't want Maria Salvatierra to find out there was a dangerous foreigner in town.

The old guy had his hands up and the two others who weren't injured did the same. The man with the crushed nose was writhing on the floor, his face bright with fresh blood. The one Diaz had clubbed with the revolver was on the floor too, conscious but on his hands and knees with a pool of vomit beneath him. Diaz seemed steady on his knees, despite breathing hard. He had a split lip and a cut beneath his left eye. The broken hand was already swelling, but if the pain bothered him, he didn't show it.

He spat out blood. 'You're dead.'

'Be glad you're alive and let this go,' Victor said.

'Never.'

The old guy said, 'Shut up before you get yourself killed.'

Victor nodded. 'You should listen to him.'

Diaz was silent.

'But you're not going to,' Victor said, 'are you?'

Diaz sneered. Blood made his teeth pink.

'You're going to do whatever it takes to salvage your pride. You're going to hunt me down, aren't you?'

Diaz didn't answer, but he didn't need to answer. Victor could see the relentlessness in his eyes. The thirst for retribution was unmistakable. Even Victor was not above acting out of a need for revenge, but he would never do so for something as insignificant as pride. Diaz wasn't like Victor. He had too much ego to let such an attack go unpunished. However much Victor wanted to avoid tipping off his target to a potential threat or the attention of the police, he wanted a vengeful cartel lieutenant even less.

'Your choice,' Victor said, and put a bullet between Diaz's eyes.

The .45 was a heavy slug with a big charge and blew out the back of Diaz's skull. A storm of bone, brain and blood followed it, plastering the wall behind.

The gun wasn't designed for recoil management and the kick was significant. The two guys on the floor didn't react – they couldn't – and though the old guy and the two others who were standing could, they didn't either. They were hoping that was the end of it.

Victor rotated on the spot, his arm following in a smooth, fast arc, squeezing the trigger twice more to deliver another two headshots, then aiming down to execute the two injured guys on the floor.

The old guy was left alive, but only long enough for Victor to tell him:

'Diaz set me up. He slipped the extra Jack on to the table.'

The old guy was scared, but he was calm, if confused. 'What? Why are you telling me?'

Victor said, 'I wanted you to know I didn't cheat,' and killed him too.

FIFTY-ONE

A petrol station, a *comedor* and a few other buildings surrounded a crossroads. No town, and not even a village. Just a place. It had no significance that Constantin could decipher. He left the bus and strolled along the side of the road. He walked with a slow gait. In part because he exerted himself only when he had to, but also because a man of his dimensions drew attention enough standing still. If he moved with haste, everyone saw him. No one forgot him.

He wore a fedora, made from pale wicker, to keep the sun from his scalp. He never tanned, and burned with little exposure. The colour had been bleached out of him long ago. Fled, perhaps.

A man sitting outside the petrol station gave him a suspicious look, so Constantin knew not to speak to him. Instead, he crossed the street and approached the bar. Inside, he removed the hat and used a handkerchief to blot his brow and the back of his neck. His face shimmered with moisture. Sweat beaded in the crook where his throat met his ribcage.

He approached the counter, removing his jacket and taking the time to fold it into a neat pile that he placed on a stool he had first checked for cleanliness. The bartender watched him the whole time. The patrons did the same.

He had come to expect a lack of air conditioning. He had come to expect heat and humidity. The bar met those expectations. It had large fans on the ceiling turning at such a slow speed that Constantin could not feel even the trace of a draught. The air was dense. It stank. Liquor and sweat fused into an invisible cloud of wretchedness. He didn't try to hide his expression of disgust, of revulsion. He placed bony knuckles beneath his nostrils as a pitiful defence.

If the patrons could smell the cloud they sat in, they made no obvious sign. They seemed happy enough, drinking and eating snacks; laughing and arguing. A transistor radio sat on one end of the bar and provided a distortion of local folk music. Constantin was only aware of the sound as he drew close to it.

'Why play music if none can hear it?' he asked to no one in particular. 'Why bother when everyone talks louder?'

A man, a regular from the relaxed ease with which he sat at the bar, heard him, and said, '*Perdóname?*'

Constantin waved a hand to dismiss further enquiries. He was in no mood to chit-chat. He had never been in such a mood. Should a conversation without purpose have any appeal to him, it would not be here, it would not be now.

'It would not be with you,' he said to the man.

'*Perdóname??*'

'Indeed, sir. Indeed.'

Insects exploded on an electrified lure. They made a pleasant sound to Constantin's ear: half fizzing, half popping.

If only it was as easy to construct his own trap, if only his targets exploded with the same fizz-pop, but then he would be in a perpetual state of boredom. He only took pleasure in killing if it had some intimacy. He wasn't here for the money, after all, but for the experience. For the satisfaction.

Constantin gestured for the bartender to approach. He was a short man, dwarfed by the Czech, and young. A child to Constantin's eye. Only the faintest trace of stubble on smooth cheeks. Constantin smiled at him in an effort to soften his otherwise severe appearance.

'Ruiz?' he asked.

The smile was, at best, of limited effect because the bartender responded with a cautious nod. '*Que está pidiendo?*'

'A man came to see you sometime in the last couple of weeks,' Constantin said, speaking in Spanish. 'A foreigner, like me. He had dark hair. He might have worn a suit. Remember?'

Ruiz shook his head. It was unconvincing, even without the backwards step, the retreat, from his questioner.

Constantin smiled wider. 'I understand. He paid you, or scared you? Which is it? I can do the same. I can pay you more. I can scare you more. Which do you prefer?'

Ruiz was confused. He was too young, too naive to make a wise choice. His eyes, wide and unblinking, showed his fear, but he refused to heed what his soul knew: that it faced true evil.

He stalled. 'You want a drink?'

Constantin rotated his head a fraction to the right, and then a fraction to the left. 'I want you to choose.'

'I don't know who you're talking about.'

Constantin drummed his long, thin fingers on the bar.

His nails were clipped short, but were hard and sharp. They rapped on the wood.

Ruiz said, 'You need to go now.'

Constantin leaned over the bar and glanced down. 'As I thought: you're wearing flip-flops.'

'So?'

'Which means you haven't walked far. You live close by, yes? I don't imagine there are too many dwellings within walking distance.'

Ruiz was confused once more, and he didn't like that confusion. 'Get out.'

Constantin used his handkerchief to wipe his scalp and place the fedora back. He removed his jacket from the stool and draped it over his left forearm that he raised to a right angle. Ruiz watched in silence.

'Thank you for your time.' He tipped his hat to the young man. 'I look forward to our next conversation.'

The street outside was pale under the hot sun. Shadows were harsh and unyielding blackness. Constantin's was long and thin, extending before him in a jagged ripple over the paving stones. He watched it watching him, mocking him.

He was a shadow, chasing a ghost, always close but always a step behind. Early days, and Constantin enjoyed the chase. So little moved him, but what did, moved him greatly. He absorbed the sights and sounds and smells of the land and was repulsed by them all. The inhabitants scattered before him, ants, tiny and insignificant. He would step on them all if time would allow.

It would not, of course, so Constantin was forced to select particular ants with care. He ignored the workers, the peasants, and sought out the soldiers, the knights, to prove his worth, and the queens to grant him satisfaction.

An imperfect system, perhaps, but it was an imperfect world.

Constantin thought of geography. He considered this rambling collection of buildings at the crossroads. A place of no significance, except that it was within one hundred miles of Maria Salvatierra's horse ranch. Surely too far to be of any importance to Constantin's competitor.

He heard a buzz that was not unlike the sound mosquitoes made. Few people would notice it, but Constantin had exceptional hearing. The buzz became a whine and he tilted his large head to the blue sky above and watched a small prop plane on its descent to land.

Ah, he thought.

FIFTY-TWO

Firefighters had tackled the blaze, but not before it had torn through the bar and barbecued the five corpses. Joanna Alamaeda circled them as the crime scene investigators did their thing. She didn't need to be told the fire was deliberate – she could smell the accelerant – and she didn't need to be told that all the men had been shot. Five shell cases were charred but obvious even before the investigators had labelled them.

The detective assigned to the case filled her in on what they knew so far, which wasn't a lot, but they knew one of the corpses belonged to Diaz thanks to his jewellery and gold teeth.

Alamaeda looked down at the blackened remains of Diaz and said, 'Well, that's one sure-fire way of avoiding indictment. No pun intended.'

Wickliffe nodded. 'He was so scared we were getting close to him that he shot himself in the head and then, just for good measure, he followed up with the old self-immolation trick.

He's thorough, I'll give him that. Also: always take credit for a pun, even when unintentional. It's a dying art.'

The detective on scene didn't speak English, so he didn't understand why they were smiling. He was a dour sort. He found nothing funny when bodies were involved. He stepped outside to light a cigarette.

'Five for five,' she said under her breath, getting a closer look at the shell cases.

'All headshots,' Wickliffe added.

She nodded. 'Three between the eyes and two in the back of the skull.'

'Because they were already on the deck.'

Alamaeda nodded again. 'One round left in the .45.' She pointed to where the gun lay.

'I'm surprised he didn't use it to make sure. Seems like a waste otherwise.'

'He didn't need it. Dead is dead.'

'Don't get many cartel hitmen with that level of self-control.'

'I'm not so sure this was in fact a hit.'

'Diaz's corpse says otherwise.'

Alamaeda took a closer look, but watched where she stepped. She had only just got her trouser suit back from the dry cleaner. Her mother would be horrified if she knew. Mama Alamaeda had worked two jobs and still found time to iron the family laundry. She had taught her children to be self-reliant, as well as frugal, and had staunch working-class values. She would think her eldest daughter to be decadent and foolish, if not a snob. Alamaeda sometimes felt a little guilty collecting the clothes, which she eased by getting to know the old husband-and-wife team who ran the joint. She had trouble understanding them and they struggled to understand her, but there was always laughter in this. A nice couple.

The bar stank of burnt wood and burnt flesh. It wasn't a pretty sight, but Alamaeda had seen a lot worse. Cartels could be brutal. They rarely just killed their enemies. There was always a message to send. Alamaeda looked for the message here, but couldn't find one. That was a message in itself, but the kind cartels didn't send.

Wickliffe said, 'Who kills a serious player like Diaz and tries to cover it up?'

'Someone not sending a message.'

'That's a first.'

The call had come through saying a cartel lieutenant had been assassinated in a bar, so Alamaeda had the whole incident played out in her head before she had even arrived. She drove to the location, picturing how sicarios would have burst through the door, emptying their AKs or SMGs, hitting their target and plenty of bystanders in the process. Fast. Loud. Messy.

That wasn't what she found. For a start, she hadn't anticipated a fire. Sicarios didn't hang around after a hit in a public place. They vanished.

Alamaeda walked the scene. Despite the fire damage, despite the bodies, it was contained. Almost neat. There were only five spent shells. She would have expected dozens, sprayed from automatic weapons, as many hitting the walls and floor as intended targets. Instead, not a single miss.

'Pools of melted plastic. They were playing cards.' Alamaeda pointed. 'One, two, three, four, five corpses, and six chairs. Where's the sixth player?'

'Can't say for sure the shooter was playing too.'

'True, but Diaz is unarmed. How many cartel guys don't carry?'

Wickliffe said, 'Are you saying that the sixth player took Diaz's gun and killed everyone in the room?'

'That's what it looks like.'

'But why?'

'Maybe he doesn't like to lose.'

Wickliffe rolled her eyes. She did that a lot, but not enough to irritate Alamaeda more than she could handle. Wickliffe could be a little condescending, a little superior, but she was an all-right partner overall. Alamaeda appreciated her. She had worked with a lot of assholes, so she appreciated it when she got to work with someone she liked. It was also nice to have a partner who never tried it on with her, which was a first.

Wickliffe said, 'Same as that crew?'

'Which crew?'

'That disappeared,' Wickliffe explained. 'Private investiga- tors,' she said, accompanied by air quotation marks. 'Sicarios in suits, you know.'

Alamaeda knew. 'What about them?'

'Strange, isn't it? Why did we never find them dangling from a lamppost?'

'The sisters are keeping their heads down. Heloise wants to get into the casino business. The word's out not to cause trouble. Don't give the gaming committee a reason to deny the licence etcetera.'

Wickliffe shrugged. The kind of shrug that said she agreed, but only to an extent. 'The timing is weird, that's all. First, four guys from the respectable wing of the cartel evaporate into the air, leaving only the faintest scent of violent death, and now Diaz is left extra crispy. We're dealing with a whole new set of rules here. I don't like the idea of the Devil Sisters developing clandestine tactics. I preferred it when they just chainsawed each other and left the pieces on the sidewalk.'

'Give it time,' Alamaeda said. 'This is a mere pretence of civility. It's not in their nature to be subtle. We'll be up to our necks in mayhem before long.'

'Is that a promise?'

'It's not just a promise, but a pinky promise.'

She offered up her left fist, little finger extended, but curled. Wickliffe did the same and they hooked their respective fingers and smiled.

They released fingers and Alamaeda said, 'I don't think this is connected. This bar isn't a cartel hangout for either side. The four other corpses look like nobodies to me. I think this was a game gone wrong. Maybe Diaz lost his temper. Maybe he had too much to drink. He pulls his gun and sticks it in someone's face, someone who isn't drunk, and that someone doesn't like it very much.'

'Then why kill the others?'

'No witnesses.'

'I don't buy it,' Wickliffe said. 'Doesn't stack with the game-gone-wrong theory. If it isn't cartel-related, then why kill the bystanders? Let's say you're right and Diaz pulled his piece and waved it around. Let's say the sixth player takes it off him and teaches him a lesson in poker etiquette. He then decides to slaughter everyone else in the room? No. Too brutal.'

'Diaz was cartel. He didn't want payback.'

'Then he's a ruthless son of a bitch because he makes that decision in a fraction of a second, and still lands another four headshots before anyone can make a break from it. What kind of poker player is he?'

'The kind you don't point a gun at.'

'Someone really should have told that to Diaz.'

'You're so insightful.'

Wickliffe smirked, then stood to approach Diaz's corpse. 'No tears will be shed for you, amigo.'

Alamaeda said, 'Everyone has a mother.'

'Not everyone. Not this guy. This guy bubbled up from some black pit of hell, I assure you. I'll toast his eternal damnation tonight.'

'Let it out,' Alamaeda said. 'Let out all of that hatred.'

'I have no hate for these guys because they aren't human. You can't hate an animal because it doesn't know any better. You kick it so it learns, and if it still doesn't learn you put it down. But you don't hate it. I'm not going to let what animals do anger me because anger is caused by stress and stress is contagious. And it's deadly. Negative energy spreads faster than any virus. You wake up late and you knock someone as you overtake them on the pavement. You didn't mean to but they have a temper and you piss them off and they take it out on the girl at the coffee shop who got up late too and is dead tired and she gets pissed and deliberately burns the coffee of the woman with the baby who was too distracted to say thank you. And that woman with the kid needs that coffee because her newborn is ill and kept her up half the night. But the coffee sucks and she's so tired and stressed and not coping with postpartum depression that her crap cup of coffee is the final straw as she waits for the red light at the crossing. Next, they're scraping up her and that newborn from the asphalt and the guy who drove the bus is never going to be the same again.'

'You wanna hug?' Alamaeda joked. 'You need someone to hold you and tell you everything's going to be all right?'

Wickliffe flipped her the double bird to punctuate the exchange and they both smiled.

'So,' Alamaeda said, 'the killer knew who Diaz was. He knew he was a serious guy. The kind of guy you should be afraid of. He knew there would be repercussions, but he killed him anyway. He killed the others to escape those repercussions. Now, what's bothering me is that this guy knew all about Diaz, but Diaz didn't know about him.'

'He was a new player.'

Alamaeda nodded. 'Exactly. Diaz hadn't known him long enough to know he was dangerous. Now, where it gets especially interesting is that a bartender remembers a foreigner getting friendly with the owner.'

'No kidding.'

'Where it gets even more interesting is when I tell you that the reason this bartender remembers the foreigner is because another foreigner came looking for him only yesterday.'

'And what does it mean?'

'I have no idea, but it's odd, isn't it? Two foreigners, one looking for the other, and then Diaz gets shot. Too much of a coincidence to be a coincidence. Something's going on that doesn't fit the narrative.'

'Screw narrative. Up to anything tonight? Fancy joining me to toast Diaz's eternal damnation, or are you seeing your new man?'

She shook her head. 'He's out of town for a few days, so sure.'

'This is the Canadian, right? He's Caucasian, yeah?'

Alamaeda shot her a look. 'Don't even go there.'

Wickliffe grinned and showed her palms. 'I'm just saying it might be worth checking he doesn't have a gun under his pillow.'

Alamaeda shot her another look. 'Don't make me hurt you.'

'Fine, bury your head in the sand,' Wickliffe said. 'But if this really was a game gone wrong it's nothing to do with us. If cartel guys kill themselves over plastic chips, not only is that a good thing, but it's none of our business. We're done here.'

'But don't you wanna know what happened here? Don't you care why?'

Wickliffe took a moment to think about it, then shook her head. 'I don't care. As far as I'm concerned, whoever killed Diaz has done this country a favour and saved us a ton of work trying to bust him. I'm not paid enough to care why a piece of shit got what he deserved.'

'You're cold,' Alamaeda said.

Wickliffe continued shaking her head. 'No,' she said, pointing at the five charcoaled corpses. '*This* is cold.'

FIFTY-THREE

You either loved Panama City or you didn't know love at all. Vinny Arturo knew this to be true because he felt both, he *knew* both. The city was a chaotic, sprawling mess, but it didn't seem to realise and wouldn't care if it did. It was a parade, a festival, a carnival of human spirit and determination. A celebration of all that was best in life. To live there was to belong there. To belong there was to be part of that celebration.

Arturo celebrated every day. Whether to smile at a pretty girl in a café or to dance a little as he walked, it was impossible not to feel the energy around him and be energised by it in turn.

Panama was the crossroads of the Americas, of South America and North America, of continents and oceans, and Arturo sat in the centre of it all. He belonged at the centre of that crossroads.

A failed state maybe, but only to those who didn't know how to succeed, only to those who embraced the failure.

Where others saw poverty, Arturo saw need. Where others saw corruption, Arturo saw opportunity.

He worked as a partner for a large law firm at the heart of the city with a client list that could be a Rolodex of demons and devils by any other name. Latin America was rich in land, in people and in greed. He was no criminal lawyer, but every one of his clients was a criminal, even if they had never been caught. In fact, some had never been caught because they were the ones who were supposed to hunt the criminals, to sentence the criminals, or to stand before cameras and take credit for it all.

Arturo's job was to keep the criminals happy, to service their needs, to keep them coming back to the firm, to encourage them to bring in more business in the form of recommendations to their criminal friends. Arturo saw himself as a professional friend. He was the handsome man in the sharp suit who a corrupt politician wanted nearby; who a warlord could respect; who a drug trafficker could invite to an orgy. He found it amusing that those who needed lawyers the most were the ones who hated lawyers the most, but that was the key to Arturo's success. He was the one lawyer who could be tolerated.

He liked nice cars and women he didn't have to call the next day. He liked the best restaurants and inserts in his shoes to give him that extra boost. He liked being good at his job and the good life it gave him.

He had a date with Grace – or was it Faith? Either way an inappropriate name for a woman that wicked, and it didn't matter because he called all his encounters *mi dulce* – my sweet – so he didn't need to remember, and to save him using the wrong name. Great to see you again, my sweet ...

the lobster here is the best, my sweet … let's go back to my apartment, my sweet.

Grace or Faith was impressed by his Maserati. She was impressed the manager shook Arturo's hand and gave him the best table in the restaurant. She was impressed by the view from his penthouse. She wasn't so impressed with something else, but Arturo still left the bedroom with a smile on his face, which was all that mattered.

A red silk kimono kept the slight chill from his skin as he stepped outside to his terrace, where an infinity pool glowed beneath the black sky. The water was heated and lights at the bottom of the pool illuminated the wisps of steam rising in gentle swirls. A glorious sight. A perfect night. A perfect life.

Arturo didn't like Scotch – he found it too harsh – but he drank it because that's what men like him were meant to drink. An unwritten rule. He sipped from the tumbler and winced despite the ice cooling and diluting the whisky's burn. He padded alongside the edge of the pool.

To dip or not to dip? It was not a question he had time to answer because he became aware he was not alone on the terrace. The sliding patio door opened behind him, and Grace or Faith stepped out into the night.

Arturo didn't take his gaze from the view. He sipped his Scotch and gazed at the city beneath him. He gazed at the possibilities spread out below, waiting for him, enticing him.

'That was amazing,' he said to Grace or Faith as she approached, to her footsteps.

Which sounded hard on the paving slabs. Heavier than they should.

A man's voice said, 'It didn't sound amazing, I'm sorry to tell you.'

The tumbler hit the ground. Scotch and ice and glass scattered.

Arturo spun around. A man in a dark suit was sliding the patio door shut behind him, but his gaze never left Arturo. He stepped closer, one slow step at a time, and Arturo could do nothing but watch the approach. Arturo had met many dangerous people. He had been scared many times. But never in his own home. Never like this.

'Who ... are ... you?'

'My name is not for you to know.'

The man was tan and dark, but was no Panamanian, no Latino at all. His Spanish was perfect, but had the unmistakable accent of a Catalonian. He walked along the edge of the pool, illuminated by the lights. He looked respectable and reasonable, and utterly terrifying.

'What do you want?'

'I'm here for you, Mr Arturo. I'm here because of what you've done.'

Step by step, the man in the suit grew closer.

'Whatever it is, whatever I've done, I can stop.'

Arturo couldn't move. He wasn't sure he had even blinked.

'Past tense,' the man in the suit said. 'It's too late to stop. You shouldn't have started.'

'You don't know who you're messing with.'

'Do you feel any conviction in those words, Mr Arturo? Because you don't project any.'

Arturo felt no conviction. It was an empty threat. He knew powerful people – dangerous people – but none who could rush to his aid now, and none that cared enough about him to avenge his death. He was a professional friend, after all. He had no true friends.

'Look,' Arturo said, dry-mouthed. 'Whatever they're paying you, I'll double it. Look at my place. Look around, look at my robe. You can see I have money. I'm rich. I'm even richer than you would think I am. I hide most of my wealth in foreign accounts. But I can get you cash. Tonight. It'll take a few hours but we can wait. You're in no hurry. How's fifty thousand dollars sound? You can walk out of here a wealthy man.'

The man was silent.

Arturo thought he was tempted, but not tempted enough, so he doubled the figure. 'One hundred thousand.'

The man in the suit stopped when he was a few metres away. Close enough for Arturo to see his eyes. He had never seen anyone with eyes as black, so empty of humanity.

'An interesting figure,' the man said, 'but nowhere near enough to buy me off. To quote a cliché: I wouldn't get out of bed for one hundred thousand dollars. That doesn't even cover my expenses, which is the reason why I'm here.'

'I don't understand. If I've done something to you, I'm sorry, but I don't know what. Tell me. Let me make it right.'

The man explained. The rifle. Jairo. The revolutionaries. Death. So much death.

'Shit,' Arturo said when he had finished. '*Shit.*'

'Don't swear.'

'I feel like swearing.'

'Trust me when I say I can change your mind.'

Arturo showed his palms. They were damp with sweat and red where his fingers had been pressed into his palms for the last couple of minutes.

'We can make this right,' Arturo said.

Arturo swallowed the moisture – and the terror – from

his mouth, but the latter didn't go down. It stuck in his throat, choking, constricting. He pushed his hair back with his fingers.

He hadn't yet worked out how, but he had to stall. He had to buy time to think of something. Anything.

'How did you find me?'

The man in the suit said, 'You're in the phone book.'

Arturo stared.

The man in the suit said, 'Jairo gave you up.'

Arturo exhaled through his nose. 'The man has no loyalty. He has no backbone.'

'Had,' the man in the suit corrected, and the casual tone cut through Arturo's core.

The man in the suit had no weapons held in hand, but he would be armed. A silenced pistol under his jacket, no doubt. A knife up his sleeve, maybe. Garrotte wire in a trouser pocket, perhaps. Or maybe there were none. Which wasn't any help to Arturo. He was no fighter. He wasn't strong. He wasn't fit. The man could beat him to death and he knew there would be nothing he could do to stop it, except maybe scream. He owned a gun, but that wasn't conveniently tucked under his kimono. It was in a drawer of his bedside table. The same drawer where he kept the condoms, water-based lubricant and little blue pills.

The same drawer that was right next to Grace or Faith. Arturo had no true feelings for her, as he had no feelings for any of the women he brought home, but he found he wasn't heartless. He realised he did care what happened to her.

'You didn't hurt her, did you?'

The man shook his head. 'She's passed out, snoring peacefully.'

'If I scream, she'll wake up.'

'If you start screaming it'll be the last noise either of you ever hears. Is that what you want?'

Arturo shook his head. 'No. I won't scream. If you leave her out of it, I'll make it easy for you.'

'You can't make it difficult for me,' the man said. 'But she never has to know I was here. She can go on sleeping peacefully. She can wake up in the morning, hungover and regretful, but alive.'

Arturo had to ask. He had to. 'What about me? Are you going to kill me?'

'I should.'

'I can pay you. I told you. I'm rich.'

'If you're so wealthy, why are you ripping off individuals buying small arms? Surely that's not a profitable use of your time.'

The stalling was working. Arturo could see a chance out of this. He had the man's interest, he had his attention. Arturo just had to close the deal.

He explained: 'I don't make any money from that. I don't get paid. That's not work for me in the traditional sense. It's like a favour. My job is to help my clients – all sorts of different people – achieve what they want to achieve. That can be as small as making a parking violation go away, or it can be as big as getting an OD'd hooker out of a hotel room before the media find out the guy snorting blow off her tits just happens to be the chief justice.'

'I said no swearing.'

Arturo's palms shot higher into the air. 'Sorry. Bad habit. But, like I say, I do favours. I help my clients sleep better at night for my very reasonable hourly rate. Then, when they owe me, when they become useful to me, they help me in return. Or, to be more precise, they help me help another of my clients. The kind who donate large sums into my numbered accounts, no questions asked. In your case, for which I'm very sorry, I have a client in Honduras who would benefit from the kind of political unrest that a few Marxists with guns running around the jungle would create. They needed to raise funds that couldn't be traced to him or anyone close to him.'

'Whose idea was it to steal from arms buyers?'

Should Arturo now lie after revealing so much truth? He wasn't sure. And in that indecision he was silent and the man understood.

'It was your idea.'

Arturo said, 'Yes.'

The man said, 'That's exactly what I was hoping to hear.'

Arturo said, 'I'm afraid I don't follow,' because he didn't.

'You're good at what you do.'

'I am?'

'I get that it was merely business for you. It's almost always business for me too. I have no grudge against you. I'm not here for revenge. If I were, I would now be drowning you in your pool, taking my time over it, letting your head up every so often to keep you alive longer, to extend the suffering. Drowning is a horrible way to die.'

Arturo couldn't help but look at the distorted reflection staring up at him, and his mind flashed an image of hands holding him beneath the surface, of underwater thrashing, of a storm of bubbles and agony.

He looked back at the man in the suit, who said, 'But I'm not, because it just so happens that our goals perfectly align.'

'They do?' Arturo asked.

'You don't want me to kill you,' the man in the suit said, so casually, so simply, that it seemed to Arturo that delivering on the words would be no more effort for him that speaking them. 'And I don't want to have to kill you.'

'I'll do anything.'

'You can start by finding out who crews the yacht *Sipak*. It's moored in Guatemala. I want a manifest.'

Such a thing would be easy for Arturo, but he resisted saying so. Instead, he nodded. 'That should be possible. Then we're even, yes?'

The man shook his head. 'No, that's half of it. That's to mitigate the loss of the rifle. That's not going to stop me killing you for trying to kill me.'

'I'll do anything,' Arturo said again.

'That's not good enough,' the man said. 'If you say that you'll make a bad deal. You'll agree to whatever it takes to save your life. That's no good to me. That's not going to help me when I need you at some later point.'

Arturo was starting to understand. The man in the suit wanted to establish a relationship. The same relationship Arturo had just described.

'You have to be happy with the deal,' the man continued.

'I will be,' Arturo was eager to assure.

'You have to convince me you're happy.'

Arturo understood. If the man in the suit doubted his sincerity, if he even suspected that Arturo would not deliver his end of the deal at some later point, then only one of them was leaving the patio.

Arturo swallowed. He composed himself. 'One favour. Five years. That's the length of the deal. Anything after that, you have to pay for. And I won't do anything that puts me in danger. I won't do anything that I deem will put me at risk, either financially or to my freedom.'

'That's more like it,' the man in the suit said. 'Ten years.'

'Seven,' Arturo said.

'Fine.'

'Weapons, ammo, information, documents, friends, whatever I can do, whoever I can put you in touch with, I will.'

'I also want you to sever ties with your German contact. Nothing hostile. Nothing overt. You just don't do any further business through them. You don't put any work her way and when she asks you for something, you can't deliver.'

'Why?'

'My reasons are my own.'

'Then it's back to five years.'

The man nodded. 'We have a deal.'

He turned and headed back towards the patio door. Arturo watched him go, not quite believing what had happened, not quite understanding that he had survived.

'Hey,' he called to the man in the suit. 'Just one question before you go: What kind of business are you in that you needed a high-powered rifle in the first place?'

'That's not an answer you want rattling around your mind,' the man said without turning around. 'Best remain ignorant, else maintain the illusion. It'll help you sleep at night.'

FIFTY-FOUR

Maybe it had been a restaurant. Maybe it had been a strip club. It was hard to tell from the weather-beaten exterior. Whatever the sign had read had been ripped away. Victor could see exposed bolt holes and slack tendrils of insulated wiring. Years of sun exposure had sucked the colour from the paintwork. Awnings had come away in places and he imagined young delinquents hanging from them by their fingertips, swinging and fooling around, delighting when they gave way under their weight. It was the kind of thing he would have done – the kind of thing he had done. Those same kids or gangs had turned the walls into chaotic murals of competing graffiti. Tags overlapped or blended into one another. Victor couldn't tell where some designs began or ended. There was no artistry on those walls, only anarchy.

Security mesh had been fixed over the windows back when the owner had still cared about the property. Like the walls, the mesh and the glass they protected were covered in graffiti. Weeds grew out of cracks in what had once been smooth asphalt, now a warped and cratered moonscape surrounding the building. A lone vehicle occupied the vastness of the otherwise empty lot.

Victor approached the building. There was only so much caution he could take when crossing a wide expanse of coverless ground. He glanced to where an old water tower overlooked the lot and the building. The tower was a couple of hundred metres away and would make the perfect spot for a waiting sniper. He had been back in Guatemala City only for a few hours, but there had been plenty of time to organise an ambush. There was no sniper on the water tower because Victor was still alive.

Inside, Victor passed an empty cloakroom and a crooked hostess station before he entered the main space. Round tables and oval-backed chairs were spread across it and around a T-shaped stage. A bar was set along the opposite wall. Once a cabaret club, he saw, from a sign. Each table had its own electric lamp in the centre, to provide the diners with a soft, flattering up-light. Semi-private booths lined the far wall.

'It was beautiful,' a voice said from the darkness. 'But it never opened.'

Victor faced the sound.

'A passion project,' the voice continued. 'But the hard realities of life always get in the way of passion, do they not?'

Victor remained silent.

'We were going for a vintage feel. Something sophisticated. A little different. We wanted to own something we could feel proud of, if that makes sense.'

Victor didn't care.

Lavandier stepped closer. He hadn't been waiting long

because he was dry. His hair was slick, but with expensive oil, not rain. 'Thank you for meeting me.'

'Why am I here?'

'Because Heloise has forgotten this place even exists. I couldn't bring myself to sell it back then, and over time it slipped out of my thoughts too as more pressing matters took precedence. Now, no one wants it.'

'That's not what I asked.'

Lavandier came closer, but he kept his distance. He stood on the far side of the stage, with plenty of tables and chairs between Victor and himself. He would be armed, of course, but the gun would be in a pocket of his coat. He was the kind of man who cared too much about his appearance to ruin the overall aesthetic with an underarm holster and rig. He also wasn't the kind of man who could draw that weapon with any kind of speed. He wouldn't be much of a shot either. A side-step, a dash, some lateral movement would be the extent of Victor's effort. Men like Lavandier let their guns be taken from them.

Lavandier said, 'Miguel Diaz was murdered.'

'You told me you didn't know who drove the yellow Lamborghini.'

The Frenchman said, 'I didn't know. I only know now because he's dead.'

'What does it matter that he's dead when he was an enemy?'

'Because you were hired to end a war, not fight it.'

'I'm not going to charge you for Diaz. Consider him a freebie.'

'That's not what I meant. We're trying to keep a low profile. Killing Diaz doesn't help us do that.'

Victor said, 'You've emptied your reserves of my goodwill

just by nature of this meeting. Don't test my patience too. You didn't ask me here to scold me over collateral damage.'

'I took you as the kind of man who never loses his temper.'

Victor said, 'I'm human.'

Lavandier smirked. 'Humanity is a construct. Life is a delusion. It isn't real. It's only real because we want it to be.'

'If I break your arm, it'll hurt whether you want it to or not.'

'You miss my point. There is a limitation to human understanding. Our ability to comprehend is finite because our brains are physical organs. We do not expect our skin to be fire resistant or our lungs to breathe seawater, so why do we expect our brains to possess all knowledge, to unravel all mysteries? Whatever our faults, arrogance is perhaps our greatest.'

'No, I understand it all too clearly,' Victor said. 'And I'm walking out right now if you don't get to the point.'

Victor knew what Lavandier was going to say before he said it, but he wanted him to say it anyway. Lavandier would have practised every point, every line. Each word would have been chosen with precision. This was the most important sales pitch of his life and it needed to be his best. Besides, even if he knew what Lavandier wanted to say, Victor didn't know how he was going to say it. How the words were delivered was just as important as the words themselves.

Lavandier took his time. He was as much a showman as he was an orator. He wanted to present himself in a stately manner. He knew he warranted no respect from Victor, so he acted as if he deserved it. Appearances were everything for men like Lavandier. They had to fool themselves first to be able to fool others.

Victor let the Frenchman do whatever he needed to do to feel as if they were meeting as equals when in fact there was no parity in the room. Lavandier was oblivious to this, of course, else he wouldn't be here.

'I want you to kill Heloise,' he said.

Victor listened.

'You're shocked by this, naturally, but hear me out. This is not a cartel war we are fighting, but a clash of civilisations. On one side we have the future, and on the other we have the past. Maria Salvatierra represents youth and vigour and a new world of opportunities. Heloise does not.'

Victor let Lavandier continue with his sales pitch.

'If she wins, the fighting will never stop. She commands no respect, only fear. Those loyal to Maria would never accept her as patron. Whereas, Heloise's men adore Maria because everyone does. They only fight for Heloise because they are scared of her. They would fight for Maria. They would fight harder for Maria. Business would boom.'

Victor cared nothing for cartel politics, loyalty, or for anyone involved.

'Heloise will be an easier target too,' the Frenchman continued. 'You have a man on the inside.' He smiled at his own perceived value. 'And when it is done, you will not only be paid for your services, but you will have gained a powerful friend. One that would no doubt wish to procure your future services from time to time.'

'You want to be patron,' Victor said. 'You've had your fill of being an advisor. You want advisors of your own.'

Lavandier took his time finding his words. He had a self-deprecating expression. 'You give my ambitions too much weight, and my cunning too much credit. I only want peace, and with it, prosperity.'

'So,' Victor began, 'in this peaceful and prosperous future

you're telling me that you can't foresee a time when you will decide that there could be even more peace, even more prosperity, with you calling the shots and not Maria?'

'I don't think we do ourselves any favours with such speculative presumptions.'

'You didn't say no.'

Lavandier stepped forward. 'Let's sit, shall we? And talk. Like men.'

'We are men. We are talking.'

'Perhaps my English is not all it could be.'

Victor said, 'It's better than mine.'

Lavandier approached a table, equidistant between them. He took the back of a chair in his hands and gestured with his chin at the one opposite. 'Shall we?'

Victor kept to the carpet. He avoided the areas of slick hardwood. Lavandier didn't pay attention to where he stood or where he walked. Victor could not comprehend how such an existence would work. What did people think about when they didn't need to consider their every step?

'I'm not tired,' Victor said.

Lavandier forced a laugh. 'Well, I am. And I prefer to save what little energy exists in his shell of flesh for more fruitful expenditure.' He sat down. 'You're considering my proposal because you are still here.'

'The rain still falls without considering snow.'

'I'm sorry, what?'

Victor said, 'No deal.'

Lavandier said, 'I'm very disappointed to hear that.'

'I'll do the job I've been hired to do, and no other. After I'm done, you want to hire me for another contract, you approach my broker with an offer.'

'You're making a mistake.'

'If you knew enough about me to know that, you'd have known that this conversation would be pointless.'

Lavandier said, 'I can make your life very difficult, Mr Wraith. You would do well to remember that.'

'And I could end yours in a second without so much as raising my heart rate.'

Lavandier had nothing to say to that.

Victor continued: 'I've been told that everyone deserves a second chance, so this is yours. Consider this my good nature getting the best of me. But the single most important thing to know about me is that I'm not a very nice person.'

Lavandier couldn't speak even if he wanted.

'Heloise will not hear about this conversation,' Victor said as he approached the exit. 'But only because this job is difficult enough without adding more complications. Be thankful I want an easy life, Mr Lavandier.' He paused, and turned around. 'Go to your restaurant and have a crème brûlée. A spike in blood sugar will put some colour back into your face.'

Lavandier managed to utter, 'How do you know about my brasserie?'

'The same way I know the name of your favourite escort and how much you pay her to make you squeal on your hands and knees.'

Lavandier paled.

Victor said, 'This city might be your house, but you're a hen, and I'm the fox you invited inside it.'

FIFTY-FIVE

Lavandier climbed into his car and engaged the lock so he could sit for a moment in the quiet and darkness with a little less fear. He hadn't expected meeting the Wraith would be so different from the previous time with Heloise. Maybe that was why it hadn't gone as well as he had expected. Perhaps Lavandier needed his patron at his side to feel powerful, to feel safe. No matter, it was over now, and he would not be seeking another face-to-face. He would stick to keeping outside of the line of fire. He would leave such dangers to those better designed for it.

The Wraith's refusal to consider his proposal was a problem, but not an immediate one. He had told Lavandier that Heloise would not hear of it, but it wouldn't make a difference if she was told. She would never believe it. Lavandier's portrayed loyalty was perfect and the Wraith meant nothing to her besides a useful tool to use. His word meant nothing. Lavandier suspected the Wraith knew this and that was the reason why he wouldn't reveal the Frenchman's treachery.

Still, all was fluid. Heloise's affections were fickle. She had torn the tongue out of a loyal man just to appear strong to her sicarios. Lavandier was forever a mouse in her claws. He already knew his existence was temporary in the trade. He had no intention of letting the Wraith walk around with the ability to shorten it. What if the Wraith killed Maria as planned, and Heloise's delight and gratitude were such that she had further jobs for him, and with each success he was drawn deeper into her confidence? She was used to Lavandier's counsel, already expectant of his skills at keeping the product flowing north and the money coming south. His novelty had long gone. His value had become routine. His talent was unappreciated. The Wraith, however, was new. New was always better, always shinier, or always more exciting. Worst still, anything Lavandier did, had done, could not compete with the singular glory of slaying the hated sister and ending the war. Heloise's gratitude would be endless. She would want the Wraith as much as Lavandier wanted Heloise.

It was quite conceivable that one day, and maybe soon, the Wraith would have Heloise's ear while she became deaf to Lavandier's loudest protestations.

Then, should the Wraith decide he had something to gain in the revelation of Lavandier's duplicity, Lavandier would be the one zip-tied to a chair and peering through swollen eyes as his love stalked closer with nails gleaming.

The Frenchman felt cold.

It was rare for him to miss the picturesque banality of Normandy, but now he longed to have another chance at picking apples.

Lavandier's phone buzzed in his pocket. He was late to meet one of his escorts, who was no doubt asking where he was, why he wasn't there, when he would be coming ... Loath as he was to keep such a delicious creature waiting, he had to attend to this more pressing matter. Whatever his insatiable levels of lust, work had to take priority. He reminded himself his lust could only be sated because of the wealth work afforded him. For a horrifying instant he imagined himself poor and driven insane with unfulfilled desires.

He drove back to the casino and was met by El Perro as he stepped out of the elevator, who was typically curt and brutish and led Lavandier into the suite to where Heloise stood with her back to the room. She was never facing him as he arrived. He was never that important.

She didn't turn around, but asked, 'How did it go?'

'He's a difficult man to converse with.'

A vague response, with more subtext than insight, and it worked, because she turned around. Always, Lavandier had to fight for her attention.

'Explain,' she ordered. 'If you would be so kind.'

Heloise's voice had a warm softness to it that belied her unmistakable strength, her casual barbarism always ready to be unleashed.

'He was curt with me,' Lavandier said. 'He was annoyed that you required an explanation for Diaz's death after our previous assurance he would be left alone.'

'I pay him,' Heloise said, 'so his annoyance means nothing to me.'

Lavandier inclined his head. 'I passed on those sentiments.'

'Good,' she continued. 'So how are his preparations going?'

He refused to kill you for me, Lavandier did not say.

'He is confident Maria will soon be dead,' Lavandier did say.

Heloise said, 'Do you share his confidence?'

'I do.'

'Perhaps his confidence was an illusion.'

'No, my dear, I would know if it was. I know how such men think. I know how to handle men like him.'

El Perro, standing guard on the periphery of the room, felt the sudden need to clear his throat.

Lavandier sneered at him, then said to Heloise, 'I advise we trust in our decision to hire him.'

She was happy with this, or happy enough to end the discussion, which she signified by turning back to the window, back to the city and all of its unfulfilled promise. What she saw with those big, beautiful eyes, Lavandier would never know. He would weep upon her death, he was sure.

Heloise then approached her pet and touched his arm. 'Would you ever put me at risk?'

'Never. I would die for you.'

She kissed him on the cheek. 'I don't deserve such devotion.'

El Perro said, 'You deserve everything.'

She gripped his arm in a long, lingering squeeze, as if she were so impressed by his strength that she couldn't let go. All part of the act, of course, but men like El Perro needed their power acknowledged to feel powerful. Heloise played him as she played them all, Lavandier included. She made El Perro feel strong, valued, even loved, and in turn he would do anything for her. Lavandier was a different but equally basic animal she had tamed by playing on his unquenchable lust. She had no need to play anyone – she paid her people well, after all – but loyalty could not be bought. She knew that better than anyone.

El Perro said, 'If I may speak freely, I advise against continuing to use this Wraith. Foreigners cannot be trusted.'

Lavandier knew the last sentence was directed at him as well.

Heloise said, 'Do you have so little faith in my judgement?'

El Perro bowed his head. 'My apologies.' He left.

He was naturally insulted that Heloise had brought in an outsider to kill her sister. He saw it both as an acknowledgement of his limitations and a dishonour. Nothing would make him happier than serving up Maria's head to Heloise. Nothing would make El Perro happier than making Heloise happy. It was a frustration to Lavandier that he could not manipulate El Perro. He could not make him an ally, because whatever the Frenchman's skills with words, whatever his cunning, nothing he could say or do would override El Perro's love of Heloise, and it was that love that made him hate Lavandier with such passion.

Heloise said, 'I'm going to bed. Please see yourself out, Luis.'

She kissed him on the cheek and left him alone.

The effect was almost instantaneous and, as was common in such moments, he turned to his phone and his list of acquaintances. As expected, one of his favourites was making it explicitly clear she was available tonight.

I know the name of your favourite escort and how much you pay her to make you squeal on your hands and knees.

Lavandier sighed. The moment was passing at an exponential rate.

A court jester, he had thought of himself. Rich, powerful, but at the beck and call of Heloise Salvatierra, dancing on the end of her strings. His tongue remained inside his mouth only because she wanted it there. It was her will. That wasn't the life of casual decadence he had envisioned for himself.

Working a few hours each week was no compensation for perpetual fear. Had he been grey when Manny had been patron?

This was not what he had signed up for and it was not sustainable.

The Wraith's refusal was disappointing, but he had not been so rash as to wager his future, his survival, on one assassin's duplicitousness, or lack thereof. Since when did hitmen have honour anyway? Lavandier considered a new weakness: was he even less honourable than a hired gun? Pah. Who cared? The single greatest weakness was loyalty. It provided no benefit to the loyal servant, only their master. Loyalty was the acknowledgement, acceptance, and, worst of all, pride in subservience. On that definition, Lavandier had no loyalty and was buoyed in that freedom from metaphysical bondage.

But, he loved Heloise. Adored her. Worshipped her. He revelled in her company. He would do anything for her. Except for anything that he didn't already want to do. He would not allow her to lead him to annihilation. He had worked hard to ensure he wouldn't have to work hard. He couldn't let anyone take that away from him. As a boy, he had thrown tantrums when asked to pick apples so his mother could bake delicious treats for him. Always inside him had been the compelling urge to do nothing. His father had chastised him for his lack of drive, for his staggering and deliberate inertia. That same father had worked hard all his life, had never seen retirement, and had died of a stroke, still toiling.

Lavandier was grateful for his father's work ethic because it meant there had been a little inheritance and a beautiful cottage left to him, mortgage-free. He had sold it within a week, banking the proceeds and using them to fund a hedonistic dalliance around the world. How Lavandier had become mixed up in the drug trade, he couldn't quite remember, but while there had never been any desire to snort or inject or swallow chemicals acquired from strangers, he saw that desire in others and he saw how little work the dealers had to do and a glorious future revealed itself to him. He invested the last remnants of his inheritance and never looked back. Until now, of course.

The Wraith had refused to kill Heloise, but it was far from over because he had another potential solution to his problem now there was a second hired gun in Guatemala. Lavandier would give the Russian time to acclimatise, time to settle in, and make the same proposal.

If he too refused, then there was one final play the Frenchman could make. A last resort, but preferable to the inevitable, grisly alternative. What did they call it?

Ah yes, Lavandier realised, they called it *scorched earth*.

FIFTY-SIX

Being poor sucked. It sucked even worse to be poor in a poor country. Which was why Petra was working as hard as she could. She had two regular jobs – washing dishes in a nice restaurant downtown and delivering mail and parcels for a courier company – and still she had nowhere near enough to pay her rent, buy food and save up to move away. She took every other job she could, as and when they appeared. Seasonal or temporary gigs. Maybe labouring on a construction site, sometimes picking fruit on a plantation. She had done stints as a waitress. She had shone shoes. She would do whatever it took to get out. Except work for the cartels.

That was her limit. She wouldn't sell her soul just to leave. She couldn't do that to herself or her country. Some childhood friends had earned a fortune as traffickers or gunmen, and all were dead. She had promised her dying mother she would never do anything illegal, which was why she was so surprised and stammering when she was stopped on her way home from a night shift by an American DEA agent.

'I work alongside your police forces,' the American told her.

He spoke Spanish well, and didn't come across as arrogant as she imagined an American would. He flashed some ID. Petra didn't really see it, but she was too nervous, too intimidated to ask to see it again.

'Don't worry,' the agent said in a soft tone. 'This isn't about anything you've done.'

'I've done nothing,' Petra was quick to say.

'Which is why it isn't about you. You haven't done anything wrong.'

'Okay,' Petra said, still unsure and still nervous, feeling as if she was guilty of something. Anything.

The American asked, 'You've been working tonight?'

'Uh huh.'

'At the restaurant?'

'Uh huh.'

'You have a lot of jobs,' the agent said. 'I respect your work ethic. Hard work gets you all that you want.'

Petra shrugged. She didn't care what this man thought of her, she just wanted the conversation to be over as fast as possible. She wanted to get home to her rented room and watch sitcoms until she fell asleep on the sofa bed. She had only eight hours before she was back to work, delivering the mail.

'Tell me about your other jobs,' the American said.

He smiled at her, trying to make her feel better. It worked, to an extent. He looked decent and honest. He looked like a nice person doing a tough job. Someone respectful and to be respected.

The American had dark hair and a deep tan, so he had been in the country a long time. For as long as Petra could remember, Americans had been in Guatemala. The War on Drugs had been raging for decades and would keep on raging so long as the drug trade was some people's only hope of climbing out of poverty. Petra wouldn't follow that route, of course, but she understood the appeal. Maybe if she had been able to afford medicine her mother would still be alive. She tried not to think about such things; she didn't want to cry in front of this stranger, this official.

'What about my jobs?' she asked.

'Would you like a cup of coffee?' he said. 'I'm paying. Something to eat, maybe? Whatever you like.'

'No,' she said. 'I never drink coffee, and I'm not hungry. I need sleep. Just sleep.'

'I'll try to be quick then. You work as a courier, yes? You also do casual jobs as and when they come in. Tell me about those.'

'About picking coffee beans?'

The American shook his head. He reached into the inside pocket of his jacket. He withdrew a piece of printer paper, which he unfolded and showed to Petra.

'Do you recognise this yacht?'

Petra nodded.

'Why do you recognise it?'

Petra swallowed. Her throat was dry. 'I sometimes work as cabin crew. In the kitchens, mostly, to clean up. I sweep the decks too sometimes. Stuff like that.'

'Do you know who owns the vessel?'

Petra hesitated. 'A rich lady.'

'Do you know why she's rich?'

Petra didn't want to admit it, but she feared being caught in a lie. She nodded. It would be silly to pretend otherwise.

'Good,' the American said. 'You can help me.'

She didn't want to know, but couldn't help but ask, 'How?'

'When are you working next on the yacht?'

'I don't know. I just get a call when the lady wants to take the boat out.'

'You get some warning though, don't you?' the American asked. 'You can't just drop everything at a moment's notice. So, how much warning do you get?'

'A few days. Maybe a week. Depends on how long she wants to go sailing for. It's the recruitment company that calls. Maybe you should be speaking to them instead. I can give you their number and you can go—'

'That won't be necessary,' he said in a tone that said more. 'Next time you get such a call I want you to call me straight away. Soon as you hang up with them, you dial my number. Okay?'

He offered a scrap of paper with a handwritten telephone number. Petra felt compelled to take it.

'Straight away,' the American repeated. 'Can you do that?'

Petra thought for a moment, because she didn't want to lie. She wanted to think and decide and then speak the truth. That was how she had been raised and that was how she wanted to live her life.

'You know what kind of work I do, don't you?' the American asked. 'You know about the drugs, about the cartels. You know my government sends people like me down here to try to help tackle the traffickers. I'm here to help make your country a better place.'

'I know.'

'So, you'll call me?'

She thought hard about the implications of her response.

She had always known who owned the yacht. Maria Salvatierra was famous. Everyone recognised her face. Everyone knew her name. Petra had gasped when she had found out who she was working for, which hadn't been until she had already agreed to wash up over a weekend excursion. Then, it was too late. She had no choice but to work. She could have declined the next offer when it came through, and she heard her mother's words in her head, but she accepted anyway. She could justify it to herself. She wasn't helping the cartel by scrubbing pans and sweeping decks. She had no blood on her hands.

Maybe giving this DEA agent information would result in Maria's arrest. Petra would lose her job working on the yacht as a result. Her dreams of a better life far away from here would be stalled.

Some things were more important than dreams, however.

'I will,' she said, and meant it.

'I want you to keep this between us, just you and me. Is that okay? If you tell anyone else ... well, let's just say it could be very bad for you further down the line. Do you understand?'

She nodded. 'I do. I won't say anything. I won't tell anyone.'

'Good,' he said. 'That's good. I want to be able to trust you, Petra.'

'You can trust me.'

FIFTY-SEVEN

Graceful, he was not. Neither was he fast nor agile. He was awkward and slow, but on land only. In water, Constantin glided. His long limbs worked in harmony, his arms slicing a path that his legs propelled him along, smooth and easy. The swimming pool was outdoors, shimmering under the hot sun. He swam whenever he could, both to keep fit and for pleasure. He took little pleasure in life, but there were things that provided small release from the unrelenting agony of existence.

He counted no lengths, but swam many kilometres before the serenity was ruined. First it was the noise, sporadic and isolated, muted by the water and his earplugs. Then, that noise grew with an escalation that could not be dampened. He exited the pool before the irritation could grow too intense and perhaps lead him to do something he wouldn't regret, but would pay for nonetheless. He used the chromed ladder to climb out into the morning – he would struggle without it – and almost collided with one of the stunted noisemakers.

It was a hideous thing, small and chubby. The fat head tilted backwards so its tiny eyes could gaze up to meet Constantin's own far above. The creature stood as if frozen, blocking Constantin's way.

A man rushed into proximity, taking the thing's hand and pulling it out of the way, mumbling apologies.

'Drown it,' Constantin said in his native Czech. 'For your benefit, and its own.'

The man shrugged his incomprehension and couldn't get away fast enough.

In his room, Constantin showered with a degree of awkwardness he was used to, lowering his chin to his chest so the spray could reach the top of his head. He thought of life. He thought of death. He thought about why he was in Guatemala and the futility of his presence here, of all presence.

Constantin's tastes were modest. That he enjoyed so little meant he required little. Somewhere to lay his heavy head was as much as he wanted out of a hotel room. The decorations were immaterial. He cared as much for the trappings of wealth as he did for anything else. He chose the hotel because it was the largest in Guatemala City, so it provided the most anonymity. It could have been the most expensive hotel or the least, and he wouldn't have minded either way. He had picked this hotel because it was old, because it was part of no chain. The locks were operated with magnetised key cards, but the windows opened. An independent hotel was a rare thing, and was becoming ever rarer.

He dressed and began his day, thinking about what was to come. Constantin had prepared himself for many considerations, many options. There wasn't much left to do because he was thorough, and he was efficient. Everything had been worked out. Planned to perfection would be a grandiose claim, but Constantin left with a feeling of calm confidence that soon the world would be a little less ugly.

No life should be ended without first understanding it. Constantin believed this to be true as much as he needed it to be so.

He understood this one. He had not had much time to do so, but some people were easier to understand than others.

She had a routine, as did everyone. Even the chaotic, the lazy, the erratic had routines. She was none of those. She was diligent and she was careful and she was predictable. She dropped off clothes at the dry cleaner every Monday evening and picked them up again every Saturday morning. She had four business suits as far as Constantin could tell, in a constant circulation – while two were worn, the other two were cleaned. She did the rest of her laundry at home. In Constantin's experience, how a person handled their laundry revealed much about their character. Her regularity was a definite mark in her favour.

She was pretty too. He had expected as much. Not to his tastes, but it had been so long since Constantin had required company of any sort that he wasn't sure if anyone would ever be to his tastes again. Even what his body needed, his mind found repulsive. In time, he had mastered himself in all things. He knew, though, that the rest of humanity revelled in that ugliness. They sought it out. The killer with the dark eyes liked this woman. Constantin wondered what was so likeable? He tried to imagine being one of them – which was hard enough without vomiting – and he saw skin and hair, and the flesh and blood beneath. A meat sack, at most.

He looked down at his long, thin fingers, and his rough

palms. He looked at the hairless skin of his forearms, thin and colourless. He was no different than her. He was uglier than all of them, he could admit. Like his body, he had mastered even his own mind, his own ego. He had risen to a higher state of consciousness, wherein his essence existed even beyond reach of impulse, desire and self-worth. That essence required a meat sack of its own, but was not of it; they occupied the same space only. Matter and dark matter in coexistence.

Joanna Alamaeda had no idea he was watching her. She saw him but she did not see into him. She saw only that which existed in the observable universe, the matter.

He was considering how to proceed when his phone rang.

It was the Frenchman. The charlatan who had no will. 'I have a proposition for you.'

Constantin said, 'I'm listening.'

'The Wraith is proving to be unpredictable,' Lavandier explained. 'He's not as discreet as we had hoped.'

'How very interesting,' Constantin said, uninterested.

'Would you consider taking over as primary on the contract?'

'I imagine if I agree this would mean removing the Wraith from the equation.'

There was a pause, before Lavandier said, 'It would.'

'What has the Wraith done to warrant such displeasure?'

Lavandier's tone was curt. 'That's none of your concern. All you need to know is that we want you to put an end to him.'

'I would end everyone if only I could,' Constantin replied, 'I would lay waste to this world and, oh, how it would thank me for that service.'

Lavandier's tone was impatient. 'A yes or no will suffice.'

'*Oui*,' Constantin sufficed. '*Je vais finir cet homme, et le reste du monde peut attendre un peu plus longtemps.*'

'Make sure it's done quickly,' Lavandier said. 'And then maybe we can talk about how to improve your accent. It's a little flat.'

The line disconnected and for once Constantin did not know how to proceed. He had not expected this, so everything had to be reconsidered. He lifted his wicker hat to wipe his brow with a handkerchief, and followed behind Alamaeda, never close but never far.

This was the best part of the job, for him. To be invisible in a world of ugliness was the highest of achievements.

FIFTY-EIGHT

Gulls squawked in the early morning mist. It was still dark, but the dawn was coming. The sky in the east was almost blue above the horizon. A tiny, almost imperceptible flicker of yellow marked the coming day. It was cold. Victor's breath misted and the steam from his coffee rose in pluming swirls. In an hour or so the temperature would have jumped by ten degrees. Puerto Barrios was quiet at this time.

He sipped his coffee from a waxed paper cup. He had removed the plastic lid. In part because he preferred his coffee without the taint of BPA and other chemicals, and in part because he could toss the hot liquid in an assailant's face should it come to it.

There was no one nearby. He stood on an empty stretch of concrete bordering the port, looking out to the harbour. A high chain-link fence rattled in a sudden gust of wind. His pickup was parked nearby, facing the exit so he could make a fast getaway if necessary. He stayed mobile out of habit, never staying in one place for too long despite the fact there were no obvious sniping lines and the coastal wind would make any shot impossible for all but the best marksman.

Nearby were low buildings. Small industry. One business made parts for refrigerators. Another recycled paper. Others had no signs and nothing in their lots to give away what they did. Victor wasn't interested in anything but the harbour. He gazed out at the horizon, at the sea. Waiting.

Across the harbour the huge shape of a cargo ship emerged through the dawn, an apparition almost slow and cumbersome. Victor liked ships, but not as much as he liked trains. Feats of engineering impressed him. He imagined the thousands of bolts and rivets, screws and welds. He pictured endless bulkheads, hatches and portholes. He could see giant rotors turned by colossal cylinders. A floating testament to human perseverance and will.

The cargo ship was right on schedule. Victor had been able to track its progress across the Atlantic, thanks to the shipping company's website. There had been no rough seas. No hurricanes. A boring voyage for the crew of the cargo ship, he had no doubt.

On occasion he would pay a captain in cash to let him travel on such a ship. A slow, but secure way to travel. The last time it had been to cross the Black Sea on his way to Russia. The captain had been talkative, happy to have someone new to pass the time with, and had many stories to share. Victor looked forward to the next such trip.

The coffee was excellent, even for takeout from a street stall. The beans were not only freshly ground, but freshly roasted. Instead of weeks from plant to cup as he was used to in Europe, it was but hours here. The downside was it was too good to take his time over. If an enemy attacked him now, he would receive nothing more than a few lukewarm drops in the face as way of discouragement.

The giant ship neared the port. On its deck were thousands of containers, piled neat and high. In one of them was a rifle. Of course, it was impossible to tell which container held the weapon, but that didn't stop Victor using binoculars to watch the ship moor and the tall cranes begin to unload.

Over the course of the morning the cranes ferried the containers to different areas of the port, stacking them in smaller piles depending on both space and consignment. Of all the crates, some were separated from the rest and delivered to an area where they were opened and their contents examined by men with clipboards. The distance was too great and the line of sight too restrictive to provide Victor with any hope of seeing if the rifle was found, but he could measure the reaction of the inspectors.

They would be used to finding undocumented cargo that no duty had been paid on, not weapons. Victor expected a rifle would cause something of a furore.

With so many containers, they might check twenty, giving only a slim chance they would open the right one. There would be other cargo within the container, and the rifle would be disguised, further reducing the chances of discovery, but hoping for the best wasn't part of Victor's professional philosophy. So, he watched and waited and tried hard to read body language and behaviour.

Should the rifle be discovered it wouldn't take any effort to find out who sent it and who was due to collect it, and a welcoming party could be arranged to greet Victor when he did. That could only happen with police involvement, which he would see coming. Officers would be sent to the port. They would inspect the container and the rifle. They would stand out from the dockers and inspectors. They would be wearing hard hats too, but smart clothes. There would be no difficulty distinguishing them from managers, because they would be treated with a certain amount of curiosity and reverence, instead of fear and disdain.

He waited all morning and all afternoon too. A hot sun burnt off the mist and blazed down on Victor, who had dressed in readiness with light clothing and a hat. He grew tired of standing. His arms were weary from holding the binoculars up so long. His eyes were feeling the strain too. He didn't get bored, however. He was never bored when his life or freedom were at stake. He took breaks when the inspectors did, but while they worked, he did too.

By the end of the working day, the inspectors with clipboards left and no more containers were inspected. No police officers arrived either.

Victor checked his email. He had a message from the shipping company.

The package would be ready for collection in the morning.

FIFTY-NINE

Assembled, the AX50 weighed over fifteen kilograms. But stripped down, no single piece weighed more than five. With the aid of some bungee cords, he was able to strap the disassembled weapon into the chassis of a Land Cruiser, utilising the plates he had welded to support the larger pieces. A thorough inspection of the vehicle would find those pieces without too much trouble, but such an inspection was almost beyond probability. If he were stopped by curious police or suspicious sicarios, they would check inside the cab and the load bed. They would need to suspect he had a weapon hidden beneath the vehicle to warrant someone sliding under there to take a look.

He took the rifle far from Puerto Barrios, far into the countryside. He already had a place picked where he could be alone, where the sound of gunshots wouldn't reach anyone else's ears. He spent most of the day practising with the rifle, familiarising himself with a weapon he hadn't used in a long time. By nightfall, his shoulder ached but his shooting was as good as ever.

He drove through the night, rifle again stored in the vehicle's chassis, crossing the country from east to west, but not as far as Guatemala City. He wanted to store the weapon where it was needed, for when it was needed.

When he was three miles from his destination he killed the headlights and drove by the light of the stars only. The roads here were not well used, and he had seen no other vehicles in half an hour. He slowed almost to a crawl to make sure he didn't miss the turning on to the dirt track that took him within a mile of the abandoned shack. The Land Cruiser was impossible to hide, and trying to disguise it would only create suspicion should it be found.

With a penlight between his teeth he slid beneath the vehicle and retrieved the AX50's parts, placing each one into a sports bag after wrapping it in newspaper to both muffle any sound and protect the more delicate parts from the heavier ones.

He switched off the penlight and spent fifteen minutes still and quiet in the darkness until his eyes had adjusted back to the starlight before he set off into the brush.

Dawn was an hour away. The night sky to the east had a thin blue line across it.

In the darkness, it was hard to check the surrounding area for signs anyone had been to the shack since his previous visit, but he did what he could. He set the sports bag down in the undergrowth and approached the building with his Glock drawn and out before him. He had been here before, which meant it was a good place for an ambush.

Such an ambush would be possible only if the ambusher or ambushers knew when he was due to return, which would be impossible. He still approached with caution, however, because the next best thing to an ambush would be a booby trap. A Claymore mine behind the door, rigged to a filament tripwire, would be perfect. Which was why Victor ignored the door and scaled the shack's north façade – simple enough to climb with lots of handholds provided by the uneven timbers – and eased up the window pane he had left a little open last time.

He slithered inside the opening and crouched in the darkness, redrawing the pistol, having tucked it into his waistband for the short climb. In his free hand he used the penlight to examine the interior of the shack.

There was no Claymore behind the door. No other booby trap or IED.

The dust-caked cobweb, however, was gone.

He checked where it had hung, stretched between timbers, and found traces of broken spider silk. Victor examined the shack. He checked everywhere. He searched for any sign, no matter how small, someone else had been here, but he found none. The web hadn't fallen apart by itself. The door, having been opened further than he himself had done, destroyed it, which meant someone had been here in the last week, but had left no other signs of their presence. No condom, no drug paraphernalia, no empty glass bottle. Whoever had opened the door hadn't used the barn for anything. So why had they been inside?

Only one answer: they were looking for Victor.

Four people knew he was in the country. Phoenix had no reason to betray him, especially so early into their arrangement, and especially given their pact of mutually assured destruction. Similarly, Georg knew better than to turn on him. Which left Lavandier and Heloise. He doubted

Lavandier had the means to organise a vengeful response to Victor's refusal of his offer and Heloise had no reason to wish him harm. If the job was a charade, they had invested more time, energy and money into it than was necessary.

There was another explanation, however. One that did make sense.

They were keeping an eye on him. Someone was shadowing him, else tracking his movements. Maybe they didn't trust his motives or his skills. Perhaps that someone was insurance. Perhaps that someone had the same objective as Victor.

We don't do things by halves, he remembered Lavandier telling him in Madrid.

So, another assassin. Another professional tasked with killing Maria. One who had come to the same conclusion as Victor regarding the shack's viability as a sniping point, and performed his or her own reconnaissance, composing their own plan.

Did that assassin know about him?

Yes, was the answer, because they had left something behind. Victor hadn't seen it at first because it was so small, almost invisible against the floor in the dim light.

A leaf.

Seemingly insignificant, seemingly a natural occurrence among the dust and the dirt and the debris, having been blown or trodden inside. It was too fresh though, not brown or blackened. Still green. Still moist. He examined it with a close eye. It had fallen, at least, instead of being picked, but it had fallen recently. Within the last few days. Victor hadn't brought it inside, and it hadn't ended up on the floor by the door by chance but by deliberate placement.

Had Victor entered through the door, the draught would

have disturbed its careful placement. He noted how it was placed with its tiny stalk lying along a gap between floorboards, making it easy to see if it had been disturbed.

Victor had seen nothing similar by the window upstairs, so he checked again. He had not missed anything. Whoever had placed the leaf by the door had not anticipated Victor entering the shack through the window. Which was interesting, and told Victor the other assassin was not much of a climber, else not limber enough to slip through small windows. A very tall man then, which was consistent with the broken cobweb. Tall and not athletic. Ungainly. Such a man would stand out to Victor's watchful gaze. He thought back through his recent experiences, scanning his memory for such a figure in the crowd of a street, on a bus or train, or sitting in a hotel lobby.

No one. Whoever he was, Victor had not encountered him yet.

The assassin also lacked the ability to envision tactics beyond those he would employ himself. He would not be able to gain entry to the shack through the window so did not conceive someone else would. So, a proficient sniper, able to deduce from his own skill set the suitability of the shack. That alone was enough to make him dangerous.

The only question remaining was whether the assassin was merely in competition with Victor, or a direct threat?

SIXTY

A client breaking the terms of his employment was neither a surprise nor something new. It was more common than not that those who hired contract killers could not themselves be trusted. Victor expected betrayal. It was part of the business he was in. He was making a fresh start, but the world remained the same around him. He wasn't yet sure how best to respond.

Another hot and humid day greeted Victor as he left the hotel. The sky was more yellow than blue, the bright sunlight diffusing through the polluted air heavy with noise and the acrid taste of exhaust fumes. Victor's sunglasses were already in place, as protocol demanded. Putting them on outside created avoidable vulnerability. For an instant he was distracted, unaware, unable to keep watch on his surroundings. Far better to do so in a hotel lobby, without the risk of potential snipers or drive-bys.

It was early afternoon and he was hungry for breakfast. He took a circular route from the hotel, often doubling back, using frequent and sudden changes of direction, sometimes walking, sometimes using public transport. A hot-dog stand was his ultimate destination, and it took him over an hour to make the ten-minute journey. He was ravenous by the time he placed his order but it would be worth it.

The guy serving the hot dogs wore sunglasses, even in the shade of the truck. He had a slicked-back ponytail wrapped up in a hairnet. He wore a single latex glove – so he could check his phone between customers, Victor realised.

It wasn't a long wait, which was one of the many reasons Victor was partial to fast food. The longer he stood in line, the longer he sat at a table, the more at risk he put himself. He liked to watch his food being prepared too. There was next to no danger of being poisoned while eating out – an enemy would need to know in advance where Victor would be eating, and he never knew himself – but by watching he could be certain.

The hot dog was big and loaded with guacamole. It came on a paper plate that bowed under the weight. The guy with the ponytail shoved a fistful of napkins Victor's way and then flopped down on to a seat of some kind – Victor couldn't see – and commenced thumbing his phone screen.

Victor took his food to a nearby bench and sat down himself. The bench was made of wood and painted white. The paint had split and chipped from sun exposure. It was hot to sit on. He ate in quiet bliss for a few minutes. He ate a little faster than he would choose to, because he knew the bliss wouldn't last long.

'Mind if I join you?' another customer asked.

Victor gestured. 'Be my guest.'

He had seen the man approach, of course. No one came

into Victor's personal space without him knowing about it, and he had seen this man long before. Even a civilian couldn't miss this man's approach given the particulars of his appearance. On the face of it, a tourist. He wasn't dressed like a tourist though. He was dressed like a traveller, an adventurer, a student on a gap year off to see what life was like outside of their comfort zone. Only a couple of decades or more too old for that. He had no camera. He had no guidebook. He had no wife or friend or companion of any sort. He was alone like Victor because he was like Victor.

The man sat down next to him, so unhurried in his movements he seemed in slow motion. 'Much obliged.' He had a hot dog of his own. 'I saw yours and thought it looked good.'

'It's excellent,' Victor assured.

The man took a bite and nodded his large head while he chewed. Whereas Victor sat perched on the bench, straight-backed and head over hips, ready to spring into action, this guy leaned backwards in a relaxed pose, elbows at his sides. His face was damp with perspiration.

'You're right,' he said after swallowing.

The accent was Czech; unmistakable to Victor's ear. He finished and wiped his mouth and hands on a serviette. He bunched it up, along with the wrapper, and tossed them into a nearby bin. He remained sitting on the bench.

'I hope you don't mind me coming over,' the man said.

'Not at all,' Victor said. 'I prefer to get introductions out of the way as soon as possible.'

The man nodded his agreement. 'It felt only polite to introduce myself.'

Victor said, 'It's a pleasure to make your acquaintance.'

'Then my presence here is no surprise to you?'

'I've suspected for a while that you might be out there. But I only knew for sure yesterday.'

'The shack?'

Victor inclined his head.

The parasol protecting the guy with the ponytail had a rainbow of colours that had been bleached pale by the sun. He played music from his phone. Something tinny and soulless.

'I've grown weary from hiding in the shadows.'

Victor said, 'I don't imagine that's easy for you.'

'It's not my forte, I'll admit.'

He was as tall as Victor had expected, but much thinner. He was pale and whatever hair he had left was cut so short as to be invisible. His eyebrows were dark, but thin and sparse. He moved in a slow, precise manner. When he smiled, he revealed yellow teeth and the skin around his eyes creased into many lines. A cream linen shirt hung loose from the man's thin frame, the shirt tails dancing around his midriff in the breeze. The sleeves were rolled up to reveal long, hairless forearms criss-crossed with jutting veins. The shirt was unbuttoned to the sternum. Victor could see ribs beneath a veneer of skin and muscle. He looked weak, but not fragile. There was more strength than that which could be measured by muscle mass, and no strength was needed to squeeze a trigger or slip a knife-point between ribs. The man projected no threat, but Victor recognised danger when he saw it.

'So you know who I am,' the man said.

'My competitor.'

'You don't seem to mind that we are in competition.'

Victor said, 'I don't see this as a competition.'

'Such a thing is beneath you?'

Victor shook his head. 'I don't see *you* as competition.'

'Ah,' he said. 'I don't see why you need to be rude about it.'

'Stating facts is rude?'

'That depends on how they're stated.'

'Then you'll have to forgive my lack of manners.'

The man said, 'I'm not sure I want to, but, as they say, to err is human, to forgive is divine. May I ask, how did you know I'd been to the shack after you?'

There was no harm in answering, so Victor said, 'There was cobweb stretched between two beams on the ceiling. When I went back, it was gone.'

The pale man nodded in a slow and thoughtful gesture. 'My hat,' he said. 'I didn't notice I had disturbed any web.'

'Then,' Victor continued, 'I knew you were very tall and your presence no happenstance because you had left that leaf near the entrance.'

He continued the slow nods. 'So, you must have entered elsewhere. Ah, you're a climber then. I must admit I find such things a little ... awkward.'

'I imagine.'

'And unnecessary.'

Victor shrugged. He wasn't prepared to argue climbing's benefits. He didn't feel the need to convince the man he was wrong. He preferred it that way.

The pale man said, 'I feel as if I've had an unfair advantage. I knew about you from the start. As I knew you didn't know about me.'

'Now we have an even playing field. If you mean to disrupt my work, you've lost your chance.'

'Who says I would have disturbed you? I might have let you get on with it in peace.'

'I bet,' Victor said. 'Let me kill Maria, then you kill me and claim my fee as your own.'

The tall man's eyes crinkled with a smile. 'The thought may have flashed through my consciousness.'

Victor raised an eyebrow. 'It would have crossed my mind too.'

'But that was before. Now, that isn't what I want. If you will permit me, I have a proposal for your consideration.'

SIXTY-ONE

The tall, pale man said nothing for a little while. The hot-dog stand was popular and the immediate area became too crowded with customers to discuss anything without the risk of being overheard. So, they sat in silence, side by side, killer next to killer. The sun was hot and the air heavy with moisture. Victor was sweating, but the pale man was drenched. His scalp was reddening. He wasn't suited to the heat, and smelled like it. There was a scent of stale sweat, bitter and strong.

In time, the queue lessened until the guy with the ponytail was serving the last customer who had been in line: an old man with trousers he kept having to pull up. He walked away with a brown paper bag stuffed with food. For himself or to be shared, Victor couldn't tell.

The tall man said, 'If you don't mind me asking, how are things progressing with your preparations?'

'I don't mind talking shop,' Victor said. 'They are progressing as expected.'

'A tricky target, isn't she? Always protected, always at her ranch.'

'Not always.'

'A long-range rifle shot is obviously the most viable course of action.'

'Obviously,' Victor agreed.

'But not the only way.'

Victor nodded. 'Are you looking for advice? Do you want to copy my homework?'

The man smirked. 'And here was I, prepared to offer you a look at my own.'

'Not necessary.'

'Are you so very arrogant?'

Victor shook his head. 'Not at all, but what works for you and what works for me are unlikely to align. But, more to the point, why would you want to help me?'

'So that we may help one another.'

'Explain.'

'For one of us to succeed, the other must fail.'

'That's how such a competition works.'

'But it doesn't have to be like that, does it? We can both succeed.'

'Fifty-fifty?'

The man said, 'Fifty per cent of something is better than one hundred per cent of nothing.'

'How could we possibly trust one another?'

'Are you a professional?'

'I am.'

'As am I,' the man said. 'Aside from being a killer, I'm a model citizen. I keep my lawn short. I pay my taxes. I even volunteer from time to time.'

Victor said, 'You're a better man than I.'

'Do you only work with those you can completely trust?'

'I generally work alone.'

'Generally?'

Victor remained silent. There was no need to elaborate and his thoughts were elsewhere. The linen shirt was transparent where it clung to the man's shoulders. His clavicles jutted out, long and obvious, and Victor couldn't help but imagine snapping them with downward strikes with the blade of his palm. They were too inviting as targets to ignore.

The man said, 'You don't have to trust me for us to work together. If you like, this can be the last time we are in close proximity. But we can share intelligence remotely. We can assist one another at arm's length.'

'Only one of us gets paid.'

'So why would the other share his purse?'

Victor nodded.

'Simple. To ensure their survival.'

Victor raised an eyebrow.

'It is no threat,' the tall man said. 'What I mean is that whichever of us collects that money will need the assistance of the other to ensure continued survival in the face of external threats.'

'From our employer?'

'Of course. You don't expect Heloise Salvatierra to honour the contract, do you?'

'Clients turning against me is not uncommon. But why do you expect betrayal in this instance?'

'She's already betrayed you by hiring me, as her consul made clear. You were not to know of my involvement. So, why wouldn't she betray you a second time?'

'Gratitude? The war with her sister will be over.'

'You don't really believe that, do you?'

'I don't know what I believe at this particular moment.'

'Understandable, of course. Take your time.'

'I wasn't planning on rushing.'

The tall man's voice rose for the first time. 'The very idea of competition is contemptible. It offends me. That offence must be punished.'

'I don't take these things personally.'

'They told me about you. They told me what you looked like. Is not such a betrayal intolerable?'

'I'm not sure I've ever had a client who hasn't betrayed me in some way.'

'I think you are dishonest in the presentation of your feelings on this matter.'

Victor shrugged. 'I'm not much of a sharer.'

'Why are you here?' the pale man asked, slow and thoughtful.

Victor said, 'It's my job.'

'That's no answer, which is why you gave it. I, however, have no fear of you seeing into my soul. You will find nothing there you can use against me. I am here in the pursuit of beauty, for the love of art. I was given a gift to share with the world and the most efficient way of sharing it is in this field of work.'

'How interesting,' Victor said without inflection.

The man continued: 'A pay cheque is merely a happy by-product. An accident, almost. They think they own me because they are paying me. They forget that they exist because I allow them to exist. All of you exist because I allow you to exist.'

'And we're very grateful,' Victor said.

The eyes crinkled and the yellow teeth appeared for a brief moment. 'You should know that the Frenchman asked if I would kill you.'

Victor thought about this. 'There's a certain sense to that. He asked me to kill Heloise.'

Many lines deepened across the pale man's forehead. 'How interesting. And you must have declined, which is why he asked me to kill you. I'm not surprised. He is without will.'

Victor said, 'And what was your own answer?'

'I agreed, of course. But, as I said, that's not what I want.'

The sun was overhead. There was no shade in the little courtyard. The man looked down at his pale, thin forearms. So white in the bright light they almost glowed.

'I don't tan,' he said with something like regret. 'I never tan. I am the shadow that light forgot.'

The guy with the ponytail was now talking on his phone, one moment laughing and joking with whoever was on the other end of the line, the next moment shouting and cursing.

'I find them so very ugly,' the pale man said, observing. 'Their lives are a plague. An insufferable, disgusting plague. They're better dead. All of them are better as corpses. Then, finally, they shut up. They're still. Then they can be beautiful. *Only* then can they be.'

He finished wiping his hands. Like the rest of him, his hands were large, but elongated – slender bones that seemed almost stretched out. In a funhouse of mirrors his squashed reflection would be that of a normal-sized man. His nails were bitten down to the quick. His cuticles were dry and cracked.

'My appetite is that of a man half my size,' the man said when there was half of the hot dog remaining. 'However

369

hungry, however good it tastes, food never satisfies me.' He presented his leftovers to Victor. 'Would you like to finish it?'

'I'll pass.'

He threw away the remnants of his meal and stood. His shadow fell over Victor.

'What is your answer to my proposal?'

'I'll think about it.'

'Take your time,' he began. 'I'll leave a number you can reach me on with your concierge. Please don't share it.'

'Not my style.'

'Of course,' he said with a note of apology in his tone. 'And I must say it is a curious thing to talk to another killer.' He did not elaborate. He lifted his wicker hat to wipe his brow with a handkerchief. The white square of cloth was soaked when he had finished. 'I hate it here,' the man said. 'I hate the people. I hate the noise. In particular, I hate the climate.'

'Personally, I like it. When the contract is complete, I might even stay.'

'How very curious,' the tall man said. 'I have enjoyed our conversation. It is unimaginably rare that I get the chance to speak with someone in this business for whom I have any respect.'

Victor said, 'It's even rarer for me.'

The tall, pale man said nothing further and went on his way. Victor watched him until he had faded into the distance and his thoughts were interrupted when his burner phone chimed. He checked the message. It was from Petra.

She'd been booked to work on board Maria Salvatierra's yacht at the weekend.

SIXTY-TWO

Victor sat on the bed while Joanna showered. She took her time, making good use of the walk-in cubicle, the overhead waterfall dispenser, the excellent water pressure. Victor missed showers. It had been years since he had felt the spray of hot water on his shoulders, on his back. He missed the efficiency too. Two minutes from that first twist of the dial to squeaky clean could not be replicated any other way. He knew. He had tried every one without success, but two minutes of sensory deprivation under a shower was close to a good night's sleep in its potential for lethality. It had been a long time since he had killed anyone who was taking a shower – he didn't count using a shower head to drown a woman trying to kill him – but it had once been one of his preferred strike points. Even hard targets took showers, and even the hardest of targets was vulnerable that way. It was only a matter of learning their time window and waiting. No one took a gun with them.

Her long shower increased the room's humidity. He had

turned off the air conditioning, as he always did. The chance of an assassin pumping poison gas was minimal – it wasn't a method he would ever even consider – but hotels were notorious for spreading disease. He didn't remember the last time he had been sick, but it wasn't worth the risk. Prevention over cure, always.

She returned looking happy. 'I don't know what you're paying for this suite, and I don't want to, but it's worth every cent just for that shower. I mean, *wow*. I never want to get out of there. Best thing ever, right?'

He nodded.

She had taken one of the white towelling robes, but left it open. She looked great as she combed her wet hair with her fingers, before pulling it back into a loose ponytail.

'Truth be told, the only reason I agreed to see you again after the first time was so I could come back here and take another shower.'

Victor shrugged. 'The end result is the same, so I don't mind.'

She shook her head, but smiled. She started gathering her things.

He said, 'You're not going to stay over?'

'No can do, buddy. Too many numbers to crunch. I need to be in the office bright and breezy.'

'You work too hard.'

'You'd better believe it. I'll be doing this when I'm in a wheelchair. They'll have to drag me away from those spreadsheets, kicking and screaming. Well, assuming I can still kick and scream when I'm ninety.'

Victor regarded her. 'You're surprisingly passionate about what you do.'

She frowned, a little uncomfortable. 'Is that a question or a statement? Or are you saying you're not passionate about what you do for a living?'

Victor shrugged. 'It's just a job. It's not me. It's not who I am.'

'You mean you didn't dream of being a commodities trader when you were a little boy?'

'Actually, I dreamed of driving a train. A steam train, ideally. Through the Alps, or the Highlands. Somewhere like that.'

She laughed. 'That's the funniest thing I've ever heard in my life.'

'Well, now you've said that, I might become a train driver just to spite you.'

She was grinning. '*Do. It.*'

'Maybe I will. Maybe I'll call you one day in the future and say you can throw coal into the engine.'

Her eyebrows rose. 'Is that a euphemism?'

'I'm ... not sure.'

'Don't make me bring out my kinky side. That's for when we really get to know each other. Would it offend you if I told you I checked you out? You know, in this day and age it's hard not to want to take a peek behind the curtain.'

'That depends on whether you did or not.'

'Well, I did, so are you offended?'

'That depends on what you found out about me.'

She shrugged. 'Nothing. You're a typical normal Canadian. Except ... ' She approached the bed. 'Since I figure we're past the treading-on-eggshells stage, I gotta ask. Some guys are covered in tattoos,' she said, looking him over. 'You're covered in scars. What gives?'

'They used to look a lot worse.'

Joanna exhaled, thinking he was joking. He wasn't. However unpleasant the scars that littered his torso, back and arms, they would have been more unpleasant had serums and lasers not improved them, little by little, year after year. Even he couldn't see some of them any longer, but there were those that had caused so much damage, else been poorly sutured – by himself more often than not – that they would never go away, and still looked as bad today as they always had.

'Seriously,' she said. 'What happened?'

'A misspent youth, mostly.'

It was a line he used to end such enquiries, but again he wasn't joking. Each scar was a lesson, a reminder, of his imperfection, of a mistake not to be repeated.

He saw by her expression that she wasn't going to let it go. Few people saw his scars, and of those who did most were satisfied with his vague answers, especially when he was paying for their company, not their questions. She was not one of those women, however, and she was more quizzical than he was used to, and more learned.

She pointed. 'That one above your clavicle. That's from a bullet.'

It wasn't a question. She knew. It would have been pointless to pretend otherwise. It would only draw more suspicion. He had cover stories for each one – *I was in a car accident ... someone jumped me outside a bar* – but they weren't going to work here. Lying would only make her more curious for the truth. Victor didn't want that.

He nodded. 'I was in the army, a long time ago.'

'Which theatre did you get shot in?'

He knew what she meant: Afghanistan or Iraq.

'Sierra Leone,' he said. 'I was attached to a British unit.'

To his knowledge no American troops had operated in that country in living memory. It was a former part of the British Empire, and British troops had been there from time to time since independence.

'The Irish Guards were in Sierra Leone,' she said, surprising him with her knowledge. 'As well as Paras, and the SAS. So, which were you attached to?'

He didn't react. 'You know your regiments.'

She shrugged. She didn't explain how. He imagined she had a cousin or a friend who had been in the military, or perhaps she just liked a certain kind of book.

'So, are you going to tell me which you were, or is it one of those you-could-tell-me-but-you'd-have-to-kill-me situations?'

'If I told you my background then I really would have to kill you.'

She laughed. 'That's so corny.'

He smiled, because he wasn't joking.

She came closer. 'May I?' She gestured to the scar on his trapezius.

He wasn't comfortable with any more intimacy than was necessary, but he didn't want her to know that. She leaned over him. He could smell the scent of the hotel shampoo in her hair. It was too floral, too powerful, as such scents always were.

'What calibre? Looks small, like a twenty-two, but I don't imagine the West Side Boys used a whole lot of those.'

'Seven-six-two, short,' he explained, and when she looked at him with surprised scepticism, he added: 'Long-range shot. Ricochet. Didn't even feel it go in.'

She checked his back. 'You're lucky it didn't come out the other side. Would have made a mess.'

He resisted telling her there was no such thing as luck, and nodded instead.

Her fingers and palms explored his chest, then abdomen, where she traced a horizontal line. 'What about this one?'

He placed his hands over hers. 'You ask a lot of questions, don't you?'

She didn't seem to hear him. She was looking at his mouth or chin. 'Where did you get that little scar?'

A groove formed between Victor's eyebrows. 'What scar?'

'Under your jawline. Here.' She pointed.

He said, 'I don't have a scar there,' thinking he knew about every one he did have, whether she had found them or not.

'You do,' she insisted. She used a thumb to touch her own chin, underneath the jawbone. 'Right here.'

Confused, he felt with his own thumb, scraping stubble and detecting a tiny groove in the skin.

'That's it,' she said.

'I ... I didn't know I had one there.'

'Really? I've only just noticed it.'

He had many scars on his arms, legs, head and torso and he knew where each and every one came from – blades, bullets, shrapnel, fire – and who had caused them. But not one under his chin. How could he not remember an injury there?

'You must have gotten it as a child,' Joanna said. 'If you don't remember it.'

'I don't.'

He shrugged as though it didn't matter to him, but it did. He didn't like not knowing, even if he preferred not to think about his childhood. He didn't like the loss of control over his own memories.

'You probably fell. Kids fall, don't they?'

'I don't really like to talk about those days.'

'Oh, okay,' she said, retreating. 'My bad.'

He had offended her in a way he didn't quite understand, but he knew enough to soften the moment. 'I'm self-conscious about my scars.'

'You shouldn't be,' she said, no longer backing off. 'They make you interesting without trying. A hidden-depth kind of thing. In your suit, no one would guess what lies beneath.'

He said, 'That's the idea.'

Joanna smiled because she was joking. Like him, she was trying to soften the moment.

She slipped out of the robe and let it fall to the floor. She held her arms away from her nakedness. 'See the difference?' She turned around on the spot. 'I'm not interesting at all.'

She expected a certain kind of response, and he was happy to play along. 'Well, I would have to disagree with you there.'

She placed her hands on her hips. 'Prove it.'

He did as requested.

Afterwards, Joanna said, 'Tell me something about you that no one else knows.'

Victor said, 'There's lots about me that people don't know.'

'Then you really have no reason to stall then, do you?'

She smiled in both challenge and self-congratulation.

'I can rub my tummy and pat my head at the same time.'

He had once said the same thing to someone else, in what seemed like another time. That person was dead. He had killed them, so it felt that he was keeping to the letter of Joanna's request, if not the spirit. That couldn't be helped, but he found it distasteful nonetheless. Any time they spent together, any moments they shared, were based on fallacy. She would never know even a hint of who he was.

She said, 'Where are you? You look sad.'

'I was momentarily thinking about work. It's hard to switch off at times.'

'Commodities getting you down?'

'Actually, things are going well. No more false starts.'

'So well you're almost finished here?'

He didn't hesitate. 'Yeah, deal is almost complete. Then it's on to the next one.'

'Ah,' she said. 'The old finite shelf life.'

'Frustratingly inevitable.'

'All good things must come to an end.'

'Don't they just?'

'Well, it was a good run we had, wasn't it? Brief but fun, and over before we got to anything messy. I'm glad we'll be able to say goodbye still liking one another.'

'Are you saying you were getting bored with me?'

'Clever. You know I'm not saying that. And it's leaving it a little late in the day to pretend you're sensitive. Don't think I'm so easily fooled. I know exactly what you're doing.'

'Which is?'

'You just did it again by asking for more. You're diverting the conversation away from us, from goodbye. I'd prefer it if you didn't do that.'

'I'm sorry.' It wasn't something he said often.

She was silent in contemplation for a long moment. He could see she was deciding on something, but he had no idea what, until she said, 'I don't work at a bank.'

'Okay,' he said, waiting for elaboration.

'I do deal mostly with finances. That part was true. It's just not the kind of finances you think. I don't so much attempt to make money, as take it.'

'You're not making a lot of sense.'

'Perhaps this will help explain.' She reached into the inside pocket of her jacket and withdrew her wallet. She took something out he couldn't see and returned to where he sat on the bed, now holding a business card in her hand. 'There are a lot of security considerations with my work, so I'm afraid I can't just tell anyone I meet what I do. I have to be sure of them first. Which . . . is a problem, naturally. So, I understand if this changes your opinion of me, which I don't want it to, but I don't want to leave things on a lie.'

She held out the card, and he took it from her.

It was nothing fancy. Off-white, with black lettering. A certain quality in the thickness, but no more than necessary. It had her full name, her email, her cell phone and landline. It also had the seal of her employer and her job title.

Special Agent Joanna Alamaeda, Drug Enforcement Agency.

'Oh,' Victor said.

SIXTY-THREE

Chartering a small fishing boat proved more difficult to do than Victor expected, but purchasing one was inexpensive. He found a hard-up fisherman in need of quick cash who was delighted that anyone would want his rundown vessel. It was sun-baked, with warped wood and marked fibreglass. The hull leaked and molluscs covered the bow. It was the kind of boat that no one wanted. Decades old and looking like a strong gust of wind would cause it to capsize, it was perfect for Victor's requirements. The Pacific off Guatemala's coast offered some excellent sports fishing, and many gleaming charter boats took tourists and enthusiasts out on a regular basis. Such charter vessels would blend in easier than the fishing boat Victor had purchased, but they would be memorable. There would be documented ownership. It would be easy to check at a later point who had bought it or when it had been stolen. That was no good to Victor. He didn't want to leave a trail. So, he needed a boat that no one wanted, that he could buy for cash from an owner who couldn't be tracked down.

He let the owner oversell because there was no reason not to. A proficient fisherman, but an old man, he told tall tales of black marlin, blue marlin and yellowfin tuna. Fifty pounds, one hundred pounds. He had caught them all, solo, with gear that couldn't handle half the weight. Victor listened with wide eyes and nods of appreciation. He let the old fisherman talk. He took a can of lukewarm beer and popped the tab and didn't ask why the fisherman poured a splash over the side, although he could guess. He laughed when appropriate and asked the kind of questions he knew the fisherman wanted to answer.

Victor listened to those answers but his focus was elsewhere. He was thinking about a rival assassin hired by his employers and the offer he had made. He was also thinking about Joanna and her newly revealed profession.

Both were the kind of problems Victor could do without, because he couldn't leave Guatemala with either of them unresolved.

Despite its sun-bleached hull, chips and dents, the boat was in good condition. It looked a wreck, but only because age had taken, little by little, the fisherman's ability to maintain its appearance. He had spent his energy wisely, however, and the engine worked, the rudder worked, the radio worked. That was all Victor needed. The exhaust smoked and sputtered at first, but he was good with engines and the fisherman gave him a box of tools and spare parts along with the boat. They were no use to him now.

It took Victor the better part of a day to get the exhaust manifold cleaned up so it wouldn't send up smoke signals to advertise his presence to every vessel in sight. The fisherman, now both cash-rich and time-rich, helped him as much as he could. He was no mechanic, but was useful passing and taking tools as required. When the sun set Victor shared final words with the fisherman, who was having a hard time saying goodbye to the boat. Victor said he would look after it, which was true, but only in part, because even in the best-case scenario the boat would be sent to the bottom of the ocean. The fisherman didn't need to know that. He had tears in his eyes as Victor untethered the mooring.

It stank, of course. Once the odour of fish had taken hold it would never let go. Victor didn't mind. A bad smell meant nothing. He had experienced a lot worse. He brought his gear on board in a series of waterproof bags and stashed them below deck. He wasn't expected to be boarded by the coastguard but it would be harder to talk his way out of it with bags on deck just begging to be opened.

Why do you have a silenced weapon? was not a question that could be explained away.

He took the time to paint over the boat's name – *Blessed Mother of Christ* – with something more generic, more forgettable – *Orca* – but otherwise let it be. If things went according to plan he would only need to use it for one night.

Based on his previous research into Maria's yacht, in the worst-case scenario there might be thirty gunmen on board, but that would mean every guest was a sicario, which wasn't the case. All the same, that's what Victor planned for to ensure there could be no surprises. To provide anything close to round-the-clock protection, half would be on day shift and half on night watch. That meant fifteen awake and wary when Victor attacked. The yacht had six decks, so with an attempt at an even spread that meant no more than three sicarios to avoid per deck. In reality he expected to encounter a fraction of this, but he never planned for best-case scenarios.

Despite being on the water, he treated the yacht as any other strike point. He would attack in the middle of the night, at four a.m., when he was awake and alert and his enemies were at their most vulnerable. Victor was always awake at that time. He slept at night only when he had no other choice. It was too dangerous. Every soldier, every killer, was taught to attack in the middle of the night, when the enemy or target was most vulnerable, when their biorhythms were at their lowest, when their threshold for disturbance was at its highest. It took a lot to wake someone so asleep. A partner climbing out of bed wouldn't do it. A shutting door wouldn't either. They could even be touched and remain asleep. It wasn't just theory. Victor had been taught the same and had proved those lessons accurate many times.

He would never go after a fellow professional at such a time, because any such professional Victor hoped to catch off guard would not be asleep at that time for that very reason. He wasn't dealing with professionals here. They may think of themselves as sicarios – hitmen – but the only similarity was in name.

With a yacht so big and so obvious it was easy to observe the arrival of Maria and her entourage. As expected, a motorcade of SUVs pulled up at the marina and dozens of people exited. The security detail had a reasonable level of proficiency, but they were no Secret Service. They allowed Maria to take her time getting to the yacht, but a shot, even if Victor had been able to set up, wouldn't have been worth taking. They surrounded her in a swarm of moving bodies. An RPG could have taken them all out in one go, but Victor might have trouble explaining that one to the nice people on the restaurant terrace he was using.

He counted twenty-six people in addition to his target, of which twelve were bodyguards. The other fourteen consisted of three men who looked like lieutenants, another four men who Victor guessed were associates or clients here to be wooed, half a dozen young women to assist with that process and a well-dressed young man whom Victor took to be Maria's boyfriend or a gigolo. The twelve-man-strong security detail carried no unconcealed weapons, and although luggage was brought on board that could conceivably include assault rifles or sub-machine guns, if they weren't brandishing them now they were unlikely to be walking around with them on deck.

Based on his previous estimates, with twelve sicarios instead of thirty, he might have to avoid only six when he attacked. Which meant no more than one to avoid per deck if they were spread out in an even security detail.

His fishing boat could fit inside the yacht many times over, and the speed disparity between the two meant he could shadow the yacht easily without appearing to do so. When the yacht dropped anchor, the Pacific stretched on to meet the horizon in all directions, so vast and beautiful it could not be quantified. The blue water met the blue sky separated by a line of pale yellow that was all that remained of the day.

Victor kept his distance, at the upper limit of his binoculars, watching the guests and guards on deck. As night fell, those shapes moved around less, and he kept his focus on the guards and their behaviour. They were amateurs, with no set routines and no real awareness. The kind of attack they were present to protect against was a full-scale assault. They would spot a speedboat thrashing towards them, but they were never going to see Victor coming.

Maria and her guests partied well into the night, drinking champagne served by waiters in crisp uniforms. Maria looked just like her sister, albeit a decade younger. She had the same dark hair, same skin tone, same height, but she dressed a little more conservatively. Heloise looked like a movie star attending a premiere. Maria dressed like one trying not to be recognised. She drank with her guests, but she had the same flute of champagne for most of the evening. She chatted and flirted and danced with those she sought to impress, and they were impressed by her, the yacht, and the young women who fawned over them, hung from their arms, kissed them on the cheek and pushed their breasts against them. It wasn't an original approach, but for middle-aged men it was close to heaven.

They partied around the pool on the stern deck, accompanied by several guards who kept a discreet distance. They were watchful, but were trying to remain as passive and absent as possible. A show of force could be impressive, but too much and it could have the opposite effect. When it was supposed to convey strength, it could demonstrate fear. Maria didn't want her guests to think she needed the protection. Hence, three or four were stationed on the stern while the rest of the sicarios were spread throughout the rest of the vessel. Victor couldn't see them all – most were inside – but he knew they were there all the same.

By one a.m. the party was winding down. Most of the guests had been dragged back to their cabins by the young women, leaving Maria and two others to converse. Maria's back was facing Victor so he couldn't read her lips, but the two men she was talking to were looking his way. One was so fat he took up an entire bench, his arms spread out along the backrest, relaxed and happy.

You know, he was saying, *when you first invited me on this trip I figured I had done something wrong and I would end up at the bottom of the ocean.*

There was a pause while Maria spoke in return. Victor saw her arms move as she gesticulated. Everyone laughed. The second man was more stilted, a little nervous, in his laughter. Maybe he wasn't as convinced as the first that he would avoid ending up on the bottom of the Pacific.

That's what I'm talking about, the man replied, *with Diaz dead, I assumed you were looking for someone to blame, not promote.*

The second man had a beard and long hair tied into a tight ponytail. He swallowed before he said, *I need to think about the proposal . . . I need time.*

Maria nodded, perhaps offering some words of reassurance. The man wiped some sweat from his brow, explaining it away with, *I think I've had a little too much to drink.*

There was more laughter. When it faded, Maria spoke again and the two men listened, nodding on occasion while she continued her proposal. Victor wasn't sure if one man was in line to take over Diaz's responsibilities, or if they were being asked to divide them between themselves. In either case, the first was enthusiastic and the second reluctant.

They conversed for a while longer, but not about her offer. They laughed and joked until Maria stood to embrace the men, one at a time, who then left her alone on the deck. She retired soon after, her champagne flute still with liquid inside.

Victor continued to wait. He waited another two hours,

watching the yacht and the guards on board. They weren't elite security, and as the night wore on and tiredness crept in, their discipline began to crumble. They smoked cigarettes and played with their phones. They left whole sections of the decks unguarded while taking trips to the latrine, which were not always quick.

At four a.m. Victor set down the binoculars and checked his things. He wore a black neoprene dry suit, to which he added a harness, fins, an oxygen tank, mask and regulator. To the front of his harness he attached a diving knife and a waterproof bag containing a pistol, suppressor and spare magazines.

He sat on the back of the boat and rolled over and into the water.

SIXTY-FOUR

He couldn't risk using a light so he navigated by compass only. It was attached to his wrist, markings visible thanks to the tritium coating that glowed in the dark. He swam just below the surface of the water, at a slow, steady rate. He didn't want to burn any energy he didn't have to. He was a strong swimmer, but didn't swim often. It had been years since he had last used a public swimming pool else swam at a beach. In a swimsuit he was too noticeable, too memorable, even without the inherent risks associated with being defenceless in the water.

The Pacific was cold, but nothing he couldn't handle. The dry suit took most of the sting out of it, and after a few minutes of swimming his body generated enough heat to push away the rest. The water was quiet. For a while he was as calm and as at peace as he had ever been.

That changed when he could see the yacht ahead, distorted through the water and illuminated by starlight. He veered towards the stern, where the anchor chain lay.

It swayed a little, pushed and pulled by the current, but was taut and secure. Victor took hold of it with one hand and removed his fins with the other, clipping them to his harness. He removed the respirator and mask, again clipping them in place, and began to climb.

The anchor chain was thick and dense, but it was slippery. He couldn't get good footholds, so he relied on his upper-body strength to pull him up. The hull above the waterline was thirty feet in height, but the anchor did not rise all the way to the deck. Victor climbed the entire length of the chain, right up to the anchor port, where he paused for a moment to take some deep breaths. Even for his fitness, the climb had been taxing.

He walked his feet up the hull until they were braced on the lip of the anchor port and he waited, contorted but comfortable, and listened. When he was certain there was no one in the immediate area above him, he pushed off with his legs and jumped for the railing above. It was only a short distance, but he was jumping at an angle to follow the curve of the hull, not straight up but out.

He caught the rail in both hands, gripping hard to fight the force of his lower body still moving with the jump, legs swinging out below him until he had used his core strength to slow and stop the momentum. He focused on his ring fingers to better activate his lats and pull himself up with enough speed to then vault over the railing, fast and smooth, dropping into an immediate crouch on the other side.

In seconds, the waterproof bag was open and he had the pistol in hand.

He was already lying flat on the deck when a sicario stepped outside. Victor lay behind one of the sun loungers, which was just high enough to hide him from casual view. The gunman took several slow steps as a disposable lighter took several thumbs for a flame to ignite. Victor could see a little from his position, peering beneath the lounger. He kept his gaze on the feet and ankles, which were parallel to the lounger, until they pivoted and Victor saw the worn heels of the man's shoes.

At that point, Victor slithered and stood, and darted across the short width of the deck, coming up behind the sicario; kicking him in the back of the knee at the same time as wrapping his arms around the man's neck, one palm snapping over the mouth and nose to catch any cries before they escaped. The sicario struggled hard, hands shooting up to grab Victor's arm in an attempt to prise it free, but weakening too fast to apply any strength. Victor maintained pressure until the sicario had ceased fighting back, and then for a little longer.

Victor tipped the man overboard.

Inside, the yacht was decorated like a gaudy hotel. Most of the lights were off, but there was plenty of starlight coming through the windows. Thanks to the extensive plans online, Victor knew the fastest way to the master bedroom. He took his time, however, keeping quiet and listening for threats. There were many rooms and hallways, and only a few guards awake and active, but they weren't patrolling. They were tired, they were bored. They were easy to avoid.

The master bedroom lay on the sixth deck, accessible via two sets of stairs – one fore, one aft – that spiralled from the fifth deck, which was laid out with a private lounge, games room, kitchen and two bathrooms, all for the exclusive use of Maria Salvatierra.

Not just Maria, Victor saw, as he followed a trail of discarded garments, female and male.

There were no guards stationed outside the master suite. No one imagined a threat could get this far. Few targets were ever prepared for someone like Victor. Besides, Maria valued her privacy.

He heard movement above him, from the master bedroom – bedclothes rustling, bare feet padding on carpet, a man's yawn.

Then a door closed with a quiet click of the doorjamb, but no catch. No lock.

Victor dashed up the spiralled steps, moving fast but still quiet, on the balls of his feet. He saw a huge, circular bed in the centre of the room. A naked woman lay on top of a sheet that had been bunched at the end of the bed. She was asleep.

On the far side of the bed was a closed door.

Victor crept past the bed and made his way to the door. He could hear a man urinating on the other side, aiming for the porcelain in an effort to be quiet.

The door was unlocked, so Victor eased it open at the same time the man was finishing up. Victor was inside the bathroom before the man had turned around.

'Shh,' Victor said, gun pointed at the man's face.

Soft palms rose belonging to the young boyfriend or gigolo Victor had seen before. Twenty-four or -five, bed-messed hair, smooth from nose to navel. He wore a pair of black silk boxer shorts and several gold chains around his neck and wrists, but nothing else. No place to hide a weapon.

He was terrified – no sicario – and was frozen to the spot as Victor glanced around the bathroom, searching for the best way to restrain the guy. He didn't want to shoot him.

Even with a suppressor, it would wake Maria up and possibly alert nearby guards. There were towels and robes, with belts.

The guy seemed to understand Victor's position, else fear took over him, because he attacked.

He was young and in shape, but an amateur. Victor slipped the clumsy punch and whipped him in the temple with the butt of the gun.

The boyfriend or gigolo was already off balance, having thrown the haymaker while on the move, so the blow to the skull took him from his feet. There wasn't enough room for him to fall straight down, and he collapsed into – then bounced away from – the marble shelf housing the washbasin. Victor caught him before he crashed to the floor tiles, limiting, but not eliminating the inevitable noise, and eased him into the bathtub.

Glazed eyes looked up at Victor, unfocused but awake, so Victor hit him again with the gun to make sure he stayed in the tub.

Maria was stirring when Victor re-entered the bedroom. The noise from the en-suite had woken her despite his efforts to reduce it. A light sleeper.

She sat up to say something, at first mistaking him for her lover, but her breath caught in her throat when she saw Victor emerge from the shadows.

'Who are you?' she demanded.

'I'm your murderer.'

SIXTY-FIVE

The pictures on Lavandier's dossier site failed to do justice to Maria Salvatierra. She was an attractive woman, even in the gloom. There were no lamps on in the room. The roof was transparent, however, and light seeped in from the bright stars. Maria's skin was silver. Her eyes were black.

She looked much like Heloise, but Maria's was an effortless beauty. In part because she was younger than her sister, but also because she didn't have the same coldness in her eyes. Maria's seemed warm, almost innocent. Victor reminded himself that she was as ruthless an individual as anyone he had encountered. People saw what they wanted to see, he had been told. Did he want to believe that she was somehow innocent?

She said, 'What are you waiting for?'

He said nothing in return. He admired her poise; afraid but not panicked, gaze locked on Victor and the gun in his hand, uncaring about her nakedness, unashamed and focused on her life and not her modesty.

'Do you think I'm scared? Do you think I haven't seen a gun before?'

'You're scared,' Victor said. 'Everyone is when a gun is pointing their way.'

'You too?'

Victor stepped closer. 'I'm different.'

Maria didn't react to the increase in proximity. She continued to stare at him with the same unblinking eyes. Her body was tense and still. There were no weapons in the room that Victor could see. She relied on her men to protect her. Without them she was vulnerable, even if she didn't act like it. There were no stalling tactics; no rapid-fire questions to distract him while her sicarios grew closer. She wasn't expecting the young guy to come out of the bathroom either. She had to know Victor wouldn't have left him in a position to do so.

'What are you waiting for?' she asked again.

'Your sister hired me,' Victor said in place of an answer.

Maria took this in without reacting, then she looked away. 'Of course she did.' There was regret in her voice. 'While I've even allowed myself to believe that one day we might stop this madness. Declare peace. Make up. Maybe one day have a relationship again. I thought I was the stronger sister too. I thought it would be me who found a way to stop this.'

'Everyone's strong until they meet someone stronger.'

'Let me guess,' Maria began. 'That effete fool Lavandier hired you. It was his idea from the start, I'm sure. I'm convinced war started because of the poison he dripped into my sister's ear. I sometimes wonder who is really my rival.'

'I met him along with Heloise,' Victor said. 'I couldn't tell you who had the original idea. I can't say I thought to ask.'

'It'll have been his, I'm telling you.'

He shrugged. 'I don't care.'

'You don't care who hired you? You don't care why?'

'I'm paid to kill, not understand.'

'Then understand that the war won't end with my death. There will be revenge attacks within hours. My lieutenants will take over and carry on in the exact same way. Nothing will change.'

'I'm sure your sister knows this.'

Maria was sitting forward now, animated. 'She doesn't have what it takes to rule this city. That she had to hire an outsider to do what she cannot says everything.'

'What does or does not happen after I'm done here is not my concern.'

'It should be your concern,' Maria said. 'She'll betray you. Heloise will turn on you as soon as she pays you. She's a snake. She is utterly empty inside. Even my father was scared of her. Can you imagine such a thing? A father scared of his child? Yet it's true. Should she actually pay you, you still won't be safe, because she'll realise that if you could get to me you could get to her too. She won't be able to sleep at night until you're dead. She's as paranoid as she is vindictive.'

Victor remained silent. Maria, however, wasn't done.

'Do you really expect to get off this yacht alive?'

Victor said, 'I do.'

'You have a silenced gun, but no gunshot is silent. I have dozens of armed men on board.'

'You have exactly a dozen to be exact,' Victor said. 'And most of them are asleep right now. Those that are awake haven't been shown to be much use.'

'You have it all worked out, don't you?'

He nodded.

'Then what are you waiting for?' she asked for the third time. 'Does Heloise want me to suffer first? Are you going to torture me?'

'She doesn't care how you die, only that you do.'

'Then a message, surely. Some cruel barb she spent weeks composing, so she can sit by her pool with a spritzer and toast my death with a smile.'

He shook his head. 'There is none.'

'You're not the first person to point a gun at me,' she said. 'But I think you might be the calmest. If I couldn't see the intensity in your eyes I might think this was some elaborate prank.'

'I'm deadly serious.'

'Then I'm really struggling to understand what you're doing right now.'

She was as impatient as she was confused.

Victor said, 'Maybe I'm not sure myself.'

'A hitman with a crisis of conscience?'

He raised an eyebrow. 'Hardly.'

'Then what is this?' Maria stared at him. 'Why haven't you killed me yet? Because you're taking a long time to pull a trigger.' She glanced down at herself. 'Or are you just getting your money's worth?'

He shook his head. 'You were right about your sister, only she's already betrayed me. She broke our agreement.'

Her poise cracked because she was surprised and eager to know more. She was silent though. She waited for him.

'She hired a second killer to come after you,' Victor said. 'I was clear that this would be unacceptable. I was explicit that the contract would be void if any of my conditions were not met. I wasn't joking.'

'Yet here you are,' Maria said.

He lowered the gun down to his side. 'I'm not here to kill you.'

She didn't blink. 'Why not?'

'Your sister needs to understand that a deal's a deal. I keep my side only if the other side keeps their own. I could kill you, collect my fee and be gone across the sea before sunrise, second killer or not. But that's not the point.'

'You broke on to my yacht just to tell me this?'

'I wanted you to know what Heloise hired me to do. I've spent the last few weeks getting to know you, Maria, and there was no other way to get close to you, let alone explain the situation. I could hardly have driven up to your ranch to talk about it over iced tea. I like the pattern on your sun loungers, by the way.'

She said, 'I think I get it now.'

'This was the best way to prove the veracity of my claim.'

'And there was I thinking you were just showing off.'

Victor said, 'Well, I do like to make an entrance.'

She gestured to the nearest bedside table, on which rested a glass of water. 'May I?'

'Be my guest.'

She shuffled closer to the table and took a sip from the glass. Her gaze never left Victor. Whatever his claims, she didn't feel safe. He hadn't killed her, but he was still an intruder with a gun.

Victor said, 'You can put some clothes on if you like.'

Maria glanced down at her nakedness. 'I'm fine like this.'

'Your choice.'

'Have you killed any of my men?'

'Fifty-fifty,' Victor said.

'What does that mean?'

'It means we'll find out soon enough. I'm afraid I had to crush your boyfriend's nose. It's going to be a long time before he's handsome again.'

She shrugged. 'He's replaceable, and it's not his nose I found so captivating.' She set the glass of water down again. 'I should probably still be enraged at this intrusion, but I find I can't be. I feel I should thank you for what you've told me tonight. I'm very grateful you're not going to shoot me.'

'How grateful?'

'Whatever Heloise promised to pay you for killing me, I'll pay you double if you kill her instead.'

'Deal,' Victor said.

'Spoken like a true mercenary. You would betray my sister so easily? You'd turn on your employer just for hiring someone else?'

Victor nodded. 'To forgive one sin is to invite another.'

'And what of your own sins? Will they be forgiven?'

'We're not here to talk about me, Ms Salvatierra.'

Maria smiled, then laughed. 'That's what you came here for, isn't it? You wanted to switch sides. Which is why you knew for certain you'd get off this boat alive.'

He nodded. 'This is a good strike point, as we are bearing witness, but it's a lousy place from which to escape. I had no interest in getting shot while swimming back to my boat. That's no kind of plan.'

Maria said, 'It's funny, because Heloise always said mercenaries can't be trusted, that they will always betray when a better deal comes along.'

'I'm an assassin, Miss Salvatierra. I'm not a very nice person just off my job description, but I was sticking to my agreement with Heloise. However, my agreement with your sister was null and void the second she hired someone else to do the job she hired me for. It would be naive of me to believe the people I deal with would honour the terms of my employment, which is why it never comes as a surprise. The kind of person who hires a killer isn't the kind of person apt to stick to their word. Hence, it's necessary for me to show them the error of their ways. Plus,' he said after a pause, 'if I'm going to forfeit my original purse, I might as well get paid for it.'

'I wish I'd had the foresight to hire you in the first place. Maybe this war would be over by now.'

'It'll be over soon,' Victor said, 'but before I go, I need something from you. If I'm going to kill your sister, she needs to think you're dead.'

'Why?'

'She's a well-connected and intelligent woman. It's reasonable to assume she will learn an intruder came aboard your yacht, and if we both live to tell the tale it won't be hard for her to deduce the reason why. If she knows I'm coming for her, there's no guarantee I'll be successful. Her casino is a fortress as it is.'

She processed this, then reached to the nightstand and scooped up a fine silver chain that she tossed Victor's way. He caught it, and saw there was a small pendant in the shape of a horse on the chain's end.

Maria said, 'A gift from my father. Heloise had one too. She despised it because I loved mine. She threw hers away after he died. Show it to her and she'll be convinced. I would never give it up.'

'Yet you are giving it up. There's no guarantee you'll ever see it again.'

'I can let it go if it means Heloise dies.'

There was a casual abruptness in her tone that Victor hadn't expected.

He said, 'You're really not fond of one another, are you?'

'The strongest love breeds the strongest hate.'

He nodded that he understood, but didn't. He didn't hate anyone.

Victor looked at the pendant. 'As good as this is, it's conceivable that I stole it, or had a copy made.'

'Did you bring a knife with you?'

He nodded. It was sheathed at his belt. He drew the weapon in his left hand.

'Hand it to me.'

He approached the bed, and presented the knife to Maria. She took it by the grip and closed her other hand around the blade.

'This is how much I want Heloise dead.'

She squeezed.

There was only the faintest flicker of a reaction in her eyes despite the horrendous pain she was inflicting upon herself. When she opened her hand again, the palm was red. She presented it to Victor, who lowered the horse pendant into the fresh blood.

Maria said, 'Will this suffice?'

'If she knows your blood type.'

Maria used a pillowcase to wrap up her hand. 'We shared the same doctor before this war began. His loyalty is to Heloise now.'

'Then yes,' Victor said. 'It'll more than suffice.'

A yell for help sounded from somewhere else on the yacht. Maria stiffened.

'What's that?'

'I threw one of your men overboard,' Victor explained. 'Sounds like someone's spotted him.'

She wasn't sure if he was serious.

'Give him a pay rise if they fish him out alive,' Victor said. 'The water's cold.'

SIXTY-SIX

The office's air conditioning was broken. It had been broken from before Alamaeda had arrived and no one seemed to know when, if ever, it would get fixed. Windows were left open all the time. Fans were on every desk. Everyone was hot and sweating for every long minute. Alamaeda had learned to take off her jacket before she was even inside the building. She knew which guys to stay clear of and where to sit to stay in the draught.

It was bad from an operational perspective to keep windows and doors open – it increased the risk of eavesdropping by outside entities or internally by corrupt cops – but if it was too hot to work then that was even better for the bad guys.

Alamaeda stared at the huge whiteboard that covered one wall of their office, where she and Wickliffe made notes and stuck pictures, reports and random thoughts and musings. She stared at a section relating to the Miguel Diaz murder, with crime-scene photographs, memorandums and a sticky note that said: foreigner?

Routine is what killed you, Alamaeda knew. She had seen it happen, in both the figurative and literal capacities. You couldn't help it. Sooner or later you repeated an action, and before long it became habit, forming a pattern. A routine. Normal people had them and so did criminals. So had Diaz, and it had got him killed. Or had it?

She stared so hard at the word 'foreigner' the letters shifted out of focus.

Wickliffe said, 'Where are you, Jo?'

Alamaeda blinked herself back to reality. 'Lost in a day-dream.' Wickliffe had her hands tucked behind her head. She'd had lunch, and Alamaeda could see a patch of pale skin at her stomach where the blouse was pulled taut, opening a gap between buttons.

Alamaeda said, 'I told him.'

'You told who what?'

'The new guy. Ryan. I told him I'm DEA.'

'I see. And how did Mr Canadian take it?'

'He was surprised, naturally. He made out that it wasn't a big deal.'

'And was it?'

'I don't know exactly. I guess we'll find out if he calls me again.'

'If he doesn't, he's an idiot.'

Alamaeda paused to change the subject. 'You ever think about retirement?'

'Yeah, all the time. I figure I won't. I'll go back into law, but small stuff. You know, getting people out of parking violations.'

'You've got it all worked out.'

She nodded with some enthusiasm. 'You need a dream,

Joanna, but not a fantasy. Something realistic. Something that can be obtained. If you shoot for the stars, all you're going to do is hit the whole lot of empty blackness around them.'

'Never let it be said that you're not bursting at the seams with wisdom.'

'You need to make the most of me while you can. Once we part ways you'll be filled with regret for wasting this opportunity.'

'Then tell me this, Oh Wise One, should I—'

Alamaeda didn't get to finish the question because her phone rang.

It was Gabriel Hernandez.

She met Hernandez in the old town. He was so nervous his knee couldn't keep still under the table. It made the cups rattle on the surface.

'You have something for me?'

He nodded. 'I was with Maria Salvatierra over the weekend.'

'At her ranch?'

'No, on her yacht. She had a party of sorts. A lot of people I didn't recognise were there. I didn't want to, of course, but you don't say no to a request like that.'

'Yeah, I get that. But why did she invite you along too? I thought you told me you hadn't had any direct dealings with her for years now.'

'Because of Diaz, because he's dead.'

Alamaeda understood. 'She offered you his job.'

'Not exactly,' Hernandez was quick to answer. 'But some of it. She wants to set up a new fund, to launder more money. A lot more money.'

'That's great.'

Hernandez shook his head from side to side. 'No, it's not. I want to get out of this, not be pulled in further.'

'I get that too, Mr Hernandez, but someone killed Diaz over a game of cards. I'm grateful you gave me his name, but it went nowhere. As I told you at the start of all of this, if you want a new life for you and your girlfriend then you need to work with me.'

'I have. I did that already.'

'Diaz died before he could be of any use, but now you have a second chance. Take the job. Be the new Diaz and you'll be more useful to us than even Diaz himself.'

'I want guarantees.'

'Take the job, and I can give them to you.'

He wiped away some sweat, and nodded. 'Okay. I'll do it. I'll do whatever it takes.'

'Good, you've made the right decision. Now tell me who else was at this boat party.'

'I don't know who they were, but something happened in the night.'

'What does that mean?'

'I don't know, but one of her guards fell overboard and had to be fished out of the water, and another one had a broken nose.'

'Sounds like your standard cerveza-fuelled punch-up. Forget about it, but not about the guests. I'll get you some pictures to go through, see if you recognise anyone.'

'If I have to.'

'Yes,' Alamaeda said, 'you have to.'

SIXTY-SEVEN

Lavandier was troubled. He was troubled by something he had believed had ceased to exist long ago: his conscience. Not for betraying Heloise, but because he had been the one to suggest hiring the Wraith in the first place. Had he suggested hiring a professional just so he could betray Heloise, to force his hand? He could not be sure. Perhaps at some subconscious level the innate drive to survive and thrive had compelled him without his knowledge, but it had taken time, it had taken a great deal of time to come to terms with the idea of betrayal, the idea of losing Heloise. He had wanted to end the war, to see Heloise become sole patron, but he could not get the image out of his head of a loyal man's tongue in her bloody claws. Lavandier dreamed of himself in that chair. He dreamed of his tongue in her hand, her cruel laughter echoing through his mind in the middle of the night.

The situation had become untenable, he had told Heloise and meant it. The whole cartel was on borrowed time. There would be no peace because there would be no winner. Even in the best-case scenario, with Maria dead by the Wraith's bullet and the war over, the cartel would still be fractured. Sicarios who had been killing one another would not forget those grievances. Traffickers who had grown rich under Maria would not welcome any loss to their income. Lavandier knew how these things worked because he understood ambition, he understood desire, and he understood weakness. He had mastered his own by not overcoming them, or even fighting them, but accepting them. If people could just recognise their own limitations and embrace them, there would be peace and prosperity the world over, but ambition trumped all. There was no limit to human greed.

He knew that better than anyone.

He sat on one of the couches in the massive open-plan lounge area of Heloise's suite. She reclined on a chaise longue, reading a book, and his heart ached just to look at her. He couldn't love her or hate her any more.

A crackle of static interrupted his thoughts as a transmission came through to El Perro's radio from the guard hut at the entrance to the compound. The volume was dialled down so as not to be a nuisance, and only El Perro could hear. Nevertheless, he took a few steps away to answer it discreetly so as not to disturb the discussion. From the corner of his eye, Lavandier saw something was wrong. El Perro's expression changed about as often as Heloise's did. He shared a brief exchange with the sentry, ended the call, and approached Heloise.

Like Lavandier, she saw it was something important.

'What is it?' she demanded.

El Perro took a moment to find the words. 'A package has arrived for you. From the Wraith.'

Lavandier said, 'Safe?'

El Perro nodded. 'My men have checked it. It's just a box. There's ... jewellery inside.'

There was far more to it than that, Lavandier could see, but El Perro was reluctant to elaborate. Heloise was impatient, and instructed him to have the package brought to her with haste.

A sicario arrived a few minutes later and presented a small gift box to El Perro. It was a pleasant little item with a black ribbon. El Perro checked inside the box, ordered the sicario away, and brought the box to where Heloise and Lavandier waited. He presented it to them, lid in one hand so they could look inside. Lavandier was eager to see what the box contained but didn't dare go first. Heloise did and he watched her, transfixed.

Her perfectly constructed face faltered and her shoulders sagged for a moment, as though all the strength flooded out of her. There could have been a hint of moisture in her eyes, but then she blinked, and when her eyes snapped open again they were clear and her poise returned.

'What is it?' Lavandier asked, desperate.

She handed him the box and he peered inside to see a small, clear ziplock bag containing a silver horse pendant smeared with blood. He didn't know the significance of the pendant, but he could guess easily enough.

'Is this what I think it is?'

Heloise nodded, her gaze far away.

Lavandier said, 'We should have the blood tested.'

Heloise said, 'That won't be necessary. The pendant was made to order. There were only two of them. Now, one.'

'What should I do with it?' Lavandier asked.

'Whatever you wish to do. Give it to one of your whores if you like.'

There was an edge to Heloise's tone despite the flippancy. Lavandier would do no such thing. He gave the box back to El Perro, who didn't know what to do with it either, so put the lid back in place and went to set it down. Heloise stopped him with a shake of her head. She didn't want to be near it.

Lavandier's phone rang. It was the Wraith.

'Congratulations,' the Frenchman said.

'I'd like to get paid.'

'Naturally.'

'I want cash.'

'As you wish. I'll have it ready by tomorrow.'

The Wraith said, 'I'll collect it from the casino,' and hung up.

SIXTY-EIGHT

The alley that Ikal called home ran along the back of a row of bars, restaurants and fast food outlets. In the daytime he stayed clear of them because the big Mexicans who ran the *cantina* would chase him away from their dumpsters if they caught him foraging for scraps and he was too damn old to be chased anywhere. So he wandered the neighbourhood, pushing his shopping trolley full to capacity with worthless possessions and trying not to get in anyone's way while hoping to collect a few quetzals from city folk.

When the sun fell, Ikal came back to the alley behind the bars to collect his dinner from what the restaurants threw away. He had to be careful because sometimes they would mix the leftover food with broken glass and other hazards to discourage him and others like him, but he always managed to find enough to eat so that these days he didn't spend the nights clutching his stomach in hunger.

Tonight, he'd found a whole half of a bean burrito that was

even still a little warm and he picked off the dirt and the other garbage and settled down to enjoy his food.

Footsteps interrupted the banquet.

He stiffened where he sat because he feared the two Mexicans had spotted him, but Ikal didn't move because he saw there was just a lone man walking towards him, and he didn't fill the alley like those two fatsos.

Ikal reached into the folds of his coat and drew out his penknife. He'd stolen it from a market stall and had kept it on him ever since because a young kid of no more than sixteen had beaten Ikal until he thought he was going to die and had only stopped when Ikal had pissed himself. Ikal had done nothing to the kid. The kid had just decided to beat him because he could, because Ikal didn't matter.

The man stopped a few feet from Ikal. His face was hidden by the darkness of the alleyway but Ikal could tell he was a foreigner.

'What you want?' Ikal snapped. 'Can't you see I'm eating my food here?'

'Do you have a criminal record?'

Ikal stared with wide eyes. 'What kind of question is that?'

'A valuable one,' the man said, 'if you answer it.'

The man held a hand into the light. Between his fingers he held a hundred-quetzal banknote.

'This can be yours if you answer me honestly. Yes, or no, it doesn't matter. You'll get paid either way.'

The man was crazy, but Ikal played along in the hope it was a genuine offer. 'No,' he said. 'I'm clean. I'm no thief.'

'Have you ever been arrested? Ever spent a night in jail?'

'No,' Ikal snarled, angry at the implication.

'Can you read and write?'

Ikal searched the darkness to try to see the man's face, to decipher what this was, but could not. 'What difference does it make to you whether I can read?'

The man produced a second banknote and Ikal's eyes glimmered at the sight of so much money, so much opportunity. Then he grew agitated. He knew a cruel scam when he saw one.

'What is this, some kind of joke? I tell you, boy, I may be old but I'll kick your ass from here till Sunday if you don't get out of my alley.'

'I want you to write something for me,' the man explained. 'No jokes. No tricks. One minute of your time for two hundred quetzals. What do you say?'

Ikal said, 'Then let's get on with it.'

There was a rustling as the man produced a packet of something and threw it to Ikal. It landed in his lap.

'First, clean your hands with these.'

'Boy, why you want me to clean my hands? What the hell is wrong with you?'

'Why do you want to question my desire to pay you well for a sliver of your time?'

Ikal grumbled and opened the packet. It contained wet wipes like the ones ladies used to clean off make-up. He used a bunch to scrub the dirt from his hands.

'Happy now, crazy man?'

'Almost.'

The man produced a thin, square object covered in a clear plastic wrap. 'Open this.'

This time he didn't throw it and Ikal took it from his hand. He tore off the plastic wrap and saw there was a greetings card inside. The man tossed him a pen.

'Write down what I say, exactly as I say it. Ready?'

'Yes. Get on with it.'

'Write "For the attention of Special Agent Joanna Alamaeda ... "'

The man then recited several pieces of information that Ikal wrote down in his neatest handwriting. There were names and times and locations that made no sense to him, but the man made sure he got it right. Ikal wanted to get it right too. He wanted all that money.

When it was done, the man said, 'Place the card in the envelope.'

Ikal did.

'Seal it.'

Ikal tore off the thin strip covering the adhesive and pressed the fold down.

'Write this on the envelope ... ' The man dictated an address.

'That it?'

'That's it.'

Ikal handed the man the envelope containing the card and the man handed Ikal the money. The man left without another word and Ikal noticed the man limped. When he was alone again, Ikal reached into his underpants and withdrew the slim roll of banknotes that were his life's savings. He unhooked the rubber band and added the two hundreds to it, happy to have earned so much for doing so little, but unable to shake the feeling perhaps he should have refused the crazy foreigner's offer.

He consoled himself by returning to the burrito banquet.

SIXTY-NINE

An empty casino felt not unlike a mausoleum, Lavandier realised. The endless rows of lightless slot machines could almost be sarcophagi; the poker tables made Lavandier think of embalming. Hundreds of millions of dollars had been poured into its construction. Heloise, one eye on her legacy, had spared no expense. No corners had been cut. Every room was luxurious. Every feature and fixture was the best money could buy. Lavandier had pleaded restraint at every turn, and at every turn had been ignored. Now, as he walked through the excess as the solitary voice of reason, he wondered if any paying customer would ever walk across the same marble floor.

They could, of course, but not while Heloise's shadow hung over the casino. He imagined a future, a year or two down the line, when, after refusal upon refusal, Heloise would have no choice but to sell the building to a reputable enterprise, taking a huge loss in both money and influence in the process. Then, half-broke and without the unfaltering loyalty and respect she enjoyed now, she would be usurped and Lavandier would be usurped with her.

If he tried to walk away before then, to ensure he survived that changing of the guard, she would have him hunted down and killed before he could make it out of the country. If he remained at her side during the inevitable decline, he would not survive the usurpation. Whoever succeeded her might kill her fast out of respect. They would make an example of Lavandier.

How had he found himself – so very clever as he knew himself to be – in a no-win situation?

It didn't matter. He couldn't change the past and there was nothing to be gained in obsessing over what could not be altered. What could happen in the future was his focus. He wanted to carry on living and carry on being wealthy and enjoying all the perks that wealth provided, particularly perkiness.

Which was why he drove to meet with Special Agent Joanna Alamaeda, who said, 'Why the face to face?'

It wasn't something they really did. Maybe once or twice over the last few years just to keep the relationship alive and well. He thought of her as his insurance policy. For the small price of a few low-level traffickers, Lavandier had established his bona fides, his usefulness to the Drug Enforcement Agency. Should he ever feel the need for a swift departure from Guatemala he could turn himself over to Special Agent Joanna Alamaeda. A worst-case scenario. A worse than worst-case, because Lavandier would rather die than go to prison, but that was now, that was today. Tomorrow, a few years in a minimum-security resort might become suddenly appealing. Especially if he could ensure a good degree of his wealth would be hidden away well enough to be waiting for him upon his return to freedom.

Then, a life of mediocrity in a programme to keep him alive. Somewhere far away from anywhere interesting. One of those small American towns, no doubt. Picket fences. Quiet. Hell. No way. Not today. Not ever.

'Today is different,' he explained. 'Today we take our relationship to the next level.'

He had always played down his role, of course. He was not Heloise's counsel, but one of many advisors. High enough up the ladder to be of use, but not so high that he should know a lot more than he ever revealed. Alamaeda wouldn't simply accept him as a source, as an inside man, but force him into testifying, and what a witness he would be on the stand. He could sit for hours and accurately recount all manner of crimes personally committed by Heloise and seen with his own eyes, let alone all those that could be tied to her through conspiracy charges.

'I'm waiting,' she said.

Lavandier said, 'Do you believe in ghosts?'

'I'm starting to believe that you're wasting my time.'

'Forgive me, but you should believe in ghosts because there is one in Guatemala City as we speak. A spirit conjured by my employer to put harm upon her sister. The Wraith.'

'Who is this guy?'

'He has no name I could find, and may not have one at all, but he's very good at what he does, I can tell you that at least.'

'What does this Wraith do exactly?'

'He kills people for considerable amounts of money.'

'You're talking about a hitman.'

Lavandier nodded. 'Hired in Madrid by Heloise herself to kill Maria, to end the war, to ensure victory.'

'How long has he been here?'

'Some weeks now.'

'And what has he been doing all of those weeks?'

Lavandier shrugged. 'Preparing, I suppose, but in truth I know nothing of his methods.'

'Are you going to give me anything I can actually use?'

'I always have, haven't I?'

They had a perfect illusion of symbiosis. He gave up traffickers whose usefulness was on the decline and in doing so established himself as a trusted informant, a man on the inside, a valuable asset who had the ear of a DEA agent. Plus, he enjoyed the subterfuge. For a coward, the thrill of taking such risks was a surprising high. He liked to think he was slowly corrupting Alamaeda. He liked that even such a supposedly stalwart champion of justice and virtue could be manipulated into betraying everything she thought she believed in.

Lavandier said, 'You know, of course, that Miguel Diaz is dead.'

She nodded.

'The Wraith killed him.'

Alamaeda stepped closer. 'Say again?'

'The Wraith killed Miguel Diaz.'

'He was paid to?'

'Oh no, not at all. I don't know, but he assures me it was to further the objective of killing Maria.'

'You have proof he killed Diaz?'

'Of course not. That's your job, not mine.'

'I'm not going to chase after some apparitional Spaniard hired by Heloise based on your assurances alone.'

'I didn't say the Wraith was Spanish, only that he was hired in Spain.'

'But he's Latino?'

'No, probably European.'

'Probably?'

'We spoke Spanish, and his was as good as mine.'

She said, 'You have a description, surely?'

'Over six feet. Dark hair. Dark eyes. Lean.'

'Notable features?'

'None.'

'That all sounds pretty generic. Kind of like you just pulled those details out of the air. Almost like he doesn't really exist.'

Lavandier showed a thin smile. 'It is not my fault he is nondescript. I suspect that my failure to provide sufficient distinguishing details of him is no accident, either a precursor to his success in his chosen profession else a deliberate act, series of acts, to ensure it.'

'I see,' Alamaeda sighed. 'So, he's either made up or some kind of chameleon. Great, and no sale. I want something solid before I leave, otherwise this conversation meant nothing and I'll walk away right now. I'll get back in my car. I'll forget this ever happened, but I won't forget you wasted my time with a make-believe assassin.'

Lavandier thought for a moment. 'What if I can prove to you that he exists? What if you can see him with your own eyes? I could arrange a face-to-face, given enough time.'

All of a sudden, Alamaeda was in no rush to leave. Her posture relaxed. She was here to stay. He hadn't even got to the best part yet.

'Agent Alamaeda,' he began. 'We're getting sidetracked by this killer, by Diaz. That's only a small part of why I'm here, only a fraction of what I know. And what I know, and you need to know, is that the Wraith was recently successful in the task he was hired to complete. Maria Salvatierra is dead. Murdered.'

Alamaeda's expression didn't change. 'Is that so?'

Lavandier nodded. Just a little nod. Understated. Classy. 'Yes, that is so. The news hasn't broken yet, and I'm not sure when it will. I imagine her lieutenants will keep it hidden for as long as possible while they seek to limit the damage to the cartel, but believe me, it's true.'

'Yeah, that's the problem. I don't believe you. Why should I?'

'Because I've seen proof, Agent Alamaeda, and because I've even met the hitman responsible for Maria's murder. I was there when Heloise hired him. It was in sunny Madrid, in a lovely suite at the Ritz no less.'

'Okay,' she said, still sceptical but too intrigued to dismiss his claims. 'Let's assume what you're telling me is true.'

'It is,' he assured.

'If you're right, if it is true that you're consul to Heloise, if it's true that Maria was killed on Heloise's orders, why are you telling all of this to me?'

'Because I'm scared. Because I've had enough.'

'Well, you're not the first guy to realise he didn't much like the bed he's made for himself and decided to cash it in for a plane ticket to a new life Stateside.'

Lavandier almost laughed. 'Oh no, you mistake my intentions. I have no plans to go anywhere. I'm willing to let you use what I know to bring down Heloise Salvatierra, I'm willing to give you the hitman that killed her sister, but when the dust settles, I want the casino.'

'You have lofty aspirations, don't you, Mr Lavandier?'

'The casino is a tiny price to pay for the complete destruction of the Salvatierra cartel, is it not?'

'It does sound like a good deal, but ultimately it's not up to me.'

'But you'll present the proposal to your superiors?'

'Not on this conversation alone.'

'How about this then?' He reached into the pocket of his coat and withdrew the small box with the black ribbon. He removed the lid and held up the ziplock bag so Alamaeda could see the silver pendant stained with blood. 'This was Maria's. This is her blood. It was taken from her by the Wraith when he killed her on her yacht this past weekend.'

Lavandier was smiling with triumph, too caught up in his own production, his own success, to notice that Alamaeda was still not convinced.

'Nice try, asshole,' she said as she walked away, 'but I know for a fact that Maria isn't dead. If the Wraith really does exist, then he's played you for a fool.'

SEVENTY

Victor had been in many casinos. Sometimes to work. Sometimes to gamble. The latter was rare, although it hadn't always been. An old acquaintance had told him he was addicted to risk, and maybe there was some truth to the observation, but Victor had no desire to understand himself any more than he already did. He didn't want any more answers.

This casino had no name, but was otherwise the finished article as far as he could tell. It was a Vegas-level super casino, just as huge, just as gaudy, just as maze-like. The sentries kept him at the gate for about as long as he expected. Enough time to pass on the message that he was here. Enough time for deliberation. Enough time for the answer to come back. He parked the car he had stolen right outside the entrance to the casino proper, where the valet station stood but where no valets waited to take his keys and park in the nearby multi-storey garage.

A well-dressed guy was waiting for him, and invited him

into the building where another search was conducted. The sentries at the gate had done the same, of course, but it would have been reckless to trust a single frisk when inviting an assassin inside. This wasn't only a business, but also a home.

The well-dressed guy did a good job with the search. Victor wouldn't have been able to get a weapon past him had he tried. Better to appear unthreatening at all times.

There were several elevators that led to the many floors of the hotel, but only a single one led to the Goddess Suite, and it was operable with only one key. Victor stepped inside and the well-dressed guy used the key. He said nothing as he kept his gaze on Victor and didn't blink for the entire ascension.

In the silence, Victor could just about hear the whir of machinery. The car was well insulated behind the mirrored walls. Victor saw no cameras, but knew they were there, somewhere. Hidden behind the glass, perhaps. They were watching him the whole time. It would be reckless not to do so.

When the car stopped, the doors opened with an automatic mechanism to reveal a short man, squat and almost boxy. He wore a suit like the well-dressed man, but it didn't fit quite right. A little too big at the chest, a little too loose at the arms and hips. Like Victor's own.

The squat man gestured for him to step out of the elevator, and proceeded to search Victor for the third time. This search was more thorough than even the well-dressed man's had been, and it was conducted without the good manners. Victor suffered the rough pat-down without comment. He understood the reasoning, after all. He agreed with it too.

Once the squat man was sure Victor had no weapons, and in the process conveyed to Victor that he disliked him as much as he didn't trust him, another wordless gesture beckoned Victor further into the suite where he found Lavandier and Heloise waiting for him.

He hadn't interrupted. Both were standing. Both were already looking his way. Lavandier was troubled by Victor's presence. The Frenchman was fidgeting with his hands and shifting his weight. Heloise, however, was motionless and emotionless. Closer, he saw the curiosity in her eyes. It reminded him of when they had first met. She hadn't expected what she had found that time in the suite in Madrid, and she hadn't expected to see him again in her own suite, or perhaps ever.

'Good evening,' she said. 'We were just talking about you.'

Lavandier managed to take control of his nerves, but instead of speaking to Victor, he said to the squat man, 'El Perro?'

The squat man shook his head.

'Interesting name,' Victor said. 'How did you come by it?'

El Perro was silent.

'Chatty, isn't he?' Victor said to Heloise.

'He's not one to waste words.'

'Perhaps I'm not as he imagined. Maybe I'm not tall enough. Perhaps I'm not as pale as he was led to believe.'

Lavandier stiffened. Just a little, but Victor saw it all the same. 'What are you talking about?'

'You hired another professional to kill Maria. I believe I was quite adamant that any violation of the terms would be unacceptable.'

Lavandier said, 'You're mistaken. There is no such professional.'

'Very tall, very pale,' Victor said. 'Very ... dead.'

Lavandier opened his mouth to say something, but Heloise silenced him with a gentle raise of a hand.

'There's no need to lie, Luis. It doesn't matter now, does it?'

Lavandier said nothing.

Heloise's gaze returned to Victor. 'You would like to get paid, I presume.'

'That's why I'm here.'

'Why shouldn't I kill you?'

'That's a good question. You don't need me any longer.'

'That's not your answer, is it?' she replied. 'You wouldn't come here if you thought you would be in danger.'

Victor nodded. 'I never walk into a room I can't walk out of again.'

'That's still not an answer.'

He pointed to the large floor-to-ceiling mirror that formed the east wall of the suite and the view spoiled by the unfinished parking garage and the construction crane.

'There's my answer,' he said. 'I have a .50 calibre rifle set up on an automated rig, pointing this way.'

'Like Madrid,' she said in response, curious, unafraid.

'Exactly like Madrid.'

She smiled. 'I don't believe you. You haven't had the time.'

'He wouldn't have been able to get past my security,' El Perro added.

Victor said, 'It's extensive, I'll give you that, but we're talking hypotheticals here, aren't we? So, hypothetically, I would need a distraction to occupy the eye of your security while I set up inside the parking garage.'

'There was no such distraction,' Heloise said. 'Which means there's no rig, there's no rifle.'

Her posture changed. El Perro noticed, and inched closer

424

to Victor. Lavandier stiffened. Both men knew their employer well enough to know where this conversation was going.

'But,' she added, 'I'm not going to kill you because I don't need you any longer. I would have paid you in full if you had actually killed Maria.'

Victor remained silent.

'You almost got away with it,' Lavandier said. 'But I'm afraid this is our town, our house.'

El Perro clapped his hands and many sicarios entered the living area from deeper within the suite. They had guns, pistols and SMGs. He took one out himself.

Victor counted thirteen new enemies.

He raised an eyebrow. 'Are you sure you have enough guys?'

Heloise asked, 'Why did you come here if you thought there was even the remotest possibility I knew you had betrayed me?'

'The best way to assault a fortress is from the inside.'

She smiled. 'You're unarmed.'

'You're forgetting about the .50 calibre rifle pointed at you.'

Heloise took the gun from El Perro. 'I think I'm going to call you on that bluff.'

She aimed it at Victor.

He said, 'You're going to shoot me here inside your casino? Seems a little reckless, doesn't it?'

'There's no risk,' she said. 'My men know how to clean up a mess.'

Lavandier approached Heloise. 'I would advise doing it elsewhere. Why risk leaving any evidence? Just one speck of blood we don't notice, just one molecule of DNA left behind ... Take him to the old cabaret club.'

Heloise took a moment to consider his counsel, then gave

the gun back to El Perro. 'Fine, do that.' To Victor, she said, 'You'll have to forgive me if I'm not there to witness your end personally, but rest assured I won't forget you anytime soon.'

'Comforting,' Victor said.

She flashed him a smile that bordered on a smirk, then walked away, done with him.

El Perro gestured for his men to approach, and as they closed, Lavandier said, 'If you didn't kill Maria, how did you come by the pendant? We can assume the blood is not hers, but how did you know the pendant would be recognised?'

Victor shrugged again. 'That's simple, and it is in fact Maria's blood. She's paying me to kill Heloise. That's the real reason I'm here now.'

Heloise stopped, and turned around, suddenly not done with him after all. She wanted to know more. She wanted more answers.

Lavandier stood before Victor. He looked confused, but also amused. Smiling. Maybe impressed. He had questions of his own, but before he could ask them, his head exploded.

SEVENTY-ONE

The .50 calibre round left the AX50's muzzle at almost two-and-a-half times the speed of sound. Even slowed by the dense, humid air, it put a huge hole in Lavandier's face half a second before the thunderous roar of the gunshot arrived. Which meant the Frenchman's head disintegrated before anyone in the suite understood why. One instant he was smiling, the next a huge amount of kinetic energy was ripping through his skull, causing a pressure wave inside the cranial cavity akin to a bomb blast. The head was erupting even before the bullet punched through the plate at the rear and sucked out half the contents of his skull along with it.

The mess was absolute. Blood spatter reached every wall. Fragments of bones and morsels of skin and brain peppered Heloise and El Perro.

Lavandier was left with only a partial face with strips of scalp flopping over it, silver-blond hair matted with blood and brain matter. He collapsed straight down, lips still poised in that final smile.

Victor was first to react, dropping to the floor an instant before El Perro launched himself at Heloise, tackling her to the carpet as more rounds split the floor-to-ceiling window.

The sicarios were slower to react, and two were killed by the next two rifle rounds, one's torso split in half, the other's arm blown clean from his shoulder.

Glass rained amidst the thunderous sound of the gunshots, one after another, blowing huge holes in the wall opposite, disintegrating anything in the path of the bullets. The air became thick and dark with dust and misting blood.

The AX50 was no automatic weapon. There was a discernible pause between each shot. *Boom. Boom. Boom ...*

Ten rounds in a full magazine meant it would be over soon, and Victor couldn't let the chaos go to waste. Aside from him, everyone was locked in a state of surprise and panic. No one was paying any attention to him – they were too busy trying to stay alive – but he would be remembered when the shooting stopped.

Lavandier's corpse was nearby, and he patted it down for weapons, finding a small .22 SIG that he used to kill the closest threat, the tinny pops of the handgun muffled and ignored while the booms of the fifty cal rushed through the suite.

Victor discarded the SIG and retrieved the weapon the sicario had been holding. It was an MP5-N. A fine weapon with ambidextrous operation. It had been set for a left-handed shooter. Victor reset it to right firing. He checked it was indeed reloaded and thumbed the selector switch to single shot. He rarely felt the need for full auto. One good shot was better than an inaccurate burst.

He searched the dead guy for spare magazines and found one tucked into the man's belt. He took it, and also the

Knights Armament suppressor protruding from a pocket of the guy's leather jacket. This was no time for stealth, but there was still a benefit to screwing it in place. He would hear enemy gunshots easier with his own quietened.

The AX50 fell silent at last and ten smoking craters lay in the floor or interior wall. Three more victims littered the floor, as did torn-off body parts and huge quantities of blood. The air was so dense it seemed as though a cloud of ochre fog had filled the suite.

Victor crouched with his back against a pillar. On the other side of it were more sicarios, and beyond them, El Perro and Heloise. Victor waited. He heard movement, shuffling, but he wasn't prepared to expose himself just yet.

He heard El Perro shout, '*Cover us.*'

The sicarios responded with automatic gunfire cutting through the air. No one had a line of sight to Victor, but it didn't matter. They filled the suite with lead, shooting at random, putting down enough suppressing fire that it would have been suicide to leave cover.

He didn't have time to shoot but he glimpsed El Perro ushering Heloise out of immediate danger, further into the suite.

Rounds cracked nearby floor tiles in a hellish rhythm. Victor dropped to the floor, staying low, lying on one hip, trying to ignore the beat of relentless gunshots and the ping of metal on stone so he could pick out—

Footsteps, nearing.

He rolled out of cover, away from the gunfire but towards the sound of footsteps, iron sights of the MP5 sweeping the dust-thick air and falling on to a shape moving out of it, trying to flank. The gun kicked three times in Victor's grip and the man contorted and stumbled backwards a step, then two, then fell.

The automatic fire paused and Victor waited a second to learn if the next shooter was responding to his fallen team-mate or reloading.

A *click, clatter, slam* told Victor the latter and he leapt up to find a line of sight through the many obstacles of the suite, but saw no gunman because he had ducked into cover while reloading. From the holes in the nearest wall, however, Victor knew which direction the rounds had come from.

When the shooter popped back up to resume firing, Victor was waiting.

The bullet blew out the back of his skull.

More shots came at Victor, tearing through a rug near his feet and cracking into the stone beneath, the gunman at an elevated position.

Victor dashed to better cover, glancing up to see a sicario on an overlooking balcony providing the advantage of higher ground and visibility, but making himself too exposed.

The first round from the MP5 struck a railing, but the second hit him in the side of the knee and he staggered and fell, screaming, over the banister. He stopped screaming an instant later when he landed head first on the hard floor five metres below.

Another gunman was rushing towards Victor's position, fast and eager, loosing rounds at Victor, who was already moving behind another pillar for more protection and using the opportunity to swap out the half-empty magazine for a fresh one. Bullets chipped at the pillar. More debris dirtied the air.

They exchanged shots, each behind cover and making

good use of it, the sicario firing in threes and fours, Victor returning single rounds.

The sicario emptied his magazine first. It took him by surprise. He squeezed the trigger a couple more times – *click, click* – before he understood. He hadn't been counting rounds.

Victor always counted. He had plenty left, but the MP5 jammed. A rare occurrence, but it hadn't been well maintained.

He waited for his enemy to drop out of sight behind a raised area of flooring on which stood a grand piano, so he was still reloading when Victor leapt up and ran over it.

The gunman gasped when Victor dropped down on the other side of the piano, landing on both feet, knees bending as he absorbed the impact, before he transferred the energy into a kick that knocked the sicario's weapon from his hands.

Victor stepped inside the guy's reach, elbows up high to deflect the incoming shots with his arms, driving the left elbow into the unprotected face beyond, twisting his hips to power an elbow strike from his right arm that slammed into the point of the man's chin. He slackened, eyes closing, dropping straight down into a heap that Victor stepped over to go after another enemy stepping out of cover.

Victor disarmed him and caught the counter-kick with his left arm, locking the leg against his flank, leaving the guy hopping to stay on his single foot. Victor stomped a heel into the guy's exposed ankle, then wrenched his leg to pull the guy closer and into an open palm. A follow-up stomp kicked the one vertical leg out from under him.

He crashed to the floor – Victor releasing the trapped leg – but he wasn't out of the fight, even with a broken ankle and a flat nose. He rolled away from Victor's stamping foot, going for the disarmed gun on the floor, half-rolling, half-shuffling.

He grabbed the pistol and shifted on to one hip to shoot, but Victor knocked the gun from his hand the instant it was in range.

A kick to the ribs flipped the guy to his stomach. He tried to push himself up, but Victor was over him, lowering to one knee and driving the other down into his spine.

Victor took hold of the guy's head and twisted in a savage, upwards spiral.

Crack.

The one he had dropped with the elbow to the chin had recovered and drew a matte-black knife, rushing to attack. Victor scooped up the pistol and shot the guy in the neck, the bullet hitting a little below the Adam's apple. Blood bubbled from the wound. It bubbled from his mouth. It bubbled from his nostrils. He gasped and spluttered and dropped to his knees, eyes wide and fingers pressed over the hole, as if they could repair the damage done to his oesophagus and arteries.

No more gunmen in sight, so Victor took a breath. Two sicarios remained, plus El Perro and Heloise, all of who were further inside the suite. The only exit was the elevator, behind him.

No way out.

SEVENTY-TWO

It was close quarters now he was out of the open-plan area so Victor kept his elbows against his chest. He didn't want to leave his arms out in front of him, exposed and vulnerable, free to be grabbed before they could be withdrawn. He stalked through the suite, never leaving a room or corner unchecked, fast but not rushed. He couldn't make a mistake. They were waiting for him, but he didn't want them to be ready for him.

He took the first sicario by surprise as he entered a kitchen. He was tall and strong, armed with a sub-machine gun, but he didn't hear Victor coming. Victor forced a palm over the guy's mouth and nose, and drove the matte-black knife into his chest, blade on a horizontal plane to slip between ribs and into the heart beyond. Not an instant kill, but close enough. The man loosened and stumbled. Victor kept hold of the knife and steered him as he started to fall, so when his legs gave out underneath him, he dropped onto a rug to lessen the noise and he lay twitching and wheezing for a second longer.

The next had better hearing, better awareness. He was already responding, entering the room before Victor was prepared to deal with him.

Victor batted the SMG from the guy's grip, and the sicario threw a punch in response, a looping right haymaker destined for Victor's jaw, but slow, predictable. Victor was dropping his head and bending his knees before the fist was halfway through its long arc, and by the time it reached the space above him, Victor's shoulder was slamming into the man's abdomen and powering him off his feet.

They struck a table, the sicario falling backwards over it and Victor falling over him in turn, but rolling with the energy, letting it take him over in a cartwheel that put him back on his feet.

His opponent tried to fight the force and failed, hitting the floor with the table tipping on top of him. He wasn't hurt, but it took time to slither out from under it.

Victor did not stand idle and let him. He used those few seconds to retrieve the sicario's SMG and used the stock as a club to crack open his skull.

Only one room remained. The master bedroom.

He approached, knowing there was only one more threat to deal with before he reached his target, who was no doubt close by and covering the door, ready and waiting for the inevitable assault. Victor wanted to catch El Perro off guard, trusting to speed when his enemy would expect stealth.

El Perro didn't wait, however. He attacked, exiting the bedroom as Victor reached it.

The gun went off as Victor pushed it away, his hand burning on the hot muzzle. He tried to shoot his own weapon, but they were too close, too in motion to get an angle before it was also grabbed.

They wrestled for control of the guns, stumbling back through the hallway, El Perro skilled enough to resist Victor's attempts to twist and wrench it from his grip. He knew how to go with the force instead of fighting it; to push when pulled and pull when pushed. He was strong and powerful. His wrists were so thick it seemed his hands were attached to his arms without joints.

Victor changed tack, attacking instead, releasing one gun to throw short looping uppercuts into the body. El Perro had a thick torso and a solid abdominal wall. He took the punches well, but he couldn't keep resisting. Each blow took its toll.

El Perro dropped the other gun so he could fight back.

The strikes came fast, forcing Victor to retreat: punches thrown in short, stinging arcs to his body; punctuated by elbow strikes aimed for his face; an intermittent knee shooting for his abdomen or groin. He blocked and slipped, parried and dodged. His enemy was as relentless as he was quick, and tireless.

He was experienced too. Whatever his speed, whatever his stamina, no amateur fought like this. He had trained and practised and learned. More than that, he had put those skills to the test. There was no substitute for the real thing. No amount of sparring could prepare for that first blow landed with intent or received in kind.

Victor had the advantage of reach. He could strike from further distance, but that came with disadvantages too. There was more of Victor to hit and to grab. El Perro's strength was condensed into a small area. The result was more explosiveness. He kept close. He didn't allow Victor to back away an inch.

He was wearing down faster than his opponent, the gap in their stamina widening to a void as Victor suffered more from their traded blows. His enemy saw it, but kept his composure. He was content to let attrition do the hard work. Had he succumbed to hubris, Victor might have fared better, but his enemy was too patient to make a mistake he didn't have to make. He wasn't going to do anything different, because what he was already doing was working.

Every strike that made its way past Victor's guard hurt and pushed him further away from his ultimate target, back into the open-plan area. His ears were ringing from the elbow jabs that connected with his skull. His ribs were on fire from the body shots. Each breath he took made him feel sick from the knee strikes he had taken.

He fought on, failing to block a fast kick to his thigh; too slow to slip an elbow to his skull; too weak to ward off the punches to his ribs.

His knees buckled, but he remained standing. Going to the floor was the last thing he wanted. It would be the end of it. Sheer will kept him on his feet.

Fresh, Victor could dictate the pace. He could exploit the inevitable gaps in defence to land vicious strikes. But fatigued, he had lost the edge of his speed. The timing was there, but he was a split-second too slow.

Victor revised his strategy. His opponent was too strong, too tough, to be defeated with counter-attacks. He absorbed them and kept on coming. Victor had never encountered such imperviousness. The longer the fight went on, the better El Perro's chances. Victor had taken far fewer blows, but he was feeling them. His head ached and a piercing whine interfered with his hearing, drowning out all but the loudest noises. Each breath felt tight and constrained. He would be vomiting blood before the night was out, he was sure. In a war of attrition, he was destined to lose.

El Perro said, 'I see the doubt in your eyes.'

'You see what you want to see.'

Victor regarded his opponent. The Guatemalan was short and square. His shoulders were wide enough to fit an extra head on each. His hands were two blocks of stone at his hips. He had thick, tanned skin, weathered and coarse. His head and face were shaved, but dark with stubble. If there was a neck, it was disguised by the triangular trapezius muscles and dense jaw. His eyes were half-hidden by drooping lids and prominent brow bones, but Victor saw an intensity in them.

Hard to recognise at first, but he understood where that intensity came from. Victor was used to intense gazes. Determination, hatred, surprise, terror were all things he was used to seeing. This look was different. He was used to people wanting to kill him, and some of those people *really* wanted to kill him. Often, because he was trying to kill them too, and nothing made a person more determined to kill than to avoid being killed in return. That kind of determination was visceral, it was instinctual. An emotional response. This guy's was of another kind. He was in no danger yet. Victor had never met him before, never seen him before, so the reverse was also true. They had no history and no association beyond Heloise. So, this guy was loyal. Fiercely so. That was why he was so determined to kill Victor. He wasn't just doing his job. He was protecting someone he cared about.

'Is she worth dying for?' Victor asked.

El Perro didn't hesitate. 'Yes.'

'And who will protect her when you're dead?'

The Guatemalan's eyes narrowed. Not angry, but afraid, only not for himself.

Victor gestured. 'Let's get this done.'

They exchanged attacks. El Perro loaded up to throw his punches with as much power as possible because he was enraged now at the thought of Heloise's death. Victor blocked and slipped, having plenty of time to see them coming and position himself for vicious counter-attacks – body shots delivered by fists and knees.

The Guatemalan took them well but each one Victor landed chipped away at El Perro's reserves of energy and will. The frustration and rage were obvious, because El Perro responded by throwing his punches with even more intent.

This made them slower and more predictable. Victor expended only as much energy as he needed to, stepping out of the way of each strike; circling around to force his opponent to turn on the spot after him, losing his balance, and in doing so letting Victor steer him to the edge of the suite, to the floor-to-ceiling window.

El Perro didn't understand. He was gasping now, exhausted from throwing all the big shots that had failed to land. Victor picked his own shots. He slipped quick elbow strikes past El Perro's non-existent defences. When the Guatemalan paused to get his breath, there was more blood on his face than sweat.

Victor caught the next punch, the fist in one hand, the elbow in the other, and locked out the arm.

Victor walked him backwards, the locked arm acting as an immovable barrier between them, preventing El Perro from making any attacks of his own. He was off-balance and his feet were working hard just to keep him upright. The left arm was thrashing, sometimes trying to reach Victor, sometimes trying to find a handhold, but failing at each.

When El Perro realised where he was going, he cried out in fear, for himself this time.

He looked over one shoulder, looking towards the inevitable, shouting and begging.

Victor kept walking him.

Of course, all El Perro had to do was lift his feet from the floor and he would fall straight down, but it was not uncommon for people to ignore the obvious when they were flooded with fear.

When they reached the edge, El Perro's free hand found something to grab hold of: the broken window itself. He gripped so hard blood bloomed out from between his fingers before the glass shattered in his hand and Victor shoved him out into the night.

He turned to see Heloise picking up one of the guns from the floor.

She looked as she always looked. She was tall and poised, in a glamorous dress, perfectly presented, ready for a night out, not fighting for her life. If she was scared, she didn't show it. Victor grimaced and took a step forward. She didn't take one back. Heloise had the pistol held out in one hand, muzzle pointed at his torso. Centre mass, the biggest target. She couldn't miss.

'You betrayed me,' she said. 'I could have made you rich

beyond your wildest dreams. You could have had a whole continent of clients based on my recommendation alone. You would be revered and feared wherever you set foot from Tijuana to Buenos Aires.'

'Some things are more important than money,' Victor said. 'And I prefer it when people are not afraid of me. They reveal their true natures so much more readily.'

'Was it the insult?' she asked. 'Was it because I commissioned another for the same job?'

'I'm a hard man to offend, I assure you. You are entitled to do what you think is best to look after your own interests, as am I.'

'Turning on your client is in your best long-term interests?'

'Few people will ever know what transpired here.'

'Even if you had been successful, your broker would know. You would have cost them a lucrative revenue stream. Would it have been worth it?'

Victor shrugged. 'A broker is an agent. They work for me, not the other way around.'

'My men would have hunted you down wherever you went.'

Victor shook his head. 'They'll be too busy fighting one another to take your seat to be thinking about the person who gave them a chance to sit on it. If anything, they'll send me a thank-you card.'

Heloise stepped closer. 'Are you so stubborn you don't understand you failed?'

'Not yet.'

'I have the gun. You should have shot me, not Luis. You wasted your best chance.'

Victor said, 'I didn't shoot him.'

'Of course,' she said with a bitter smile. 'Another auto-mated rig wirelessly linked to your phone.'

He shook his head. 'Not this time. This time I have a partner.'

Victor threw himself to the floor and a final shot rang out.

SEVENTY-THREE

Constantin didn't really care who he killed, only that he killed. Whether it was a nameless sicario or a cartel boss, it was all the same to him. They were all ugly, all unworthy of life. He didn't like to discriminate. After all, who was he to judge? His soul was even uglier than the meat sack it resided inside. So, it had been an easy decision to join forces with the Wraith and kill Heloise on behalf of her sister.

He left the unfinished parking garage and drove away with the rifle to rendezvous with the Wraith as planned. There were no celebrations, no congratulations either. They still had work to do.

The Wraith arranged the meeting with Maria over the phone while Constantin waited. The details were discussed briefly and agreed upon without fuss. Constantin envied his ability to deal with clients so closely, so personally. Constantin preferred to keep his distance from clients and people in general. He was not one of them, and had no longing to be near them, unless it was to elevate them to a higher state of aesthetics.

The Wraith had worked out the plan, knowing his presence would distract Heloise's security and provide Constantin the opportunity to sneak into the compound. He really was quite the tactician.

Which meant Constantin had to be very careful how he killed him. Before, he had not understood just whom he was up against. He had killed other professionals in the past, of course. One could not thrive in this business without doing so, but the Wraith was a cut above the norm. But so was Constantin.

It was nothing personal, and it wasn't even business. It was for the satisfaction, the amusement, the irony of the universe, because there was no reason to kill him beyond his innate ugliness. As things stood, they would each receive a considerable amount of money from Maria for a successful hit on Heloise. Constantin could retire with his share, and go back to murdering people pro bono.

Where was the fun in that?

'Set up here,' the Wraith said.

They were on the walkway of an old water tower overlooking an expanse of empty brownfield space. At the centre of the space was a low building. A former cabaret club, the Wraith had explained.

'You'll have a good view, wherever they approach from.'

Constantin nodded. He assembled the rifle, a beautiful brand-new AX50. It had been a joy to use it against Heloise and that snake Lavandier. The one-way windows had been no barrier to the sophisticated infrared scope.

Should he shoot the Wraith first, or Maria? he wondered.

The Wraith was the greater threat, and so from a purely tactical viewpoint he should be killed at the earliest available opportunity. Which would be before Maria even arrived. Constantin pictured the Wraith walking across that expanse of empty space and understood the problem. He would be looking at the Wraith's back. The Wraith wouldn't be looking at Constantin. He wouldn't know what was happening. He wouldn't understand the betrayal.

Constantin said, 'Would you like to hear something funny?'

'Always.'

'What's funny is that this isn't the first time we've met.'

The Wraith was unconvinced. 'I find it hard to believe that I don't remember you.'

The man smirked. 'I was sitting down. It was only for a moment. You were distracted. We didn't actually meet, of course, but I saw you. I can picture it clearly. You were wearing a charcoal suit, white shirt and no tie. You had longer hair, and a beard then. The same tan though. It was in Minsk, and I was part of a crew that was hired to kill you. I was new to this particular group, so I was tasked with little more than being a lookout. It was outside a railway station, on a cold November's day. Does any of that sound familiar?'

The Wraith remained silent.

'I shall take your reticence as confirmation, although I don't need it. In case you've forgotten, you killed most of the crew. I had to saw up the three corpses you left in a back room. How did a large shard of mirror glass end up pinning one of their hands to a table?'

'That would be telling.'

'It was something of a curiosity to me then, truth be told. There were no broken mirrors anywhere in that station. I checked every conceivable one. Of course, then I realised it must have been from a toilet on a train. They obviously didn't frisk you very well.' He flexed the fingers of his hand. 'Must have been very painful.'

The Wraith said nothing.

'You look different now, of course. Your face isn't quite the same, but it is still you. We cannot change our essence, can we?'

'I'll keep trying.'

'I want you to know that I bear you no ill will from that day. I didn't even realise I knew you before I sat down with that hot dog, and it wouldn't have changed things had I known. You lost me a job and a sizeable reward, but it's happened before and will no doubt happen again. It's not personal.'

The Wraith understood. He was a professional.

'Here,' the Wraith said, presenting a burner phone. 'I'll call you when I'm inside and we'll keep an open line. You can let me know when they're close.'

'Good idea,' Constantin said, taking the phone and thinking he would call the Wraith in a few minutes' time, when he was halfway to the abandoned club.

I don't mean to interrupt, he would say, *but could you please turn around so I can see your eyes before you die?*

After that, who knew what Constantin would do? Maybe he would wait for Maria to show up and he would kill her too and anyone else who couldn't make it to cover fast enough. The AX50 had a ten-round magazine, and there was still a full spare even after the shootout at the casino. Twenty anti-armour bullets was more than enough to take out a sizeable entourage. Or ... maybe he would just go. Kill the Wraith and take the first flight to a cooler climate.

Either way he would leave Guatemala in a better mood than he had arrived in.

He had a thought, sudden and glorious. He should kill the DEA agent before he left. Of course. He was angry at himself for almost missing such an opportunity. He could have real fun with that. He could imagine her face as he explained to her just who her new boyfriend really was.

I killed him purely because I wanted to. Which is why I'm here now . . .

The Wraith checked his watch. 'They won't be long. I'd better get in position.'

Constantin nodded. He had finished assembling the rifle and set it in place on the walkway of the water tower.

'All set,' he said.

The Wraith had explained the plan: 'Maria will bring the money here, in person but not alone. It'll be cash, so it will be cumbersome. She'll have her men carrying it into the club. That will keep them occupied. They can't lug suitcases and wield AKs at the same time. Wait until you see them and they're out in the open, and start shooting. Once they drop, the rest won't hang around. They'll scatter.'

'Maybe Maria will play fair,' Constantin offered.

The Wraith was adamant. 'I show her proof Heloise is dead and she no longer needs to pay me. She no longer needs me alive at all.'

Constantin said, 'We stick to the plan then,' because he didn't care who he killed as long as he killed.

He lay down behind the rifle, which was awkward, given his dimensions and the walkway's restrictions. The Wraith stepped back to allow him room to test the positioning and Constantin settled as much as he could. The metal walkway was uncomfortable, biting at his kneecaps and elbows, but he would not suffer for long. Maria would be here soon and then it would all be over.

Constantin imagined putting half a dozen sicarios out of their eternal misery, but their ends were meaningless. No worth. No satisfaction. That would come from the Wraith. Constantin was eager to see the surprised look on the Wraith's face when the first shot hit him, severing a leg or arm perhaps. Anywhere else would mean instant death, and where was the fun in that? Constantin peered down the sight, and focused it on the centre point of the empty lot.

Constantin said, 'I'm ready.'

He pictured bright mists of pink and perfect arcs of crimson.

It was his gift to the world, transforming the ugly into the beautiful.

SEVENTY-FOUR

The air was saturated in moisture. It had been raining all afternoon. A light, fine mist of a downpour that seemed without
end. Puddles reflected the night sky and the gleam of distant
streetlamps. There was a chill in the night too. The first time
Victor had really felt the temperature drop since he had been
in Guatemala. When the weather changed, so did people.

The tall, pale man said, 'I'm ready.'

I'm ready too, Victor thought.

He shot him in the back of the head.

A single round, fired point-blank to the brainstem. Very
little happened. The tall, pale man was already prone, so he
remained so, albeit with a slackness where there had been
rigidity before. His long, thin body became relaxed in death,
each lifeless component coordinating with a seamless grace
that he had lacked while alive. The bullet made a neat little
hole and only a narrow trail of blood trickled from it, snaking
down over his skull and neck and beginning to drip to the
metal walkway in a slow, steady patter.

It was nothing personal, but it was only ever going to end one of two ways: Victor killing him, or being killed in return. People said there was no honour amongst thieves, but there was even less between killers.

Besides, Victor needed a corpse.

Maria Salvatierra and her entourage arrived in two motorcades. The first delivered her sicarios, who formed a perimeter around the club's car park, scouting and guarding in preparation for their patron's arrival. Victor kept track of them by the glowing cigarettes even if they were too far away for him to see their faces. Even in the days when he had smoked, he had never done so when working. He had never turned up to fulfil a contract stinking of tobacco. He had never performed surveillance with glowing embers to give his position away. Though it came as no surprise, it was never easy to understand why his enemies so often failed to maintain even the most basic level of professional competence.

They were keeping out of the way, at least. Close enough to help out, but only if needed, while the second motorcade, which consisted of three vehicles, parked up right outside the building. Her bodyguards knew enough to make sure she wasn't exposed for long, and they were out of the vehicles first, making sure it was safe for her to step outside. The three vehicles were cheap and nondescript. No blacked-out windows, let alone armour. Passing through Guatemala City, no one would look at them twice.

He counted eleven men, each with a sub-machine gun or assault rifle. A sizeable force, Victor noted as he watched them. He in turn could not be seen inside the building. He was armed with the gun that had killed the pale assassin,

449

which he would use if things went wrong, but he didn't plan on needing the gun at all. At least, he didn't need it for shooting.

Maria entered the cabaret club with a single bodyguard, who was wheeling two large hard shell suitcases he had taken from the boot of one of the vehicles. The rest of her men remained outside, as per the agreement.

Inside, the club was no drier. The flat roof hadn't held up without maintenance. Rainwater came through holes and cracks, in places as snaking rivulets down walls and pillars, else in staccato streams from the ceiling. The whole floor was wet. Where it was carpeted, the carpet was soaked and stank of rot. It squelched underfoot. The air was more humid inside, and even colder as a result. The VIP section looked better than the rest of the interior. It was a little raised, so its carpeted floor had been spared the worst of the water damage.

The sole surviving daughter of Manny Salvatierra was dressed all in black and looked neither pleased nor displeased to find Victor waiting on the stage before the curtain that hung across the back of the space. It was still red, but the colour had been muted by rainwater, dust and dirt. It was soaked with moisture. The brass rings that held it up had not been designed to support the weight of a soaked curtain. Some had distorted to ovals.

Maria said, 'It's been a long time since I felt safe enough to come into the city.'

The bodyguard had his nose splinted and bandaged. He was the guy Victor had knocked out in the en-suite of the yacht's master bedroom. He looked angry, even with his face half-hidden by dressings, but said nothing – no doubt under strict orders. He released the suitcases, which stood on their own thanks to four wheels, and approached Victor. He motioned for him to come forward and raise his arms.

Victor stepped off the stage, and did as instructed. The carpet squelched underfoot. Decay soiled the air.

'Back of my waistband,' he said.

The bodyguard with the broken nose took the pistol, and frisked him with a quick, thorough pat down. He then returned to Maria's side.

'You made quite a mess at my sister's casino,' she said.

'Like you,' Victor said, 'she was not easy to corner.'

Maria said, 'Did she suffer?'

'Not at all.'

'Something, at least. And her death means dozens more will not have to die. Maybe hundreds.'

Victor didn't bother to say that violence always begat violence. Whatever peace Maria had created for herself would be temporary.

'I suppose you would like to get paid.'

He nodded. 'That's why I'm here.'

She considered something. She looked around. 'You're on your own, yes?'

'That was the deal.'

'No booby traps?'

He shook his head.

She pursed her lips. 'Then why do I need to pay you at all?'

'Why did you bring the money if you weren't going to pay me?'

'I imagined someone as resourceful as yourself would have a contingency plan in place to ensure cooperation.'

'A deal's a deal,' he said.

'Only when it's equally beneficial.'

Victor remained silent.

'My sister was an awful woman. The world is better off with her no longer sullying it.'

Victor waited.

She gestured to the suitcases. 'Here's your money. By killing Heloise you'll earn me a hundred times what's in those suitcases.'

'I told you I'm good value.'

Maria said, 'I hope you don't intend to count it now. We'll be here all week.'

She motioned and the guy with the nose splint wheeled the suitcases closer to Victor, and then backed away with the same perma-angry expression. Maria's gaze remained on Victor. There was an intensity in her eyes, growing stronger and more powerful with every passing second. Victor had seen such looks before, eyes full of emotions he could guess at but not truly understand.

When the bodyguard was next to her again, Maria said, 'Hand me his gun.'

The guy with the nose splint did as instructed.

Maria took it from him, feeling the weight of it in her palm. An unfamiliar weight. 'I've never shot anyone before.'

'I believe you.'

'I've never needed to,' she continued. 'Heloise was always the one who did that when it was necessary. She didn't ever give me the chance to.' Maria paused. 'I suppose it was her way of protecting me.'

Victor remained silent.

Maria had never shot anyone, but she knew how the gun worked. She gripped the slide and pulled it back to check there was a round in the chamber, then pointed the gun at Victor.

She said, 'What's to stop me shooting you now?'

'Your good character.'

She smiled. 'I might need a little more convincing than that.'

He held her gaze. Like her sister, her eyes were large and full of cunning and strength. She had no fear of him. She hadn't even been scared of him while she had been at his mercy on the yacht. Now, she held a gun, but she didn't need it. She had eleven guys with her. Guys with automatic weapons. Guys who would fight to the death for her. The gun was just a tool. She didn't need it to be powerful. She couldn't be more powerful.

'You're not scared,' she said.

'I'm not,' Victor admitted.

'Why?'

'I don't get scared.'

She didn't believe him. 'Why not? What makes you so very special?'

'I never walk into a room I can't walk out of again.'

She didn't understand. 'I decide whether you can walk out of here or not.'

'You'll let me.'

She asked, 'Why?'

'There are two reasons, but only one matters in this instance. If you squeeze that trigger, the gun will blow up in your hand.'

She glanced down at the weapon. 'You said no booby-traps.'

'I lied.'

'You're bluffing.'

He didn't blink. 'Do you really want to risk it?'

No one spoke for a moment. The bodyguard with the nose splint shifted his weight. He was the only person in the room who was scared. He didn't know what either of the other two might do.

'You killed my sister,' Maria said.

Technically, he didn't, but there was no need to correct her.

'I should kill you,' she continued. 'Even if I could let my sister's murderer walk free, you're too dangerous to keep alive.'

'I agree.'

Maria smiled.

'But you can't shoot me,' Victor said.

Her large eyes grew larger. 'Why ever not?'

'Because in a matter of minutes a lot of police are going to surround this club and flood the area with men. You see, a good citizen has tipped them off you're going to be in the city. Here. Now. And that you have killed a foreign national. So, the very last thing you want is for them to show up with you standing over a fresh corpse. Even your no-doubt exceptional lawyers would struggle to get you out of that one.'

'You're bluffing.'

He nodded. 'About the exploding gun, yes. About the cops, no. Remember, at this precise moment in time you've committed no crime.' He glanced at the suitcases full of money. 'Well, aside from failure to report earnings.'

Maria was silent for a long moment, and then the gun lowered in a slow, smooth arc. She pushed it back into the bodyguard's hands.

'You're right,' she said. 'I've committed no crime. I'm just a woman in a derelict building sheltering from the weather.'

'Credible,' Victor said.

'But that's now. That's this moment as you made clear. There will be many more moments once this one is over. And know this: in one of those coming moments, whether soon or a long time from now, I'll find you.'

'Unlikely,' Victor said.

There was no scowl, no frown. Only her eyes showed her anger, but even that was restrained. That restraint made her a far more dangerous enemy than her sister had been. A patient foe was the deadliest of all.

She said nothing further, and motioned to the guy with the nose splint, and together they left the club. Before they had gone out of Victor's line of sight the bodyguard looked back over his shoulder like he wanted to deliver some final insult or threat, but then thought better of it.

A minute later Victor heard the sound of engines revving outside. He took one suitcase in each hand, climbed up on to the stage, stepped behind the curtain, and disappeared.

SEVENTY-FIVE

Maria Salvatierra didn't get far. Her convoy had barely made it out of the old cabaret club's car park before police swarmed the scene, blocking off the road and surrounding her and her men. Dozens of weapons were pointed their way. Dozens more were close by, securing the perimeter but ready to act should it prove necessary. Alamaeda watched it all. It was quite a show. A huge operation that had started with her. She had been the one to receive the anonymous tip-off, but it wasn't her place to make the arrest. That went to a senior police officer, who took great satisfaction in ordering Maria out of her SUV and even more pleasure putting the cuffs on her himself. She didn't try to fight her way out. Instead, she came willingly, happily, even. She wasn't expecting to stay in custody long.

'What have I done wrong?' she asked in an innocent tone.

Within moments, the Guat cops had her men out of the vehicles too, stripped of weapons and their hands on bodywork. Maria watched, smiling as if it was all a big joke. The search didn't take long.

'Found it,' a cop said.

The smile slipped from Maria's face as she saw a gun, a handgun, bagged as evidence. It was a beautiful moment. Wickliffe and Alamaeda hugged when the smug smile slipped from Maria's face and doubt crept in.

The logistics of rounding up her entourage were significant and it took time. Alamaeda and Wickliffe used it to join the crime scene investigators already at work at the water tower.

The John Doe they found there was more Giant Doe. A foreigner. He looked like a pencil, long and thin and white. The only colour was the trickle of red at the back of his skull that pooled at the base of his neck and then snaked in a jagged pattern along the curvature of his throat before dripping into a little puddle beneath. A neat bullet hole. No excess mess. No signs of a struggle.

'An execution,' Wickliffe said.

Alamaeda agreed. There was no room for debate. Next to the corpse was a huge military-grade sniper rifle. No signs it had been fired in the last few hours, but the muzzle stank of cordite and it fired the same massive .50 calibre bullets that had torn up Heloise's casino the previous night.

Wickliffe said, 'So, our mystery foreign hitman wasn't simply a rumour.'

'But why kill him?'

Wickliffe shrugged. 'Served his purpose. Heloise is dead, so why keep him around longer than necessary?'

A press conference was hastily organised once the ballistics had come back from the lab. A rush job, trumping all other tests, but no mistakes. Orders from on high. If there was even the slightest problem with the evidence then everyone knew Maria would walk. Once they were sure, or even when they were pretty sure, the word went out to the media, so a whole host of police officials and politicians could claim credit for the arrest of Maria Salvatierra, only surviving patron of the Salvatierra cartel, previously untouchable.

Alamaeda watched the press conference from the back of the room, trying to keep a straight face at the exaggerations and untruths. There was no mention of any tip-off. No mention of DEA assistance. Just talk of excellent police work, excellent tactics, excellent resolve.

'He must be a contortionist,' Wickliffe said.

Alamaeda glanced at her for elaboration.

Wickliffe said, 'To pat himself on the back like that.'

Alamaeda remembered that three-million-dollar bust, way back. She remembered her pride and then her embarrassment when she watched the video they sent her. There would be no video this time. Maria Salvatierra had been arrested for conspiracy to murder, with a gun in her entourage's possession that had killed a foreign national.

Of course, it wouldn't be anything like open-and-shut, Alamaeda was sure. No slam dunk, despite the gun that was, almost literally, smoking. Maria wasn't answering questions right now, but would no doubt deny any involvement in the murder, plead her innocence, claim a conspiracy of corrupt cops had set her up, or anything else that might work once a defence strategy had been put together. An entire law firm's worth of lawyers would rise from the pits to represent Maria and her people, the best money could buy, and fierce and effective. Alamaeda could see it all playing out before her eyes, even if she hoped – prayed – it would be different. She imagined the guy who had been found in possession of the gun would claim the weapon was his, only his, and Maria had had no knowledge of it nor what he had done, or not done, with it. He would admit to the murder, plead guilty like a loyal soldier, and his family would be buying new cars for cash before the year was out.

What would ultimately stick, Alamaeda didn't know, but what she did know was that Maria was done. Maybe down the line she would confess to some minor charge to make the big one go away. Maybe she would give up some of her Mexican customers to reduce her sentence. Or, perhaps her wealth and influence would be enough to make sure she walked free, unscathed and unsullied, but not now and not for a long time and certainly not in time to realign the fractured cartel.

'Stop thinking about what might happen further down the road,' Wickliffe said. 'Enjoy this victory. It might be a long time before we get another one.'

'I'm enjoying it, I assure you, but I don't like to have unanswered questions rattling around my head.'

'Such as?'

'Such as: who tipped us off?'

'A good Samaritan,' Wickliffe said.

'Maybe,' Alamaeda said. 'Or maybe he got something out of it too.'

Wickliffe shrugged, dismissive. 'I hope he did, because he deserved it. I'd like to thank him.'

Alamaeda stared into the middle distance. 'I have a horrible feeling I might be able to.'

SEVENTY-SIX

The money itself presented a problem. There was only so far Victor could conceivably drive with it and he couldn't just walk into a bank and deposit it in one of his offshore accounts. Suitcases full of money were a little unsubtle, so he had unpacked the stacks of hundred-dollar bills and redistributed them into toolboxes, gasoline canisters, fuselage and the inside of the truck's spare tyre. None of which would survive a thorough examination, but would hide the money from a cursory glance.

Given that he hadn't been paid by Heloise for the original contract because he hadn't executed it, Phoenix had no claim to the cash Maria had given him. He planned to pay her commission anyway, because it wasn't her fault things had transpired the way they had. A deal was a deal, after all.

When Joanna arrived at the beach, it was clear she hadn't slept. Her skin was a little pale and her eyes were red with bags beneath. Her clothes were yesterday's outfit. There were wrinkles on her jacket and trousers. No one looked their best tired, but she still looked good, though.

It was windy on the shores of Lago de Amatitlán. They were on a narrow strip of beach, facing distant mountains. The water shimmered orange and red in the sunset.

'I haven't slept since yesterday,' she said, then rested an elbow on the load bed of his pickup. 'You have a cut lip, and you're going to have a black eye come tomorrow.'

'I had an unfortunate encounter with a very angry gentleman.'

'Is that so?'

Victor nodded. 'I spilled his drink. He had a temper. It was messy.'

'He beat you up?'

'Just a couple of punches and it was all over.'

She took this in, or didn't. 'I don't suppose you happened to see the news?'

Victor shook his head.

'Well, just to catch you up on proceedings, out of the two warring patrons of the Salvatierra cartel, one is dead and one is in police custody. I've been after them for years, and now ... Now, it's kind of over.'

'Kind of?'

'Getting a boss in handcuffs is only half the fight.'

'Sure,' Victor said. 'Congratulations.'

'Thanks.' She removed her sunglasses to look at him uninterrupted. 'But it was all down to an anonymous tip-off. A handwritten note, if you can believe it, telling us where and when we could find Maria, the rifle that shot up her sister's casino, and the gun that killed the sniper she hired to assassinate Heloise.'

'Are you allowed to tell me this?'

She shook her head. 'But I'm figuring it won't do any harm.

461

Or perhaps I should say that I'm hoping it won't. Man, am I hoping.' She reached into her inside jacket pocket to fetch a notebook with a black leather cover. It had a pen attached with a thin cord. She presented the pad to Victor.

'What's this?' he said.

She pressed a fingertip against the side of her head, as if trying to force it through her skull. 'It's an unreachable itch buried deep inside my mind and only you can scratch it.'

'I'm afraid I don't understand.'

'I'd like you to write something for me.'

'Like what?'

'Like: "For the attention of Special Agent Joanna Alamaeda ... "'

She kept her gaze fixed on his eyes the whole time, watching for a reaction. There was none, but he asked, 'Why?'

'So that we can stay friends.'

There was a lightness in her tone, but a harshness in her expression, a fear. Her hands didn't move, but he could tell she was thinking about their proximity to her sidearm. He took the notepad, he took the pen. He wrote out the words she had requested. He could see the tension in her posture, the expectation. The fear.

He finished writing. He turned the pad around so she could see what he had written. The effect was immediate. Either she didn't try to hide it, or couldn't. The tension left her shoulders and she exhaled. He pretended he didn't see that relief.

'I'm confused,' he said.

She smiled as she shook her head. 'Don't be. Forget it. You scratched my itch just fine.'

'Happy to be of service.'

He held out the notepad for her, but he released it just

before her fingers fully closed around it and the pad dropped to the ground.

'My bad,' he said. 'Sorry.'

'Butterfingers.'

He squatted to retrieve it, now a little dusty with sand. This time he made sure she had a hold on it before releasing the pad. She gave it a quick wipe before putting it away again in the pocket where it came from. Maybe there would be another itch inside her mind she couldn't scratch, which would lead her to check the pad for fingerprints. With the sand, with the wipe, there was a credible excuse for not finding any if she ever looked.

The wind was whipping at her hair. She pushed some from her face, but it kept coming back. Victor liked watching the unwinnable fight.

'So, this angry guy who beat you up, did you get any digs in yourself?'

'I'm more of a lover than a fighter.'

She winced, sucking in air. 'Well ... that's not saying much, is it?'

Victor raised an eyebrow. 'That hurt more than the three punches.'

'I thought it was two punches.'

'I must have a concussion.'

She cracked first and smiled. 'You didn't joke this much when I first met you. Truth be told, I thought you were a little boring when we met on that bus. Cute, but boring.'

'Some people have stunted growth. I have a stunted personality. Just be glad I'm a late bloomer.'

She laughed. 'Seriously, where's all this coming from?'

'I'm in a particularly jovial mood.'

She pursed her lips. 'I'm not sure anyone has ever used the word jovial in my presence. Or even this whole century so far.'

'Then I'm honoured to be the first.'

She said, 'Any particular reason why you're so *jovial*?'

'I'm standing on a beautiful beach with a beautiful woman. Life is feeling pretty good right now.'

Her eyes narrowed. 'Don't think you're getting any, pal. Sand gets everywhere.'

Now it was his turn to crack. 'Perish the thought.'

'So,' she said, pointedly. 'This is goodbye, right?'

'I didn't want to do it over the phone.'

'Where are you off to?'

He looked into the distance. 'New pastures.'

'Sounds exciting. You closed your deal? It went well then?'

Victor nodded. 'I could probably retire if I wanted to.'

Alamaeda said, 'And do you?'

'Right now, that's anyone's guess.'

'Then what's next?'

He inhaled and shrugged. 'At this point I have no idea, and I kind of like that. Maybe I'll just take each day as it comes for a while. See where that gets me.'

'Sounds nice,' she said. 'Sounds really nice.'

'Those new pastures,' he began. 'I could give you a call when I'm there. You could join me if you wanted to.'

'Didn't we agree this had a finite shelf life?'

'It still does,' he said. 'I'm talking of an extension only.'

'I've already had my vacation, remember?'

'Surely you're a hero for bringing down the cartel. They'll give you some leisure time if you want it. Or just take it, and deal with the fallout when you get back.'

She thought for a moment, a smile forming. 'The weekend's

coming up anyway. I suppose I could be back in the office on Tuesday. One day won't hurt, I guess. But do I bring my bathing suit or my snowboard?'

'I have no idea.'

She frowned, surprised and confused. 'You don't know where you're going?'

'It's usually better if I don't know my destination. But it'll be somewhere secluded, somewhere quiet.' He thought for a moment. 'Somewhere ... peaceful.'

'I'm sold. Count me in, buddy.'

'Then I'll give you a call.'

'You'd better.'

She climbed inside her car and started the engine. She said nothing else and neither did Victor. He watched her drive away, tyres throwing up plumes of swirling sand.

He checked the money was still secured and hidden inside the pickup and called a number from his current burner phone.

'Arturo, it's time to honour our deal,' he said when the line connected. 'I hope you have plenty of detergent because I have a considerable amount of laundry for you.'

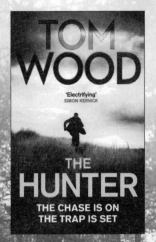

TOM WOOD

'Electrifying'
SIMON KERNICK

THE
HUNTER
**THE CHASE IS ON
THE TRAP IS SET**

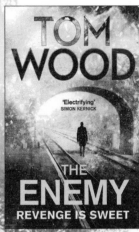

TOM WOOD

'Electrifying'
SIMON KERNICK

THE
ENEMY
REVENGE IS SWEET

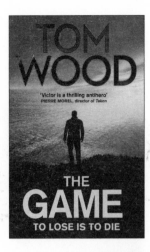

TOM WOOD

'Victor is a thrilling antihero'
PIERRE MOREL, director of *Taken*

THE
GAME
TO LOSE IS TO DIE

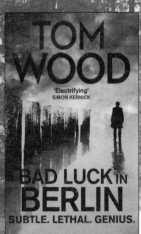

TOM WOOD

'Electrifying'
SIMON KERNICK

BAD LUCK IN
BERLIN
SUBTLE. LETHAL. GENIUS.

TOM WOOD

'Electrifying'
SIMON KERNICK

LONER. KILLER. HERO.
BETTER OFF
DEAD

'Victor is a thrilling antihero'
Pierre Morel – Director of *TAKEN*

TOM WOOD

REVENGE IS BEST SERVED COLD
THE DARKEST
DAY

'Very few British writers are as good at the all-action thriller'
Sunday Express

TOM WOOD

A KILLER CAN BE A HERO
A TIME TO
DIE

A VICTOR THRILLER

TOM WOOD

'Explosive'
Gregg Hurwitz
author of
Orphan X

THE
FINAL
HOUR
**He tried to kill her.
Now she needs his help**

A VICTOR THRILLER

TOM WOOD

'Great,
page-turning,
with a hard edge'
James Swallow
author of
NOMAD

KILL
FOR ME
**A family at war.
Only one man can end it.**